THE CHRONOS FILES
TIME TRIAL

THE CHRONOS FILES

TIME TRIAL

Bestselling author Rysa Walker *(Timebound)* takes readers on a stand-alone adventure set in the **CHRONOS** Files world!

Nineteen-year-old Clio Dunne has lived a life of secrecy. Her world-saving, time-traveling parents have kept a low profile in a boring, small town…but Clio yearns for her own adventure. In the fall of 1931, Clio packs her bags and heads to the big, modern city of Chicago. While following her dreams of becoming a famous illustrator, Clio's own nascent skills as a time traveler will be put to the test…

STORY BY: RYSA WALKER

WRITTEN BY: HEATHER NUHFER

ART BY: AGUSTIN PADILLA

COLORS BY: CHRIS SUMMERS

LETTERS BY: DERON BENNETT

COVER BY: AGUSTIN PADILLA AND ANDREW DALHOUSE

EDITOR: PAUL MORRISSEY

SENIOR PRODUCTION MANAGER: JILL TAPLIN

JET CITY COMICS

www.apub.com ISBN 10: 1503938859 ISBN 13: 9781503938854 EISBN: 9781503993846

CHAPTER 1

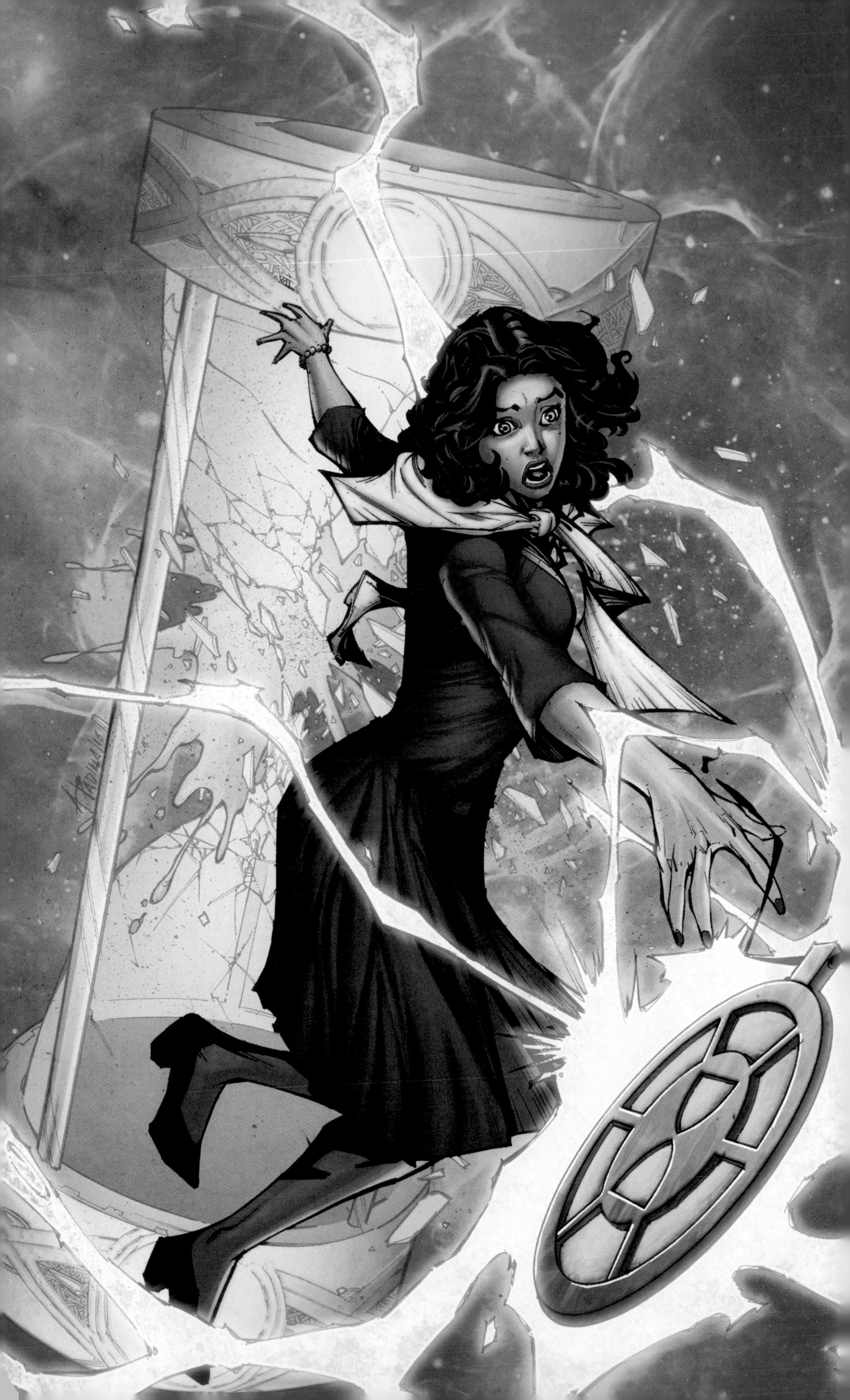

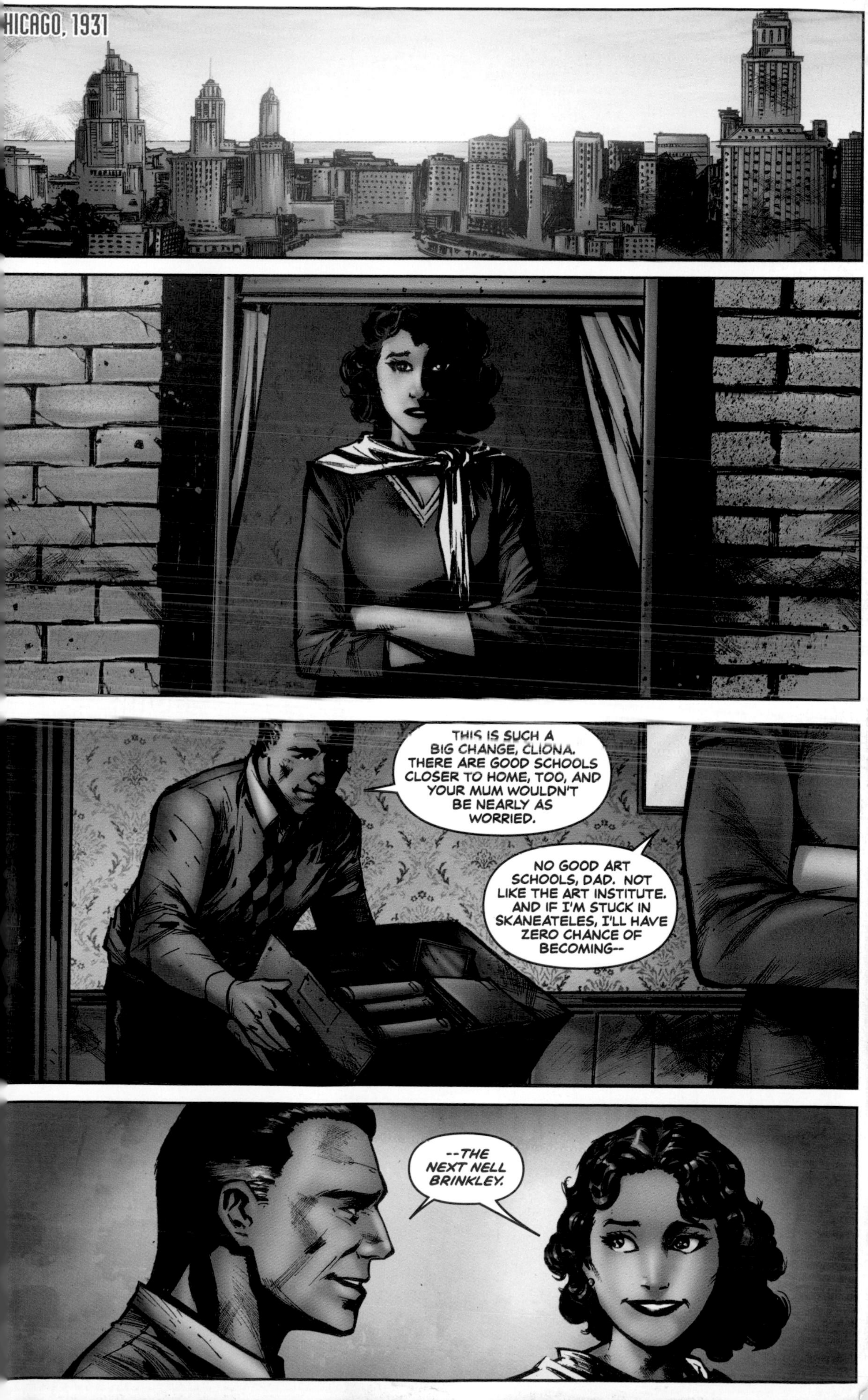
HICAGO, 1931
THIS IS SUCH A BIG CHANGE, CLIONA. THERE ARE GOOD SCHOOLS CLOSER TO HOME, TOO, AND YOUR MUM WOULDN'T BE NEARLY AS WORRIED.
NO GOOD ART SCHOOLS, DAD. NOT LIKE THE ART INSTITUTE. AND IF I'M STUCK IN SKANEATELES, I'LL HAVE ZERO CHANCE OF BECOMING--
--THE NEXT NELL BRINKLEY.

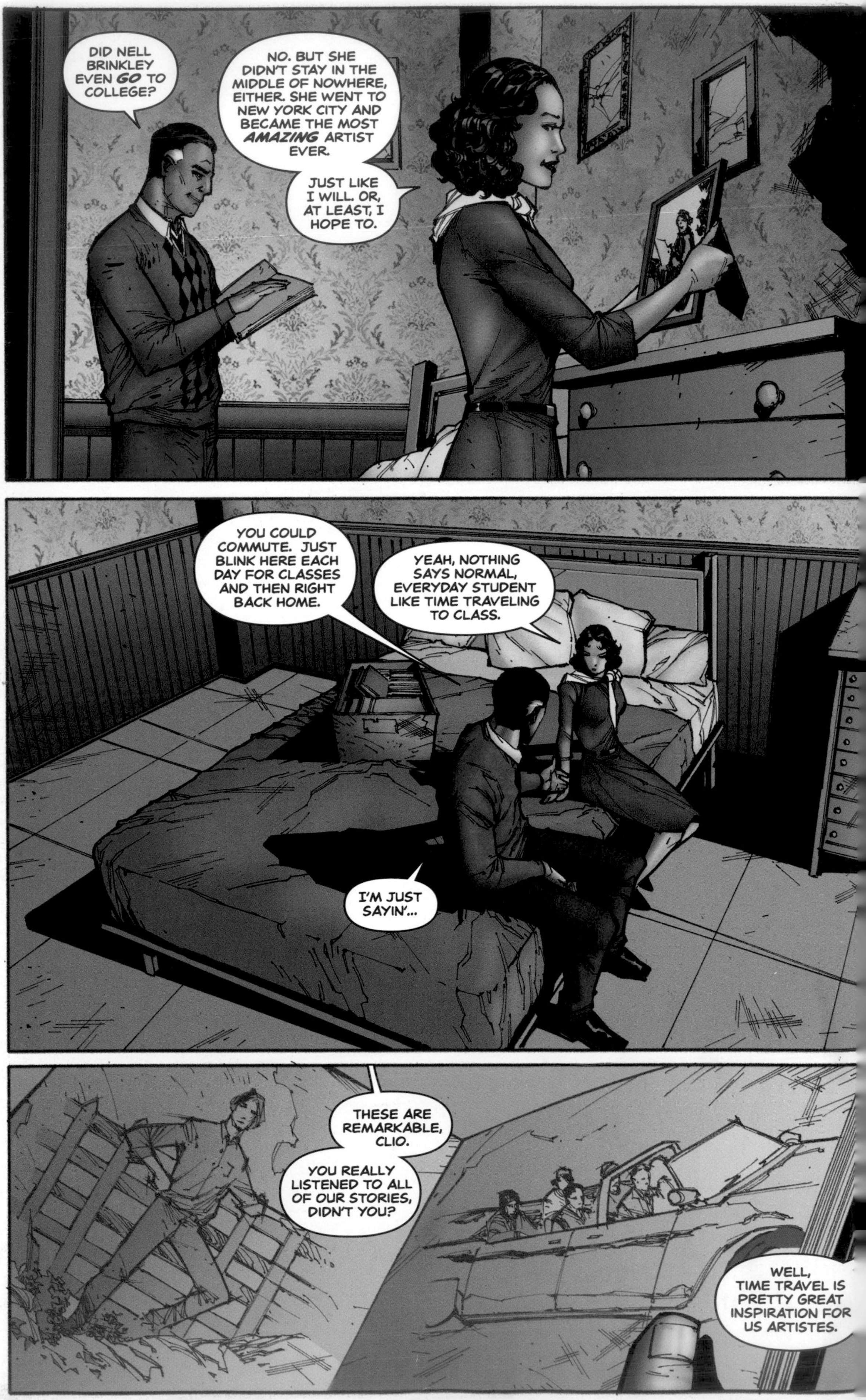
DID NELL BRINKLEY EVEN GO TO COLLEGE?
NO. BUT SHE DIDN'T STAY IN THE MIDDLE OF NOWHERE, EITHER. SHE WENT TO NEW YORK CITY AND BECAME THE MOST AMAZING ARTIST EVER.
JUST LIKE I WILL. OR, AT LEAST, I HOPE TO.
YOU COULD COMMUTE. JUST BLINK HERE EACH DAY FOR CLASSES AND THEN RIGHT BACK HOME.
YEAH, NOTHING SAYS NORMAL, EVERYDAY STUDENT LIKE TIME TRAVELING TO CLASS.
I'M JUST SAYIN'...
THESE ARE REMARKABLE, CLIO.
YOU REALLY LISTENED TO ALL OF OUR STORIES, DIDN'T YOU?
WELL, TIME TRAVEL IS PRETTY GREAT INSPIRATION FOR US ARTISTES.

THIS IS MY FAVORITE.

I CAN'T LIVE AT HOME FOREVER, DAD. IT WON'T MATTER WHETHER I'M IN CHICAGO OR JUST WALKING DOWN TO THE LAKE--MOM WILL ALWAYS WORRY THAT I'LL LOSE **BOTH** OF MY CHRONOS KEYS AND VANISH INTO THIN AIR.

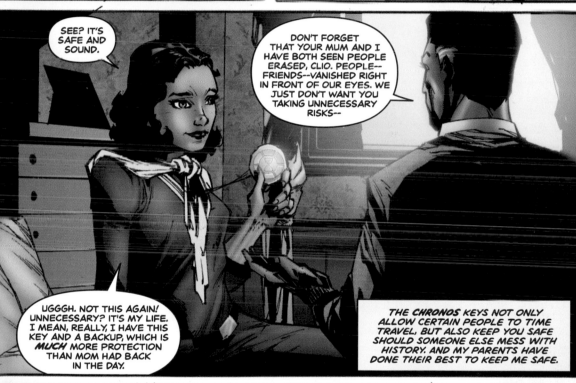

SEE? IT'S SAFE AND SOUND.

DON'T FORGET THAT YOUR MUM AND I HAVE BOTH SEEN PEOPLE ERASED, CLIO. PEOPLE--FRIENDS--VANISHED RIGHT IN FRONT OF OUR EYES. WE JUST DON'T WANT YOU TAKING UNNECESSARY RISKS--

UGGGH. NOT THIS AGAIN! UNNECESSARY? IT'S MY LIFE. I MEAN, REALLY, I HAVE THIS KEY AND A BACKUP, WHICH IS **MUCH** MORE PROTECTION THAN MOM HAD BACK IN THE DAY.

THE **CHRONOS** KEYS NOT ONLY ALLOW CERTAIN PEOPLE TO TIME TRAVEL, BUT ALSO KEEP YOU SAFE SHOULD SOMEONE ELSE MESS WITH HISTORY. AND MY PARENTS HAVE DONE THEIR BEST TO KEEP ME SAFE.

AND I'M NOT EVEN TRYING TO SAVE THE WORLD, DAD! JUST TRYING TO GO TO SCHOOL.

BUT YOU KNEW THAT KATE DUNNE WOULD NEVER BE CONTENT JUST SITTING AT HOME THE REST OF HER LIFE. AS MUCH AS I LOVE ALL OF YOU, SIMPLY *EXISTING* ISN'T ENOUGH FOR ME, EITHER.

I WASN'T EXACTLY HAPPY ABOUT HER TAKING THOSE RISKS EITHER, BUT--

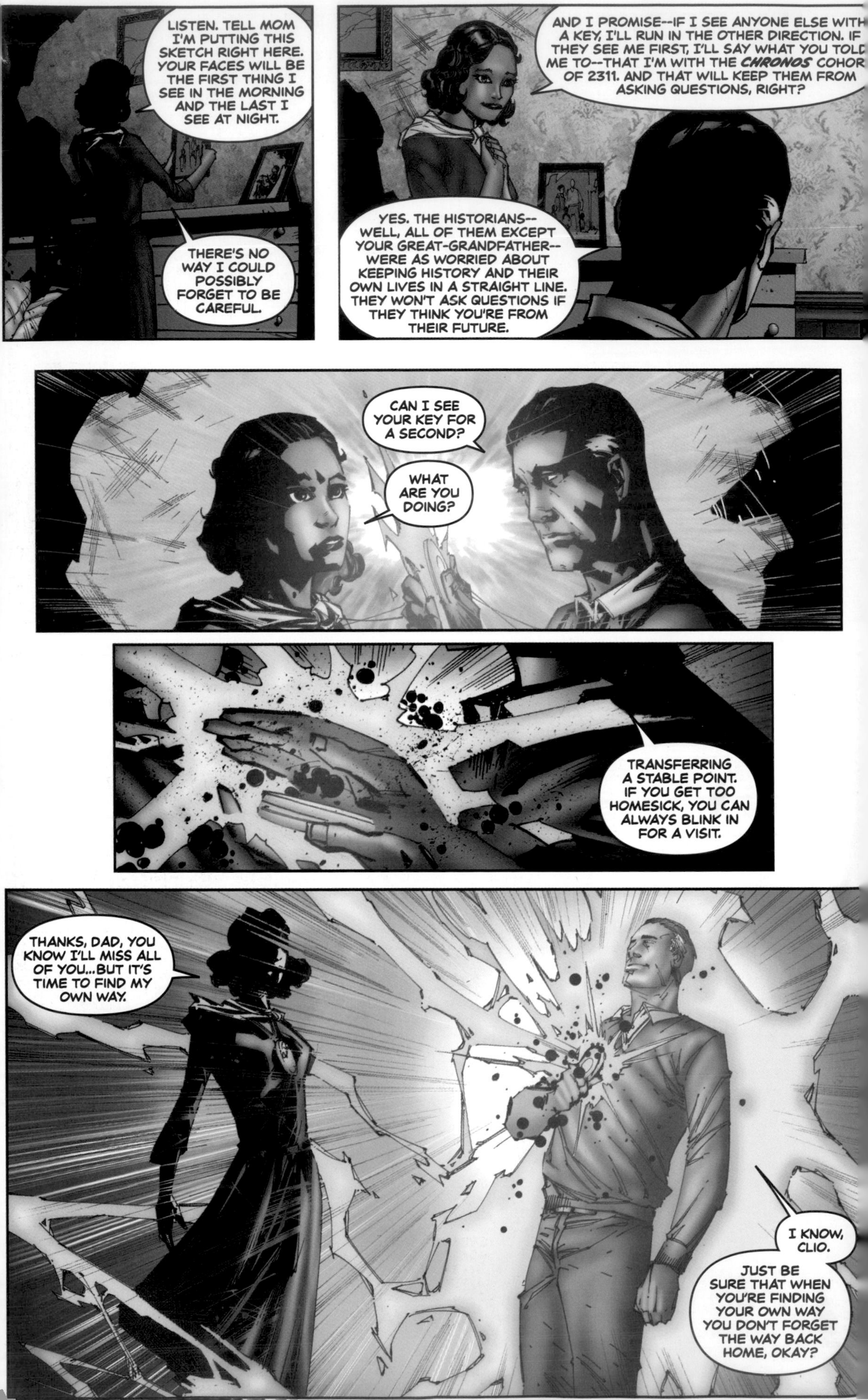
LISTEN. TELL MOM I'M PUTTING THIS SKETCH RIGHT HERE. YOUR FACES WILL BE THE FIRST THING I SEE IN THE MORNING AND THE LAST I SEE AT NIGHT.
THERE'S NO WAY I COULD POSSIBLY FORGET TO BE CAREFUL.
AND I PROMISE--IF I SEE ANYONE ELSE WITH A KEY, I'LL RUN IN THE OTHER DIRECTION. IF THEY SEE ME FIRST, I'LL SAY WHAT YOU TOLD ME TO--THAT I'M WITH THE CHRONOS COHORT OF 2311. AND THAT WILL KEEP THEM FROM ASKING QUESTIONS, RIGHT?
YES. THE HISTORIANS--WELL, ALL OF THEM EXCEPT YOUR GREAT-GRANDFATHER--WERE AS WORRIED ABOUT KEEPING HISTORY AND THEIR OWN LIVES IN A STRAIGHT LINE. THEY WON'T ASK QUESTIONS IF THEY THINK YOU'RE FROM THEIR FUTURE.
CAN I SEE YOUR KEY FOR A SECOND?
WHAT ARE YOU DOING?
TRANSFERRING A STABLE POINT. IF YOU GET TOO HOMESICK, YOU CAN ALWAYS BLINK IN FOR A VISIT.
THANKS, DAD, YOU KNOW I'LL MISS ALL OF YOU...BUT IT'S TIME TO FIND MY OWN WAY.
I KNOW, CLIO.
JUST BE SURE THAT WHEN YOU'RE FINDING YOUR OWN WAY YOU DON'T FORGET THE WAY BACK HOME, OKAY?

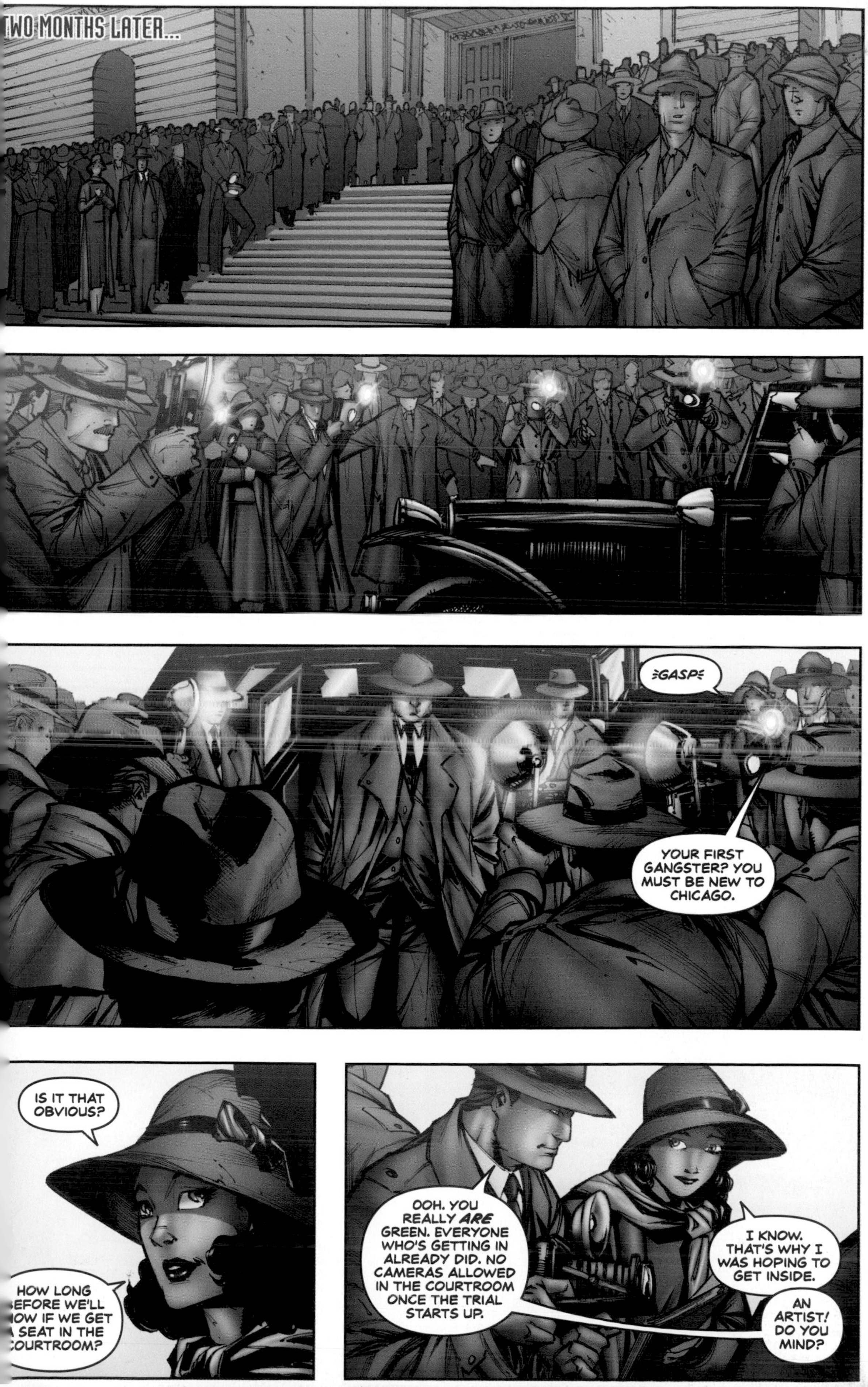
TWO MONTHS LATER...
GASP
YOUR FIRST GANGSTER? YOU MUST BE NEW TO CHICAGO.
IS IT THAT OBVIOUS?
HOW LONG BEFORE WE'LL KNOW IF WE GET A SEAT IN THE COURTROOM?
OOH. YOU REALLY ARE GREEN. EVERYONE WHO'S GETTING IN ALREADY DID. NO CAMERAS ALLOWED IN THE COURTROOM ONCE THE TRIAL STARTS UP.
I KNOW. THAT'S WHY I WAS HOPING TO GET INSIDE.
AN ARTIST! DO YOU MIND?

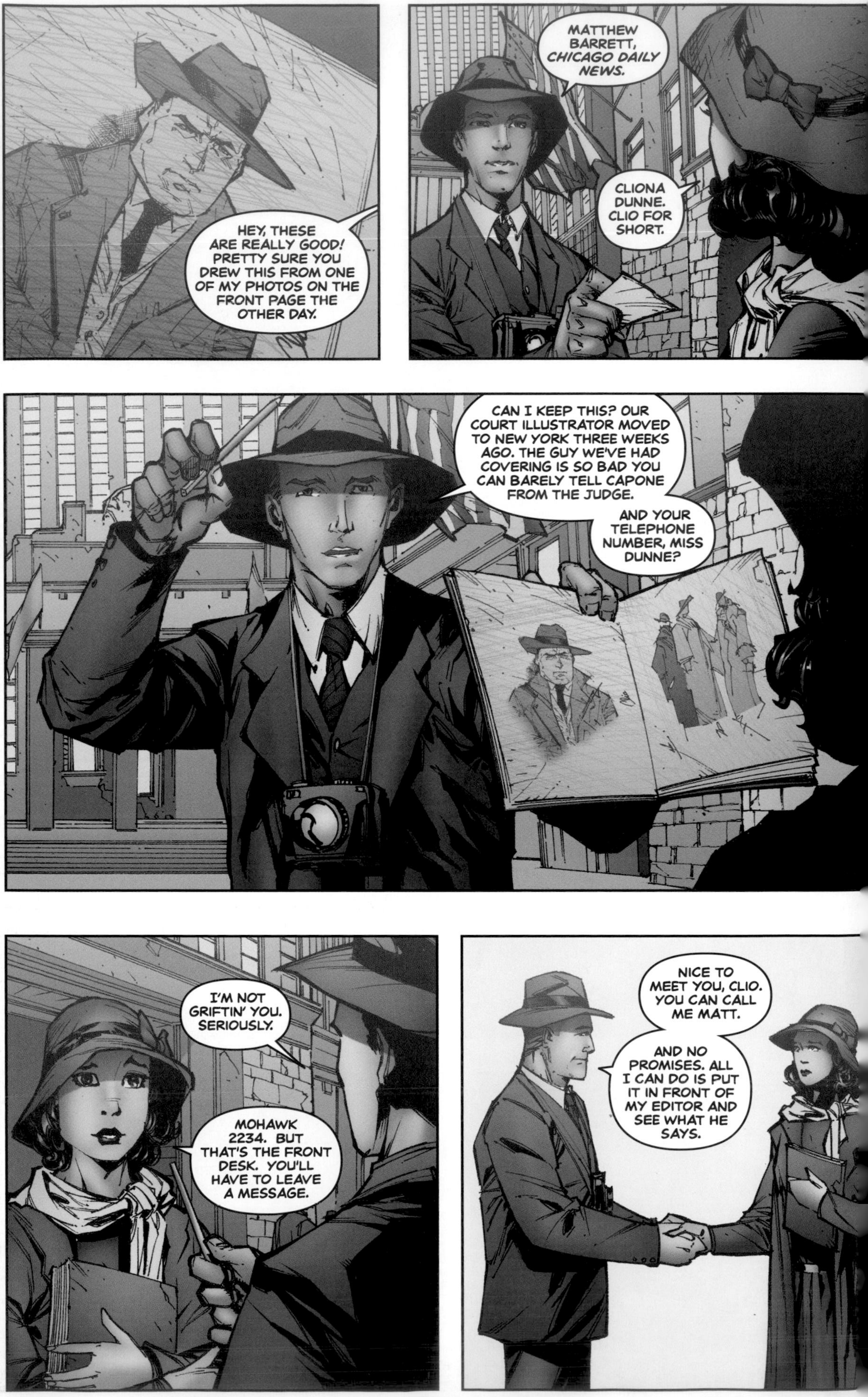
HEY, THESE ARE REALLY GOOD! PRETTY SURE YOU DREW THIS FROM ONE OF MY PHOTOS ON THE FRONT PAGE THE OTHER DAY.
MATTHEW BARRETT, *CHICAGO DAILY NEWS.*
CLIONA DUNNE. CLIO FOR SHORT.
CAN I KEEP THIS? OUR COURT ILLUSTRATOR MOVED TO NEW YORK THREE WEEKS AGO. THE GUY WE'VE HAD COVERING IS SO BAD YOU CAN BARELY TELL CAPONE FROM THE JUDGE.
AND YOUR TELEPHONE NUMBER, MISS DUNNE?
I'M NOT GRIFTIN' YOU. SERIOUSLY.
MOHAWK 2234. BUT THAT'S THE FRONT DESK. YOU'LL HAVE TO LEAVE A MESSAGE.
NICE TO MEET YOU, CLIO. YOU CAN CALL ME MATT.
AND NO PROMISES. ALL I CAN DO IS PUT IT IN FRONT OF MY EDITOR AND SEE WHAT HE SAYS.

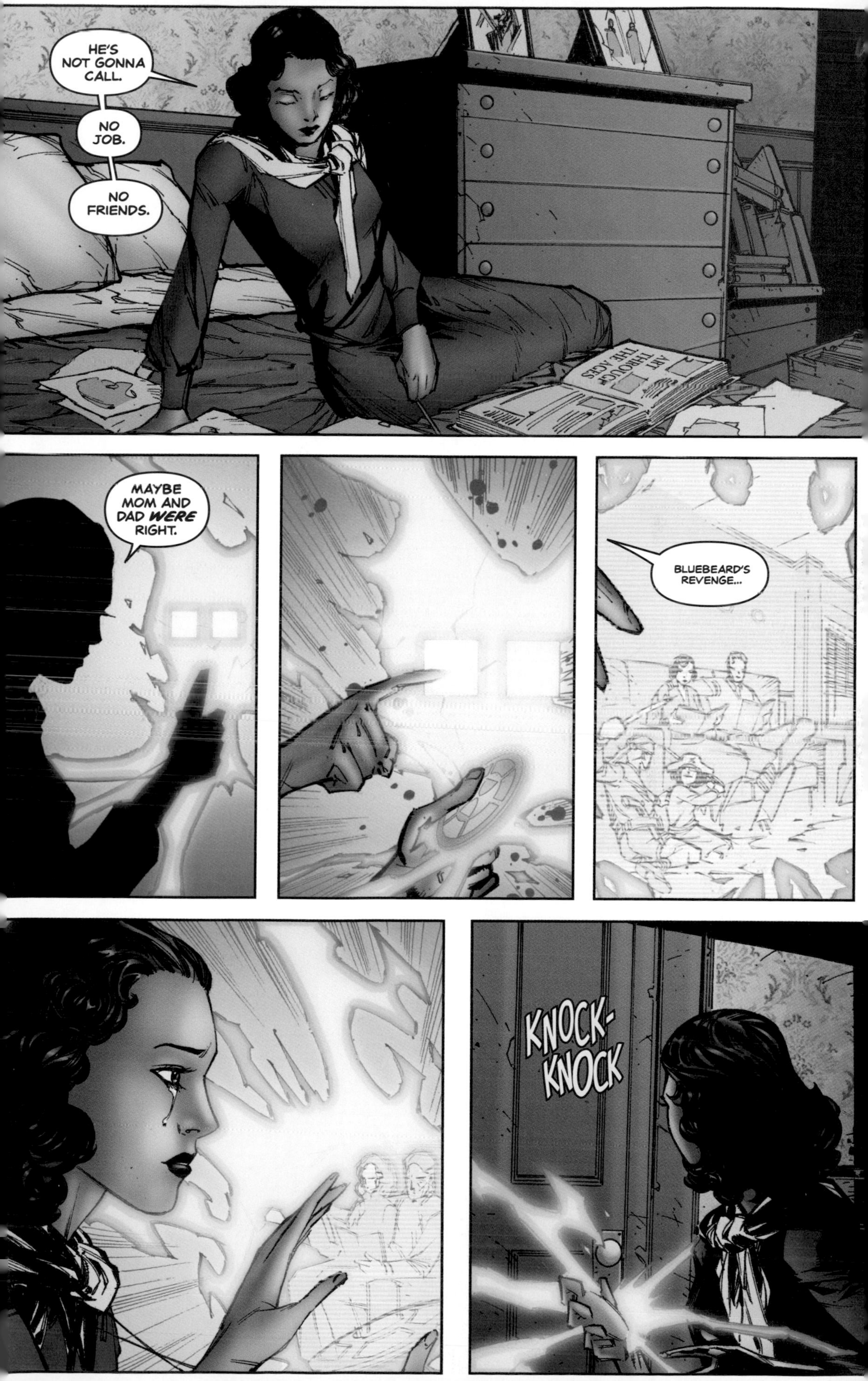
HE'S NOT GONNA CALL.
NO JOB.
NO FRIENDS.
MAYBE MOM AND DAD *WERE* RIGHT.
BLUEBEARD'S REVENGE...
KNOCK-KNOCK

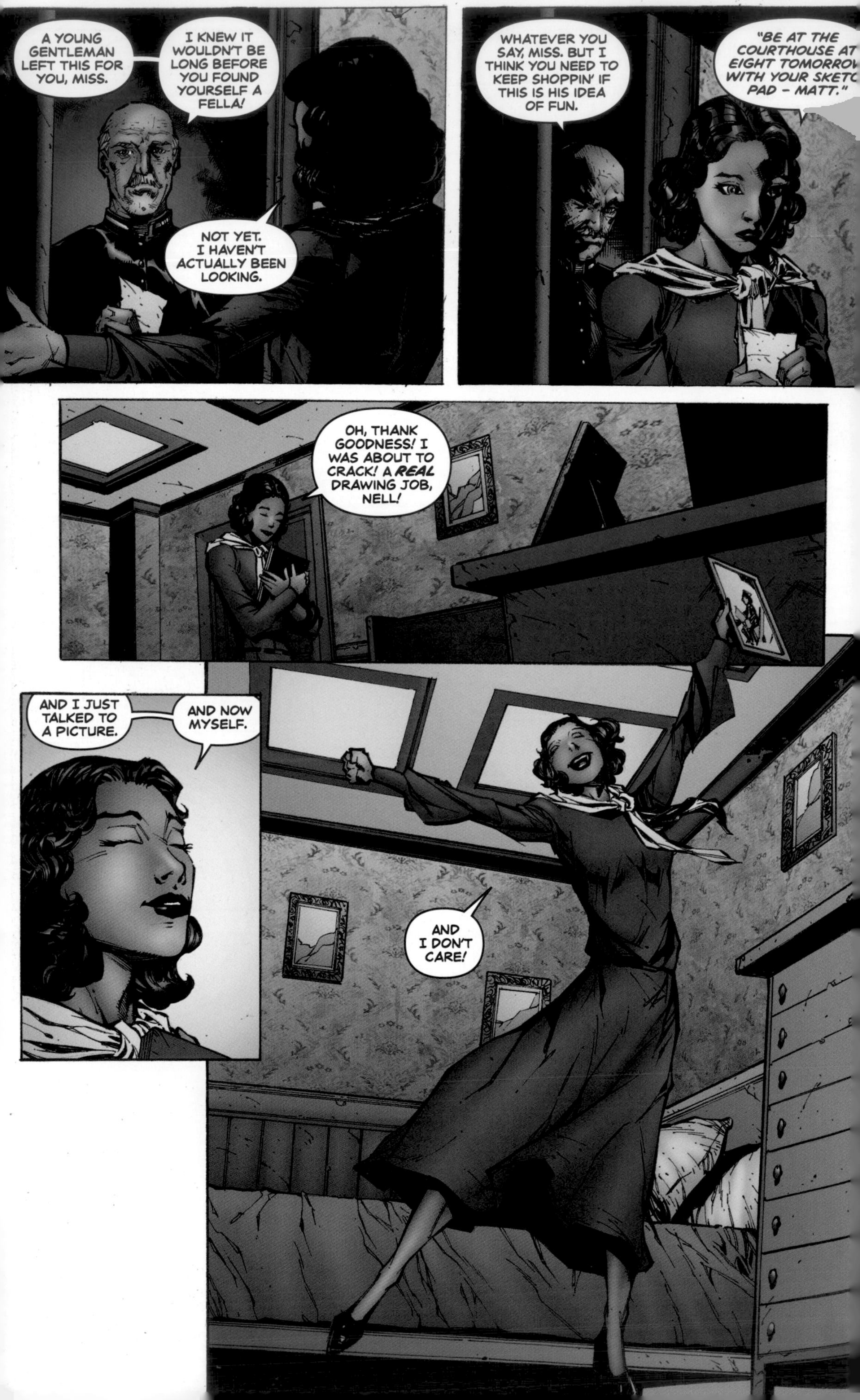
A YOUNG GENTLEMAN LEFT THIS FOR YOU, MISS.
I KNEW IT WOULDN'T BE LONG BEFORE YOU FOUND YOURSELF A FELLA!
NOT YET. I HAVEN'T ACTUALLY BEEN LOOKING.
WHATEVER YOU SAY, MISS. BUT I THINK YOU NEED TO KEEP SHOPPIN' IF THIS IS HIS IDEA OF FUN.
"BE AT THE COURTHOUSE AT EIGHT TOMORROW WITH YOUR SKETC PAD – MATT."
OH, THANK GOODNESS! I WAS ABOUT TO CRACK! A *REAL* DRAWING JOB, NELL!
AND I JUST TALKED TO A PICTURE.
AND NOW MYSELF.
AND I DON'T CARE!

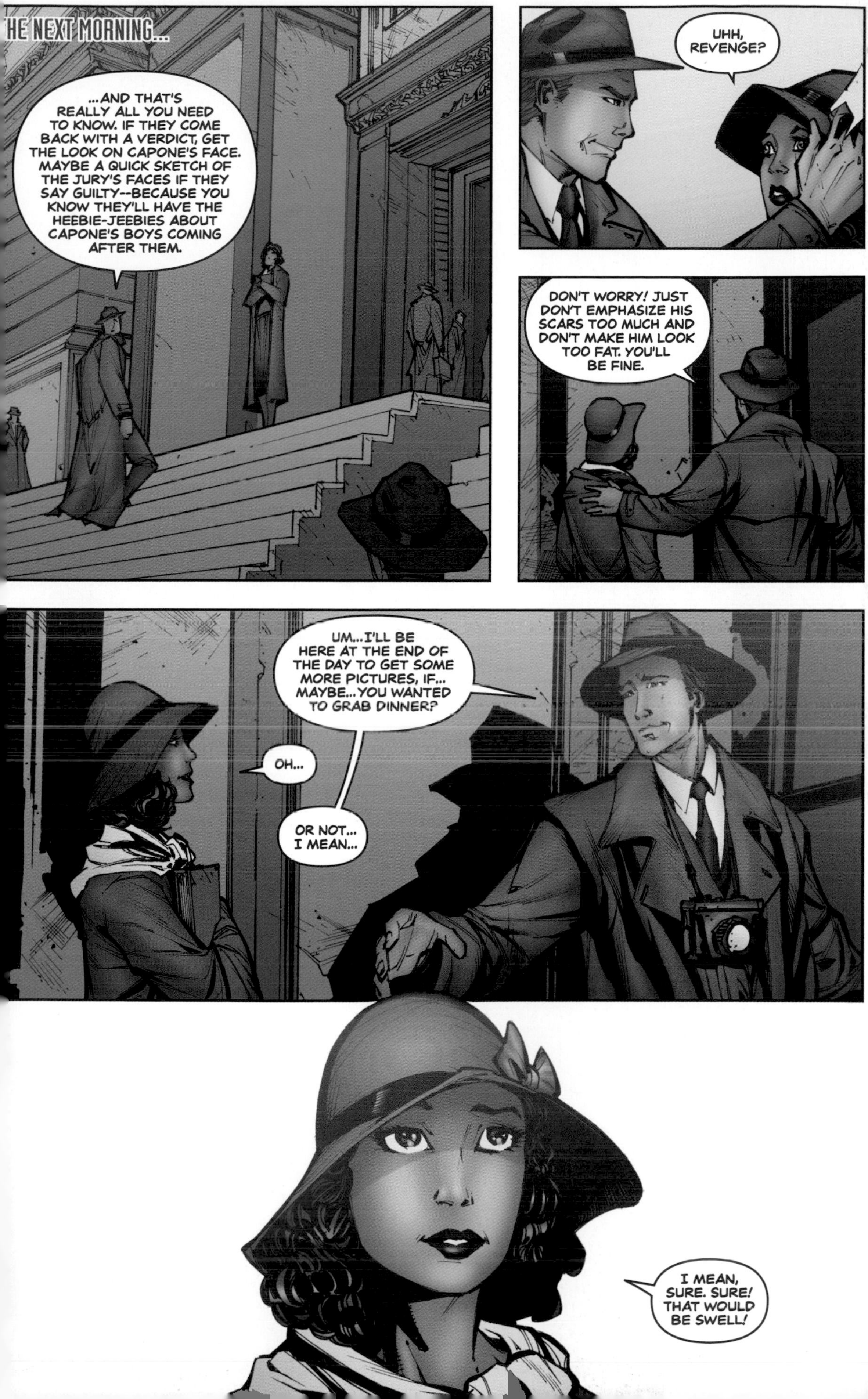
HE NEXT MORNING...
...AND THAT'S REALLY ALL YOU NEED TO KNOW. IF THEY COME BACK WITH A VERDICT, GET THE LOOK ON CAPONE'S FACE. MAYBE A QUICK SKETCH OF THE JURY'S FACES IF THEY SAY GUILTY--BECAUSE YOU KNOW THEY'LL HAVE THE HEEBIE-JEEBIES ABOUT CAPONE'S BOYS COMING AFTER THEM.
UHH, REVENGE?
DON'T WORRY! JUST DON'T EMPHASIZE HIS SCARS TOO MUCH AND DON'T MAKE HIM LOOK TOO FAT. YOU'LL BE FINE.
UM...I'LL BE HERE AT THE END OF THE DAY TO GET SOME MORE PICTURES, IF... MAYBE...YOU WANTED TO GRAB DINNER?
OH...
OR NOT... I MEAN...
I MEAN, SURE. SURE! THAT WOULD BE SWELL!

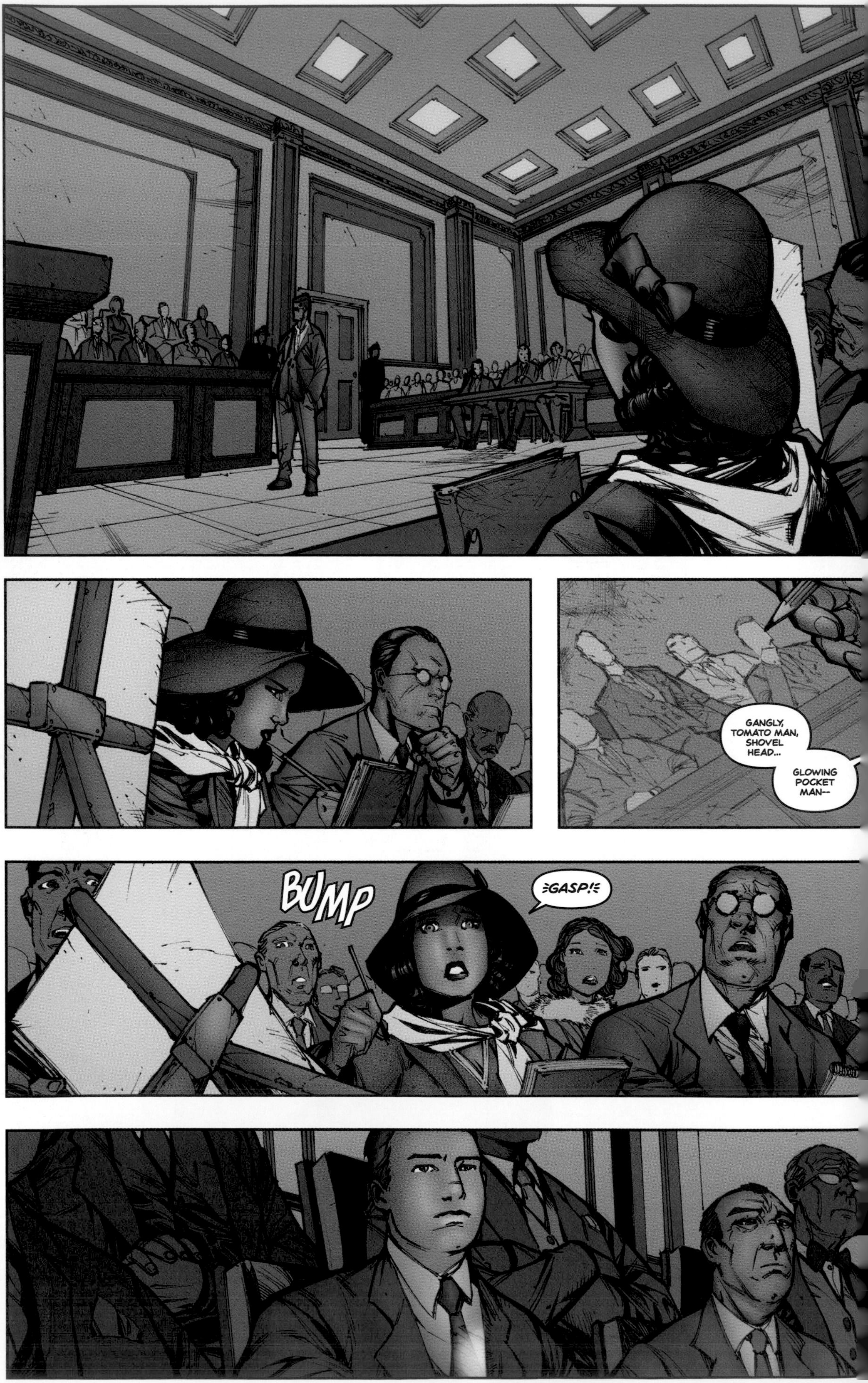
GANGLY, TOMATO MAN, SHOVEL HEAD...
GLOWING POCKET MAN--
BUMP
GASP!

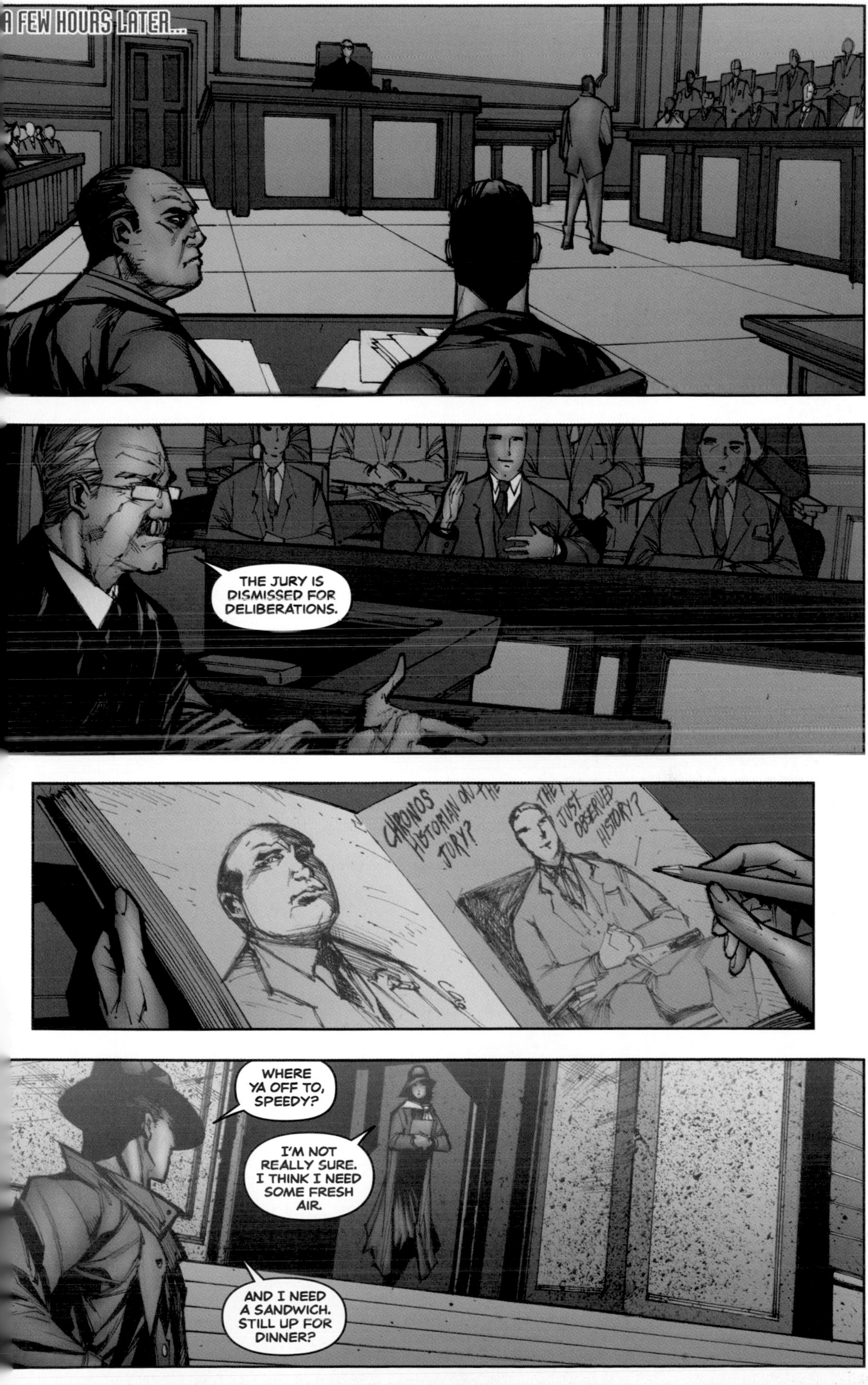
A FEW HOURS LATER...
THE JURY IS DISMISSED FOR DELIBERATIONS.
CHRONOS HISTORIAN ON THE JURY?
JUST OBSERVED HISTORY?
WHERE YA OFF TO, SPEEDY?
I'M NOT REALLY SURE. I THINK I NEED SOME FRESH AIR.
AND I NEED A SANDWICH. STILL UP FOR DINNER?

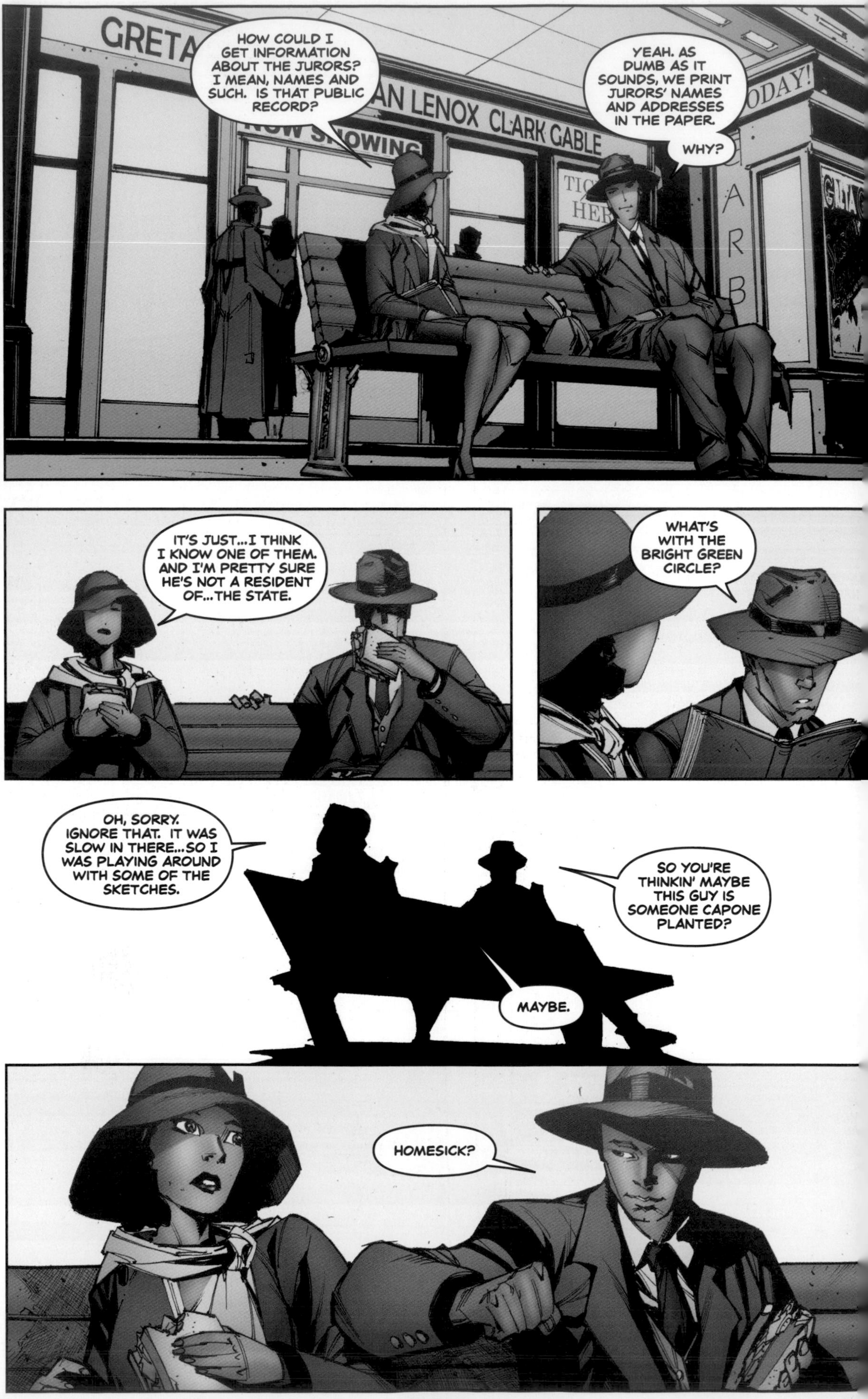
GRETA
HOW COULD I GET INFORMATION ABOUT THE JURORS? I MEAN, NAMES AND SUCH. IS THAT PUBLIC RECORD?
AN LENOX CLARK GABLE
NOW SHOWING
YEAH. AS DUMB AS IT SOUNDS, WE PRINT JURORS' NAMES AND ADDRESSES IN THE PAPER.
WHY?
ODAY!
IT'S JUST...I THINK I KNOW ONE OF THEM. AND I'M PRETTY SURE HE'S NOT A RESIDENT OF...THE STATE.
WHAT'S WITH THE BRIGHT GREEN CIRCLE?
OH, SORRY. IGNORE THAT. IT WAS SLOW IN THERE...SO I WAS PLAYING AROUND WITH SOME OF THE SKETCHES.
SO YOU'RE THINKIN' MAYBE THIS GUY IS SOMEONE CAPONE PLANTED?
MAYBE.
HOMESICK?

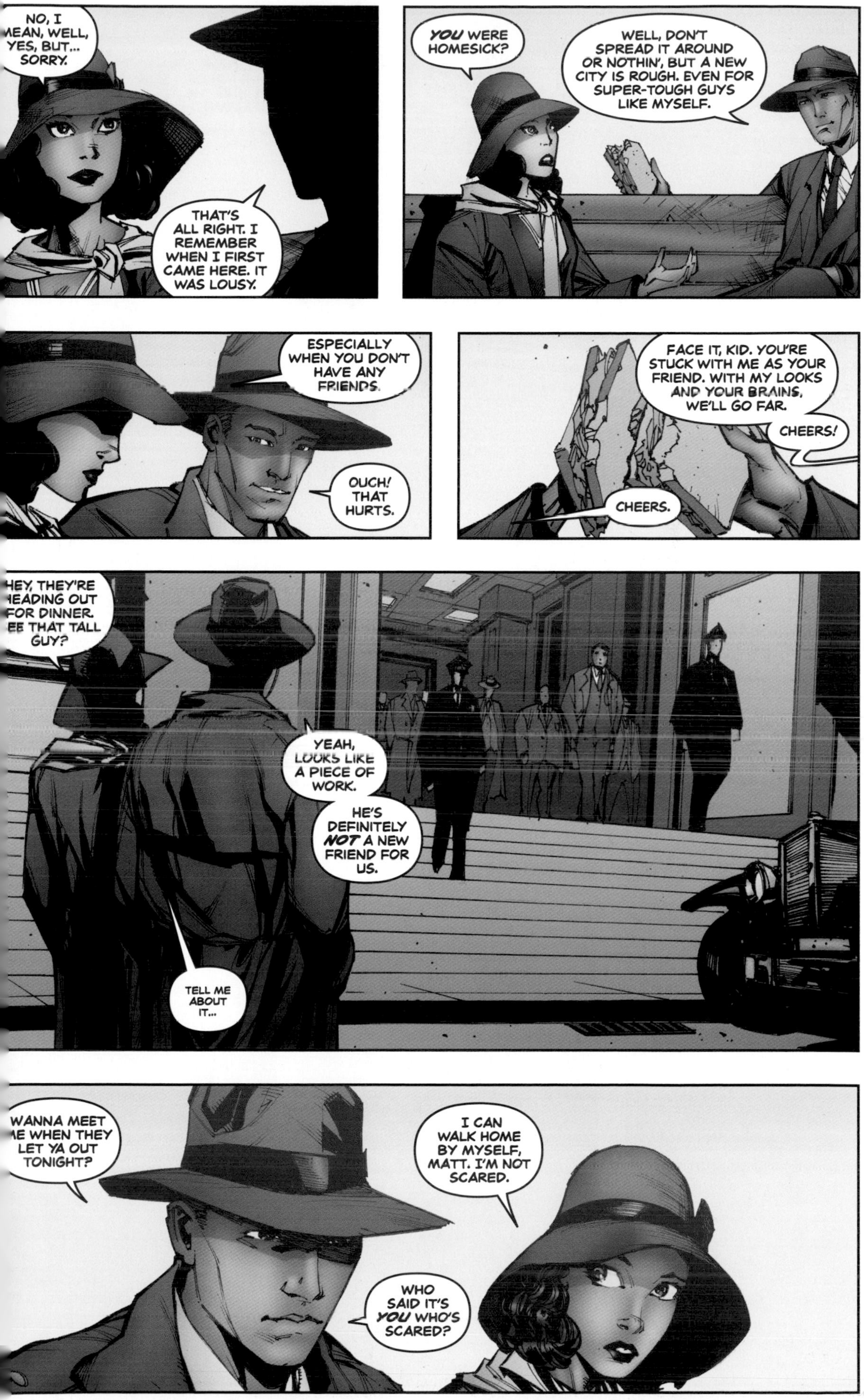
NO, I MEAN, WELL, YES, BUT... SORRY.
THAT'S ALL RIGHT. I REMEMBER WHEN I FIRST CAME HERE. IT WAS LOUSY.
YOU WERE HOMESICK?
WELL, DON'T SPREAD IT AROUND OR NOTHIN', BUT A NEW CITY IS ROUGH. EVEN FOR SUPER-TOUGH GUYS LIKE MYSELF.
ESPECIALLY WHEN YOU DON'T HAVE ANY FRIENDS.
OUCH! THAT HURTS.
FACE IT, KID. YOU'RE STUCK WITH ME AS YOUR FRIEND. WITH MY LOOKS AND YOUR BRAINS, WE'LL GO FAR.
CHEERS!
CHEERS.
HEY, THEY'RE HEADING OUT FOR DINNER. SEE THAT TALL GUY?
YEAH, LOOKS LIKE A PIECE OF WORK.
HE'S DEFINITELY NOT A NEW FRIEND FOR US.
TELL ME ABOUT IT...
WANNA MEET ME WHEN THEY LET YA OUT TONIGHT?
I CAN WALK HOME BY MYSELF, MATT. I'M NOT SCARED.
WHO SAID IT'S YOU WHO'S SCARED?

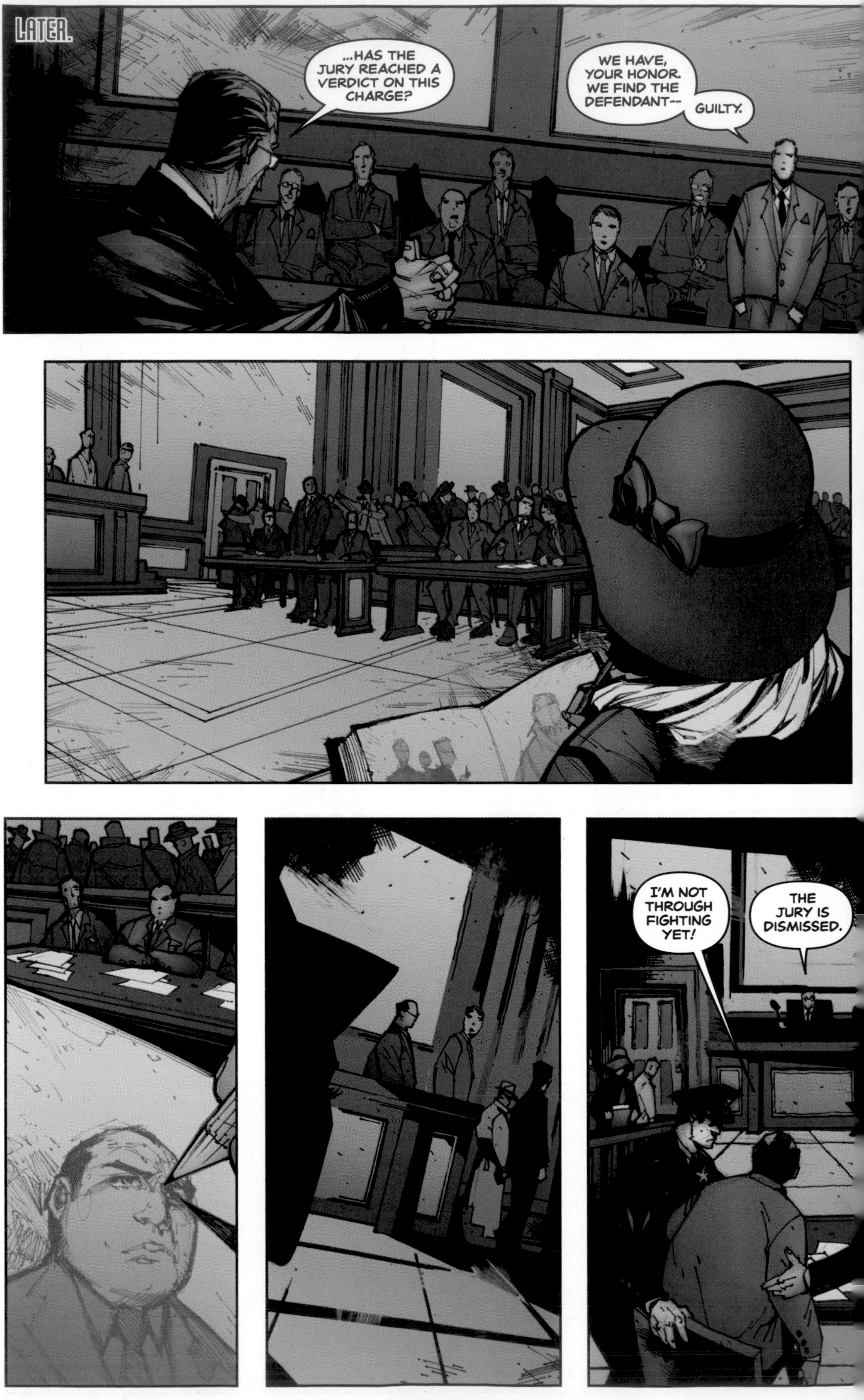
LATER.
...HAS THE JURY REACHED A VERDICT ON THIS CHARGE?
WE HAVE, YOUR HONOR. WE FIND THE DEFENDANT--
GUILTY.
I'M NOT THROUGH FIGHTING YET!
THE JURY IS DISMISSED.

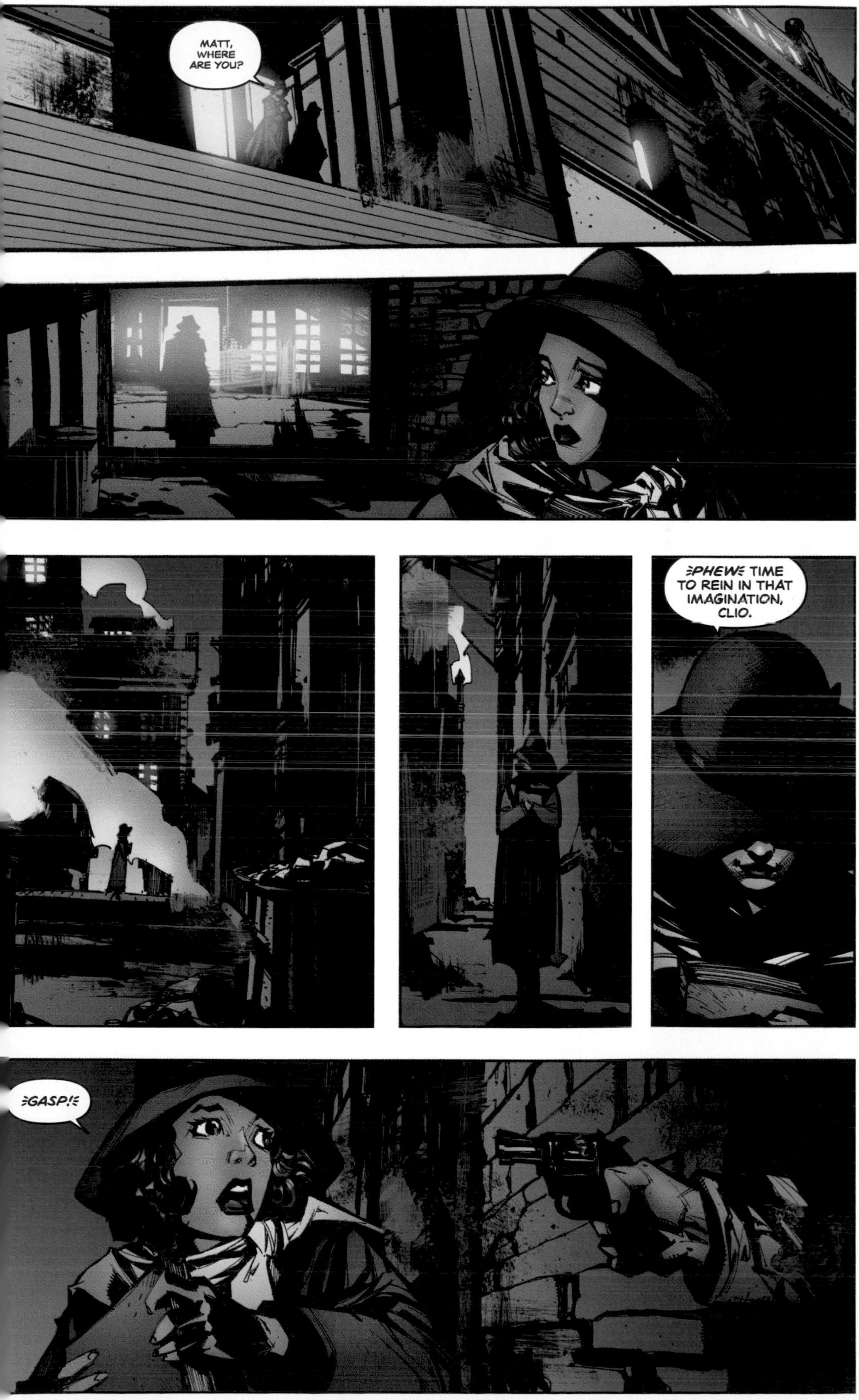
MATT, WHERE ARE YOU?
=PHEW= TIME TO REIN IN THAT IMAGINATION, CLIO.
=GASP!=

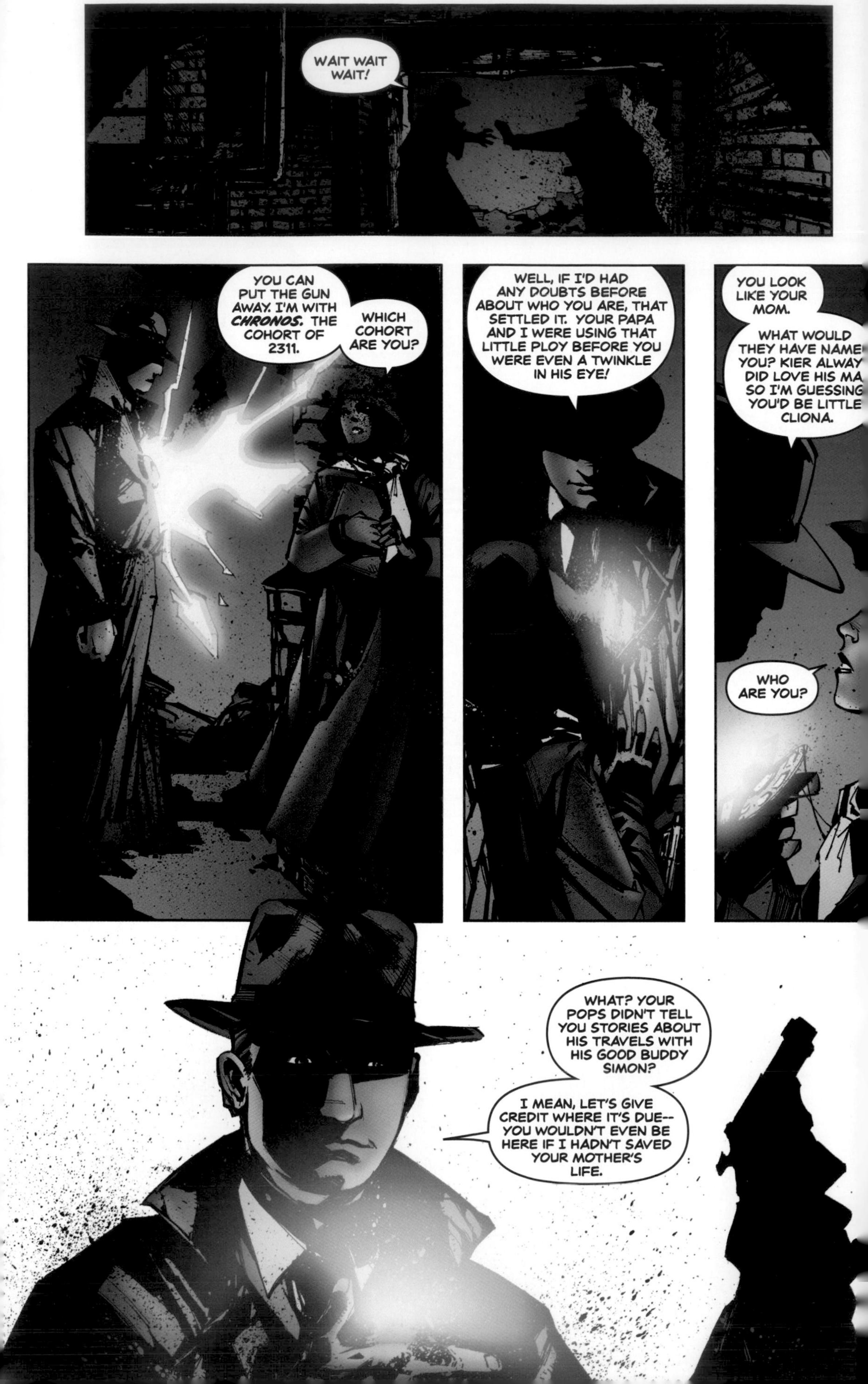
WAIT WAIT WAIT!
YOU CAN PUT THE GUN AWAY. I'M WITH ***CHRONOS.*** THE COHORT OF 2311.
WHICH COHORT ARE YOU?
WELL, IF I'D HAD ANY DOUBTS BEFORE ABOUT WHO YOU ARE, THAT SETTLED IT. YOUR PAPA AND I WERE USING THAT LITTLE PLOY BEFORE YOU WERE EVEN A TWINKLE IN HIS EYE!
YOU LOOK LIKE YOUR MOM.
WHAT WOULD THEY HAVE NAME YOU? KIER ALWAY DID LOVE HIS MA SO I'M GUESSING YOU'D BE LITTLE CLIONA.
WHO ARE YOU?
WHAT? YOUR POPS DIDN'T TELL YOU STORIES ABOUT HIS TRAVELS WITH HIS GOOD BUDDY SIMON?
I MEAN, LET'S GIVE CREDIT WHERE IT'S DUE-- YOU WOULDN'T EVEN BE HERE IF I HADN'T SAVED YOUR MOTHER'S LIFE.

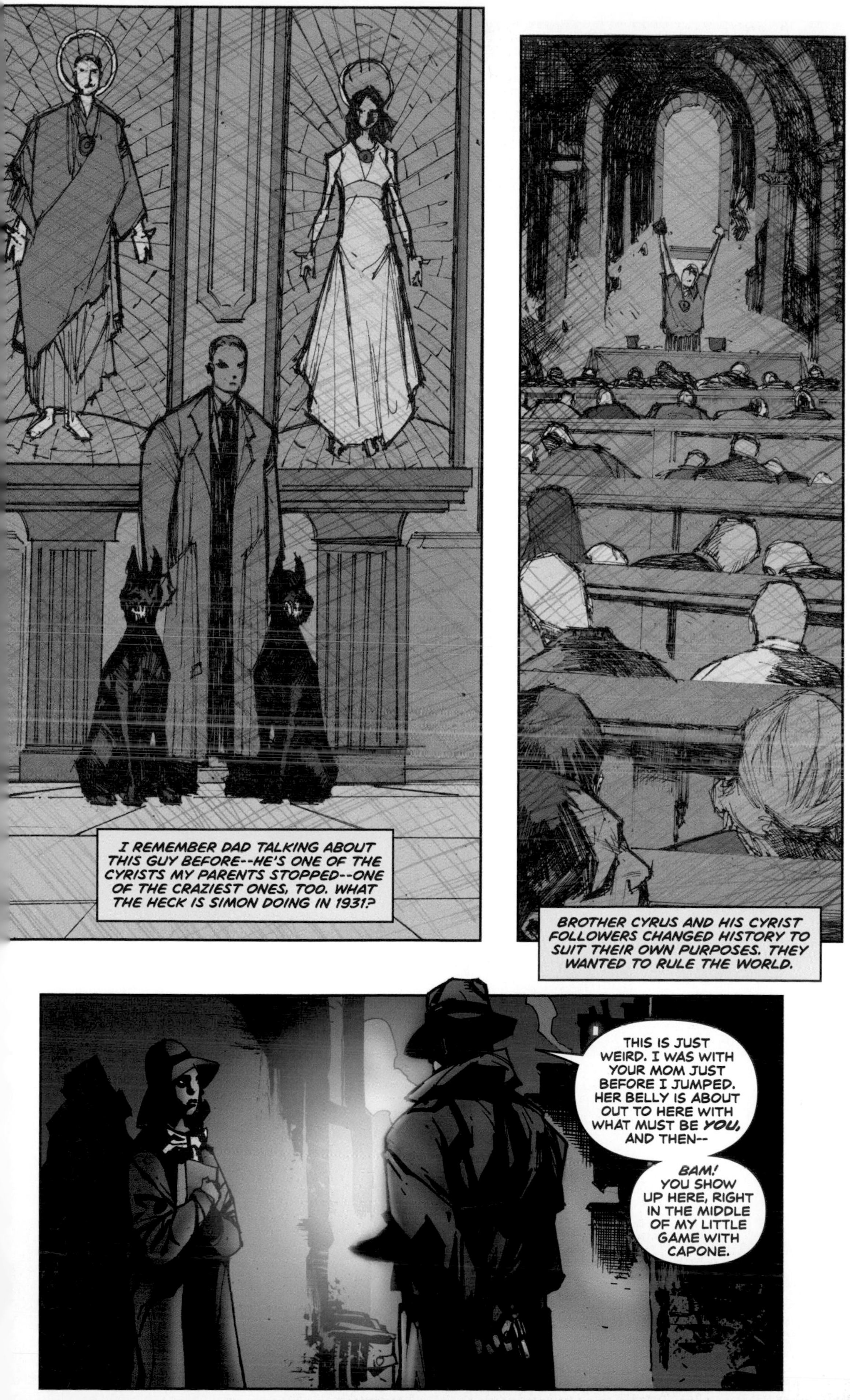

I REMEMBER DAD TALKING ABOUT THIS GUY BEFORE--HE'S ONE OF THE CYRISTS MY PARENTS STOPPED--ONE OF THE CRAZIEST ONES, TOO. WHAT THE HECK IS SIMON DOING IN 1931?
BROTHER CYRUS AND HIS CYRIST FOLLOWERS CHANGED HISTORY TO SUIT THEIR OWN PURPOSES. THEY WANTED TO RULE THE WORLD.
THIS IS JUST WEIRD. I WAS WITH YOUR MOM JUST BEFORE I JUMPED. HER BELLY IS ABOUT OUT TO HERE WITH WHAT MUST BE *YOU,* AND THEN--
BAM! YOU SHOW UP HERE, RIGHT IN THE MIDDLE OF MY LITTLE GAME WITH CAPONE.

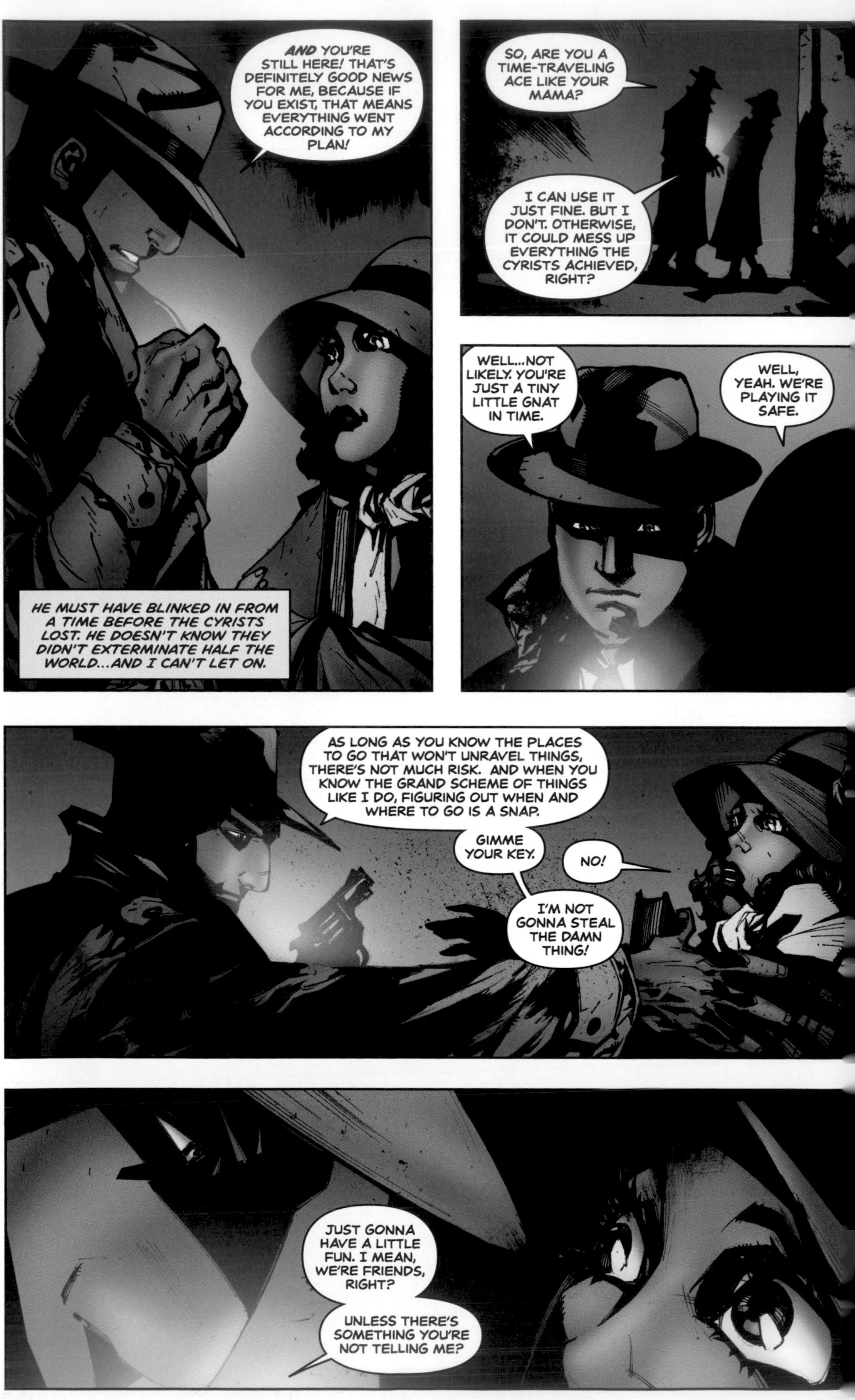
AND YOU'RE STILL HERE! THAT'S DEFINITELY GOOD NEWS FOR ME, BECAUSE IF YOU EXIST, THAT MEANS EVERYTHING WENT ACCORDING TO MY PLAN!
HE MUST HAVE BLINKED IN FROM A TIME BEFORE THE CYRISTS LOST. HE DOESN'T KNOW THEY DIDN'T EXTERMINATE HALF THE WORLD...AND I CAN'T LET ON.
SO, ARE YOU A TIME-TRAVELING ACE LIKE YOUR MAMA?
I CAN USE IT JUST FINE. BUT I DON'T. OTHERWISE, IT COULD MESS UP EVERYTHING THE CYRISTS ACHIEVED, RIGHT?
WELL, YEAH. WE'RE PLAYING IT SAFE.
WELL...NOT LIKELY. YOU'RE JUST A TINY LITTLE GNAT IN TIME.
AS LONG AS YOU KNOW THE PLACES TO GO THAT WON'T UNRAVEL THINGS, THERE'S NOT MUCH RISK. AND WHEN YOU KNOW THE GRAND SCHEME OF THINGS LIKE I DO, FIGURING OUT WHEN AND WHERE TO GO IS A SNAP.
GIMME YOUR KEY.
NO!
I'M NOT GONNA STEAL THE DAMN THING!
JUST GONNA HAVE A LITTLE FUN. I MEAN, WE'RE FRIENDS, RIGHT?
UNLESS THERE'S SOMETHING YOU'RE NOT TELLING ME?

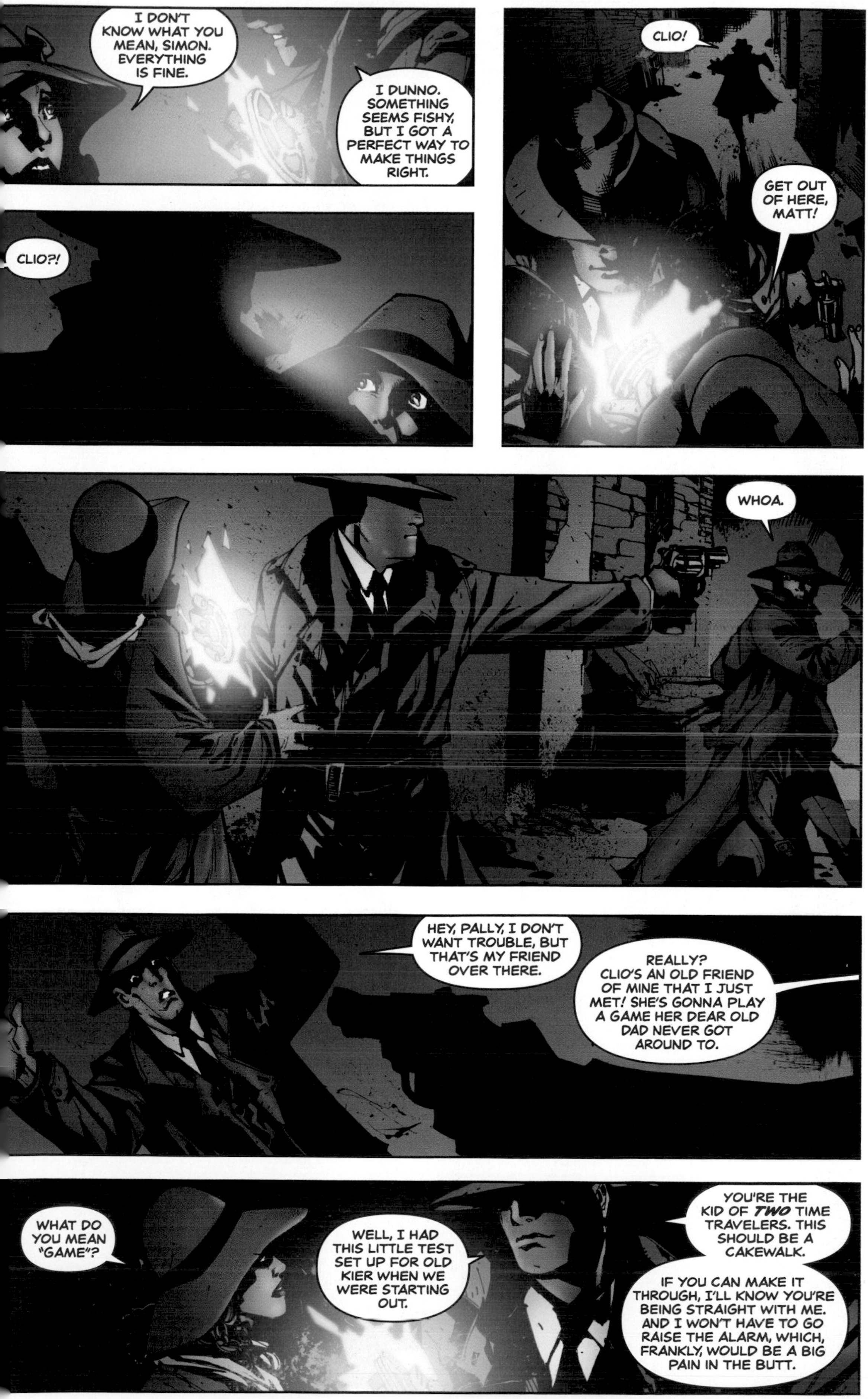
I DON'T KNOW WHAT YOU MEAN, SIMON. EVERYTHING IS FINE.
I DUNNO. SOMETHING SEEMS FISHY, BUT I GOT A PERFECT WAY TO MAKE THINGS RIGHT.
CLIO?!
CLIO!
GET OUT OF HERE, MATT!
WHOA.
HEY, PALLY, I DON'T WANT TROUBLE, BUT THAT'S MY FRIEND OVER THERE.
REALLY? CLIO'S AN OLD FRIEND OF MINE THAT I JUST MET! SHE'S GONNA PLAY A GAME HER DEAR OLD DAD NEVER GOT AROUND TO.
WHAT DO YOU MEAN "GAME"?
WELL, I HAD THIS LITTLE TEST SET UP FOR OLD KIER WHEN WE WERE STARTING OUT.
YOU'RE THE KID OF *TWO* TIME TRAVELERS. THIS SHOULD BE A CAKEWALK.
IF YOU CAN MAKE IT THROUGH, I'LL KNOW YOU'RE BEING STRAIGHT WITH ME. AND I WON'T HAVE TO GO RAISE THE ALARM, WHICH, FRANKLY, WOULD BE A BIG PAIN IN THE BUTT.

GO AHEAD AND PULL UP MY FIRST STABLE POINT. I'VE GOT YOUR ITINERARY ALL SET. EVERYTHING ELSE IS BLOCKED OUT.

START THERE AND YOUR LITTLE VACATIONS WILL OPEN UP IN ORDER.

I'M NOT GOING *ANYWHERE*. I-I'M NOT ALLOWED.

I SEE YOU, REPORTER BOY. DON'T EVEN.

I WASN'T...

THWACK

GAH!

RUN, MATT!

NEED MORE INCENTIVE, HUH? YOU NEED TO BREAK MOMMY AND DADDY'S RULES SOME DAY, LITTLE GIRL.

JUMP IN THE NEXT TEN SECONDS OR I'M GONNA TAKE A LITTLE TRIP THROUGH TIME AND ALTER HIS PAST.

I CAN BLINK BEFORE THAT BULLET GETS ME, BUT CAN HE SURVIVE BEING ERASED FROM HISTORY?

TIME TRAVEL? YOU'RE A LOO... MISTER!

N-NO, SIMON.

COME ON, BABY TIME TRAVELER, THIS WILL BE EASY PEASY FOR YOU.

PLUS, YOU WOULDN'T WANT YOUR BOY TOY TO GO POOF, NOW WOULD YA?

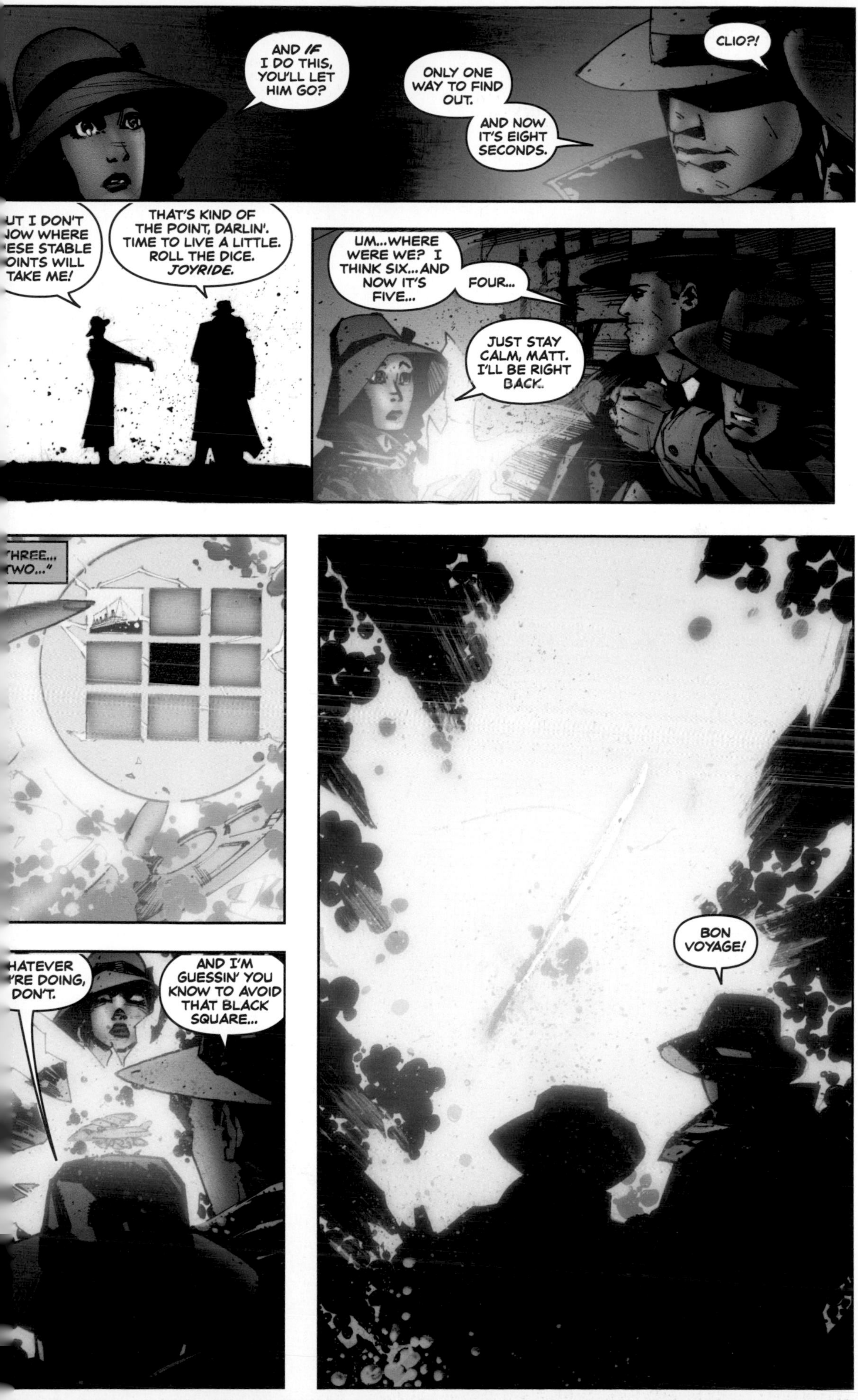
AND *IF* I DO THIS, YOU'LL LET HIM GO?
ONLY ONE WAY TO FIND OUT.
CLIO?!
AND NOW IT'S EIGHT SECONDS.
UT I DON'T NOW WHERE ESE STABLE OINTS WILL TAKE ME!
THAT'S KIND OF THE POINT, DARLIN'. TIME TO LIVE A LITTLE. ROLL THE DICE. *JOYRIDE.*
UM...WHERE WERE WE? I THINK SIX...AND NOW IT'S FIVE...
FOUR...
JUST STAY CALM, MATT. I'LL BE RIGHT BACK.
THREE... TWO..."
HATEVER 'RE DOING, DON'T.
AND I'M GUESSIN' YOU KNOW TO AVOID THAT BLACK SQUARE...
BON VOYAGE!

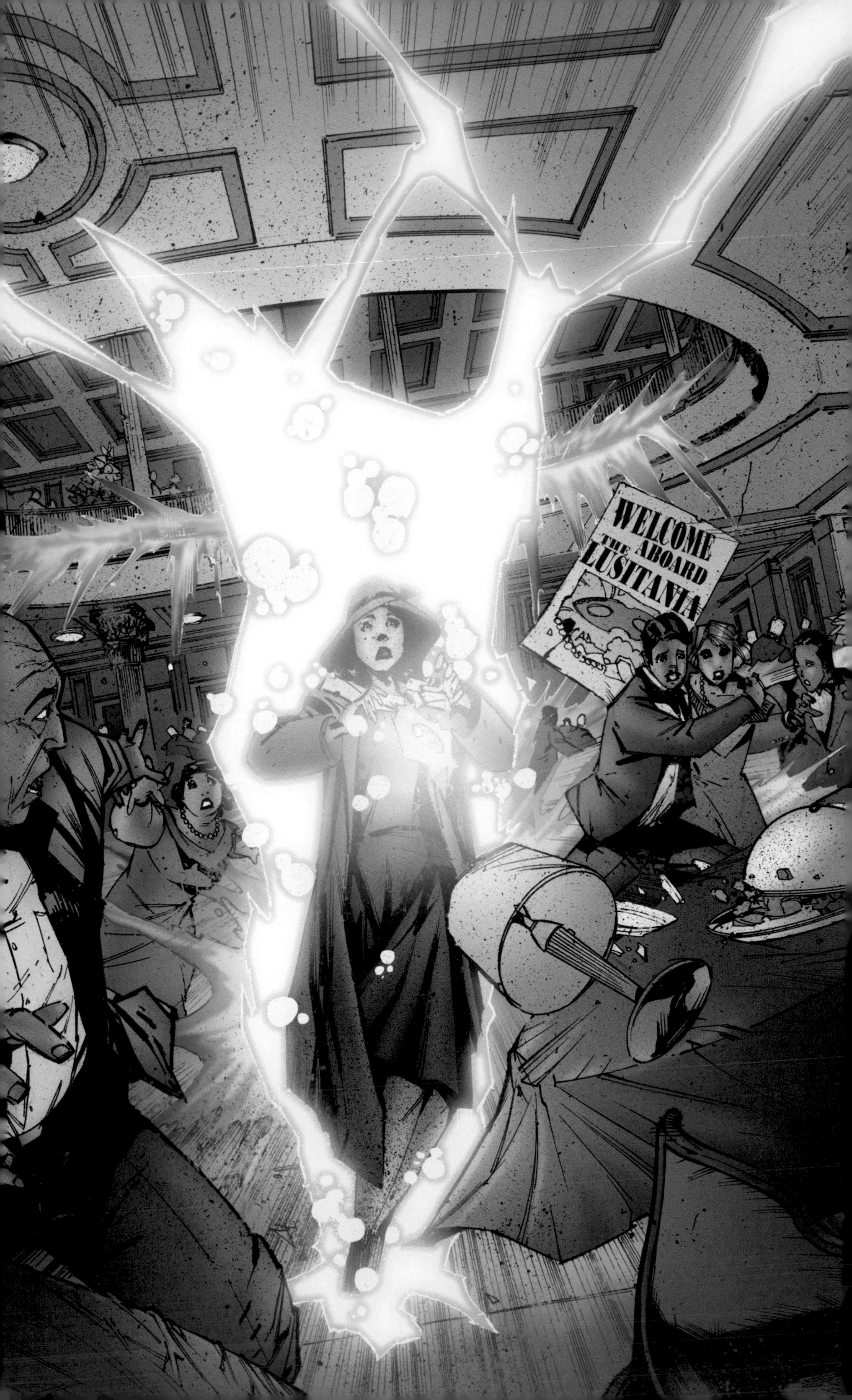

WELCOME
ABOARD
THE
LUSITANIA

CHAPTER 2

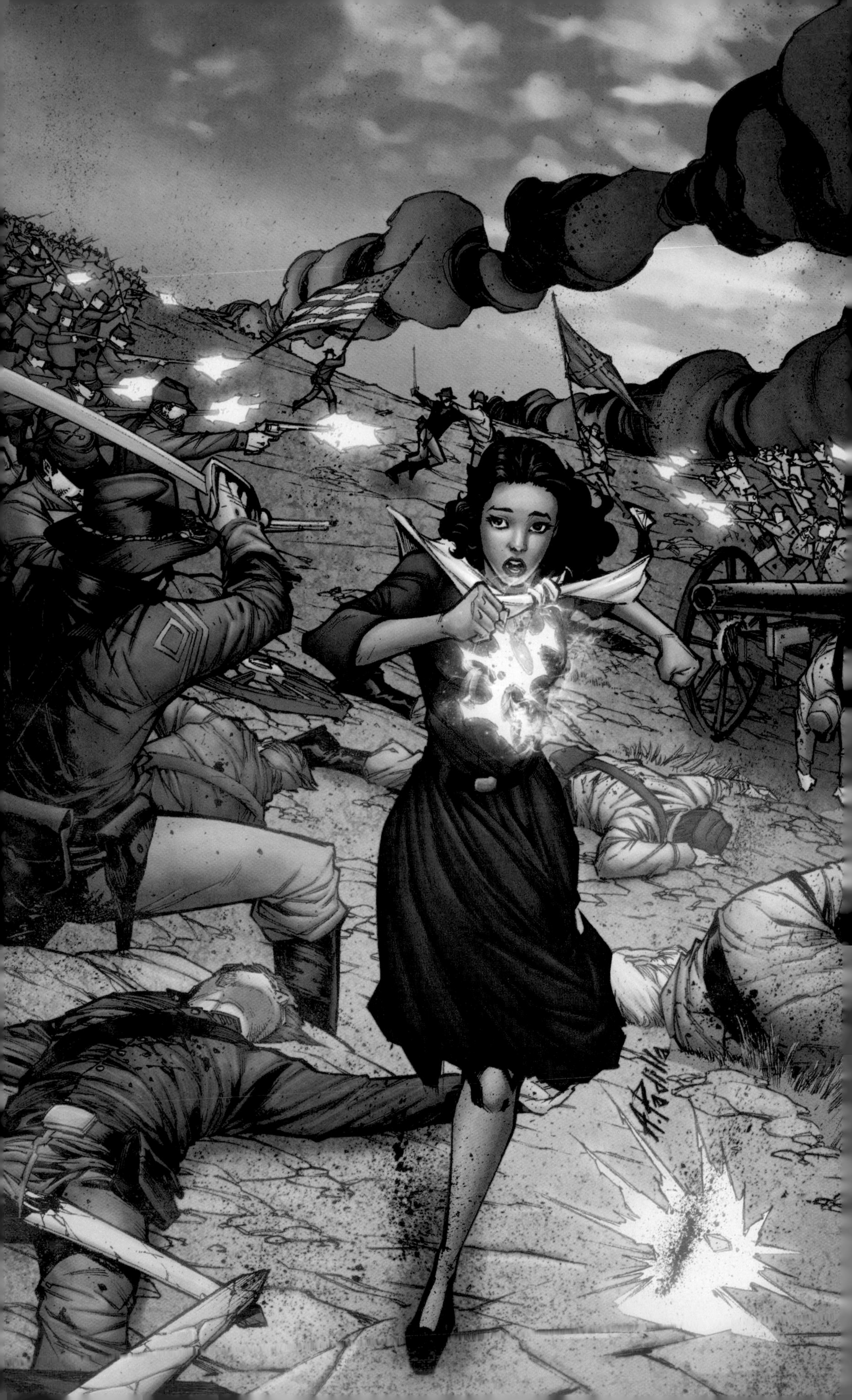

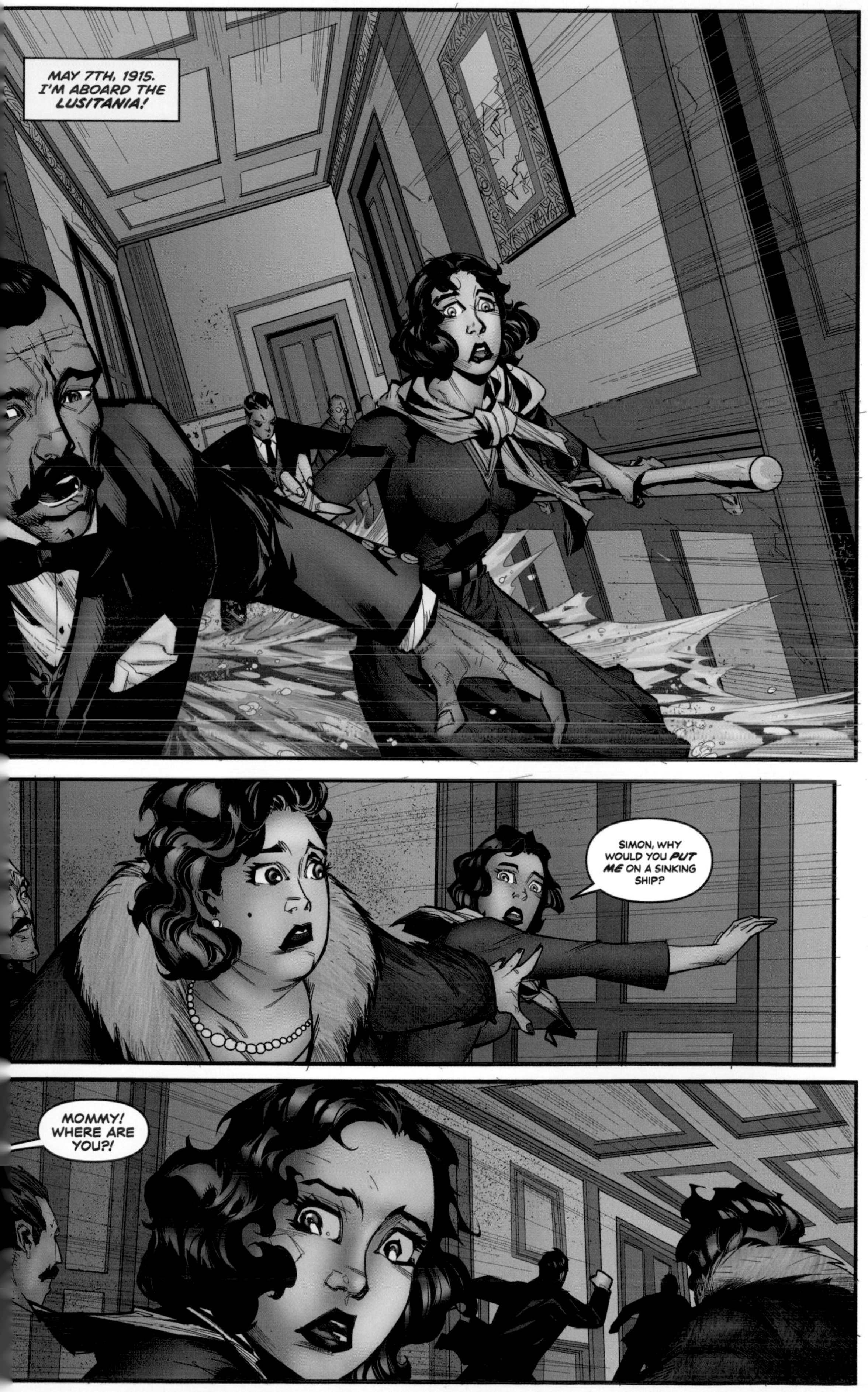
MAY 7TH, 1915. I'M ABOARD THE LUSITANIA!
SIMON, WHY WOULD YOU PUT ME ON A SINKING SHIP?
MOMMY! WHERE ARE YOU?!

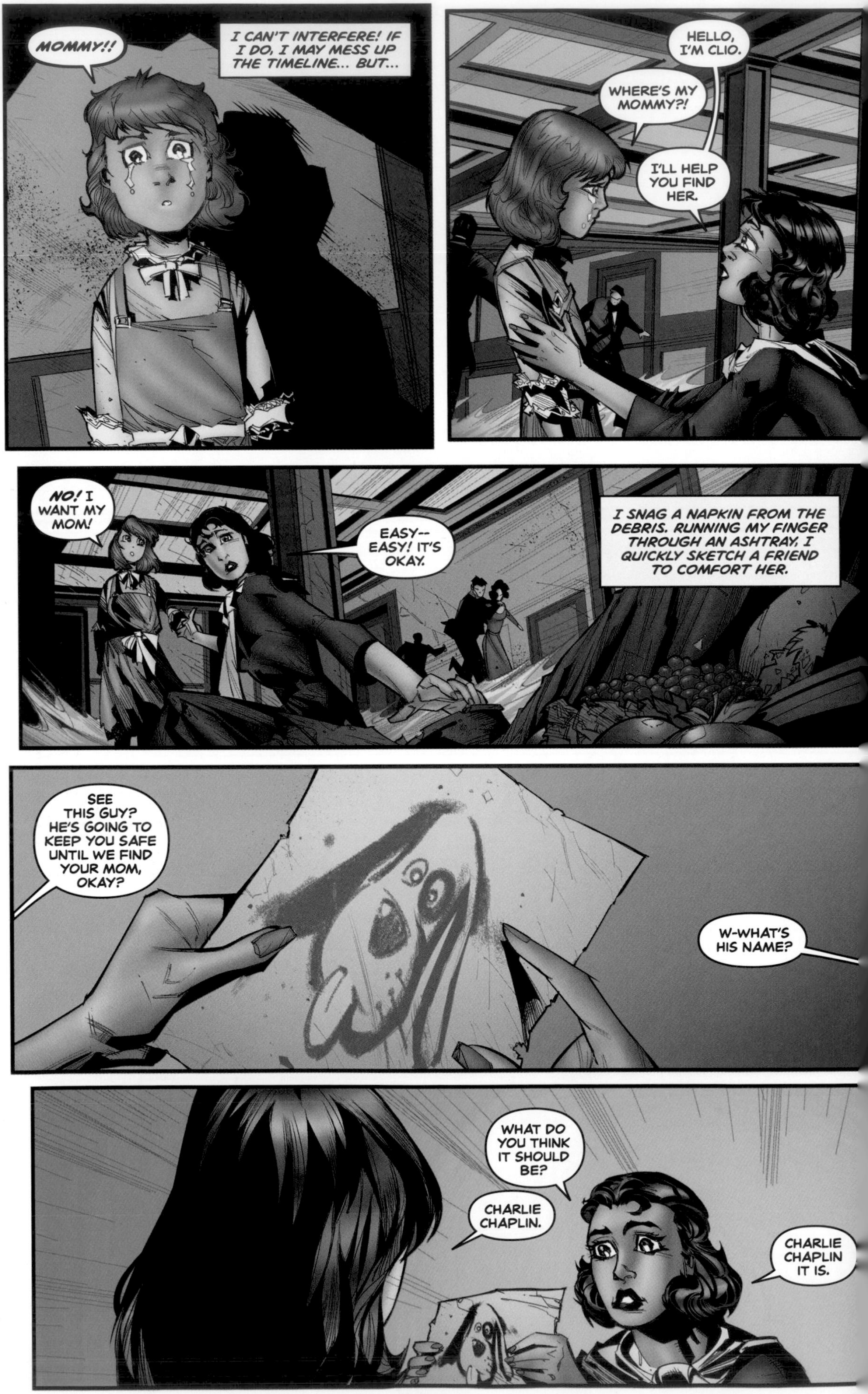
MOMMY!!
I CAN'T INTERFERE! IF I DO, I MAY MESS UP THE TIMELINE... BUT...
HELLO, I'M CLIO.
WHERE'S MY MOMMY?!
I'LL HELP YOU FIND HER.
NO! I WANT MY MOM!
EASY-- EASY! IT'S OKAY.
I SNAG A NAPKIN FROM THE DEBRIS. RUNNING MY FINGER THROUGH AN ASHTRAY, I QUICKLY SKETCH A FRIEND TO COMFORT HER.
SEE THIS GUY? HE'S GOING TO KEEP YOU SAFE UNTIL WE FIND YOUR MOM, OKAY?
W-WHAT'S HIS NAME?
WHAT DO YOU THINK IT SHOULD BE?
CHARLIE CHAPLIN.
CHARLIE CHAPLIN IT IS.

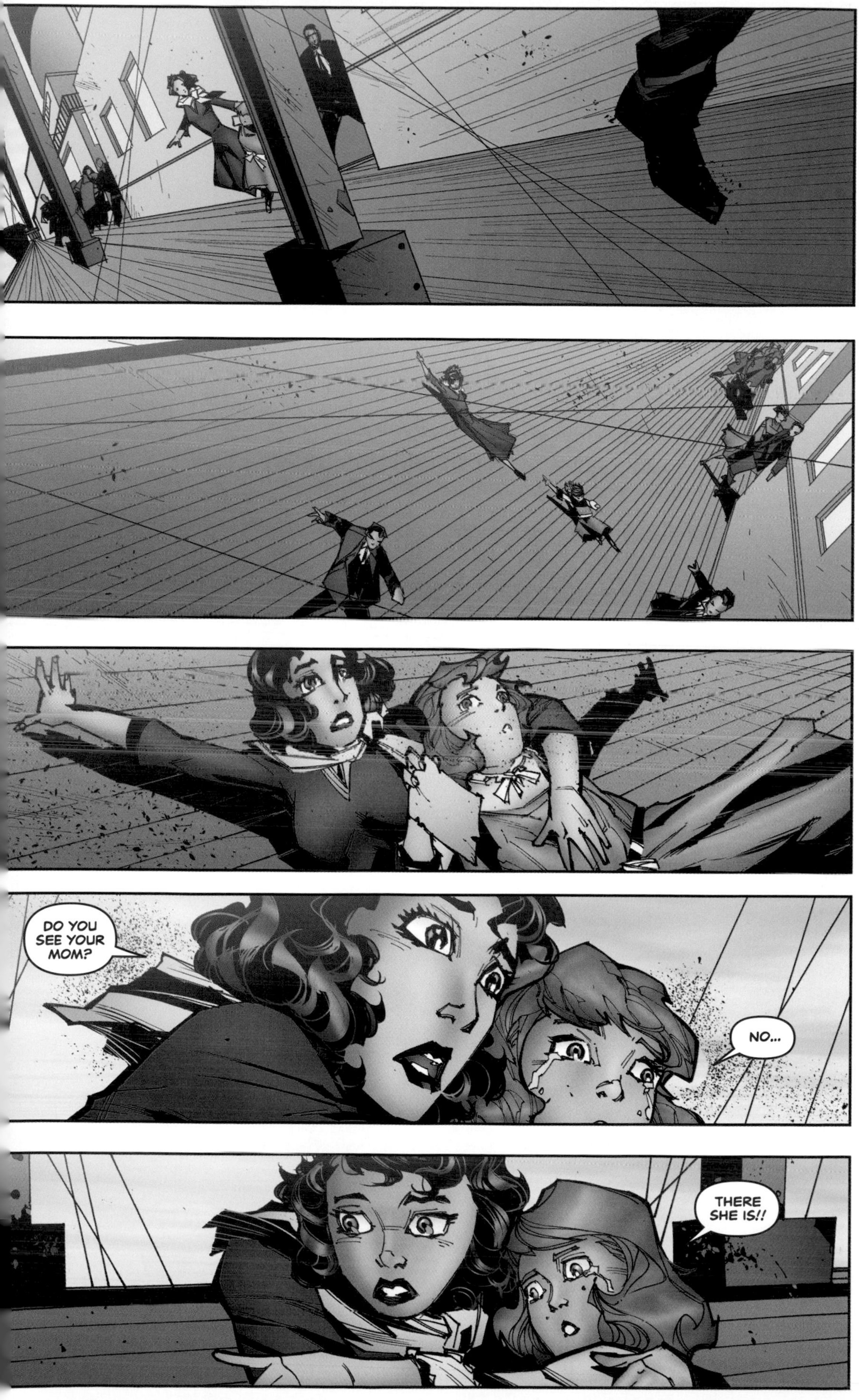
DO YOU SEE YOUR MOM?
NO...
THERE SHE IS!!

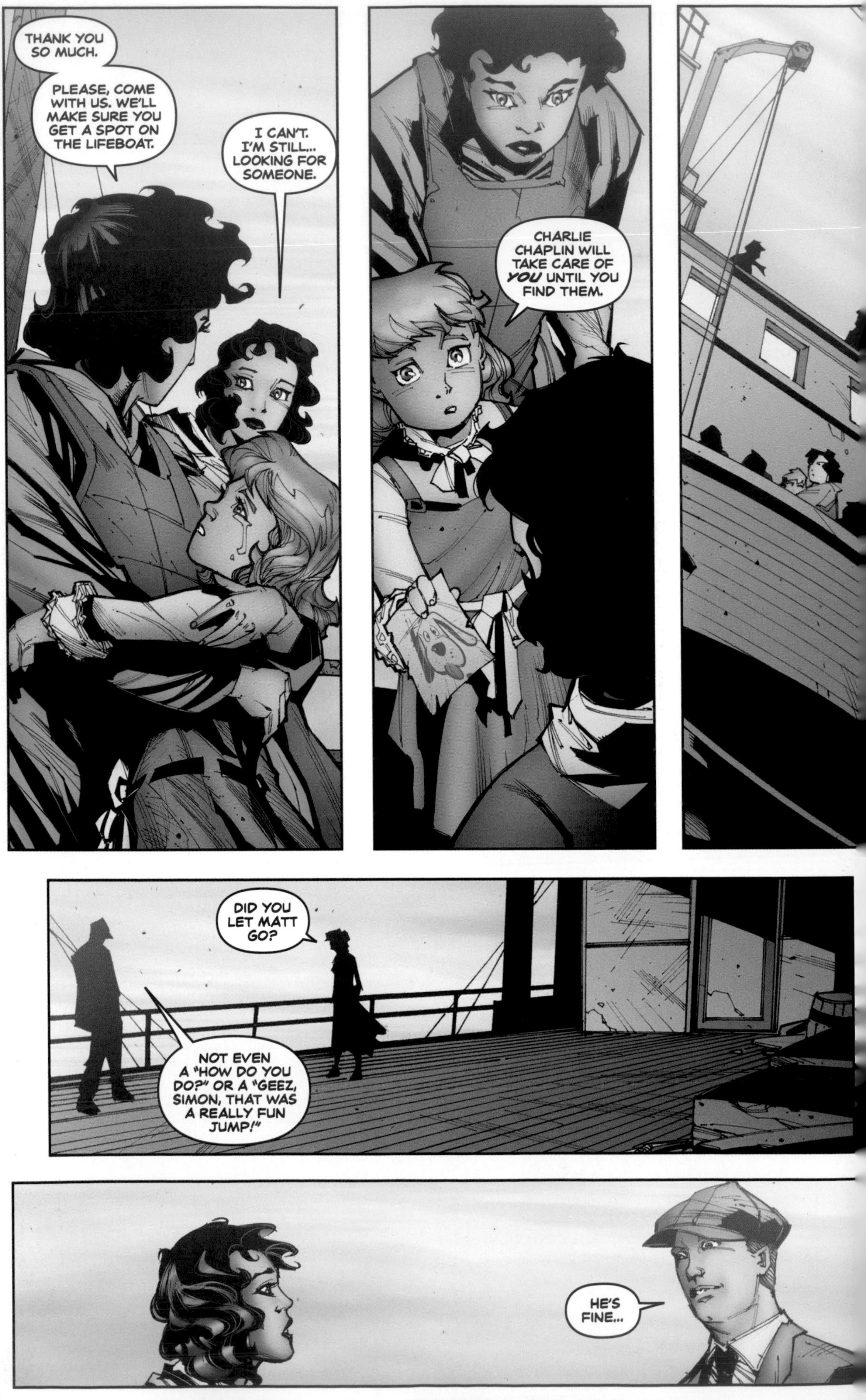
THANK YOU SO MUCH.
PLEASE, COME WITH US. WE'LL MAKE SURE YOU GET A SPOT ON THE LIFEBOAT.
I CAN'T. I'M STILL... LOOKING FOR SOMEONE.
CHARLIE CHAPLIN WILL TAKE CARE OF YOU UNTIL YOU FIND THEM.
DID YOU LET MATT GO?
NOT EVEN A "HOW DO YOU DO?" OR A "GEEZ, SIMON, THAT WAS A REALLY FUN JUMP!"
HE'S FINE...

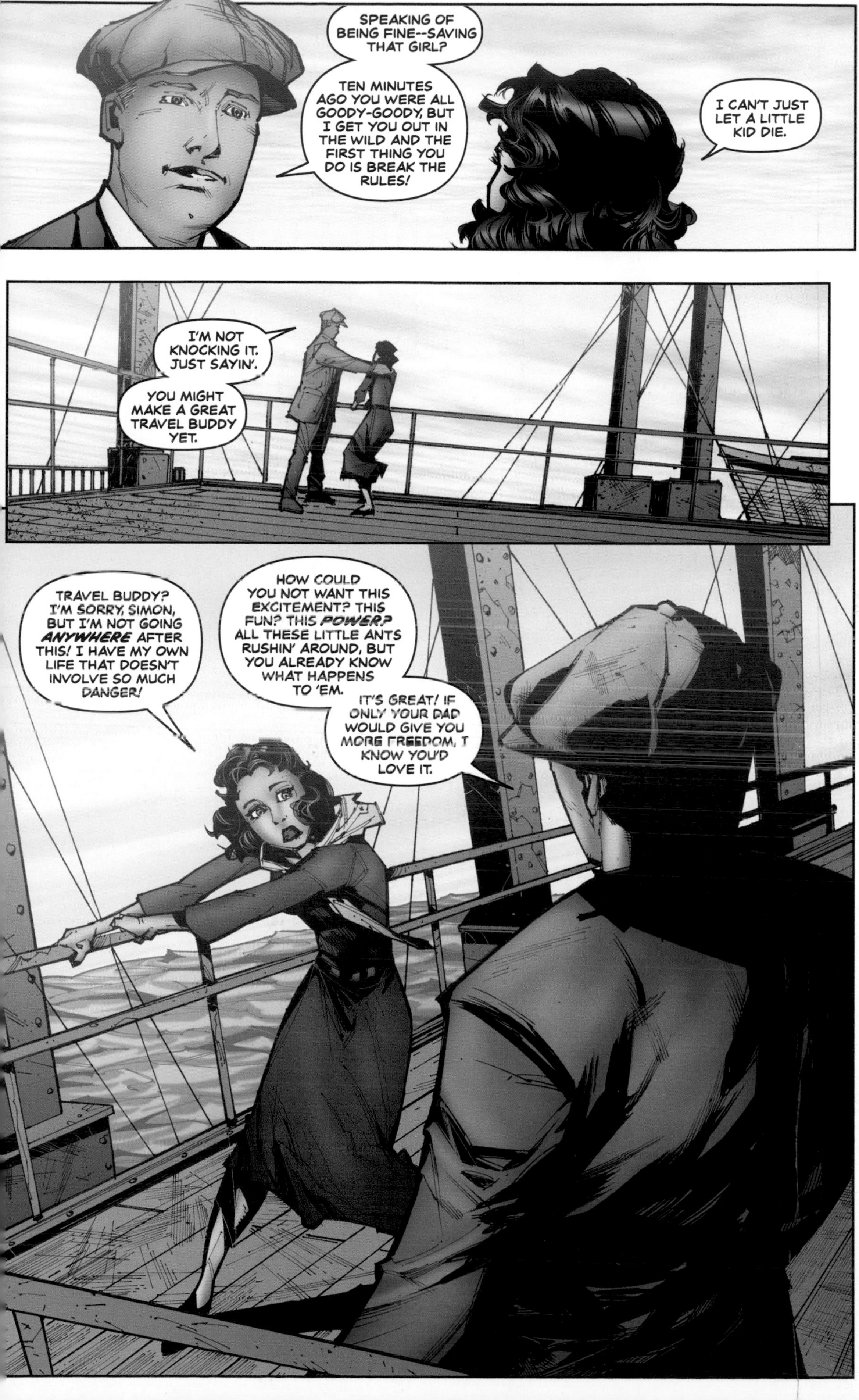
SPEAKING OF BEING FINE--SAVING THAT GIRL?
TEN MINUTES AGO YOU WERE ALL GOODY-GOODY, BUT I GET YOU OUT IN THE WILD AND THE FIRST THING YOU DO IS BREAK THE RULES!
I CAN'T JUST LET A LITTLE KID DIE.
I'M NOT KNOCKING IT. JUST SAYIN'.
YOU MIGHT MAKE A GREAT TRAVEL BUDDY YET.
TRAVEL BUDDY? I'M SORRY, SIMON, BUT I'M NOT GOING *ANYWHERE* AFTER THIS! I HAVE MY OWN LIFE THAT DOESN'T INVOLVE SO MUCH DANGER!
HOW COULD YOU NOT WANT THIS EXCITEMENT? THIS FUN? THIS *POWER?* ALL THESE LITTLE ANTS RUSHIN' AROUND, BUT YOU ALREADY KNOW WHAT HAPPENS TO 'EM.
IT'S GREAT! IF ONLY YOUR DAD WOULD GIVE YOU MORE FREEDOM, I KNOW YOU'D LOVE IT.

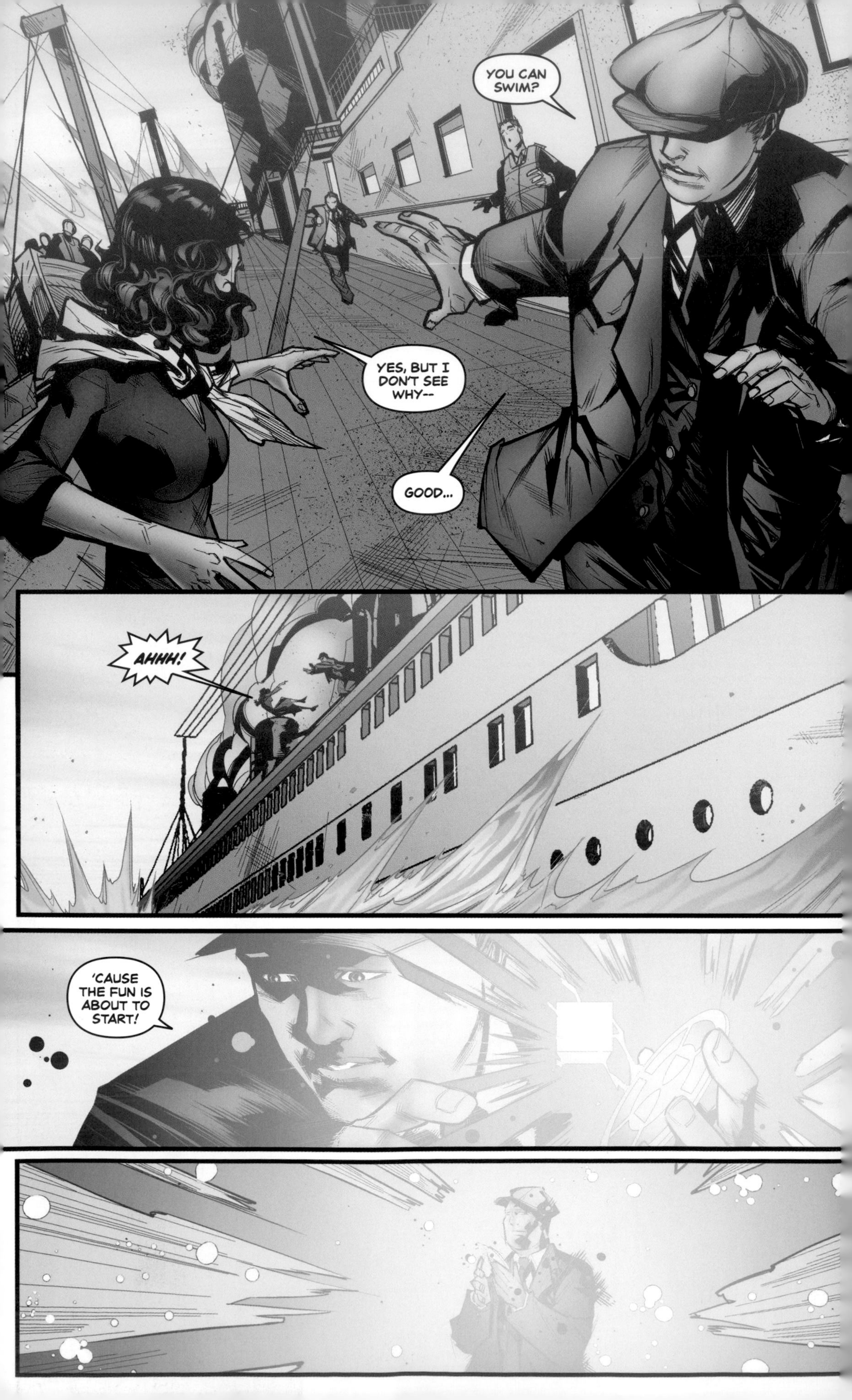
YOU CAN SWIM?
YES, BUT I DON'T SEE WHY--
GOOD...
AHHH!
'CAUSE THE FUN IS ABOUT TO START!

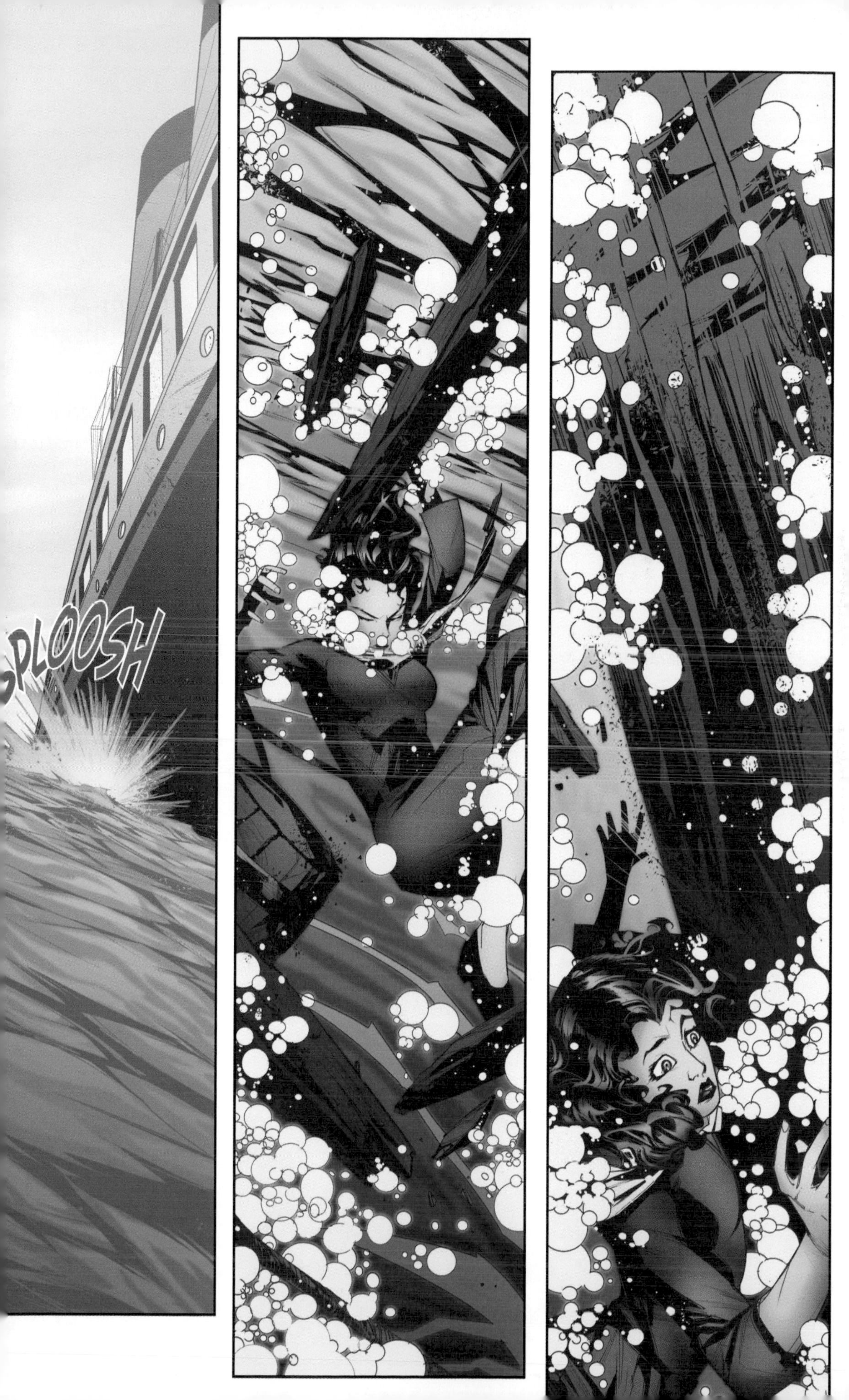
SPLOOSH

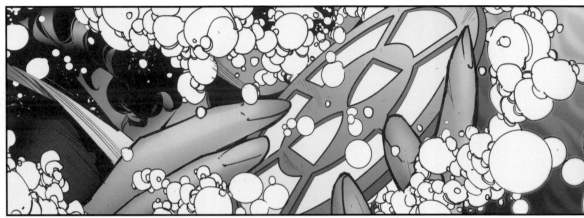

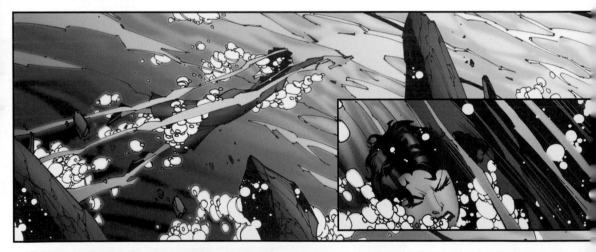

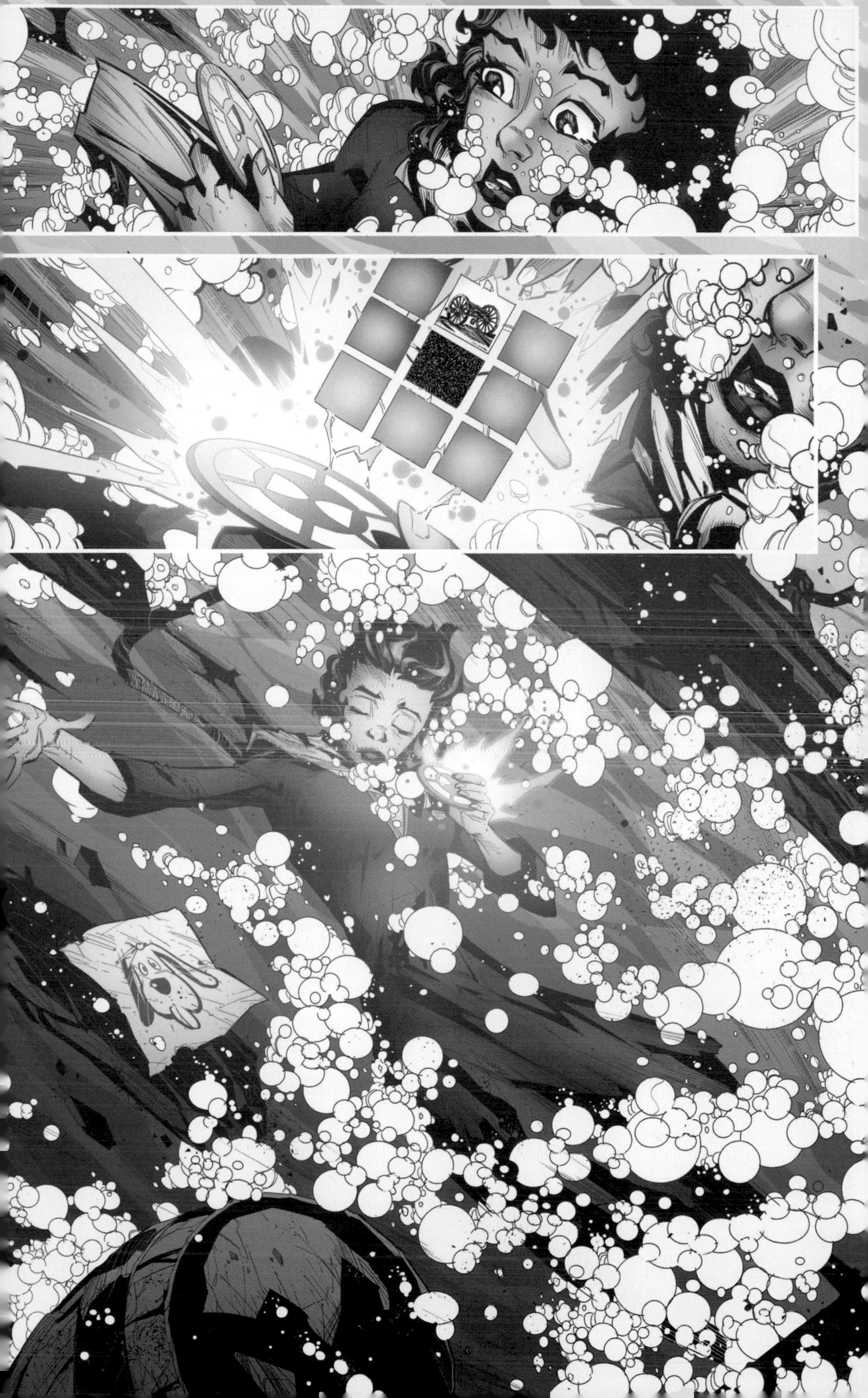

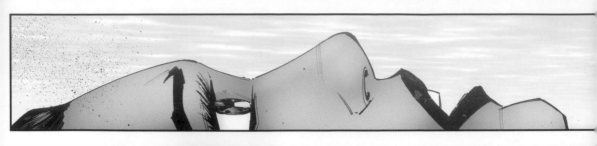

GETTYSBURG.
JULY THIRD, 1863.
10:22 A.M.

WHY DO
I HAVE THE
FEELING THIS
IS ABOUT TO
GET REALLY
NOISY?

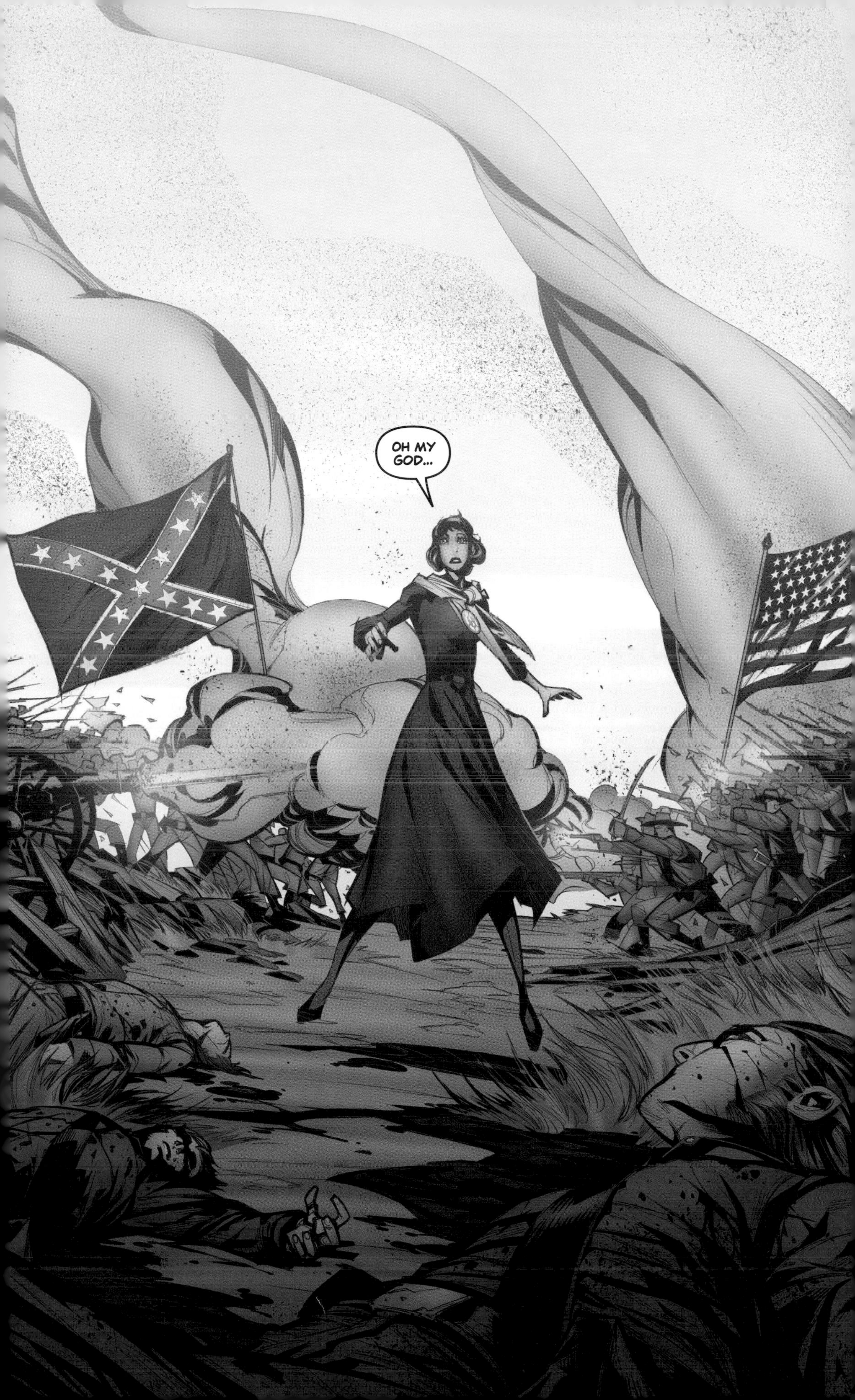
OH MY GOD...

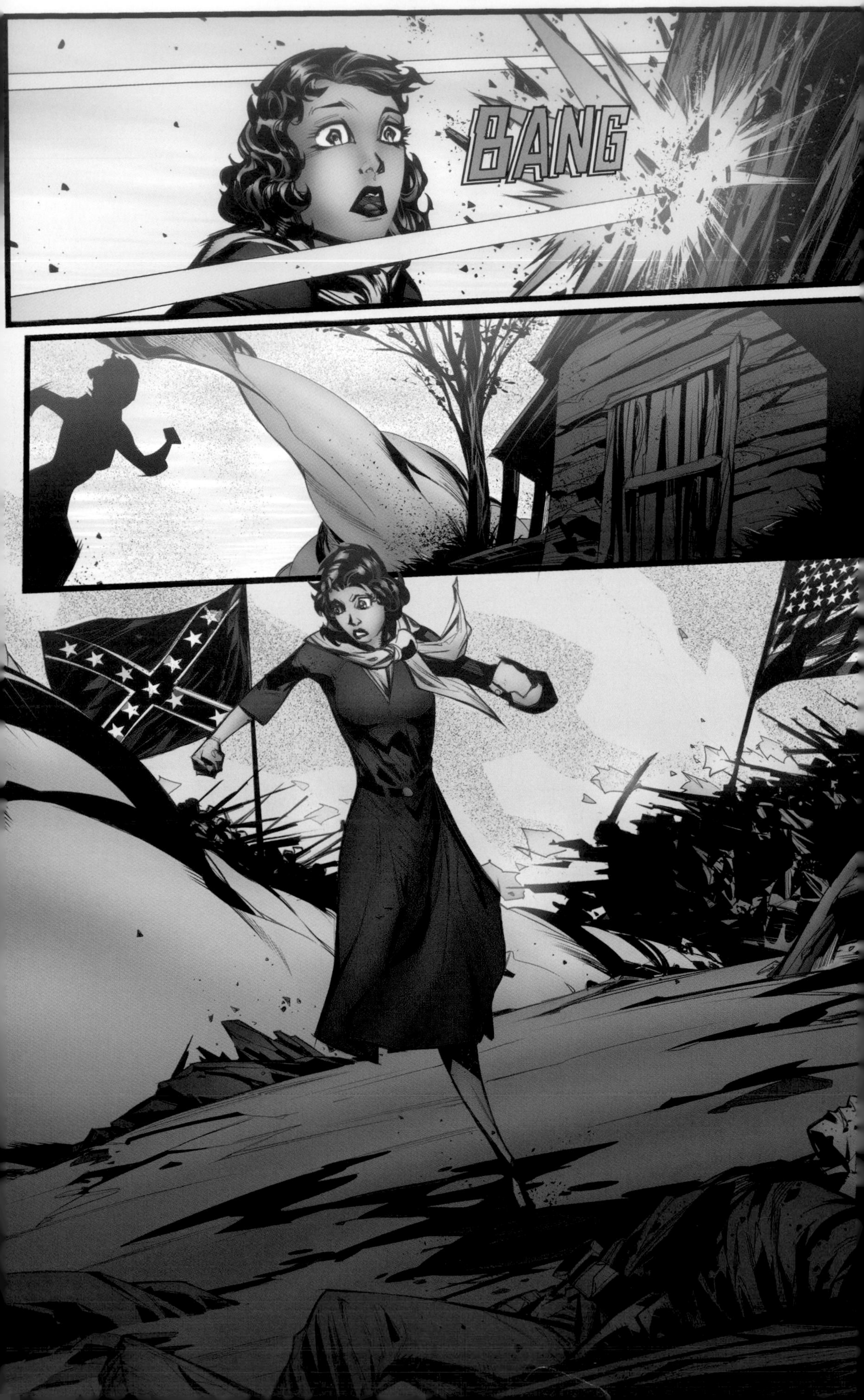
BANG

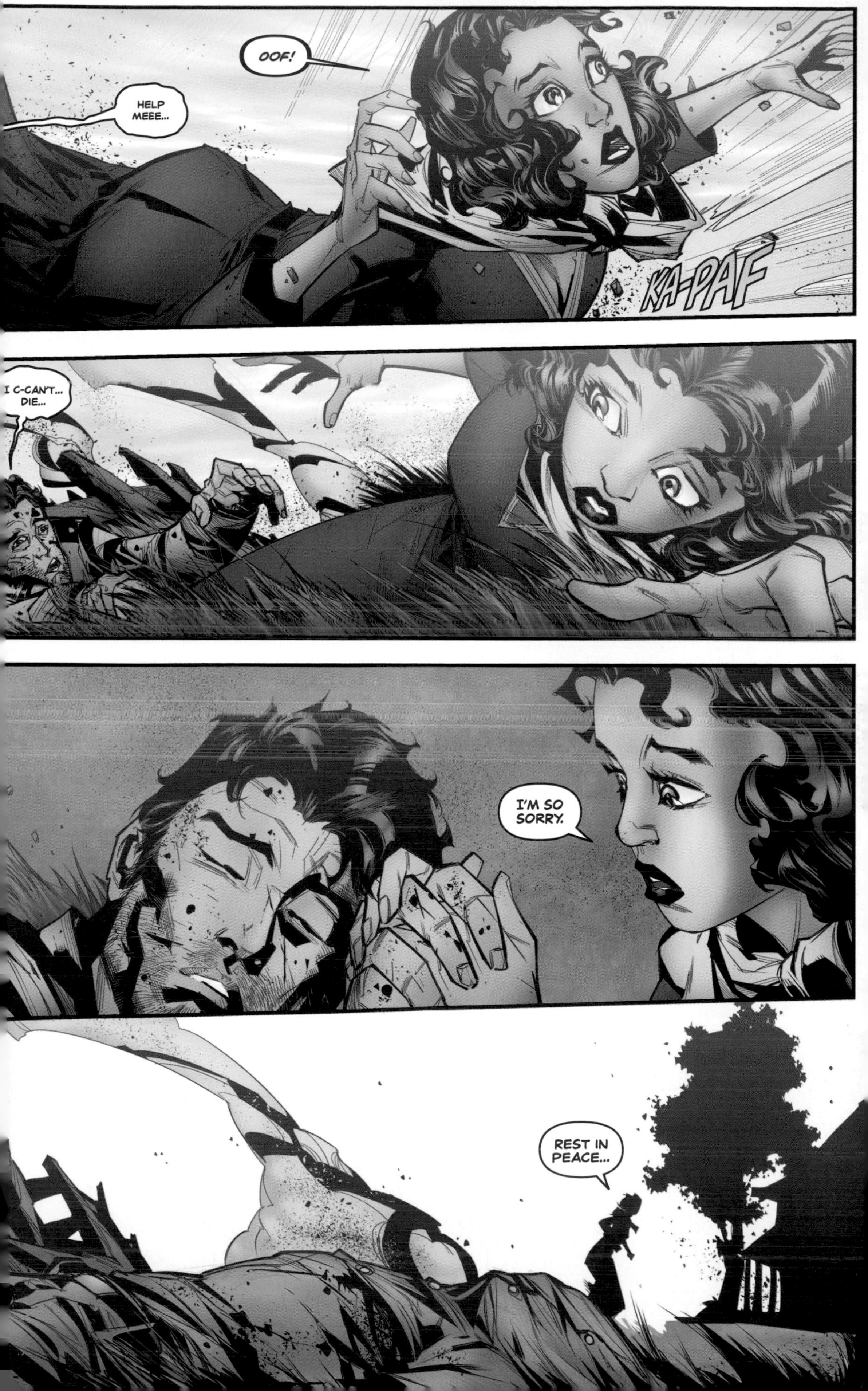
OOF!
HELP MEEE...
KA-PAF
I C-CAN'T... DIE...
I'M SO SORRY.
REST IN PEACE...

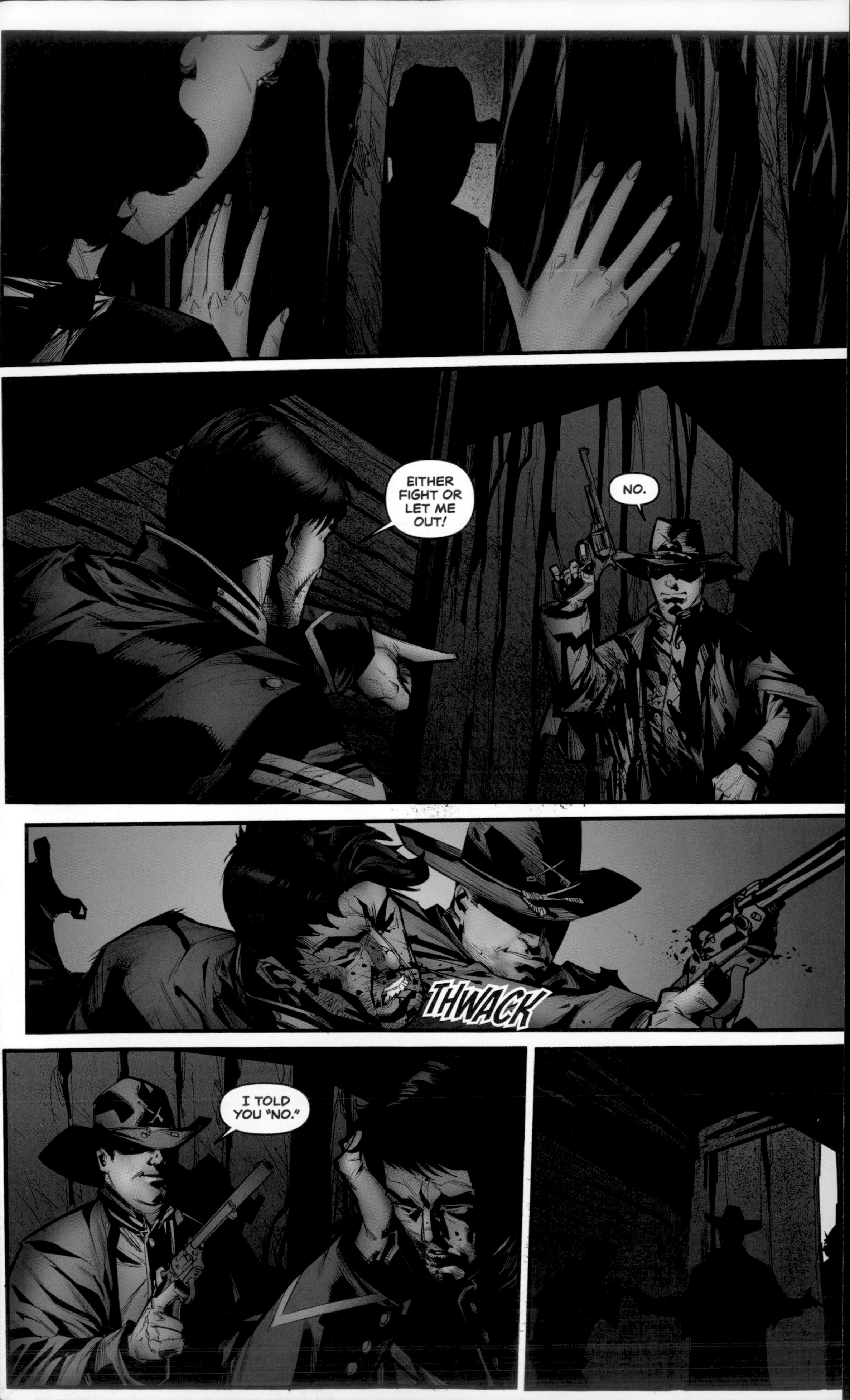
EITHER FIGHT OR LET ME OUT!
NO.
THWACK
I TOLD YOU "NO."

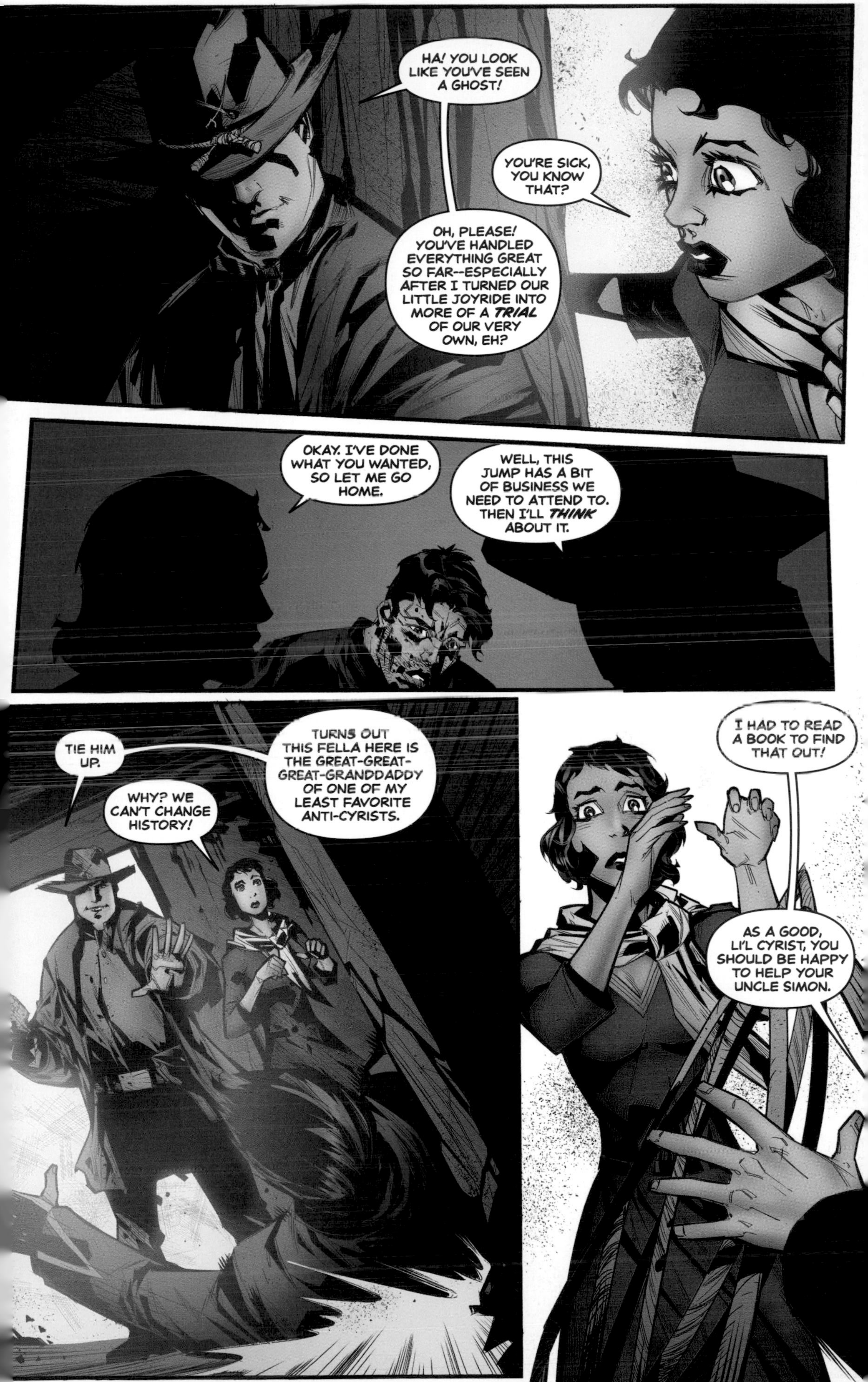
HA! YOU LOOK LIKE YOU'VE SEEN A GHOST!
YOU'RE SICK, YOU KNOW THAT?
OH, PLEASE! YOU'VE HANDLED EVERYTHING GREAT SO FAR--ESPECIALLY AFTER I TURNED OUR LITTLE JOYRIDE INTO MORE OF A *TRIAL* OF OUR VERY OWN, EH?
OKAY. I'VE DONE WHAT YOU WANTED, SO LET ME GO HOME.
WELL, THIS JUMP HAS A BIT OF BUSINESS WE NEED TO ATTEND TO. THEN I'LL *THINK* ABOUT IT.
TIE HIM UP.
WHY? WE CAN'T CHANGE HISTORY!
TURNS OUT THIS FELLA HERE IS THE GREAT-GREAT-GREAT-GRANDDADDY OF ONE OF MY LEAST FAVORITE ANTI-CYRISTS.
I HAD TO READ A BOOK TO FIND THAT OUT!
AS A GOOD, LI'L CYRIST, YOU SHOULD BE HAPPY TO HELP YOUR UNCLE SIMON.

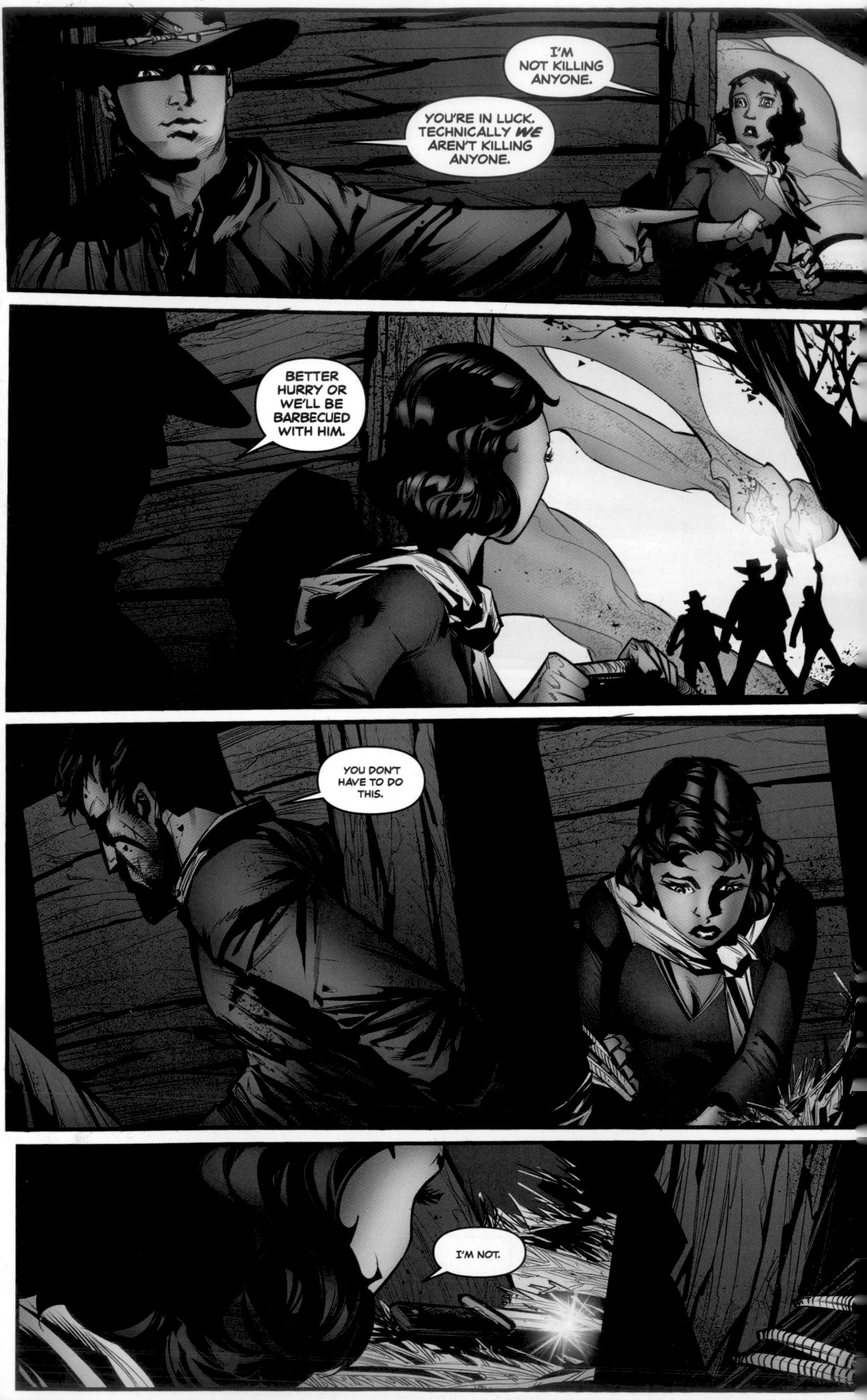
I'M NOT KILLING ANYONE.
YOU'RE IN LUCK. TECHNICALLY *WE* AREN'T KILLING ANYONE.
BETTER HURRY OR WE'LL BE BARBECUED WITH HIM.
YOU DON'T HAVE TO DO THIS.
I'M NOT.

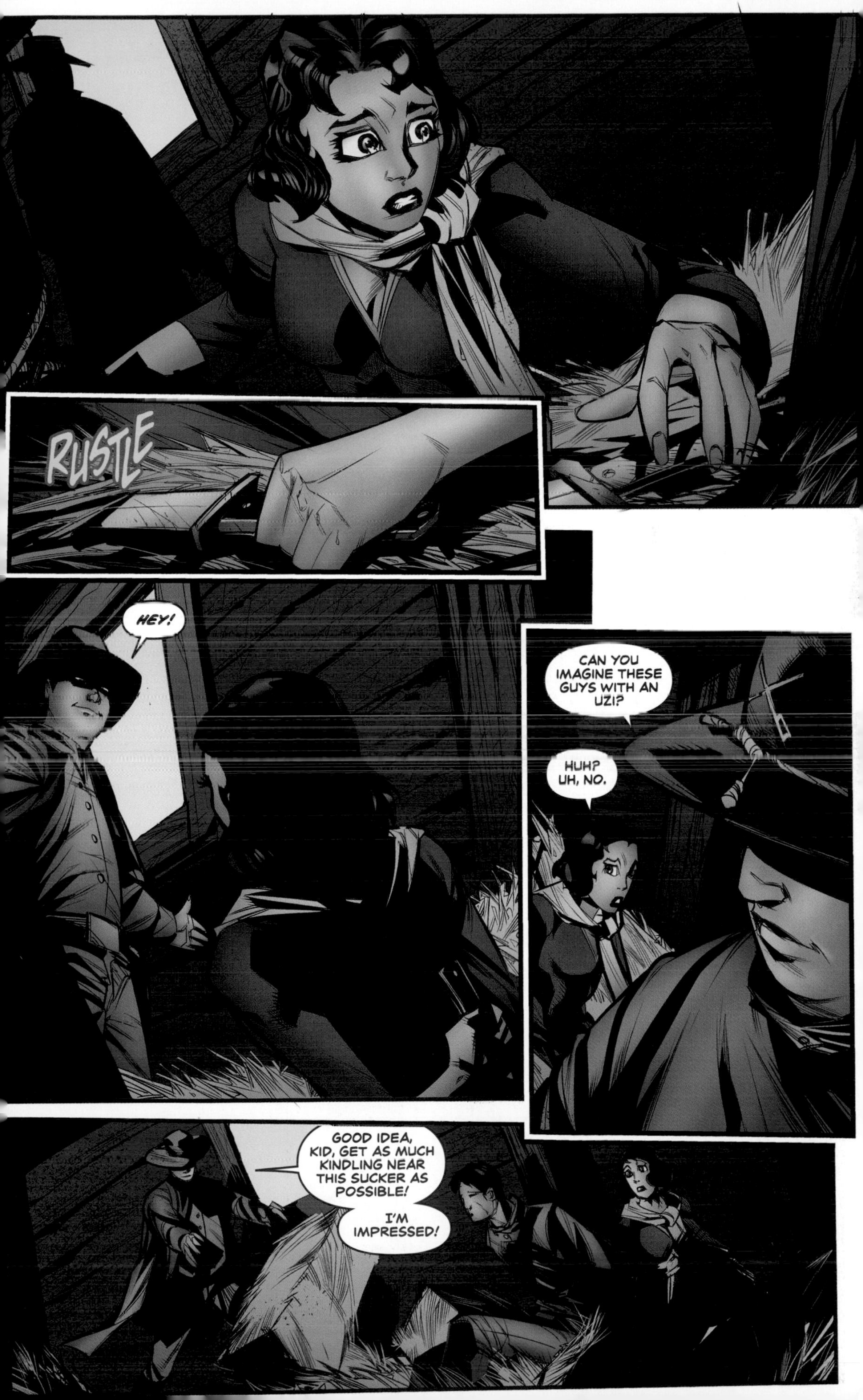
RUSTLE
HEY!
CAN YOU IMAGINE THESE GUYS WITH AN UZI?
HUH? UH, NO.
GOOD IDEA, KID, GET AS MUCH KINDLING NEAR THIS SUCKER AS POSSIBLE!
I'M IMPRESSED!

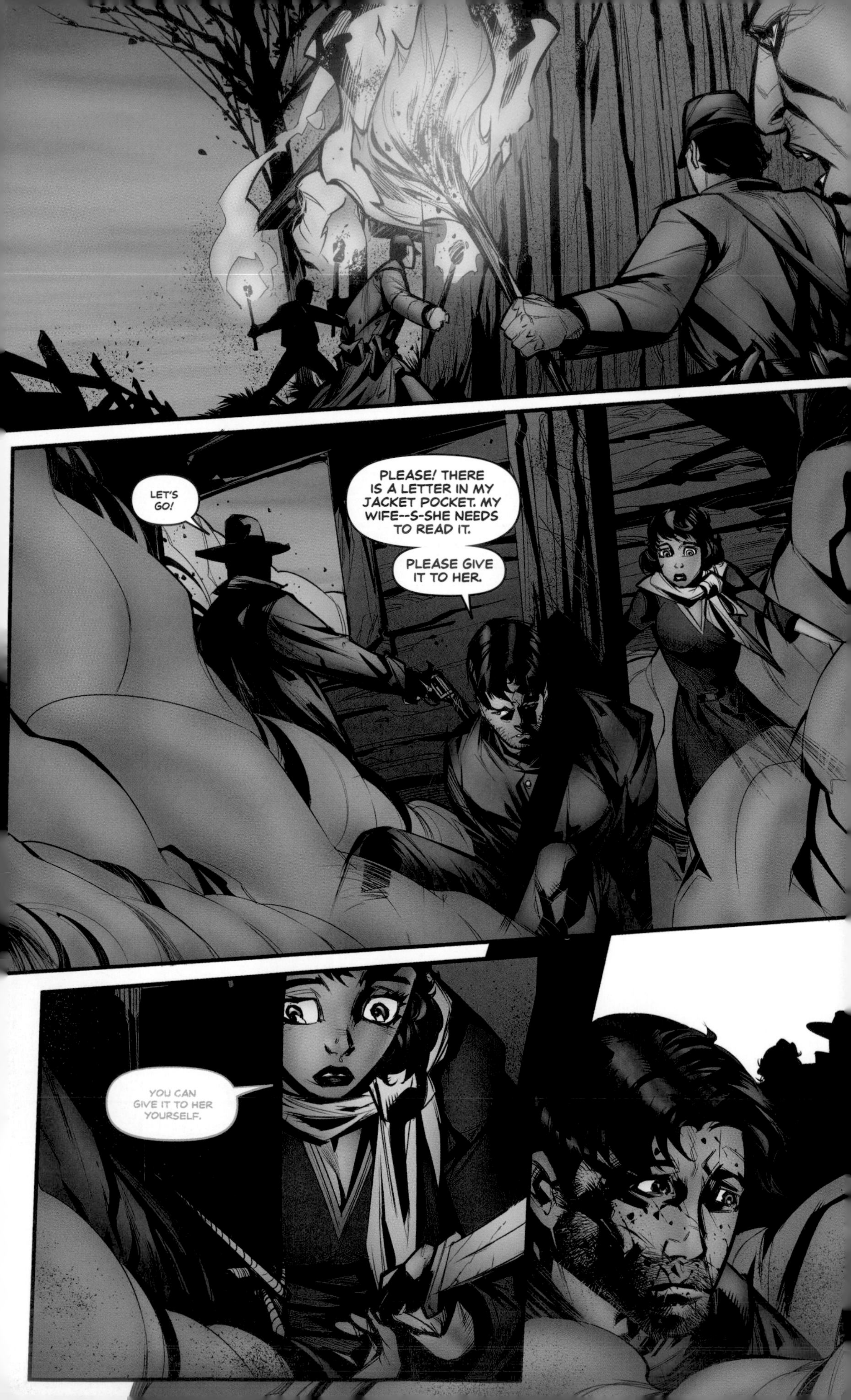
LET'S GO!
PLEASE! THERE IS A LETTER IN MY JACKET POCKET. MY WIFE--S-SHE NEEDS TO READ IT.
PLEASE GIVE IT TO HER.
YOU CAN GIVE IT TO HER YOURSELF.

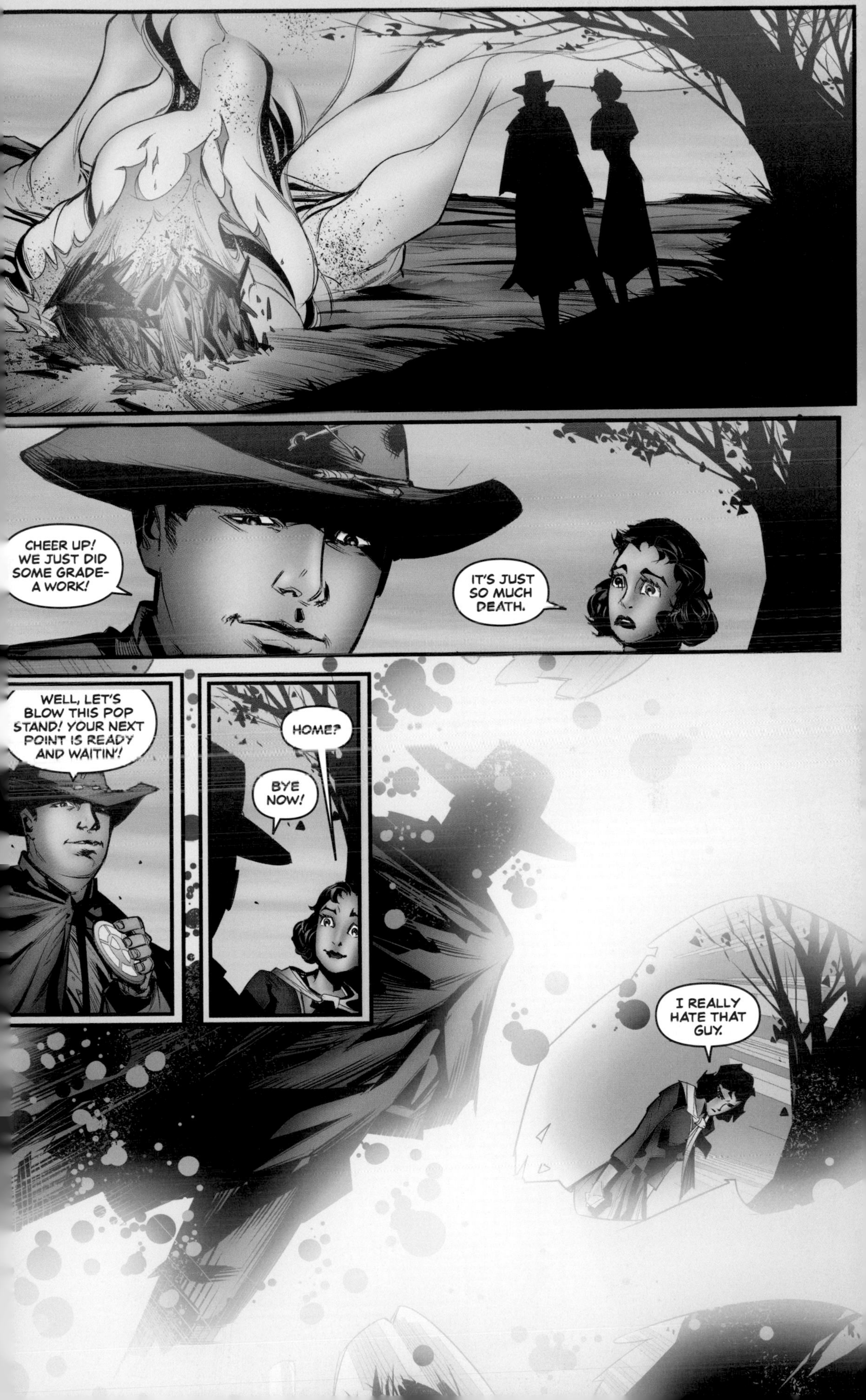
CHEER UP! WE JUST DID SOME GRADE-A WORK!
IT'S JUST SO MUCH DEATH.
WELL, LET'S BLOW THIS POP STAND! YOUR NEXT POINT IS READY AND WAITIN'!
HOME?
BYE NOW!
I REALLY HATE THAT GUY.

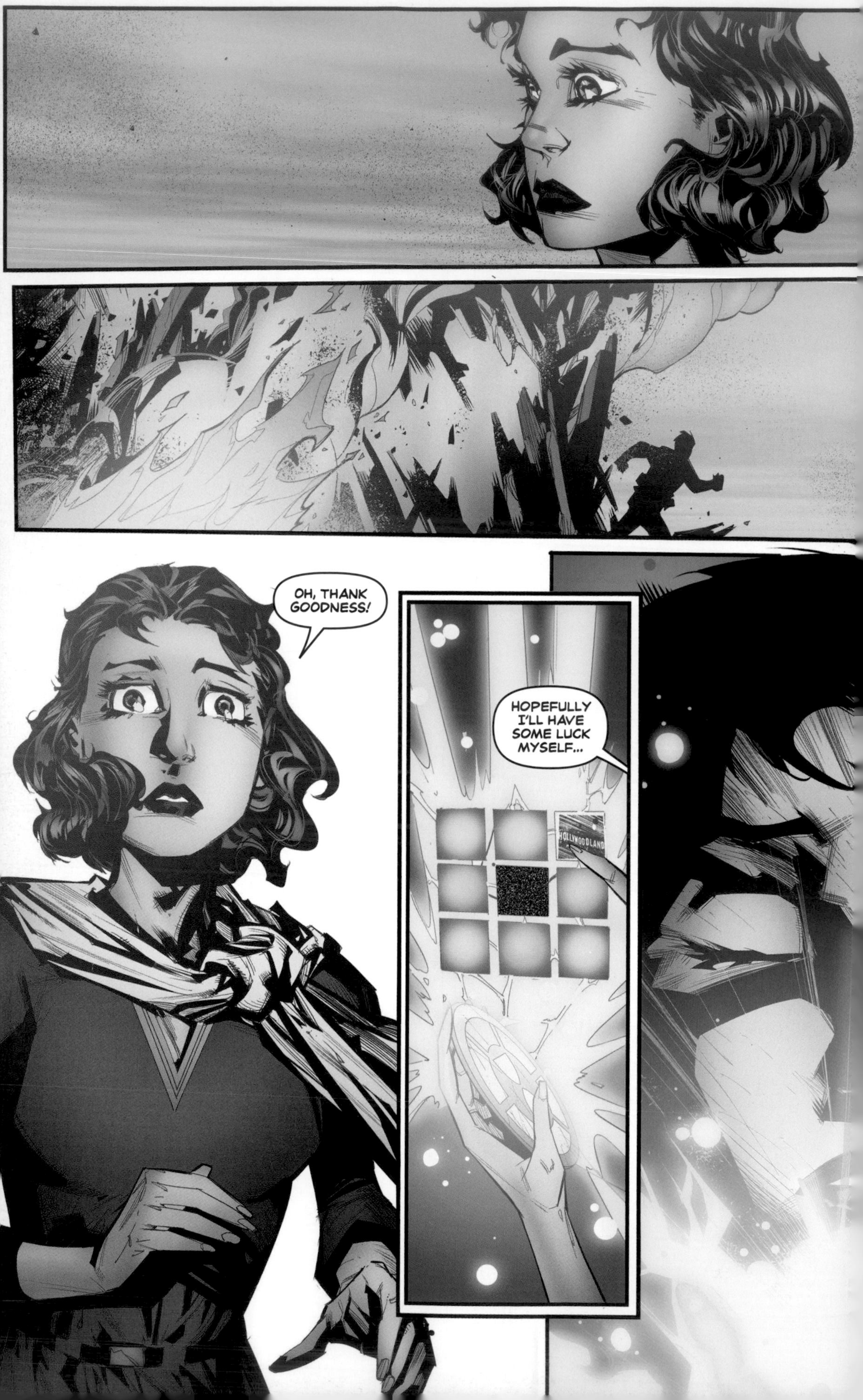
OH, THANK GOODNESS!
HOPEFULLY I'LL HAVE SOME LUCK MYSELF...
HOLLYWOODLAND

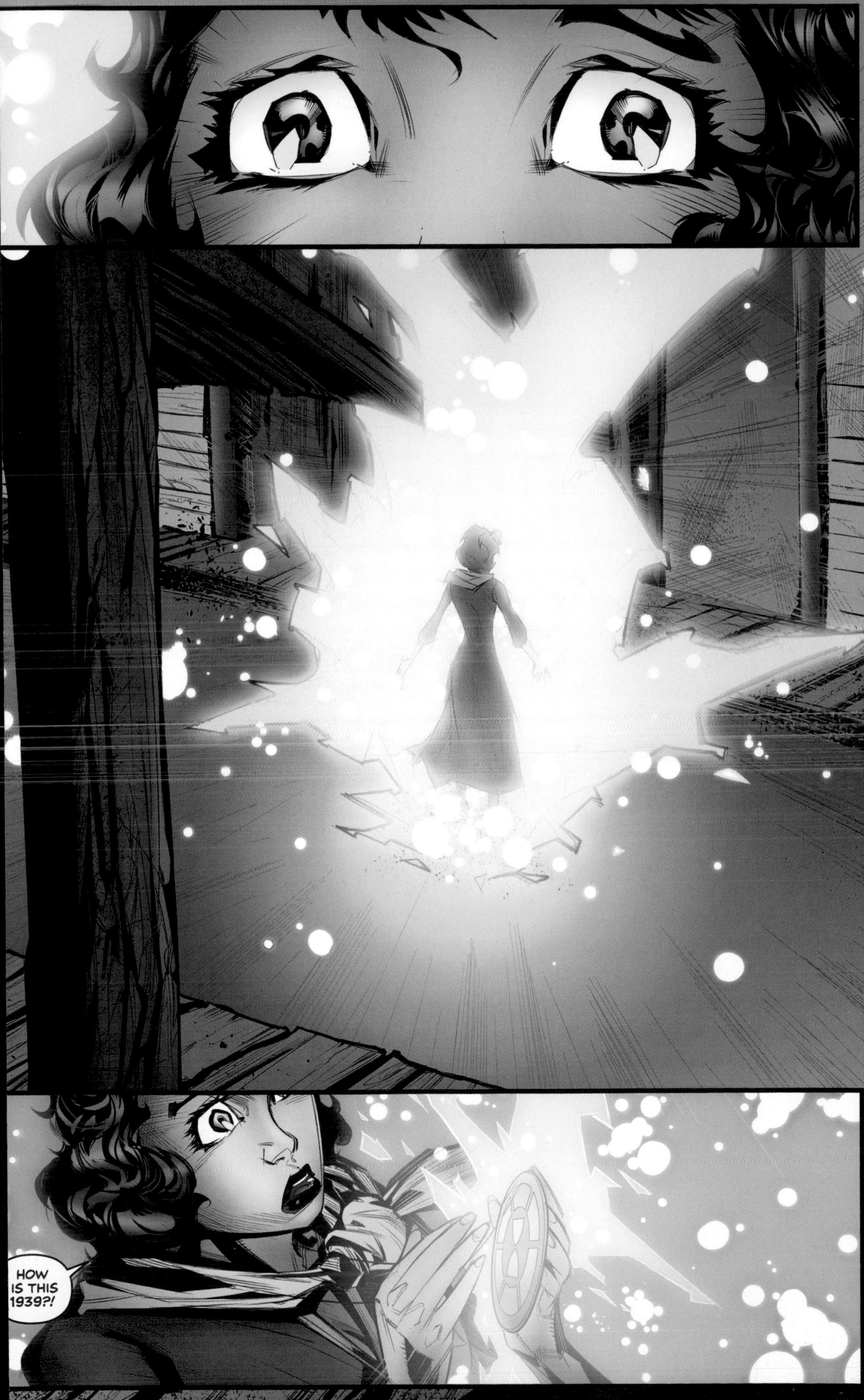
HOW IS THIS 1939?!

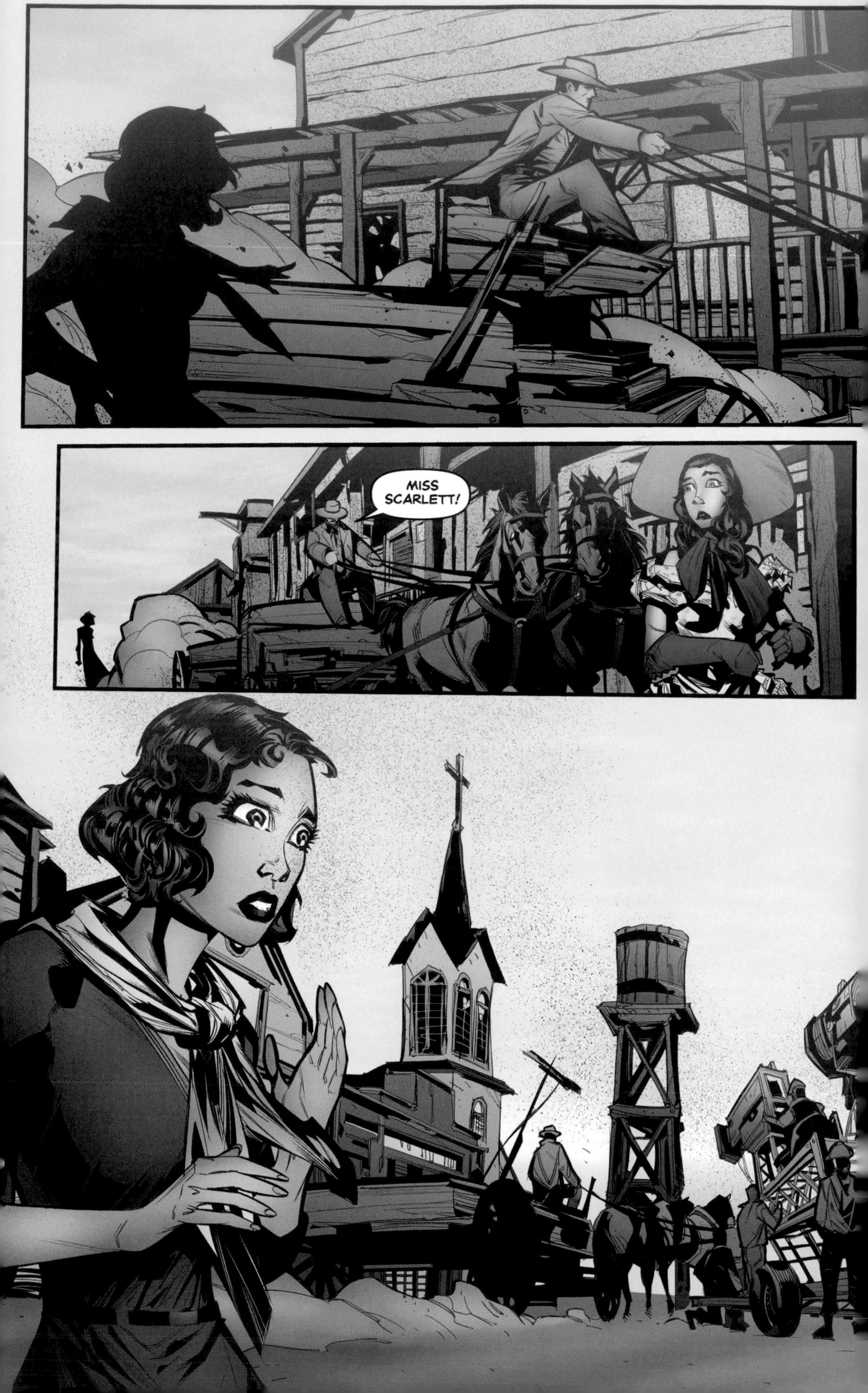
MISS SCARLETT!

CHAPTER 3

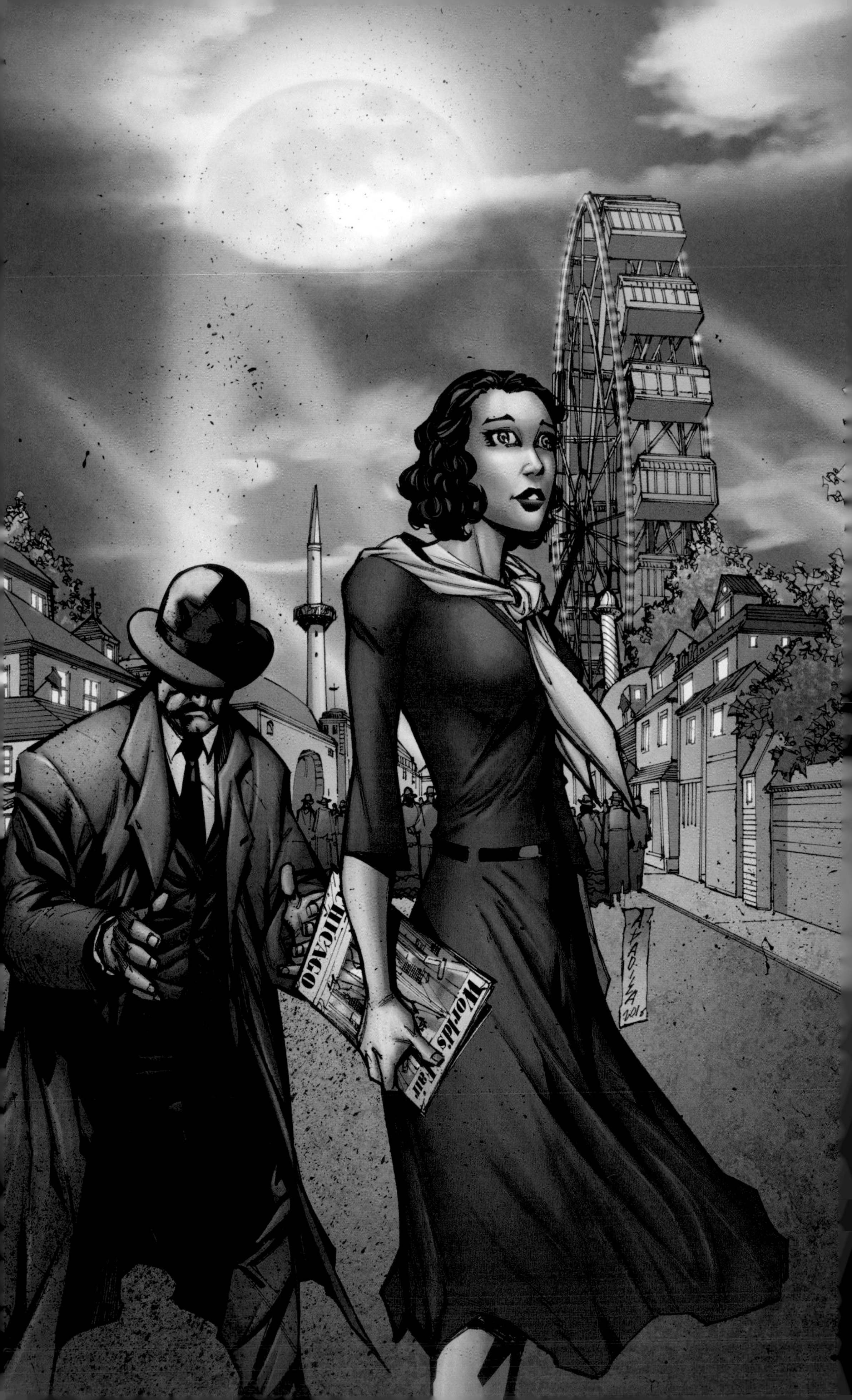
CHICAGO
World's Fair

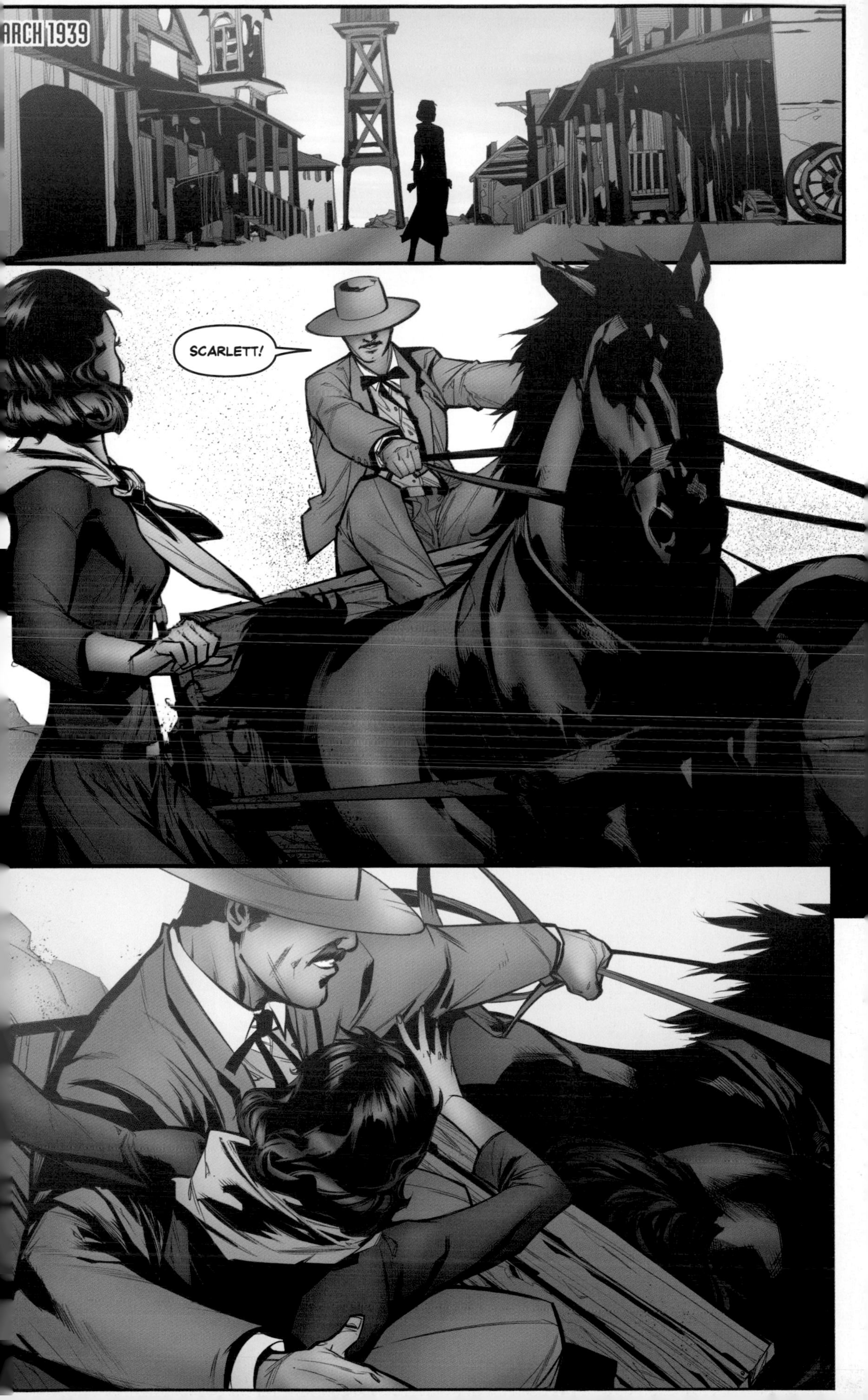
ARCH 1939
SCARLETT!

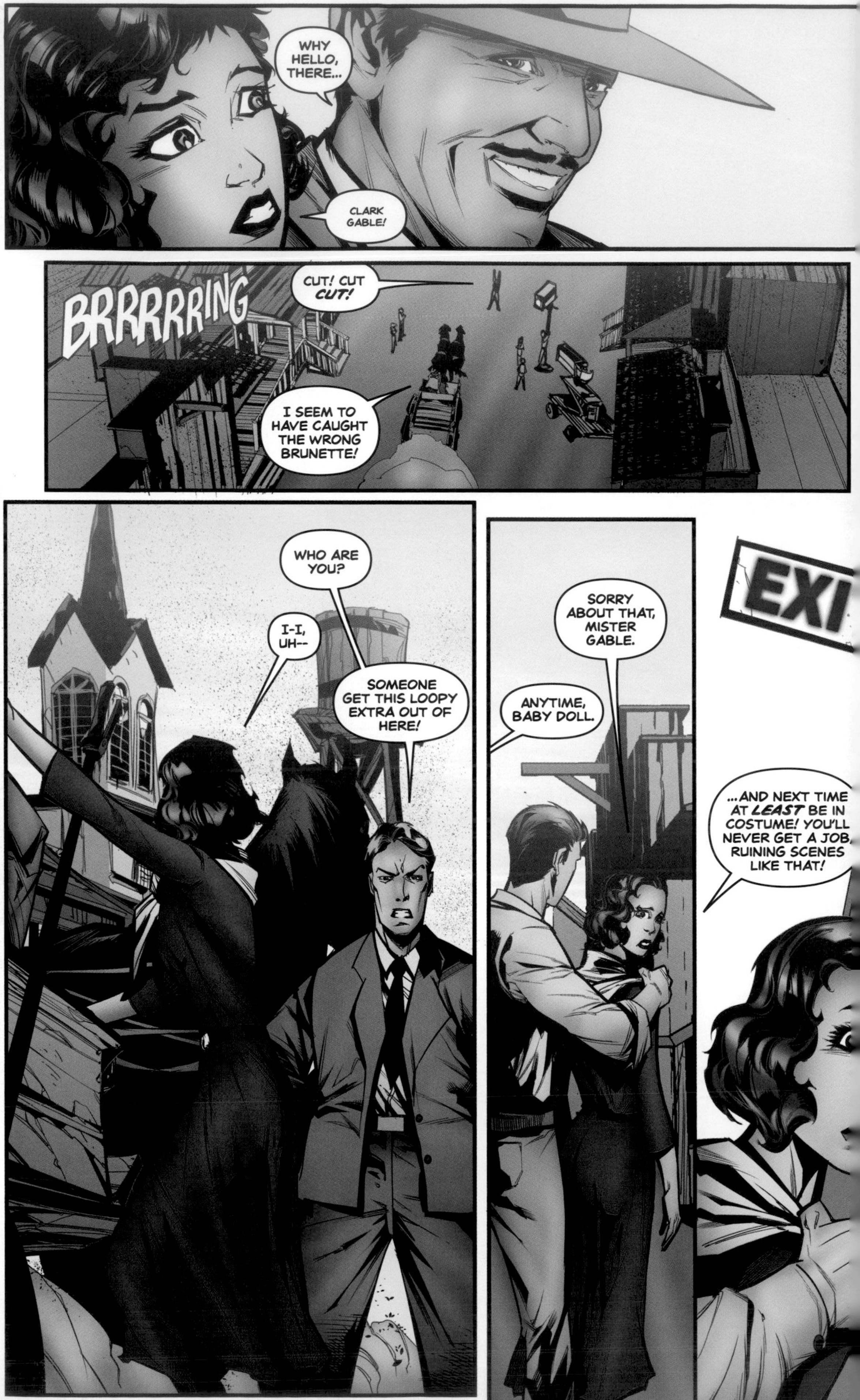
WHY HELLO, THERE...
CLARK GABLE!
BRRRRRING
CUT! CUT *CUT!*
I SEEM TO HAVE CAUGHT THE WRONG BRUNETTE!
WHO ARE YOU?
I-I, UH--
SOMEONE GET THIS LOOPY EXTRA OUT OF HERE!
SORRY ABOUT THAT, MISTER GABLE.
ANYTIME, BABY DOLL.
EXI
...AND NEXT TIME AT *LEAST* BE IN COSTUME! YOU'LL NEVER GET A JOB, RUINING SCENES LIKE THAT!

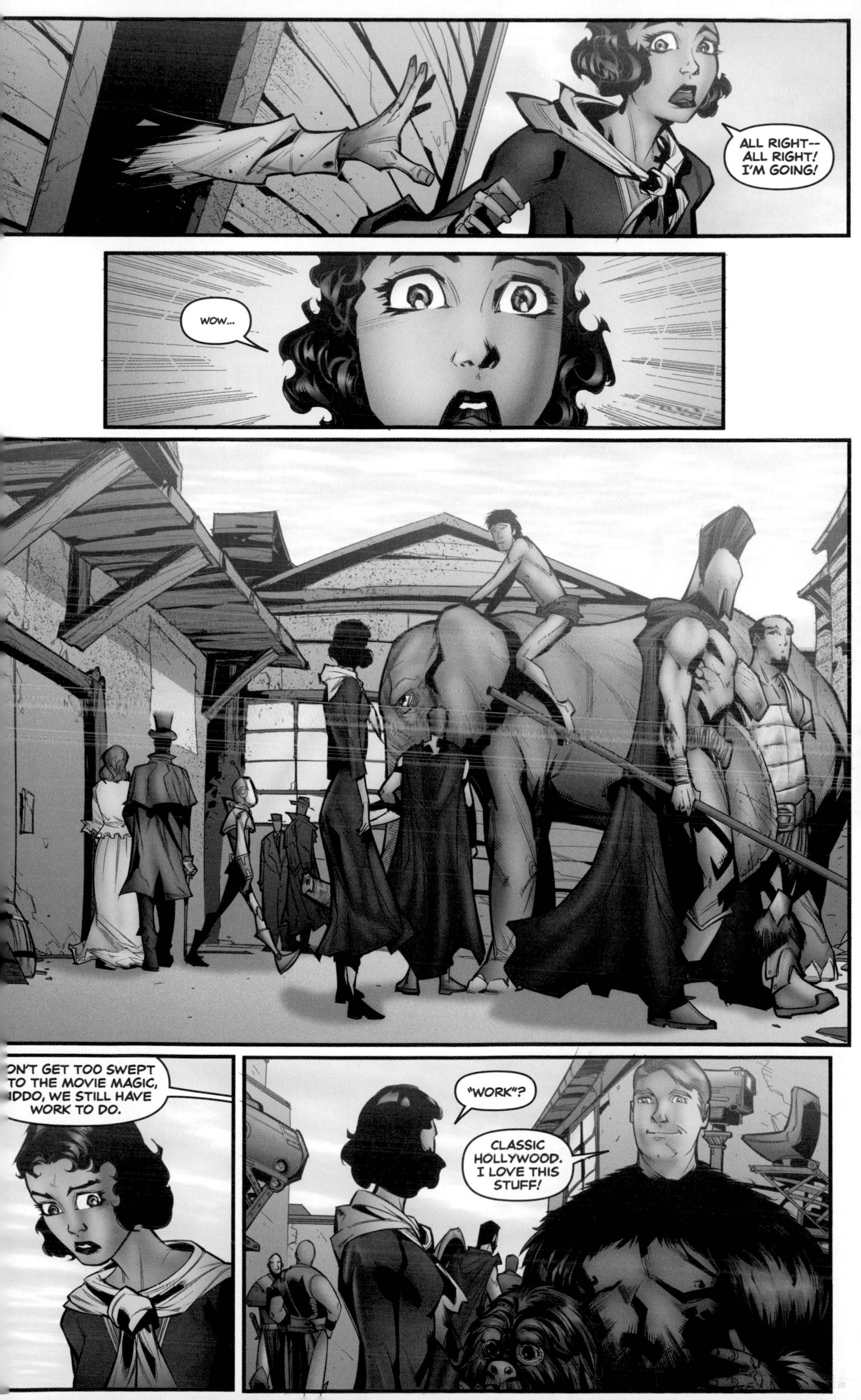
ALL RIGHT-- ALL RIGHT! I'M GOING!
WOW...
ON'T GET TOO SWEPT TO THE MOVIE MAGIC, IDDO, WE STILL HAVE WORK TO DO.
"WORK"?
CLASSIC HOLLYWOOD. I LOVE THIS STUFF!

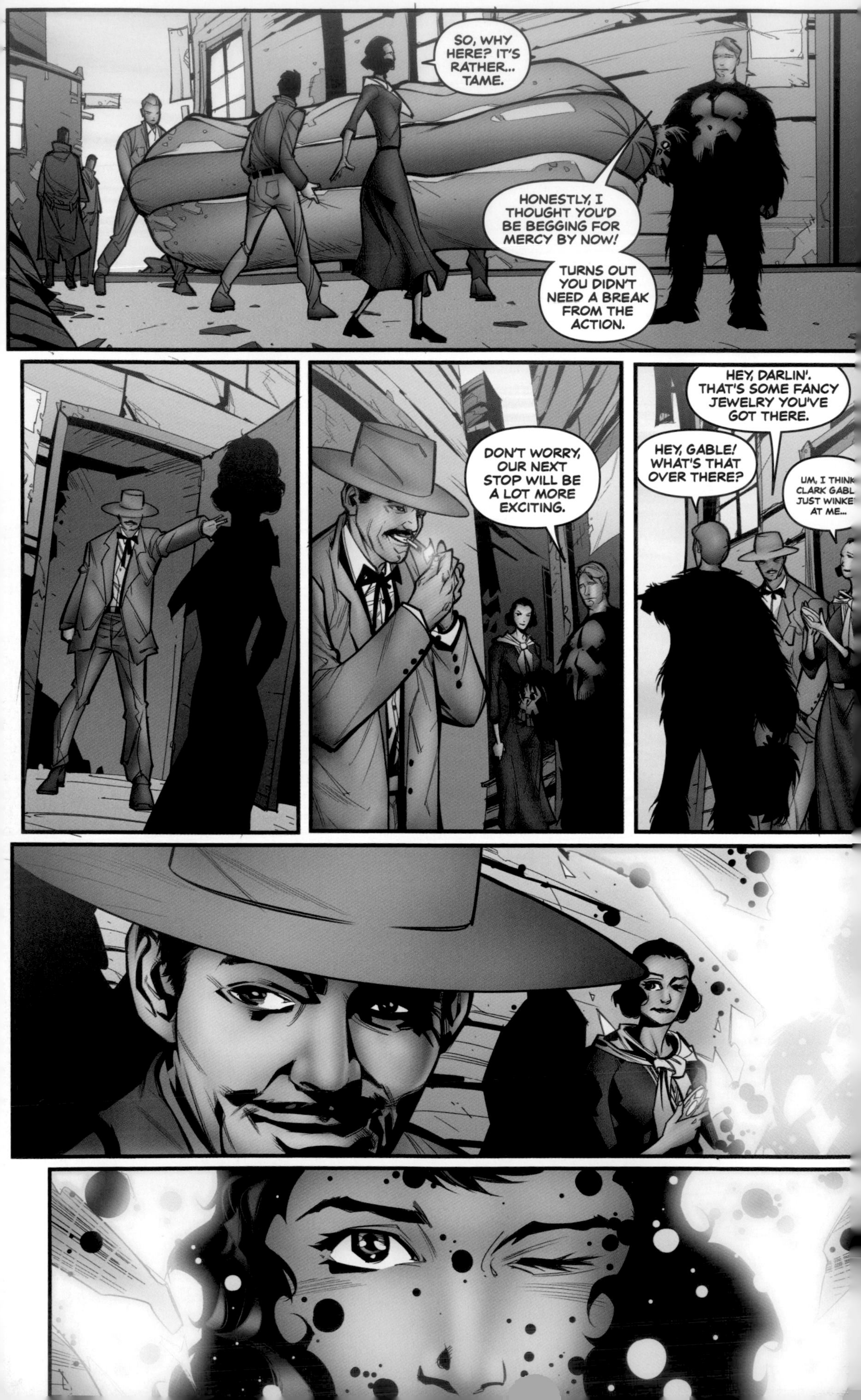
SO, WHY HERE? IT'S RATHER... TAME.
HONESTLY, I THOUGHT YOU'D BE BEGGING FOR MERCY BY NOW!
TURNS OUT YOU DIDN'T NEED A BREAK FROM THE ACTION.
DON'T WORRY, OUR NEXT STOP WILL BE A LOT MORE EXCITING.
HEY, DARLIN'. THAT'S SOME FANCY JEWELRY YOU'VE GOT THERE.
HEY, GABLE! WHAT'S THAT OVER THERE?
UM, I THINK CLARK GABL JUST WINKE AT ME...

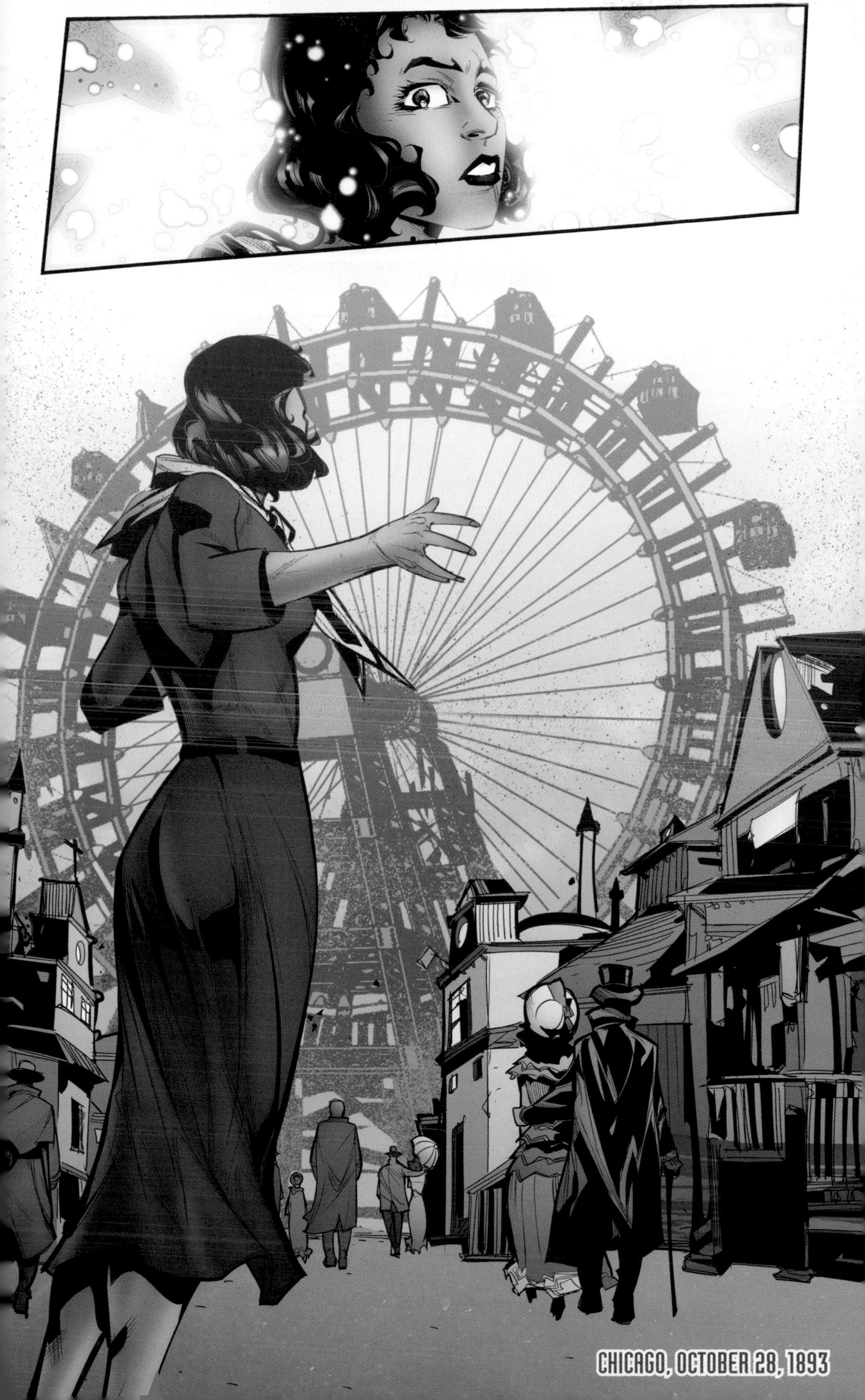
CHICAGO, OCTOBER 28, 1893

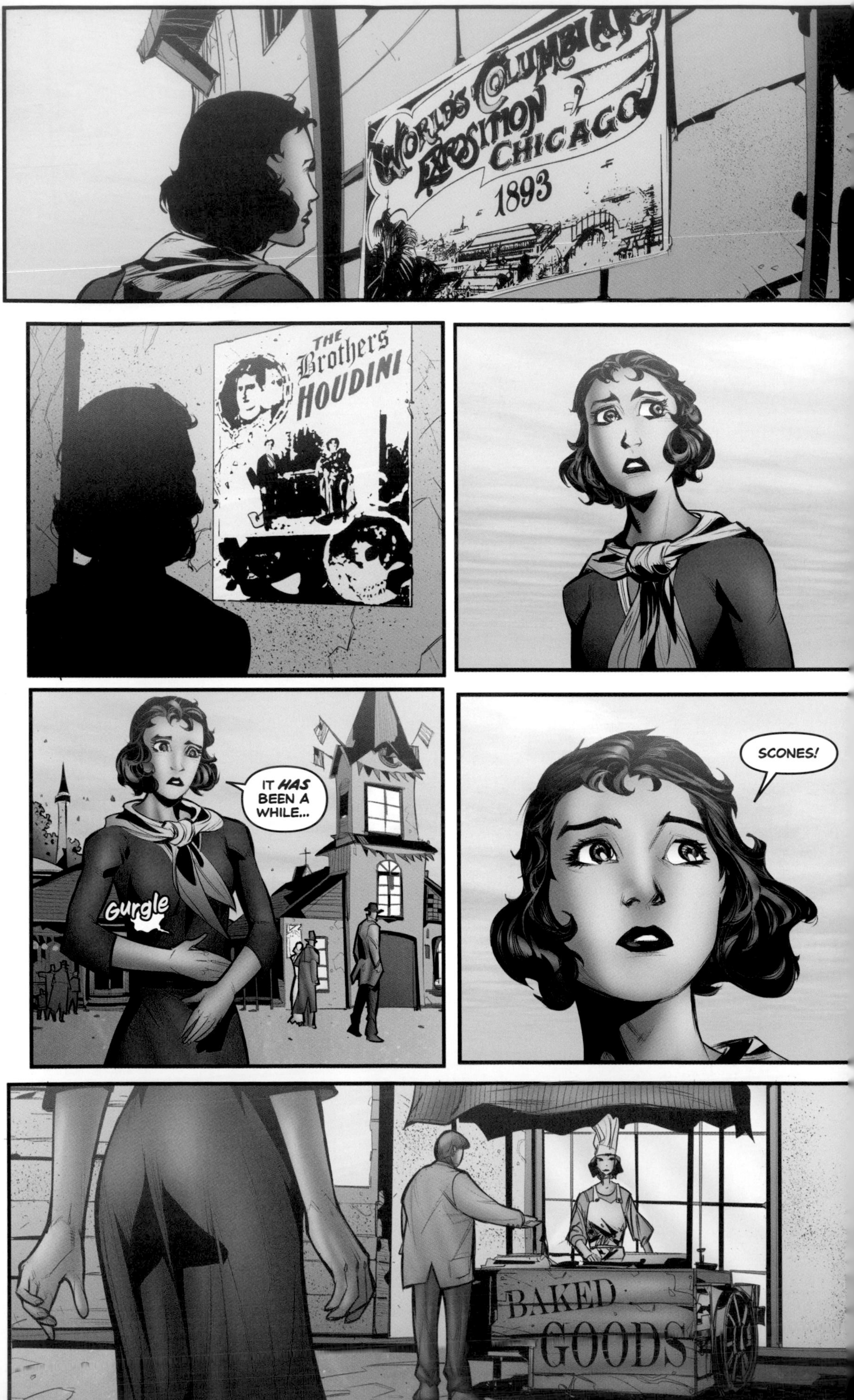
WORLD'S COLUMBIAN EXPOSITION CHICAGO
1893
THE Brothers HOUDINI
IT HAS BEEN A WHILE...
Gurgle
SCONES!
BAKED GOODS

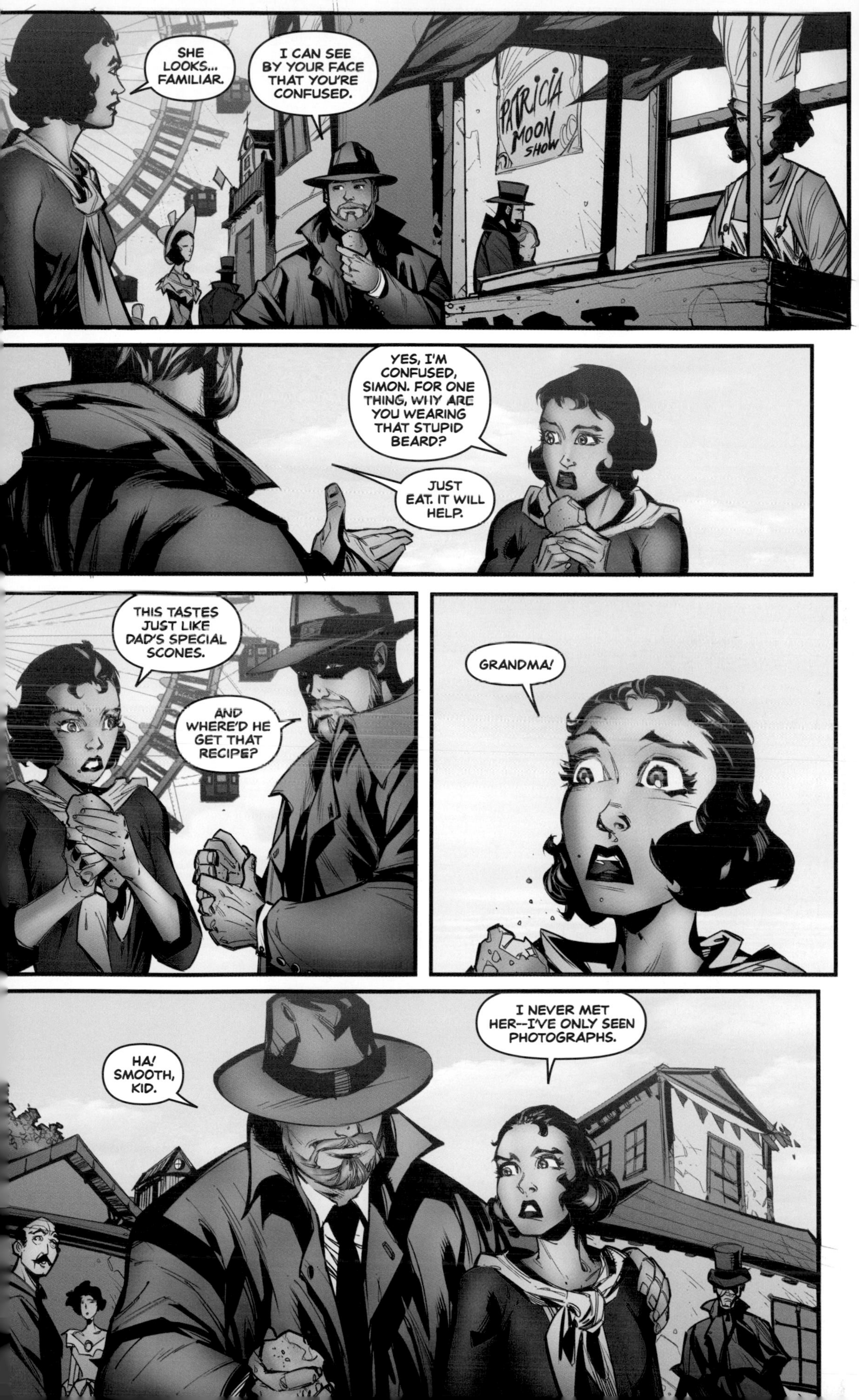
SHE LOOKS... FAMILIAR.
I CAN SEE BY YOUR FACE THAT YOU'RE CONFUSED.
PATRICIA MOON SHOW
YES, I'M CONFUSED, SIMON. FOR ONE THING, WHY ARE YOU WEARING THAT STUPID BEARD?
JUST EAT. IT WILL HELP.
THIS TASTES JUST LIKE DAD'S SPECIAL SCONES.
AND WHERE'D HE GET THAT RECIPE?
GRANDMA!
I NEVER MET HER--I'VE ONLY SEEN PHOTOGRAPHS.
HA! SMOOTH, KID.

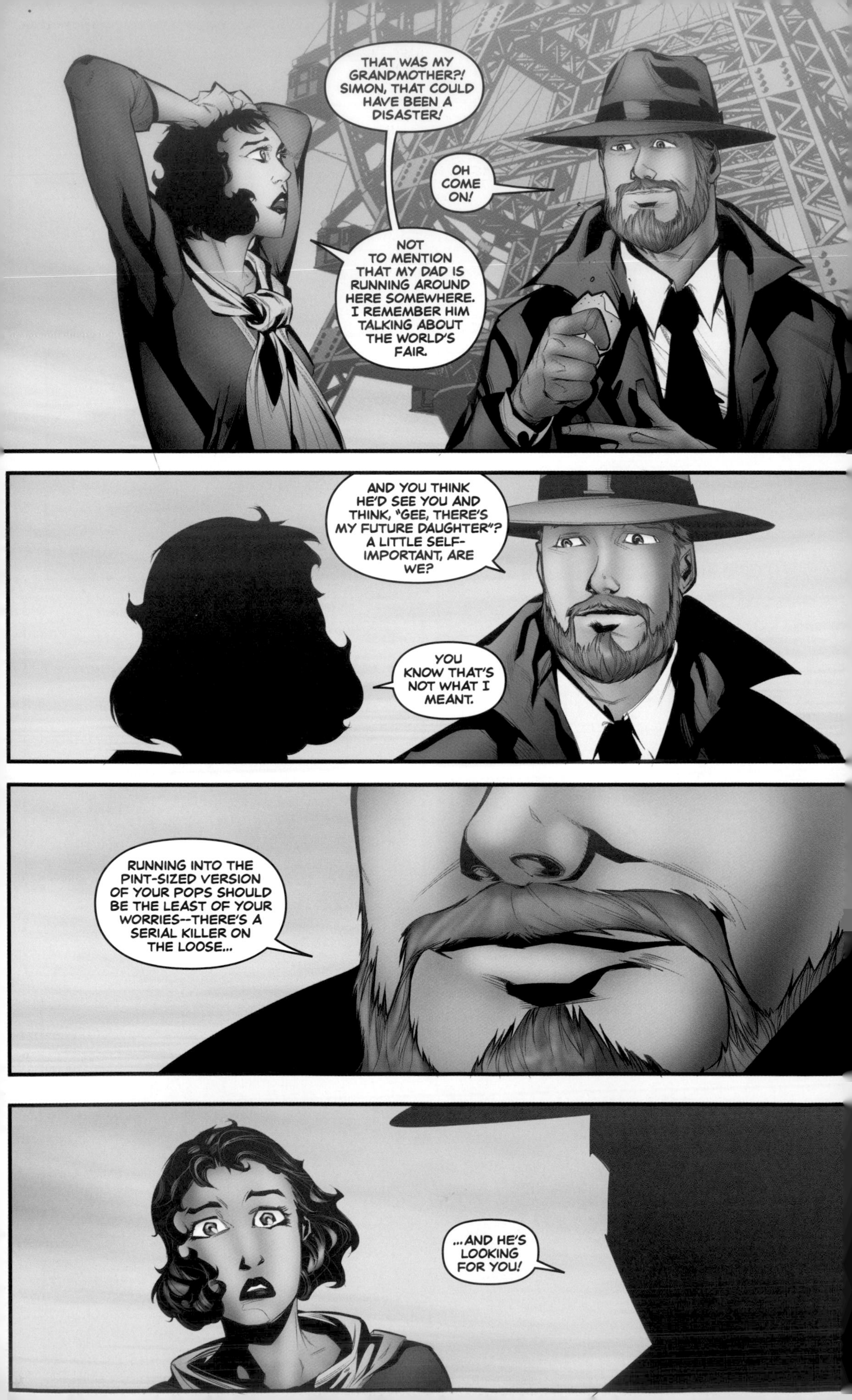
THAT WAS MY GRANDMOTHER?! SIMON, THAT COULD HAVE BEEN A DISASTER!
OH COME ON!
NOT TO MENTION THAT MY DAD IS RUNNING AROUND HERE SOMEWHERE. I REMEMBER HIM TALKING ABOUT THE WORLD'S FAIR.
AND YOU THINK HE'D SEE YOU AND THINK, "GEE, THERE'S MY FUTURE DAUGHTER"? A LITTLE SELF-IMPORTANT, ARE WE?
YOU KNOW THAT'S NOT WHAT I MEANT.
RUNNING INTO THE PINT-SIZED VERSION OF YOUR POPS SHOULD BE THE LEAST OF YOUR WORRIES--THERE'S A SERIAL KILLER ON THE LOOSE...
...AND HE'S LOOKING FOR YOU!

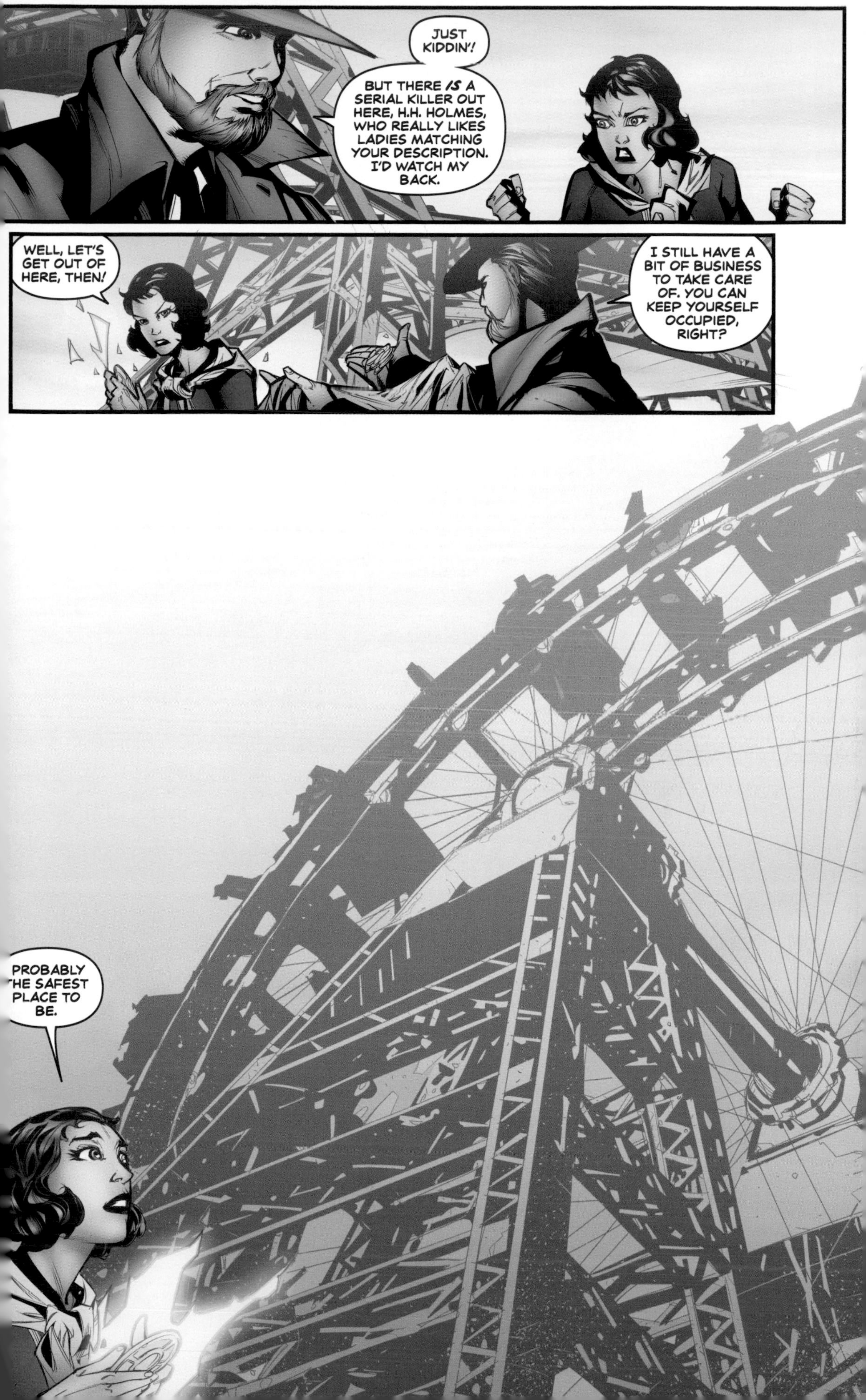
JUST KIDDIN'!
BUT THERE *IS* A SERIAL KILLER OUT HERE, H.H. HOLMES, WHO REALLY LIKES LADIES MATCHING YOUR DESCRIPTION. I'D WATCH MY BACK.
WELL, LET'S GET OUT OF HERE, THEN!
I STILL HAVE A BIT OF BUSINESS TO TAKE CARE OF. YOU CAN KEEP YOURSELF OCCUPIED, RIGHT?
PROBABLY THE SAFEST PLACE TO BE.

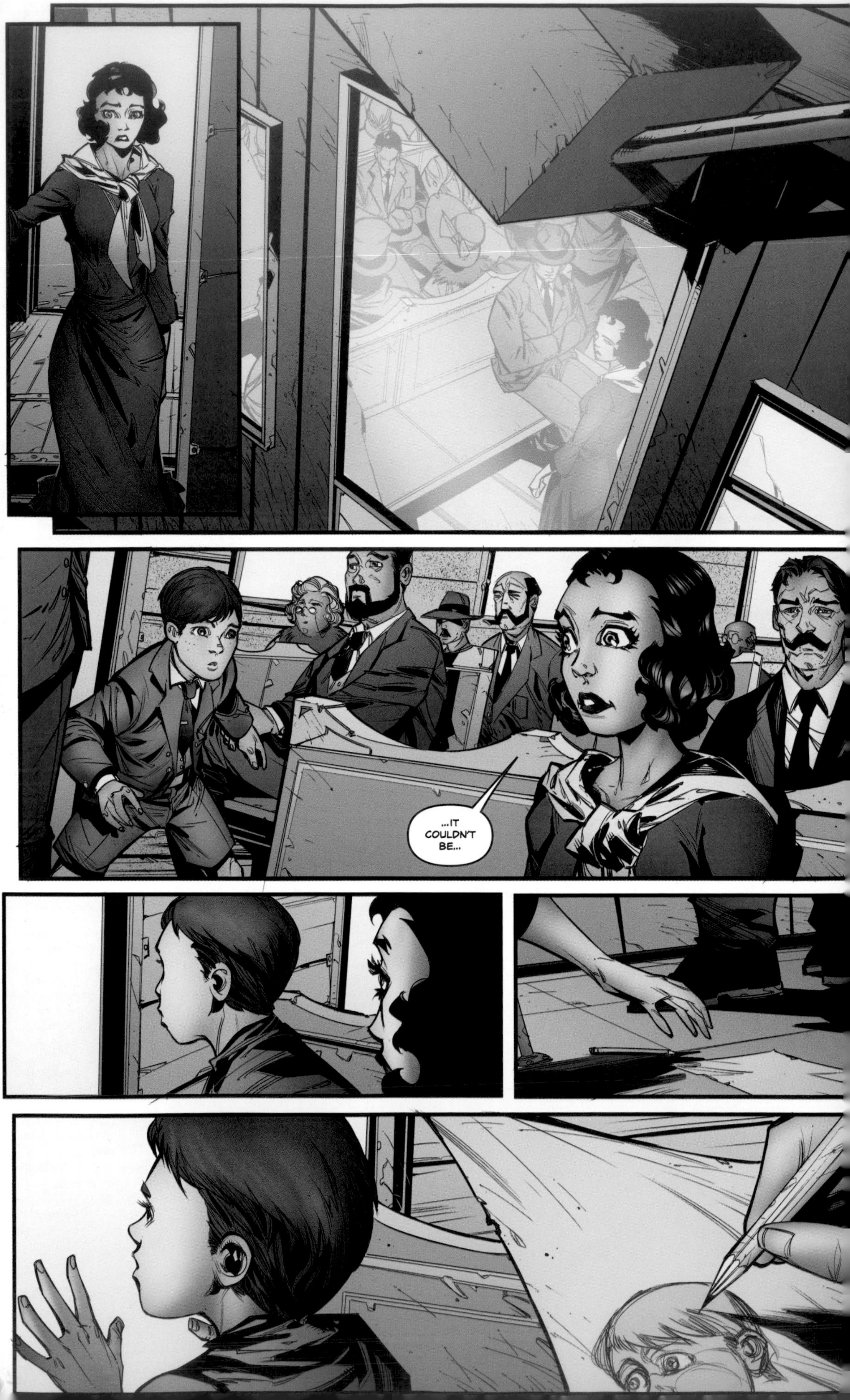
...IT COULDN'T BE...

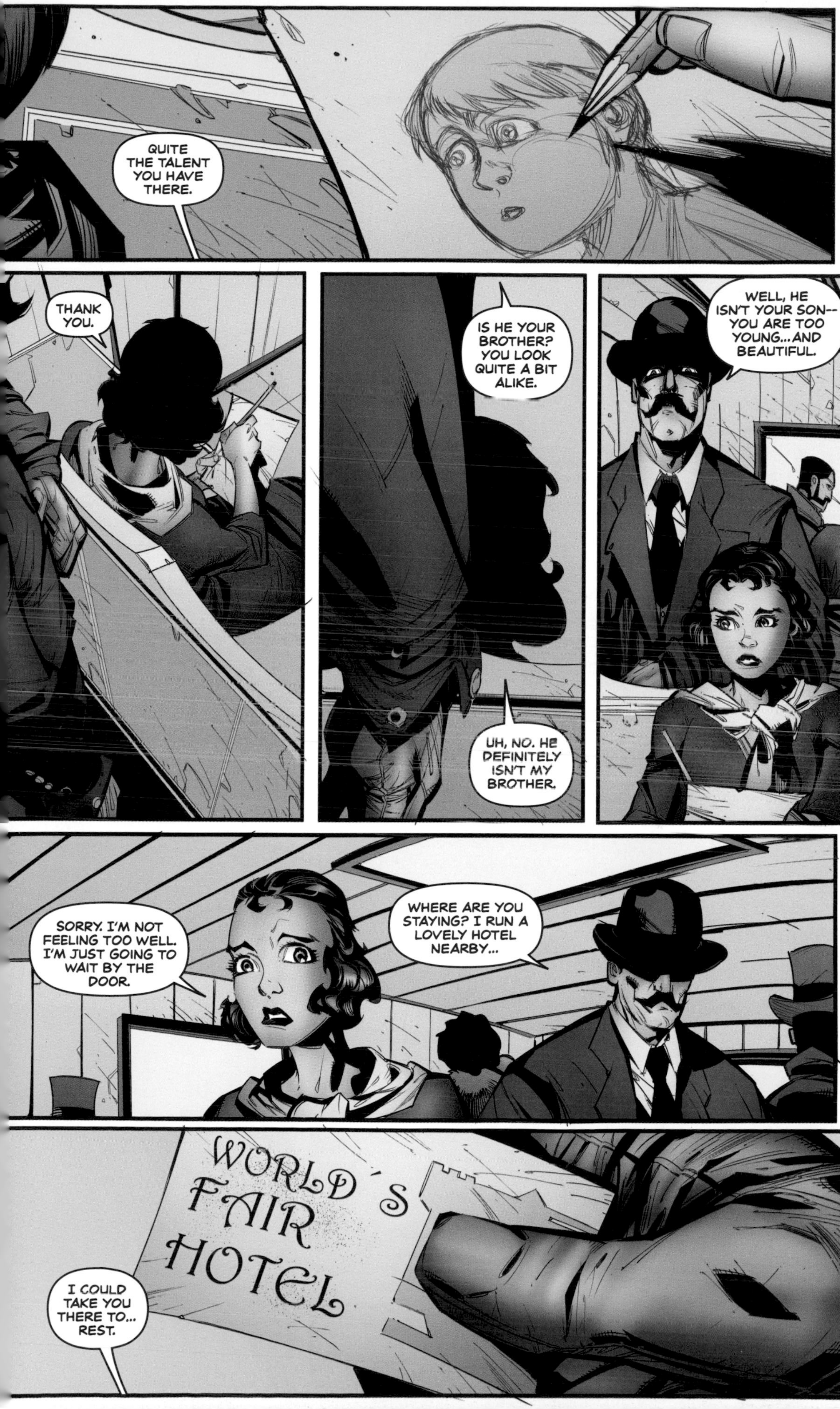
QUITE THE TALENT YOU HAVE THERE.
THANK YOU.
IS HE YOUR BROTHER? YOU LOOK QUITE A BIT ALIKE.
UH, NO. HE DEFINITELY ISN'T MY BROTHER.
WELL, HE ISN'T YOUR SON-- YOU ARE TOO YOUNG...AND BEAUTIFUL.
SORRY. I'M NOT FEELING TOO WELL. I'M JUST GOING TO WAIT BY THE DOOR.
WHERE ARE YOU STAYING? I RUN A LOVELY HOTEL NEARBY...
WORLD'S FAIR HOTEL
I COULD TAKE YOU THERE TO... REST.

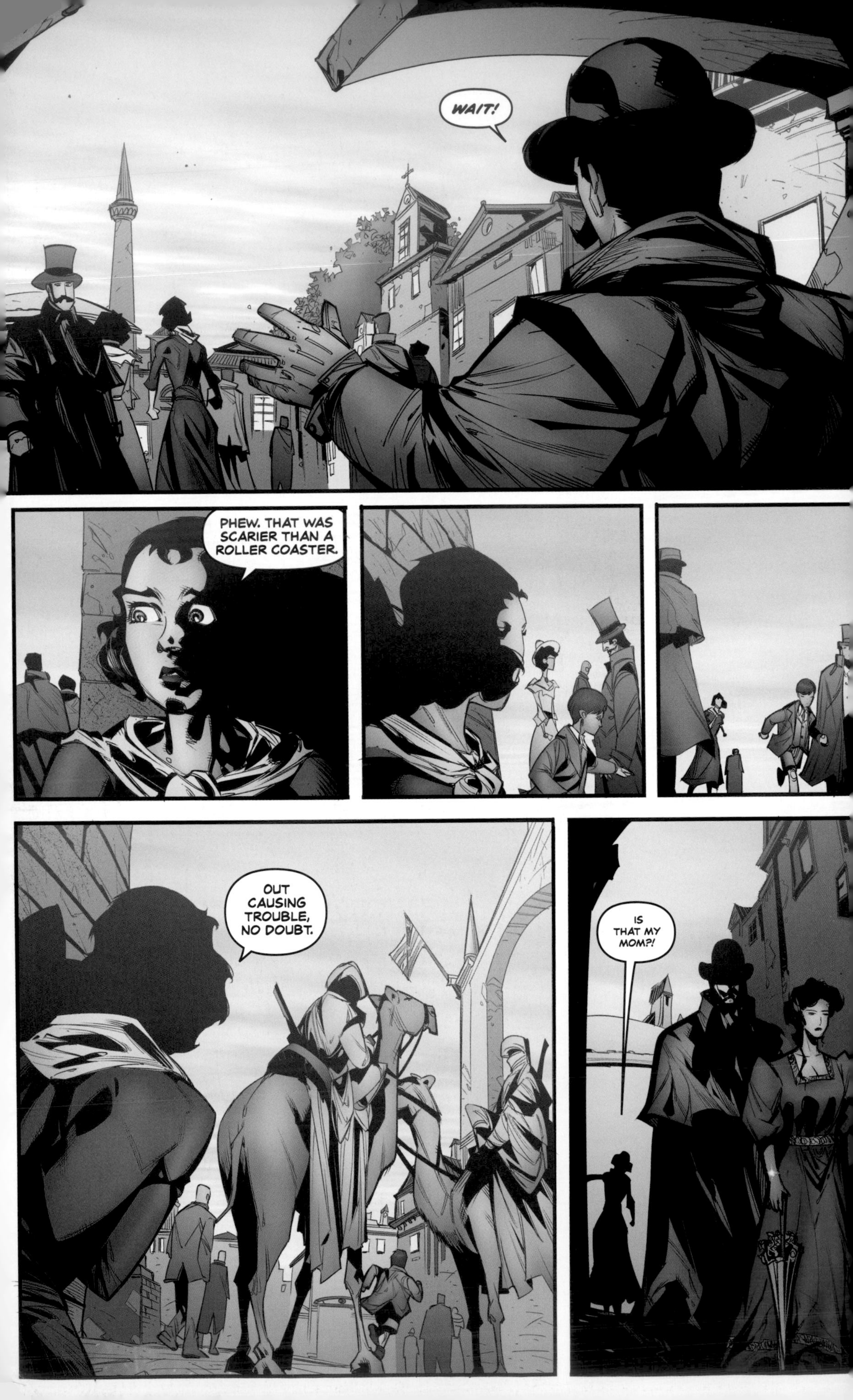
WAIT!
PHEW. THAT WAS SCARIER THAN A ROLLER COASTER.
OUT CAUSING TROUBLE, NO DOUBT.
IS THAT MY MOM?!

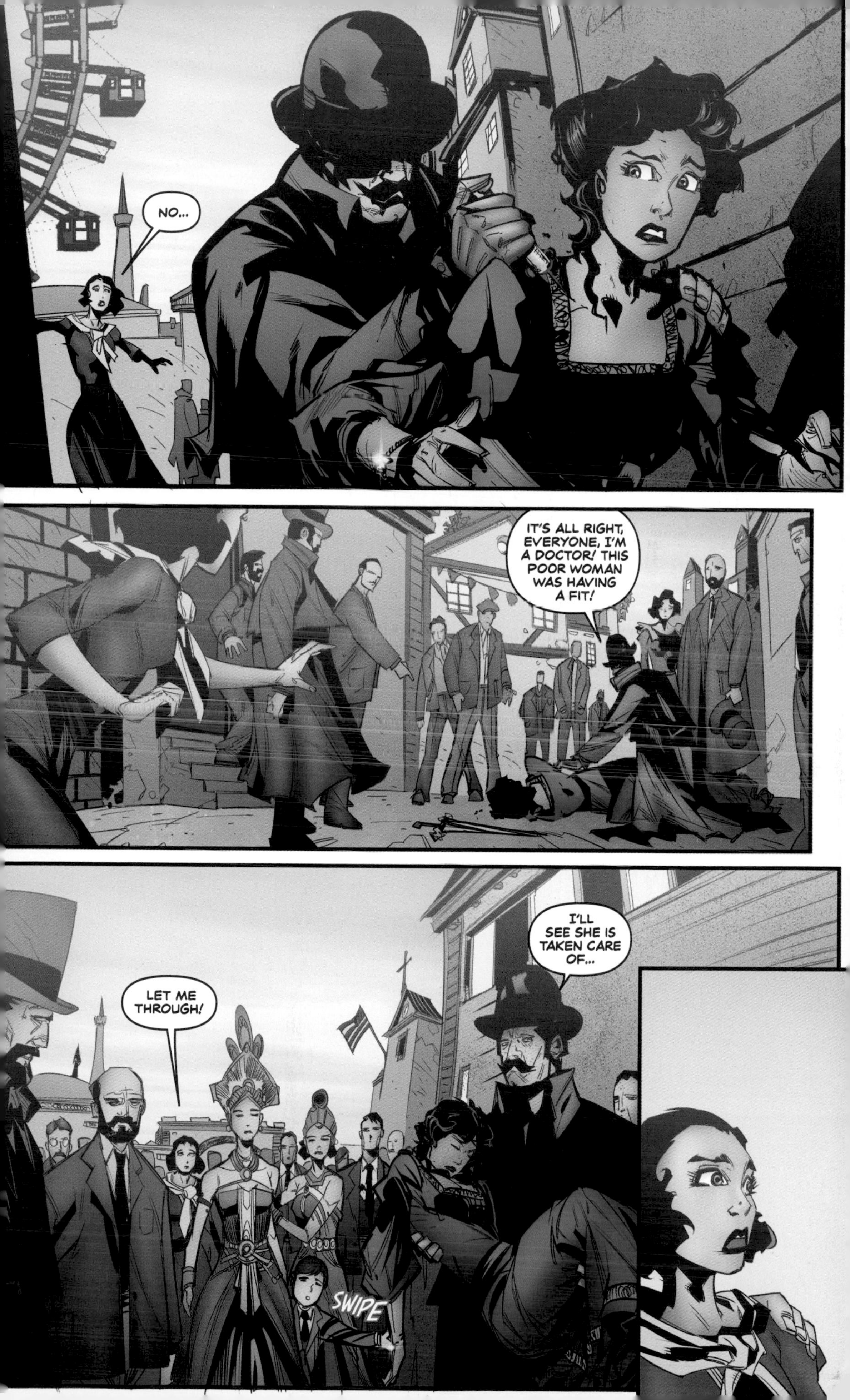
NO...
IT'S ALL RIGHT, EVERYONE, I'M A DOCTOR! THIS POOR WOMAN WAS HAVING A FIT!
I'LL SEE SHE IS TAKEN CARE OF...
LET ME THROUGH!
SWIPE

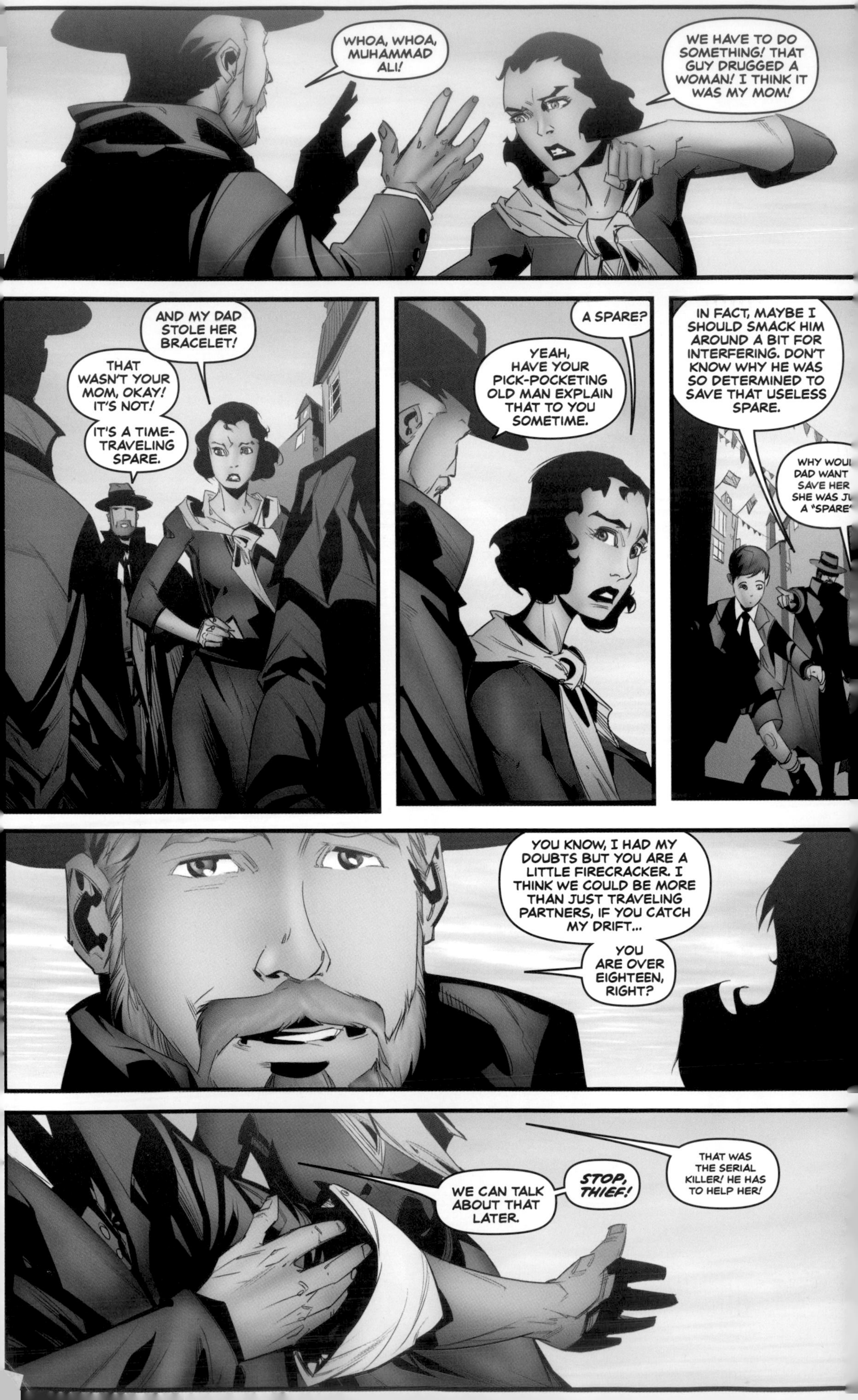
WHOA, WHOA, MUHAMMAD ALI!
WE HAVE TO DO SOMETHING! THAT GUY DRUGGED A WOMAN! I THINK IT WAS MY MOM!
AND MY DAD STOLE HER BRACELET!
THAT WASN'T YOUR MOM, OKAY! IT'S NOT!
IT'S A TIME-TRAVELING SPARE.
A SPARE?
YEAH, HAVE YOUR PICK-POCKETING OLD MAN EXPLAIN THAT TO YOU SOMETIME.
IN FACT, MAYBE I SHOULD SMACK HIM AROUND A BIT FOR INTERFERING. DON'T KNOW WHY HE WAS SO DETERMINED TO SAVE THAT USELESS SPARE.
WHY WOUL DAD WANT SAVE HER SHE WAS JU A "SPARE"
YOU KNOW, I HAD MY DOUBTS BUT YOU ARE A LITTLE FIRECRACKER. I THINK WE COULD BE MORE THAN JUST TRAVELING PARTNERS, IF YOU CATCH MY DRIFT...
YOU ARE OVER EIGHTEEN, RIGHT?
WE CAN TALK ABOUT THAT LATER.
STOP, THIEF!
THAT WAS THE SERIAL KILLER! HE HAS TO HELP HER!

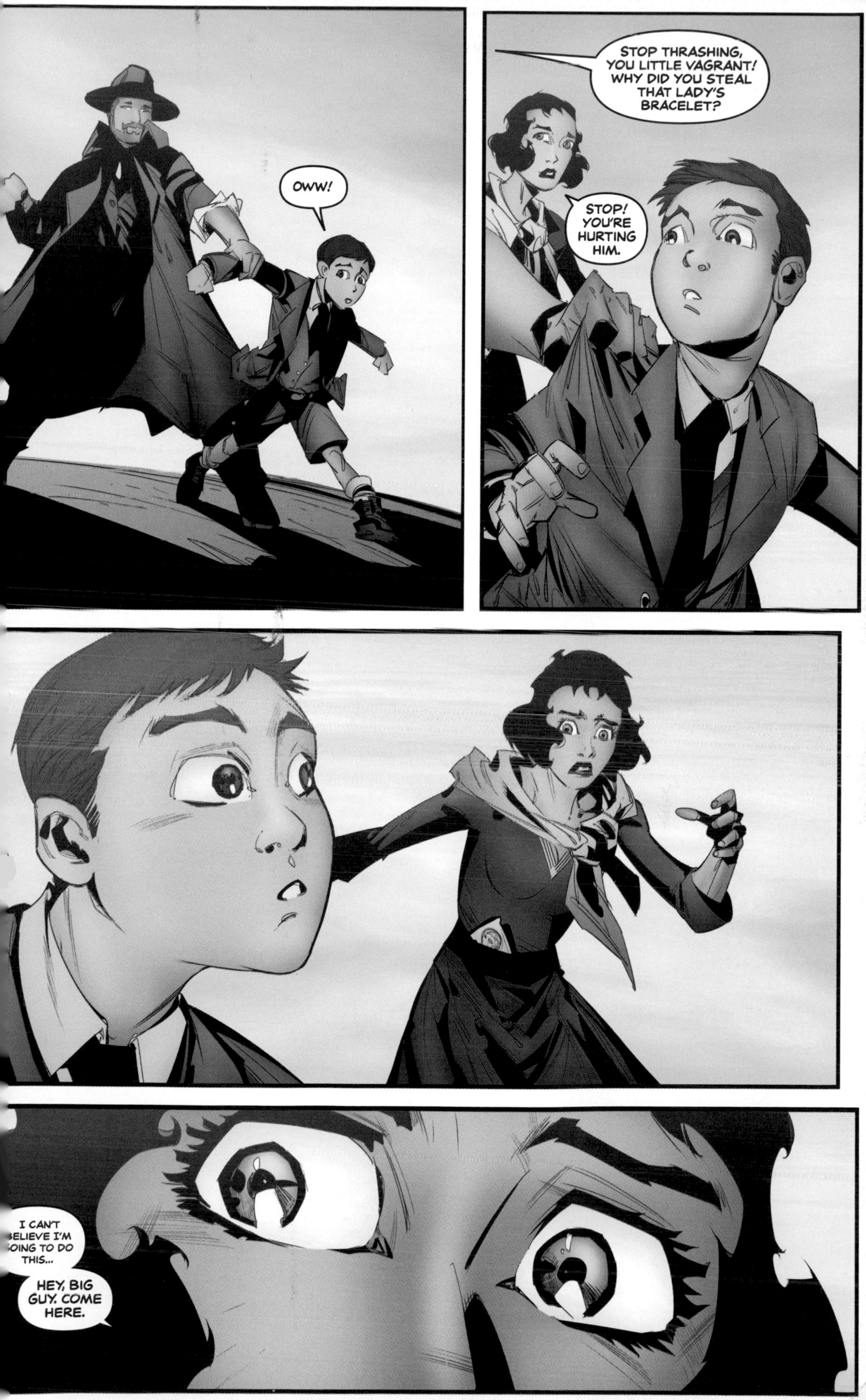
OWW!
STOP THRASHING, YOU LITTLE VAGRANT! WHY DID YOU STEAL THAT LADY'S BRACELET?
STOP! YOU'RE HURTING HIM.
I CAN'T BELIEVE I'M GOING TO DO THIS...
HEY, BIG GUY. COME HERE.

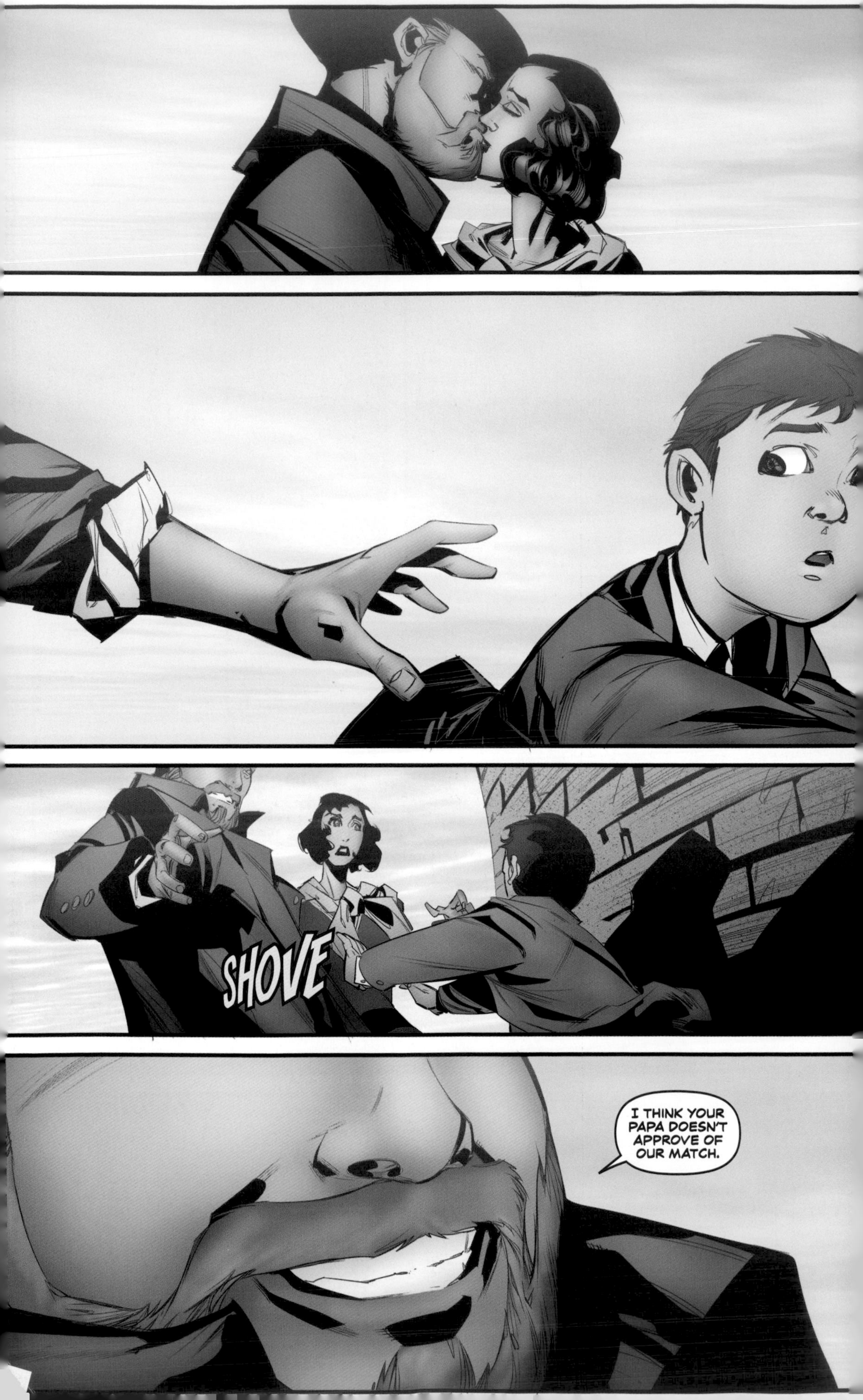
SHOVE
I THINK YOUR PAPA DOESN'T APPROVE OF OUR MATCH.

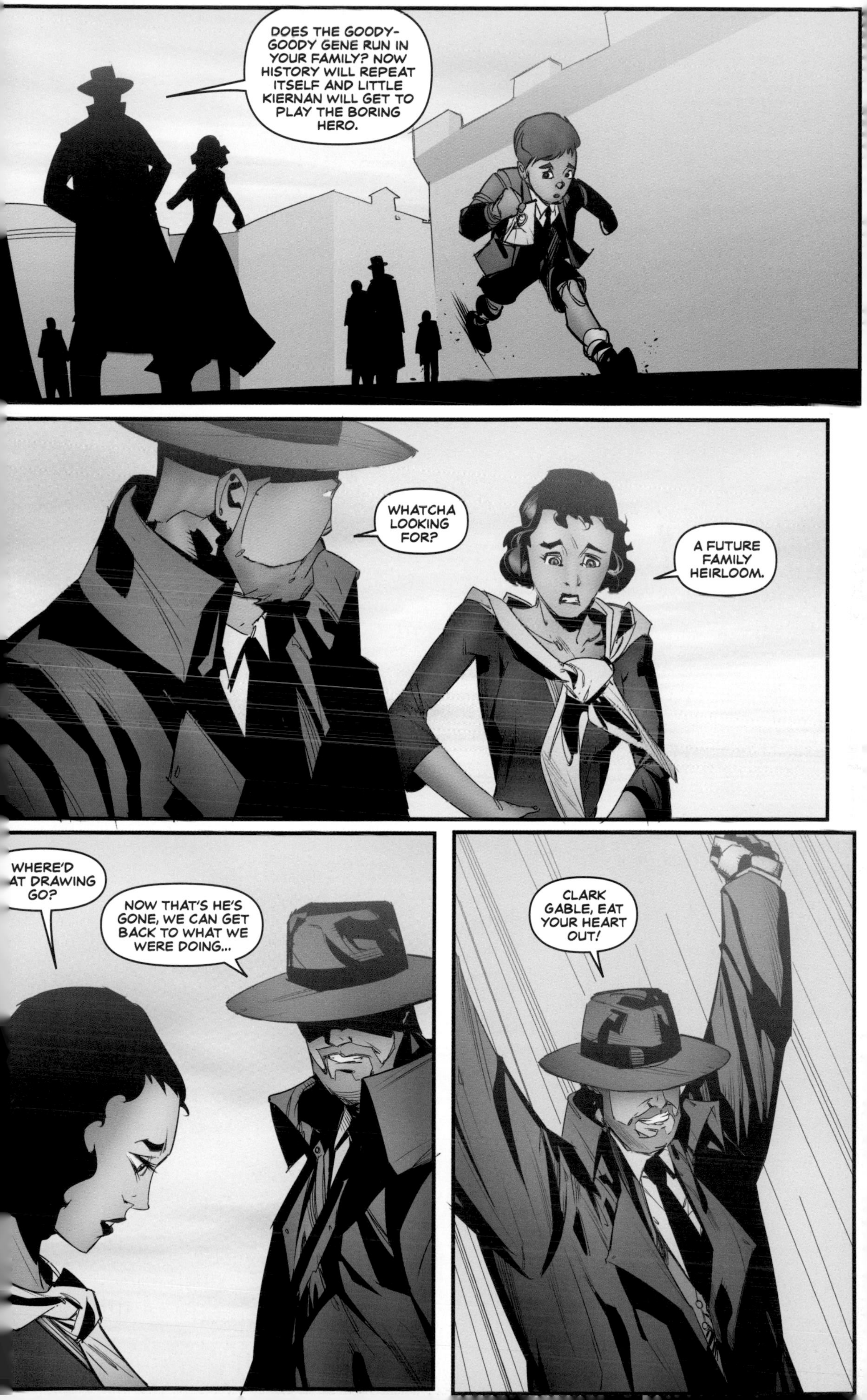
DOES THE GOODY-GOODY GENE RUN IN YOUR FAMILY? NOW HISTORY WILL REPEAT ITSELF AND LITTLE KIERNAN WILL GET TO PLAY THE BORING HERO.
WHATCHA LOOKING FOR?
A FUTURE FAMILY HEIRLOOM.
WHERE'D AT DRAWING GO?
NOW THAT'S HE'S GONE, WE CAN GET BACK TO WHAT WE WERE DOING...
CLARK GABLE, EAT YOUR HEART OUT!

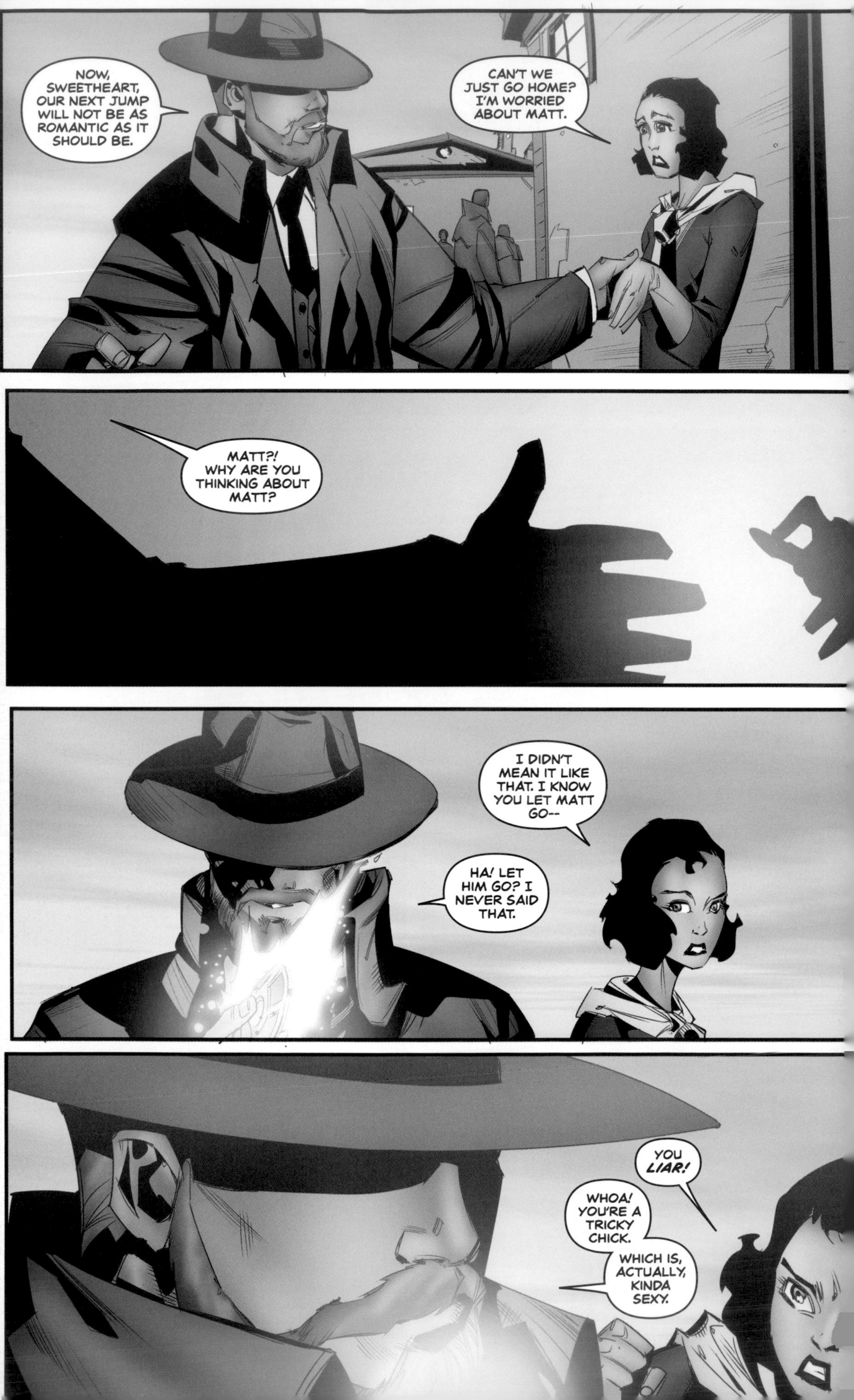
NOW, SWEETHEART, OUR NEXT JUMP WILL NOT BE AS ROMANTIC AS IT SHOULD BE.
CAN'T WE JUST GO HOME? I'M WORRIED ABOUT MATT.
MATT?! WHY ARE YOU THINKING ABOUT MATT?
I DIDN'T MEAN IT LIKE THAT. I KNOW YOU LET MATT GO--
HA! LET HIM GO? I NEVER SAID THAT.
YOU *LIAR!*
WHOA! YOU'RE A TRICKY CHICK.
WHICH IS, ACTUALLY, KINDA SEXY.

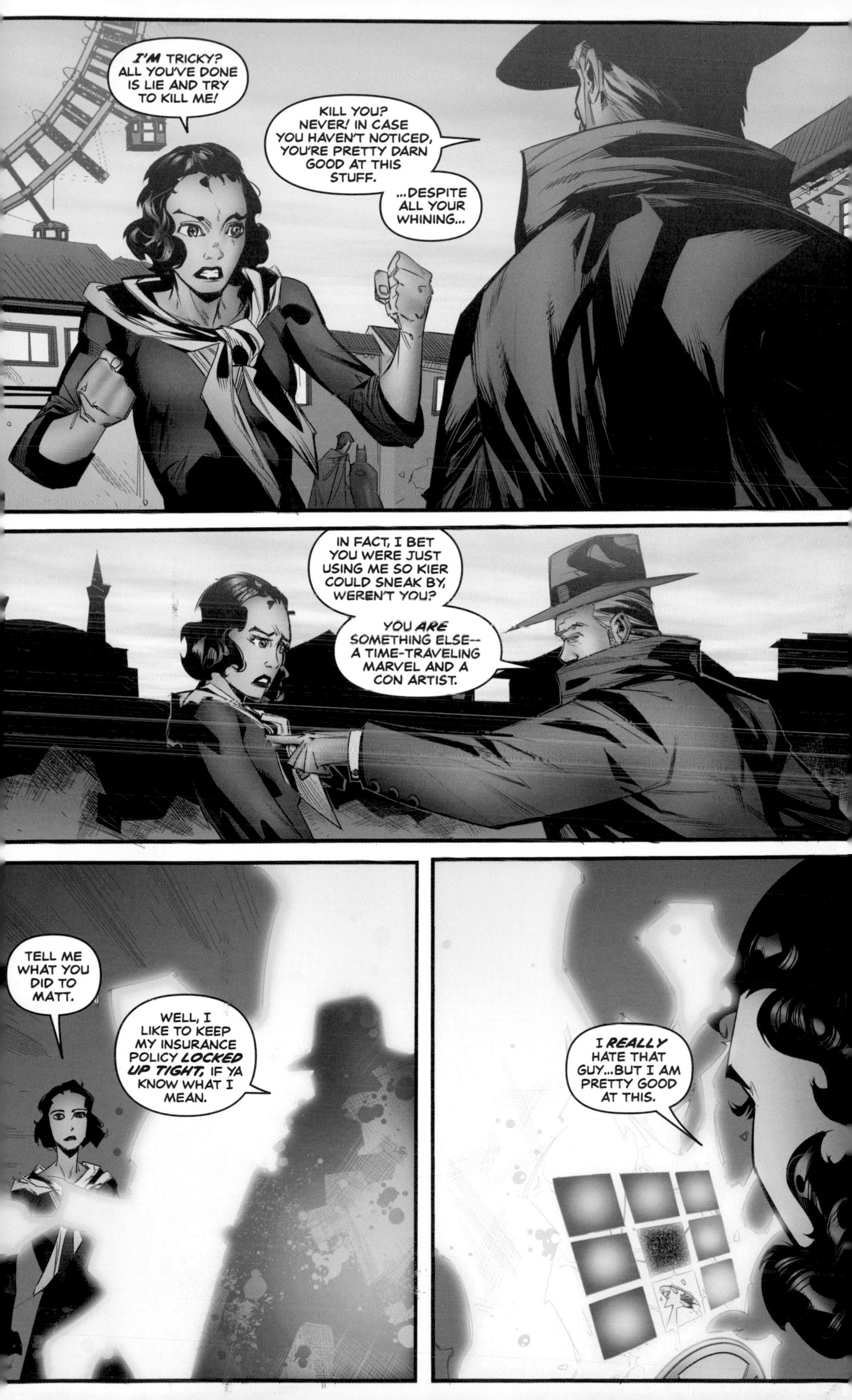
I'M TRICKY? ALL YOU'VE DONE IS LIE AND TRY TO KILL ME!
KILL YOU? NEVER! IN CASE YOU HAVEN'T NOTICED, YOU'RE PRETTY DARN GOOD AT THIS STUFF.
...DESPITE ALL YOUR WHINING...
IN FACT, I BET YOU WERE JUST USING ME SO KIER COULD SNEAK BY, WEREN'T YOU?
YOU *ARE* SOMETHING ELSE-- A TIME-TRAVELING MARVEL AND A CON ARTIST.
TELL ME WHAT YOU DID TO MATT.
WELL, I LIKE TO KEEP MY INSURANCE POLICY *LOCKED UP TIGHT,* IF YA KNOW WHAT I MEAN.
I *REALLY* HATE THAT GUY...BUT I AM PRETTY GOOD AT THIS.

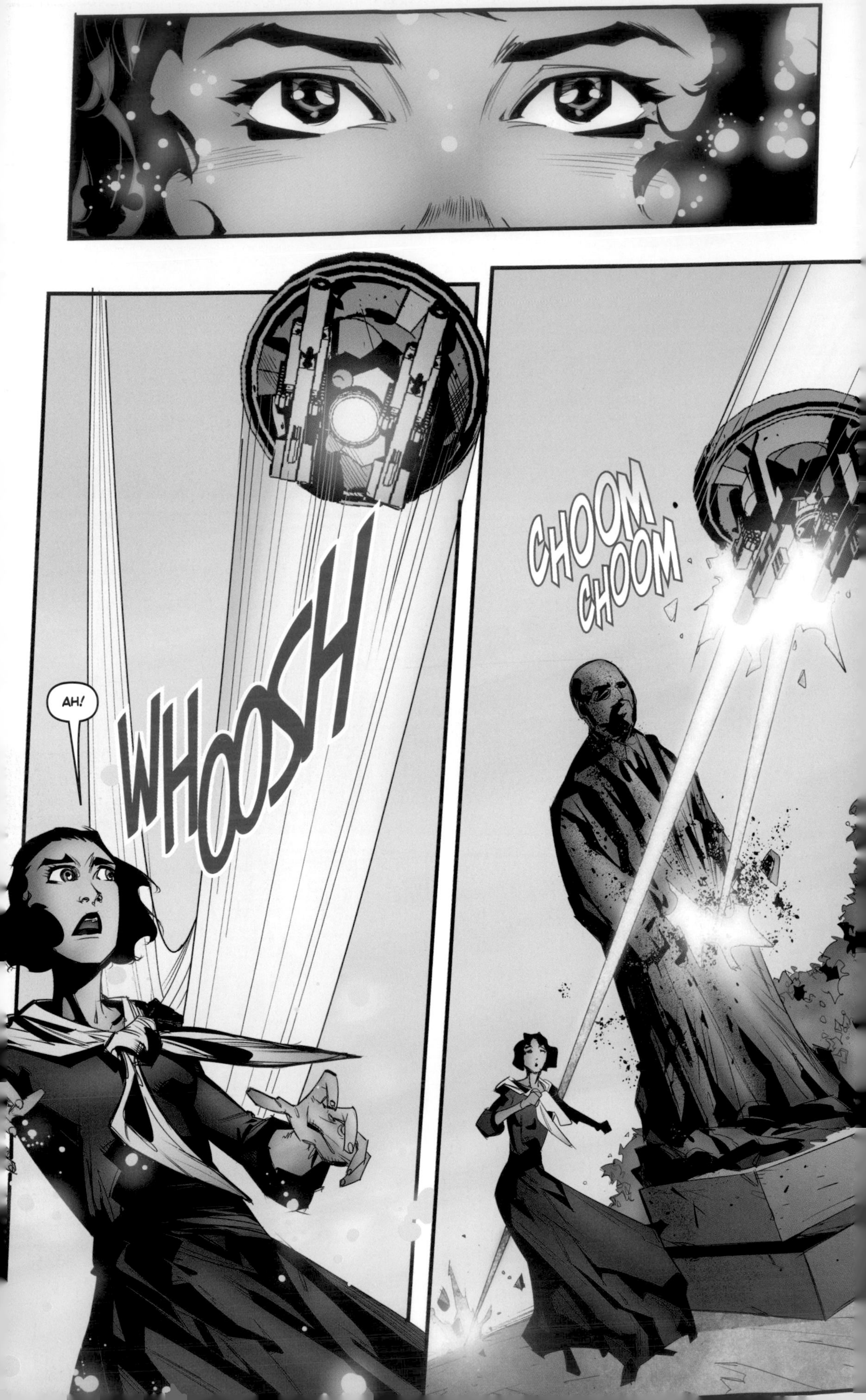
AH!
WHOOSH
CHOOM
CHOOM

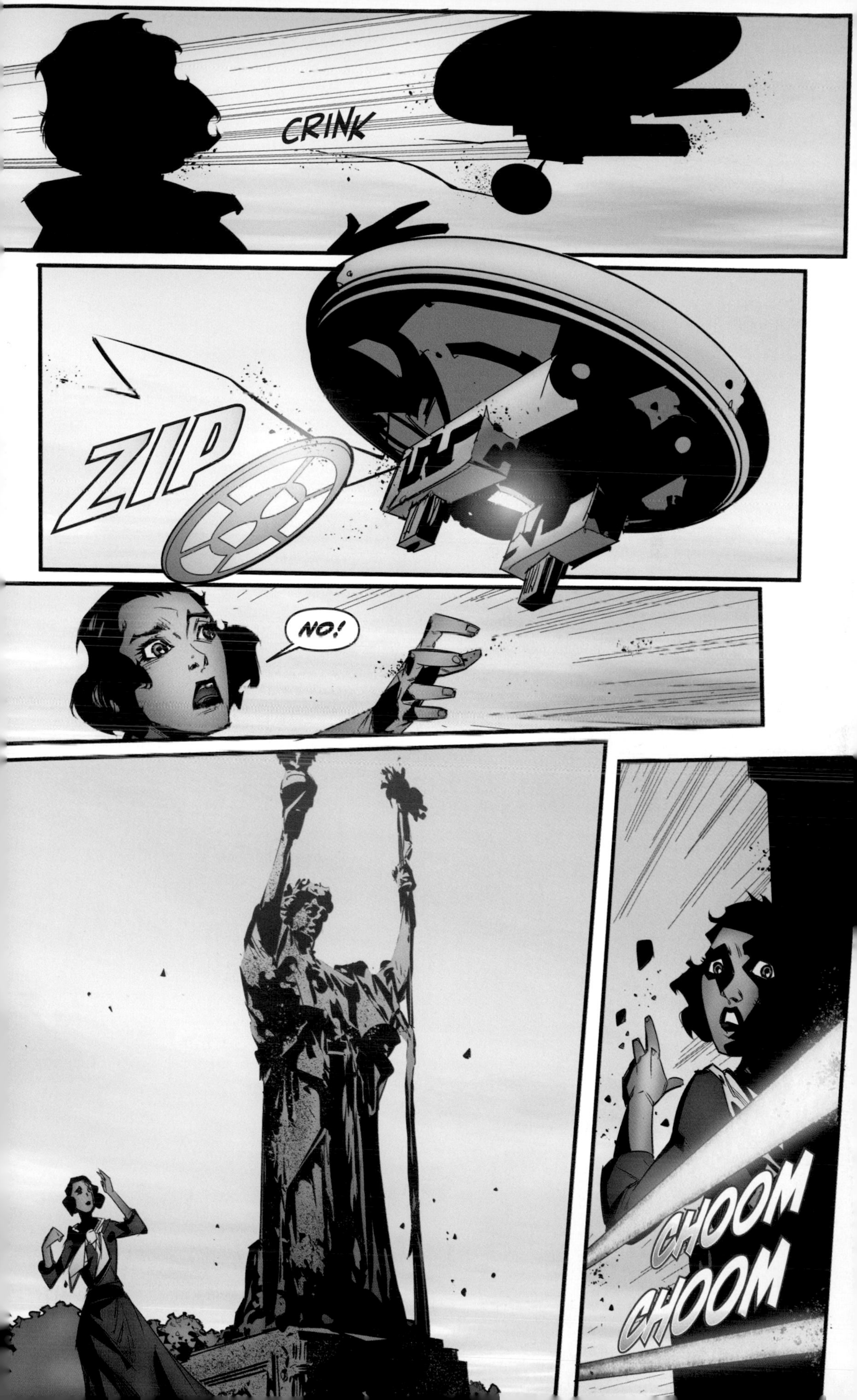
CRINK
ZIP
NO!
CHOOM
CHOOM

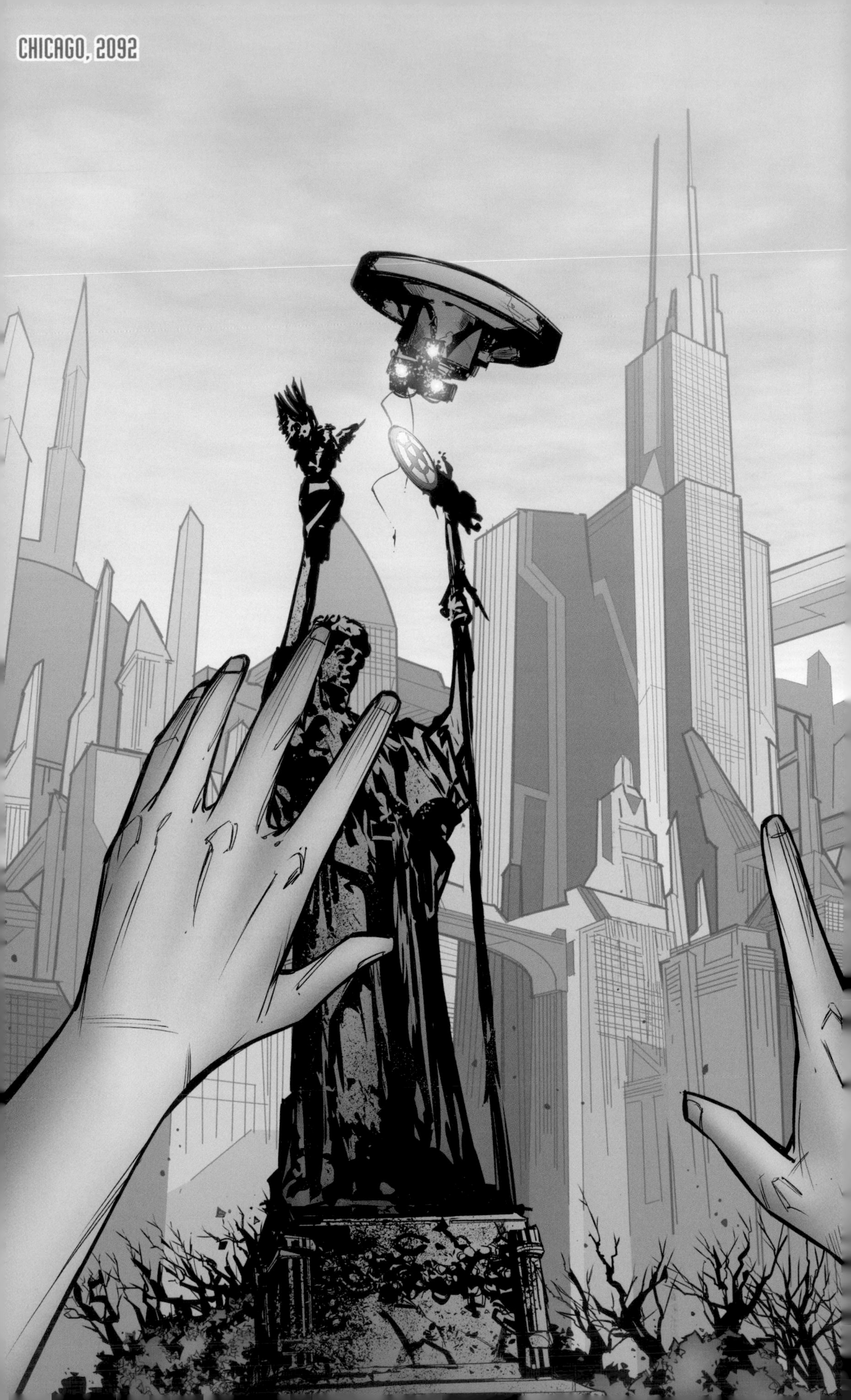
CHICAGO, 2092

CHAPTER 4

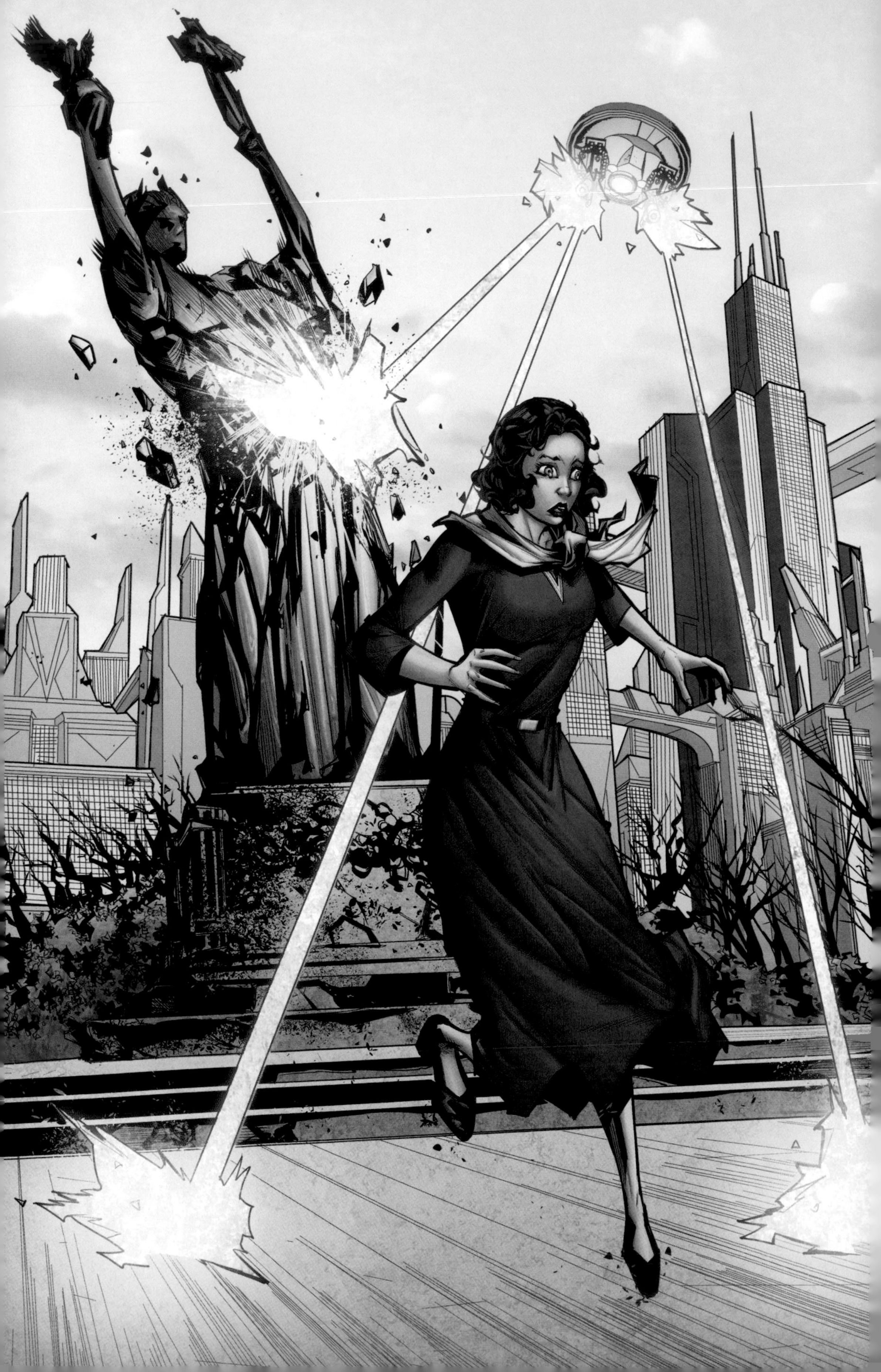

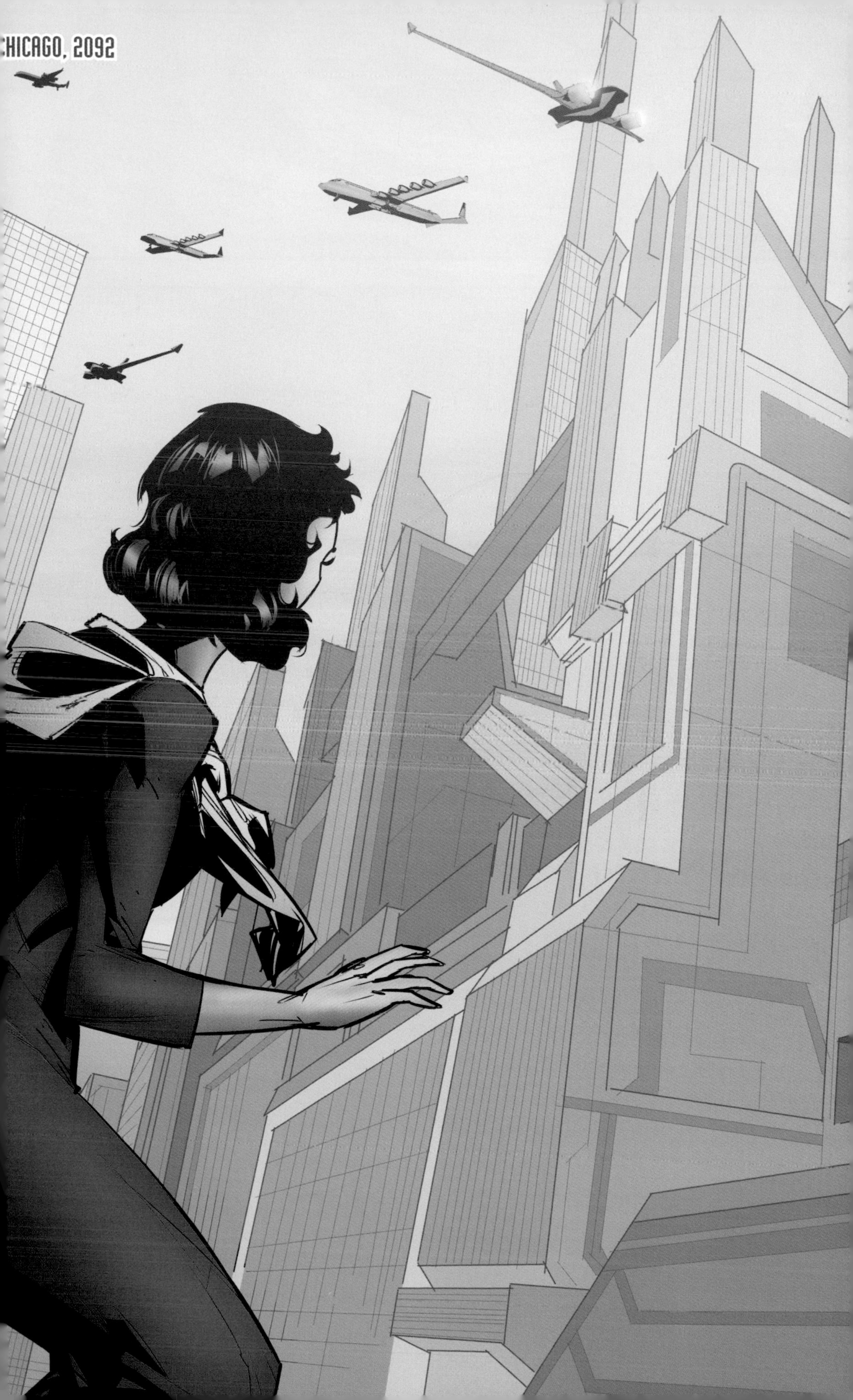
HICAGO, 2092

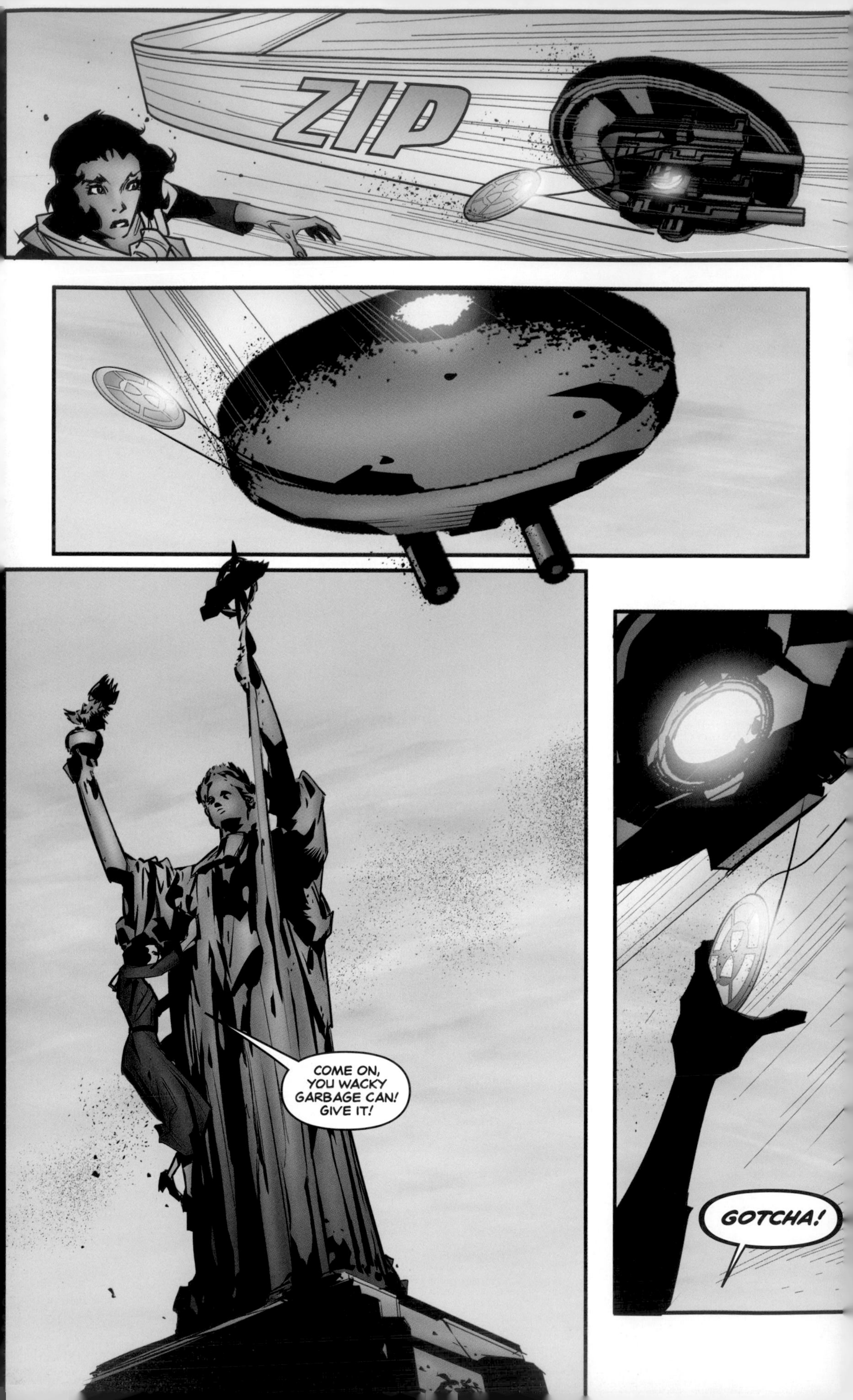
ZIP
COME ON, YOU WACKY GARBAGE CAN! GIVE IT!
GOTCHA!

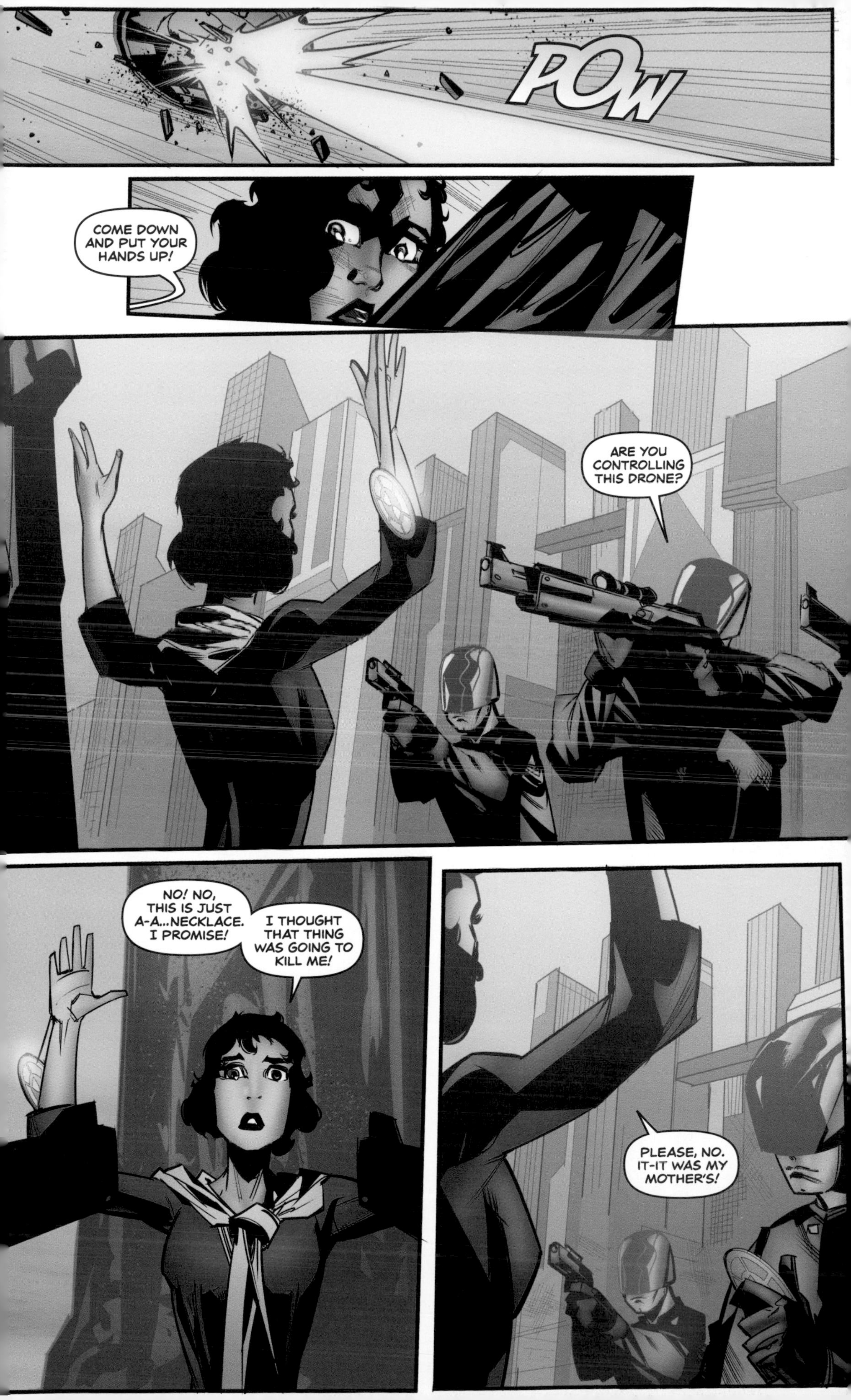
POW
COME DOWN AND PUT YOUR HANDS UP!
ARE YOU CONTROLLING THIS DRONE?
NO! NO, THIS IS JUST A-A...NECKLACE. I PROMISE!
I THOUGHT THAT THING WAS GOING TO KILL ME!
PLEASE, NO. IT-IT WAS MY MOTHER'S!

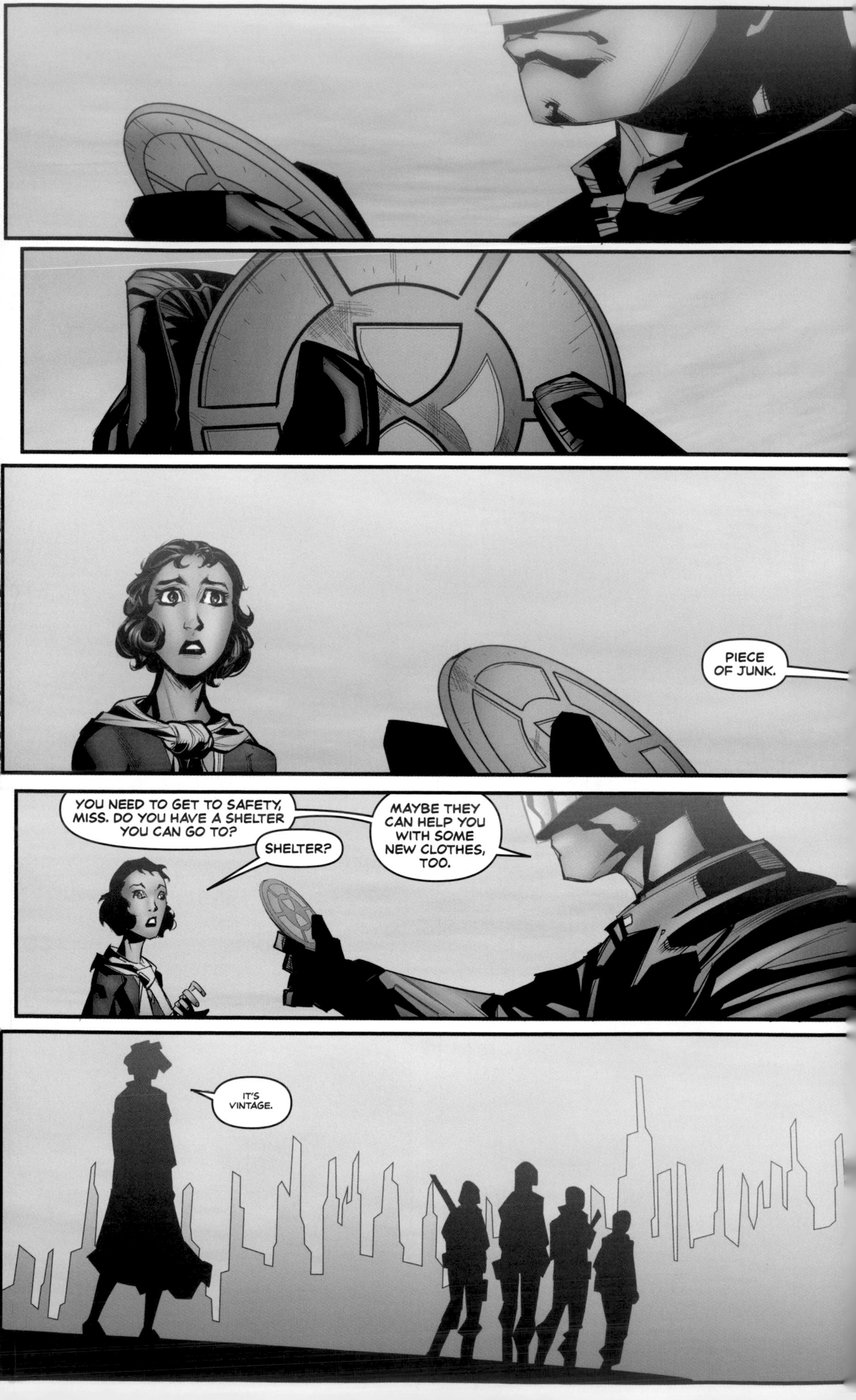
PIECE OF JUNK.
YOU NEED TO GET TO SAFETY, MISS. DO YOU HAVE A SHELTER YOU CAN GO TO?
SHELTER?
MAYBE THEY CAN HELP YOU WITH SOME NEW CLOTHES, TOO.
IT'S VINTAGE.

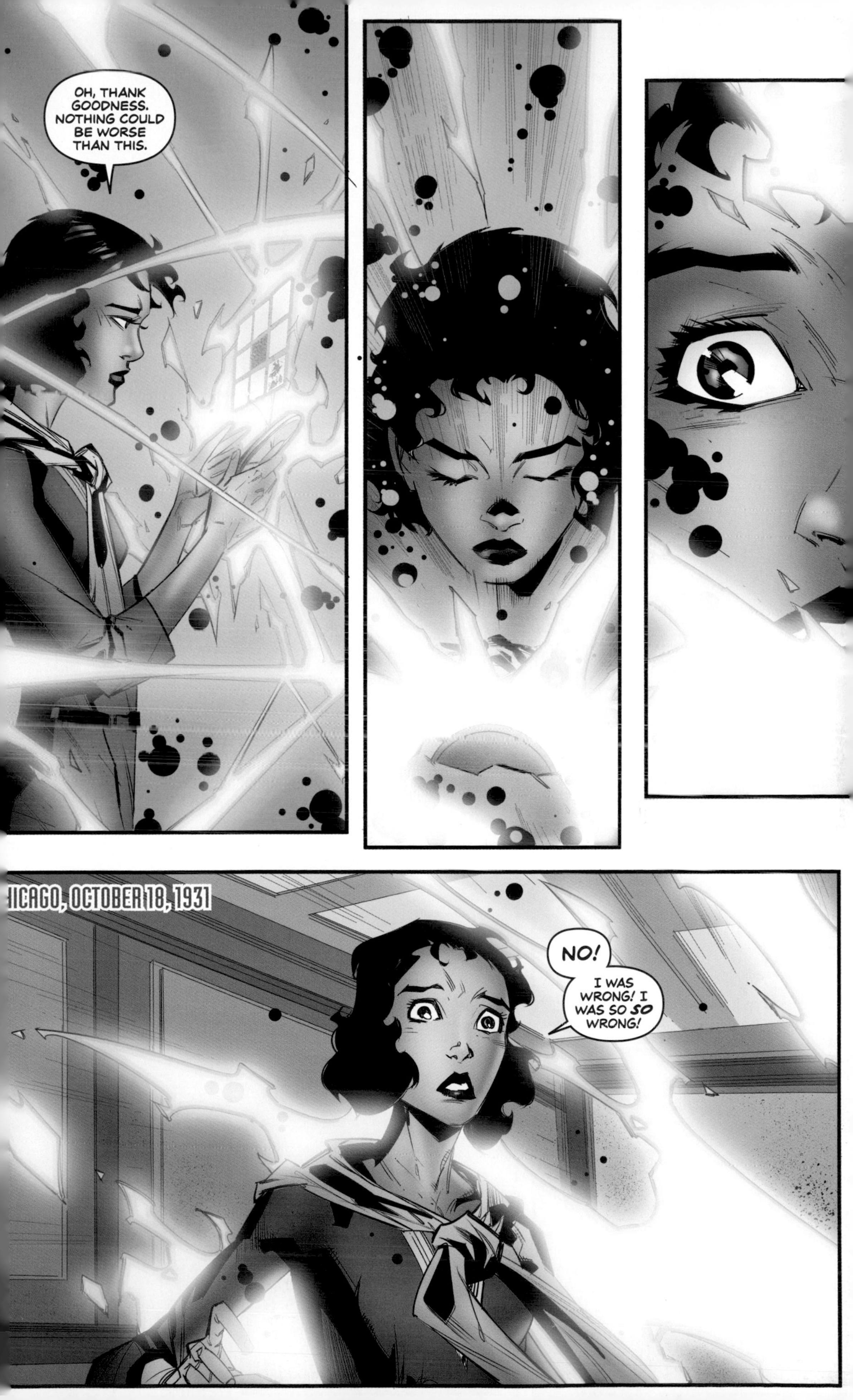
OH, THANK GOODNESS. NOTHING COULD BE WORSE THAN THIS.
ICAGO, OCTOBER 18, 1931
NO!
I WAS WRONG! I WAS SO SO WRONG!

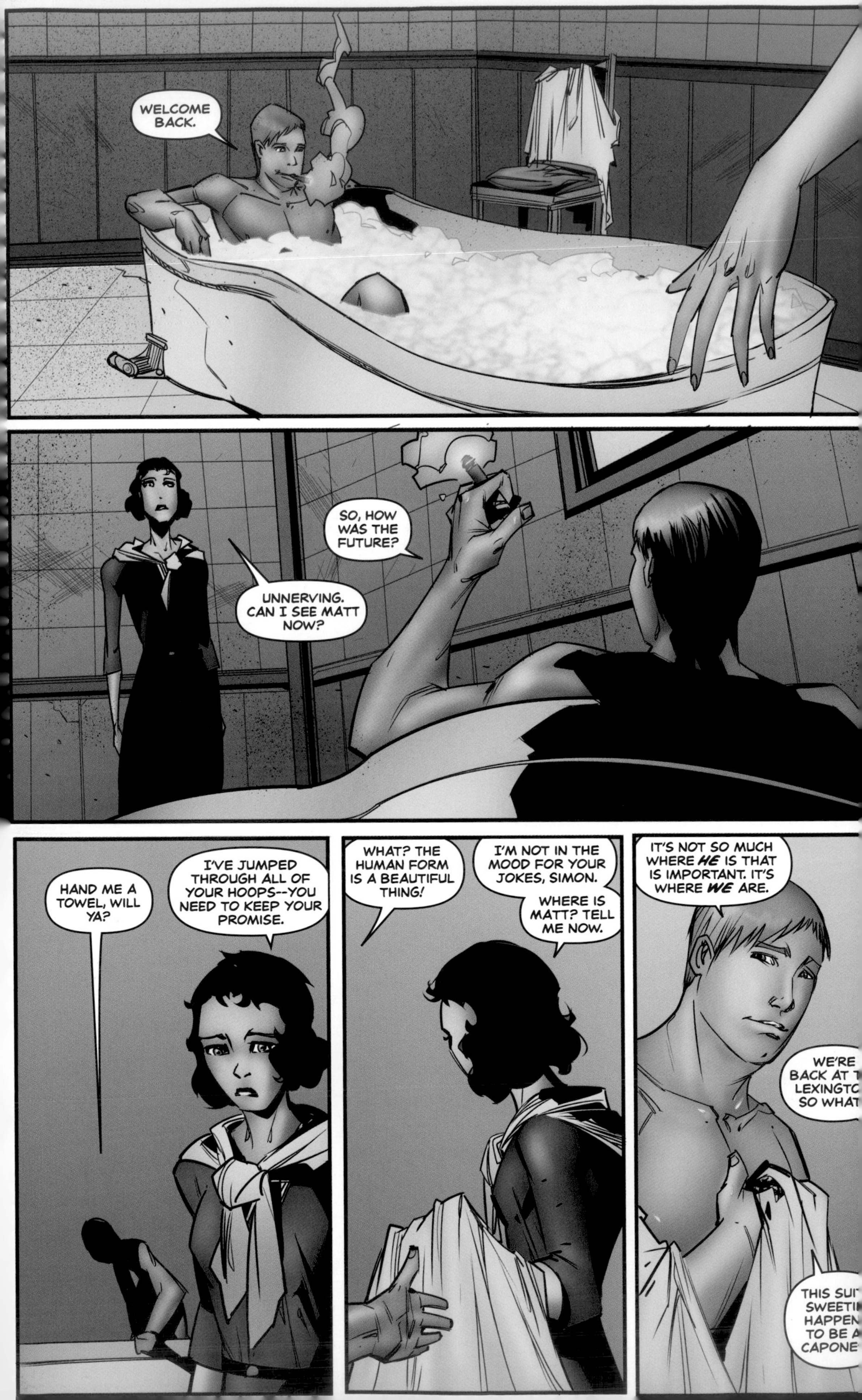
WELCOME BACK.
SO, HOW WAS THE FUTURE?
UNNERVING. CAN I SEE MATT NOW?
HAND ME A TOWEL, WILL YA?
I'VE JUMPED THROUGH ALL OF YOUR HOOPS--YOU NEED TO KEEP YOUR PROMISE.
WHAT? THE HUMAN FORM IS A BEAUTIFUL THING!
I'M NOT IN THE MOOD FOR YOUR JOKES, SIMON.
WHERE IS MATT? TELL ME NOW.
IT'S NOT SO MUCH WHERE *HE* IS THAT IS IMPORTANT. IT'S WHERE *WE* ARE.
WE'RE BACK AT
SO WHAT
THIS
HAPPEN
TO BE A
CAPONE

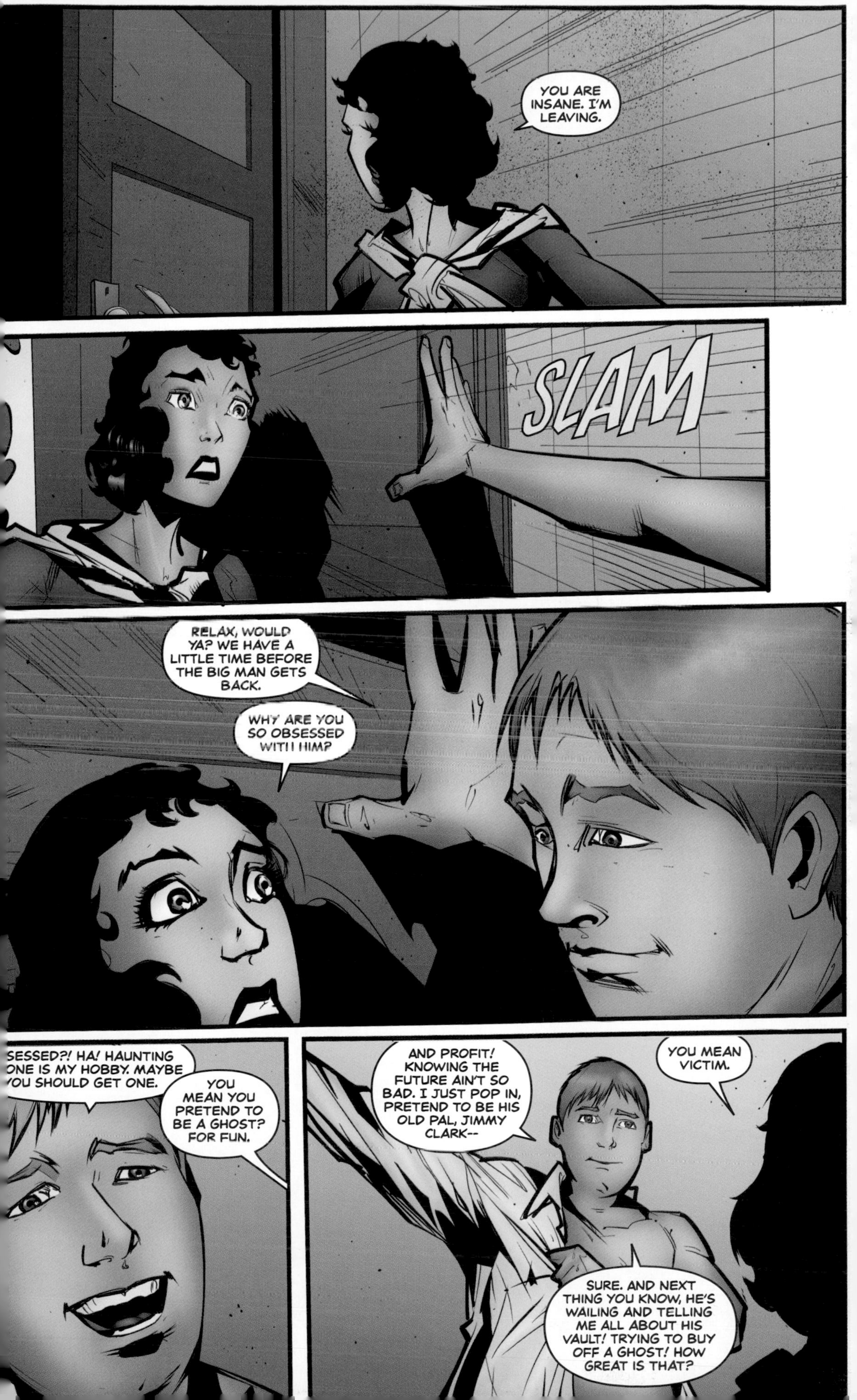
YOU ARE INSANE. I'M LEAVING.
SLAM
RELAX, WOULD YA? WE HAVE A LITTLE TIME BEFORE THE BIG MAN GETS BACK.
WHY ARE YOU SO OBSESSED WITH HIM?
SESSED?! HA! HAUNTING ONE IS MY HOBBY. MAYBE YOU SHOULD GET ONE.
YOU MEAN YOU PRETEND TO BE A GHOST? FOR FUN.
AND PROFIT! KNOWING THE FUTURE AIN'T SO BAD. I JUST POP IN, PRETEND TO BE HIS OLD PAL, JIMMY CLARK--
YOU MEAN VICTIM.
SURE. AND NEXT THING YOU KNOW, HE'S WAILING AND TELLING ME ALL ABOUT HIS VAULT! TRYING TO BUY OFF A GHOST! HOW GREAT IS THAT?

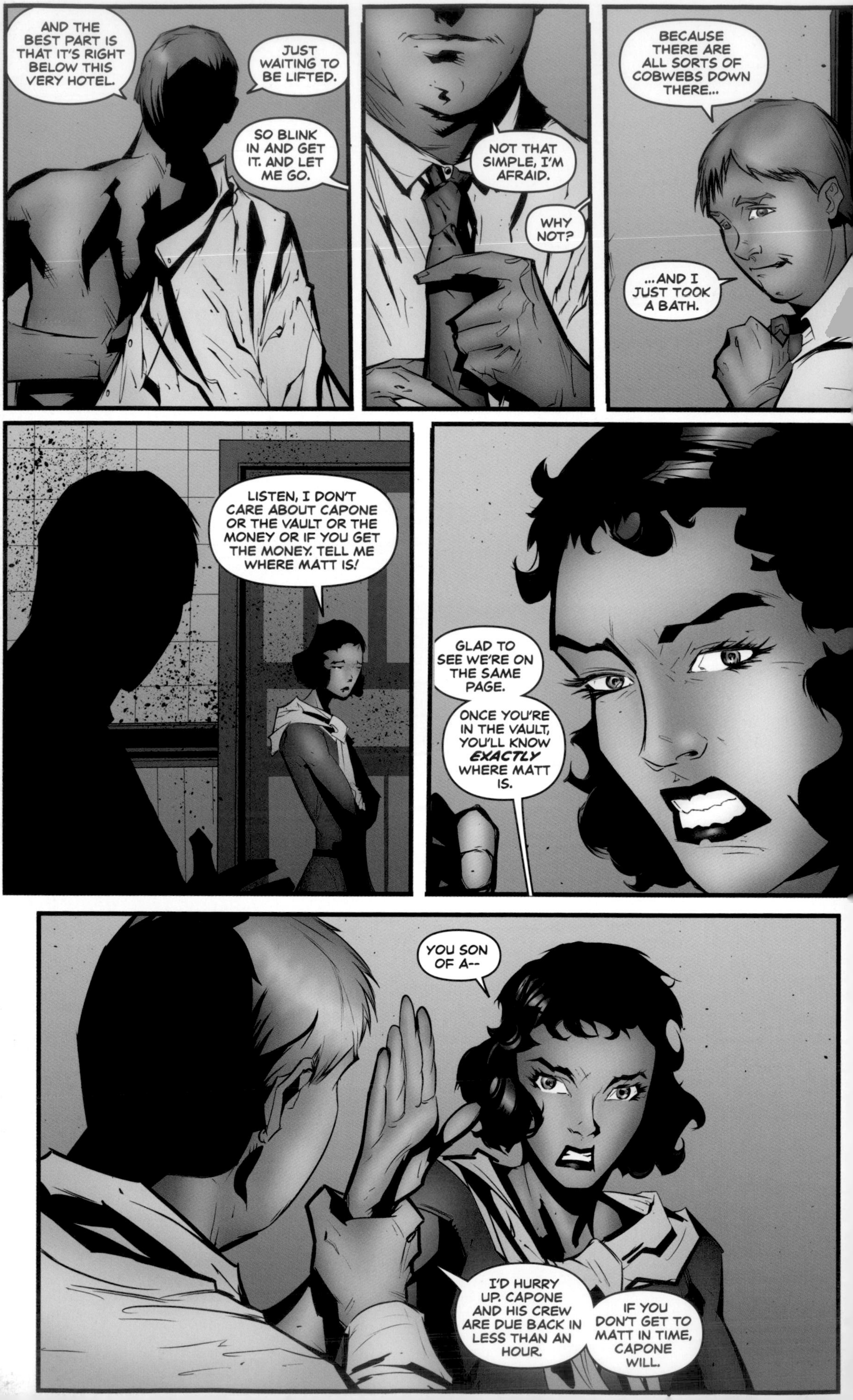
AND THE BEST PART IS THAT IT'S RIGHT BELOW THIS VERY HOTEL.
JUST WAITING TO BE LIFTED.
SO BLINK IN AND GET IT. AND LET ME GO.
NOT THAT SIMPLE, I'M AFRAID.
WHY NOT?
BECAUSE THERE ARE ALL SORTS OF COBWEBS DOWN THERE...
...AND I JUST TOOK A BATH.
LISTEN, I DON'T CARE ABOUT CAPONE OR THE VAULT OR THE MONEY OR IF YOU GET THE MONEY. TELL ME WHERE MATT IS!
GLAD TO SEE WE'RE ON THE SAME PAGE.
ONCE YOU'RE IN THE VAULT, YOU'LL KNOW *EXACTLY* WHERE MATT IS.
YOU SON OF A--
I'D HURRY UP. CAPONE AND HIS CREW ARE DUE BACK IN LESS THAN AN HOUR.
IF YOU DON'T GET TO MATT IN TIME, CAPONE WILL.

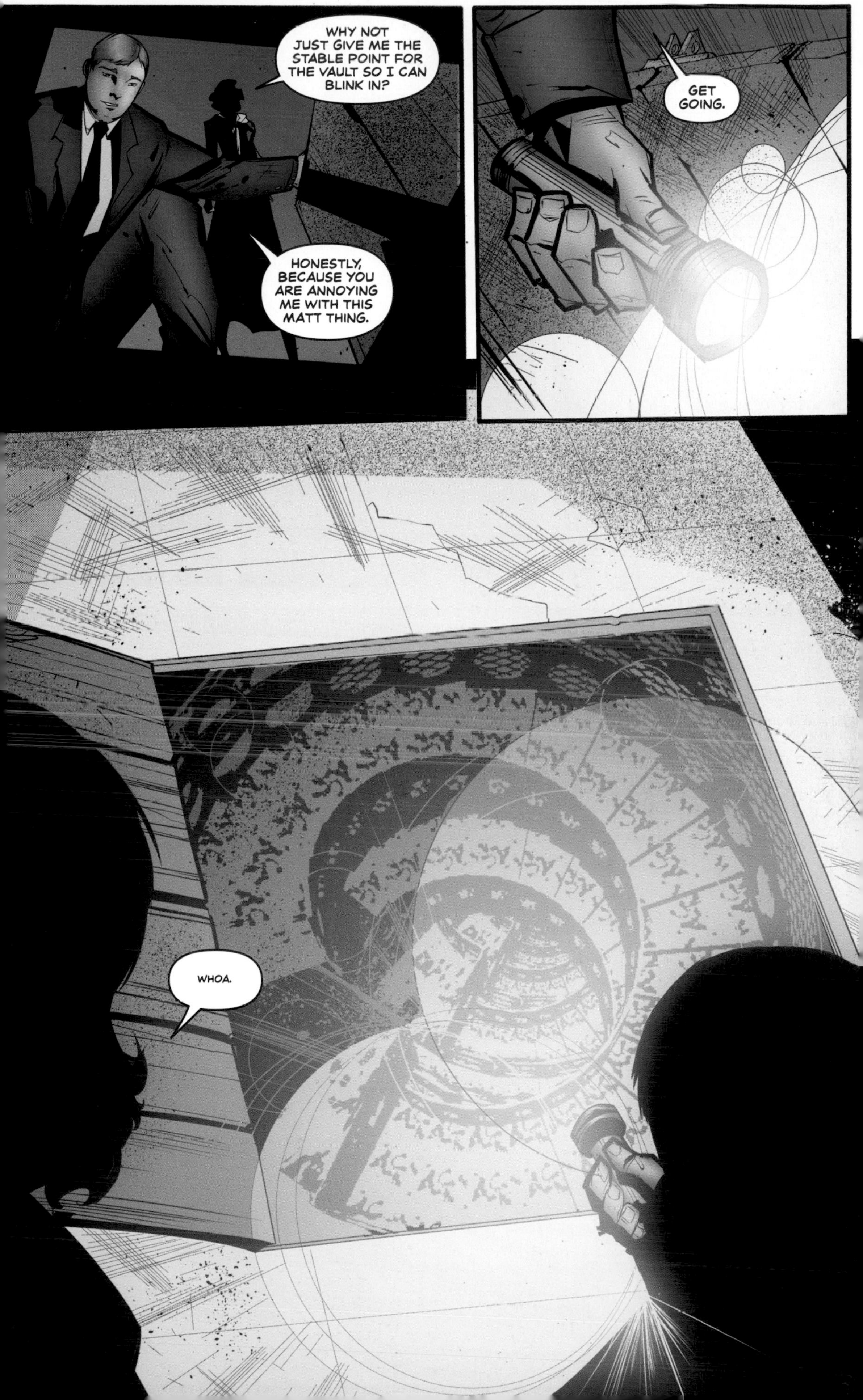
WHY NOT JUST GIVE ME THE STABLE POINT FOR THE VAULT SO I CAN BLINK IN?
HONESTLY, BECAUSE YOU ARE ANNOYING ME WITH THIS MATT THING.
GET GOING.
WHOA.

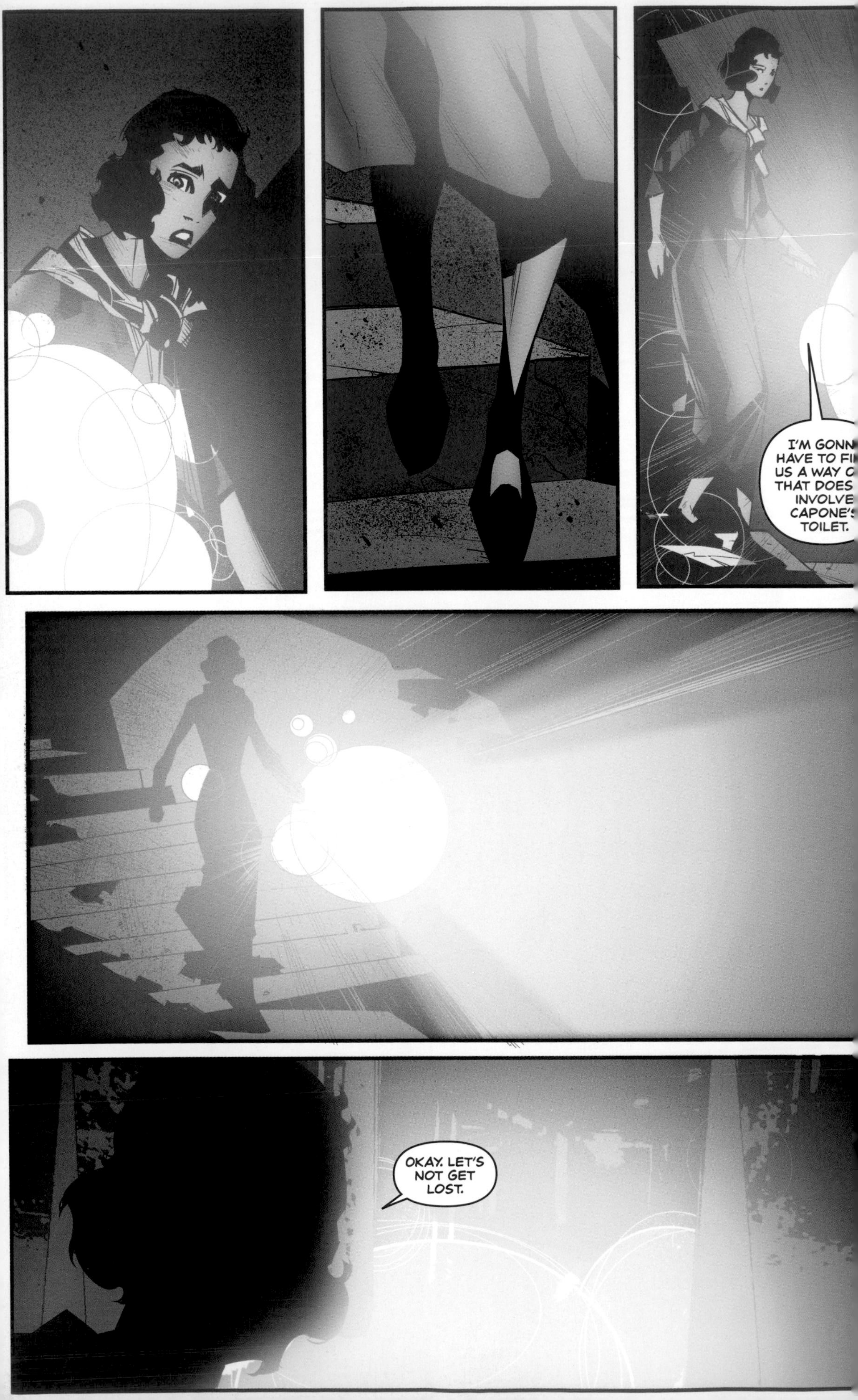
I'M GONN HAVE TO FI US A WAY C THAT DOES INVOLVE CAPONE'S TOILET.
OKAY. LET'S NOT GET LOST.

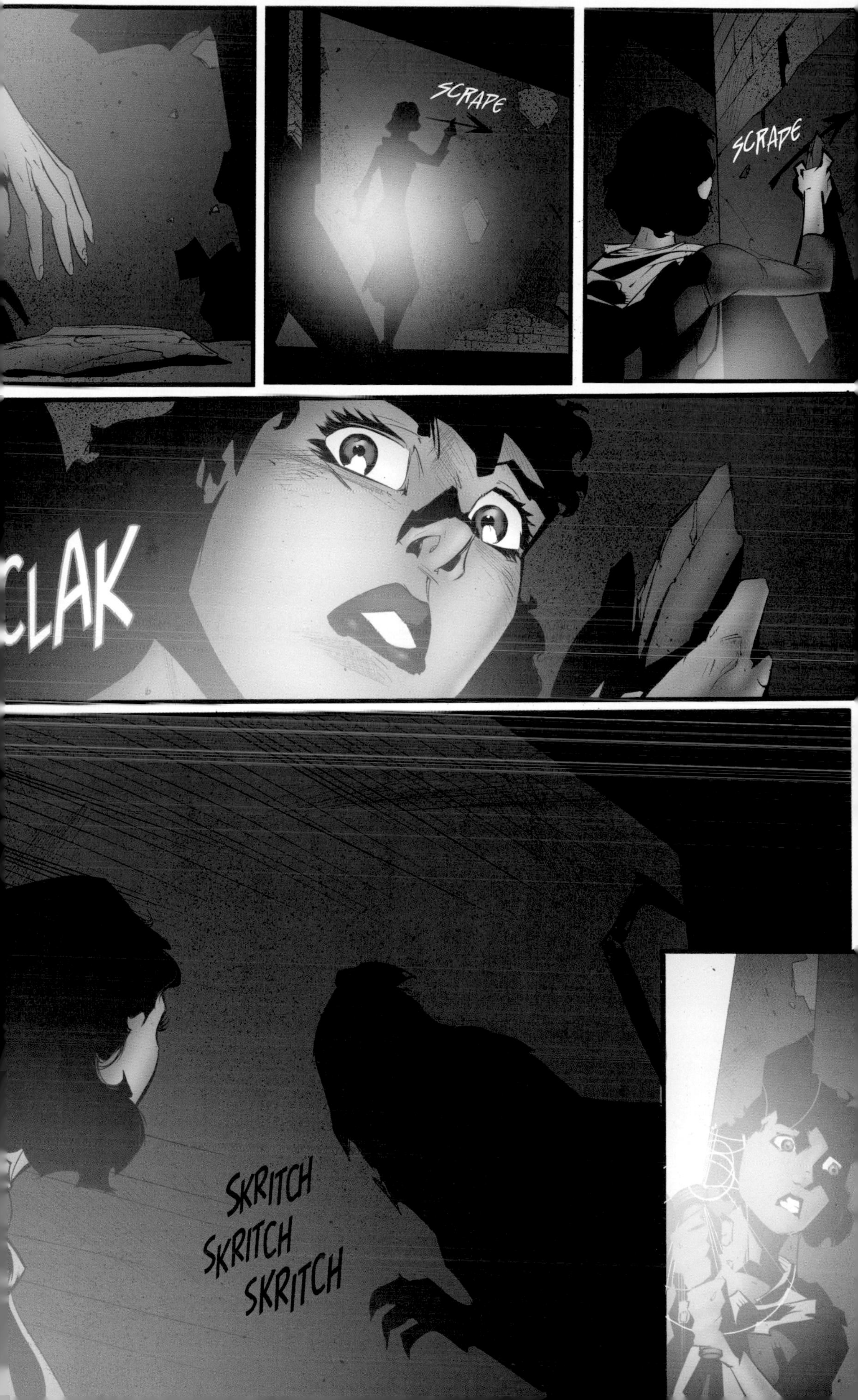
SCRAPE
SCRAPE
CLAK
SKRITCH
SKRITCH
SKRITCH

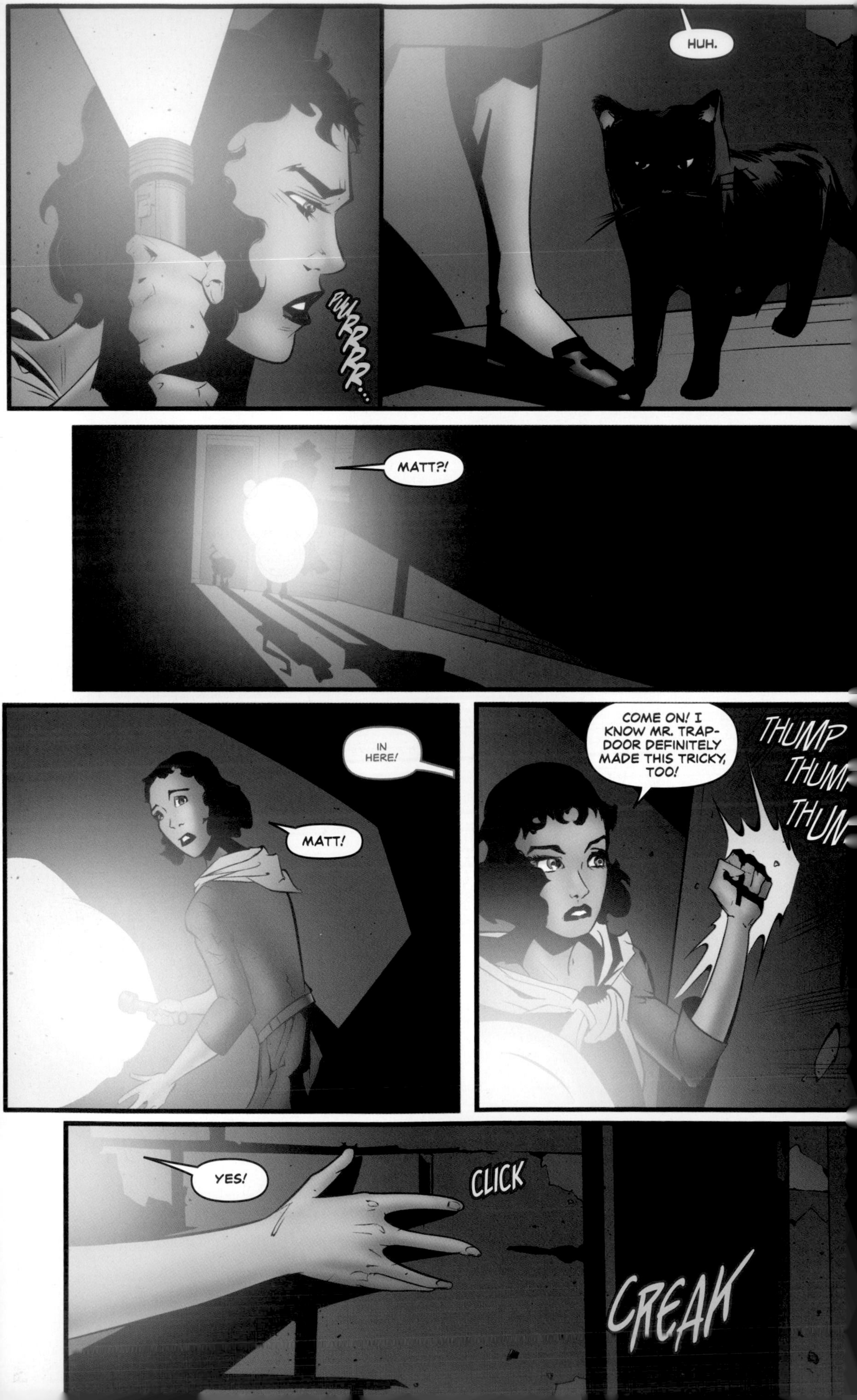
PURRRRR...
HUH.
MATT?!
IN HERE!
MATT!
COME ON! I KNOW MR. TRAP-DOOR DEFINITELY MADE THIS TRICKY, TOO!
THUMP
YES!
CLICK
CREAK

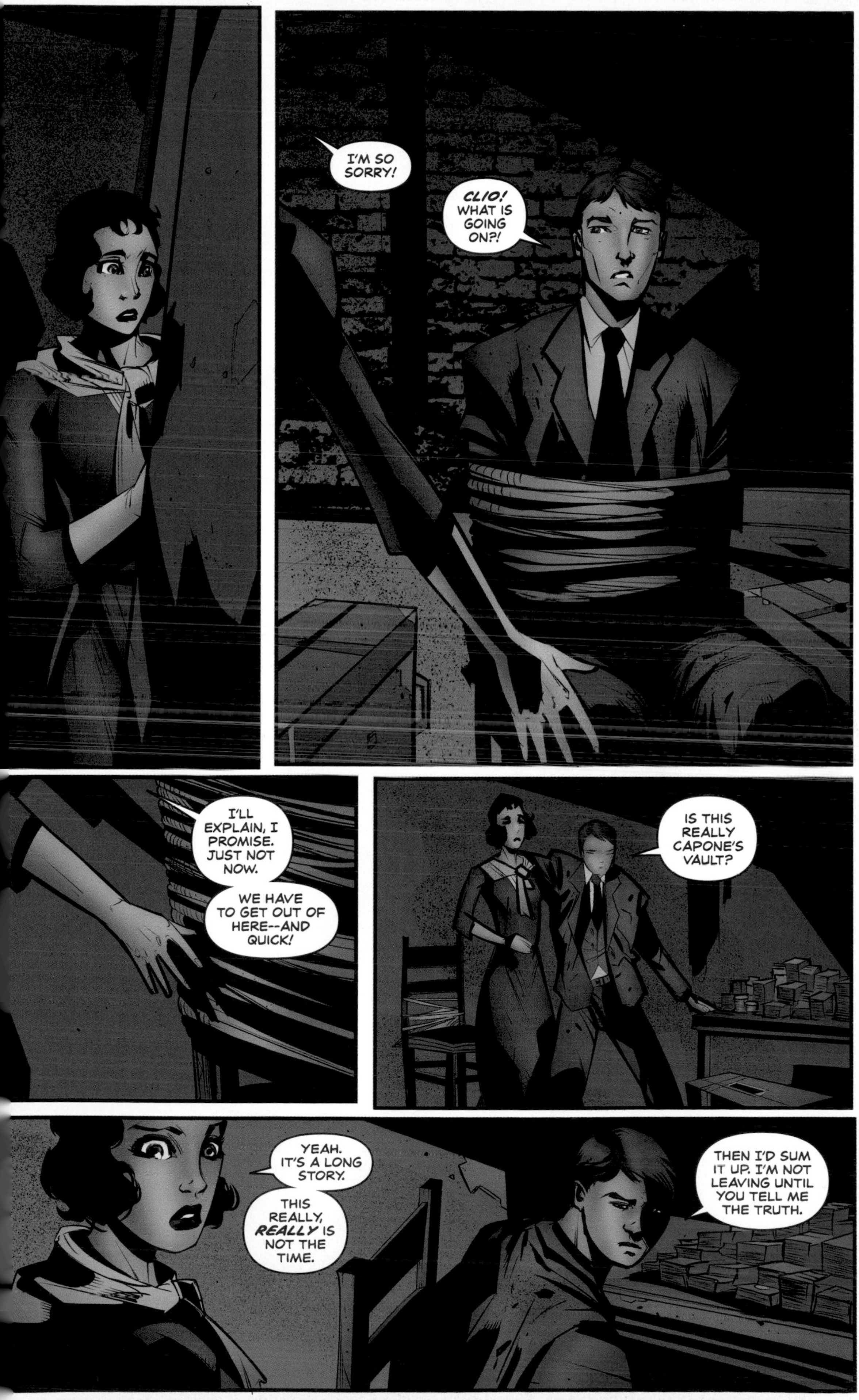
I'M SO SORRY!
CLIO! WHAT IS GOING ON?!
I'LL EXPLAIN, I PROMISE. JUST NOT NOW.
WE HAVE TO GET OUT OF HERE--AND QUICK!
IS THIS REALLY CAPONE'S VAULT?
YEAH. IT'S A LONG STORY.
THIS REALLY, REALLY IS NOT THE TIME.
THEN I'D SUM IT UP. I'M NOT LEAVING UNTIL YOU TELL ME THE TRUTH.

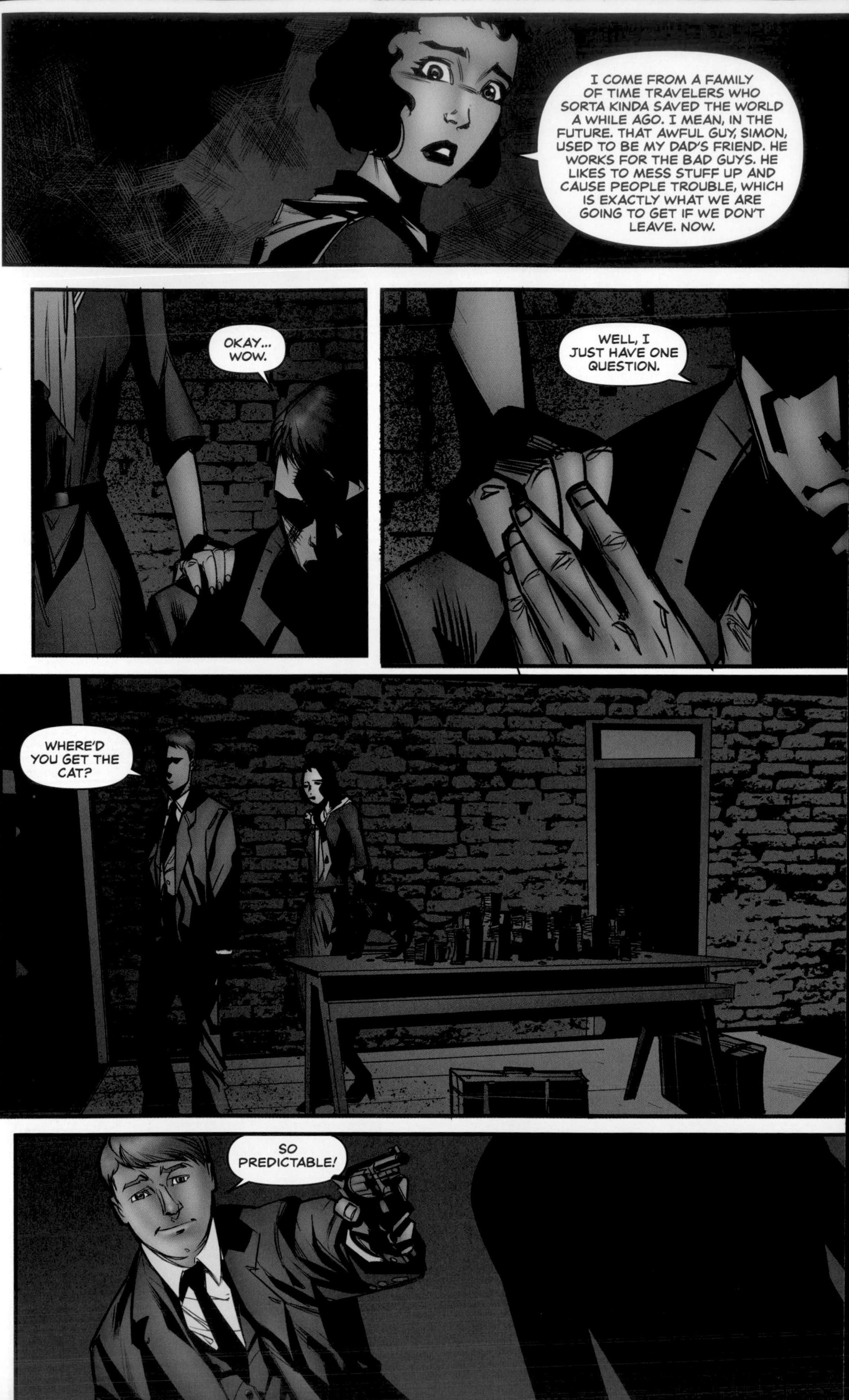
I COME FROM A FAMILY OF TIME TRAVELERS WHO SORTA KINDA SAVED THE WORLD A WHILE AGO. I MEAN, IN THE FUTURE. THAT AWFUL GUY, SIMON, USED TO BE MY DAD'S FRIEND. HE WORKS FOR THE BAD GUYS. HE LIKES TO MESS STUFF UP AND CAUSE PEOPLE TROUBLE, WHICH IS EXACTLY WHAT WE ARE GOING TO GET IF WE DON'T LEAVE. NOW.
OKAY... WOW.
WELL, I JUST HAVE ONE QUESTION.
WHERE'D YOU GET THE CAT?
SO PREDICTABLE!

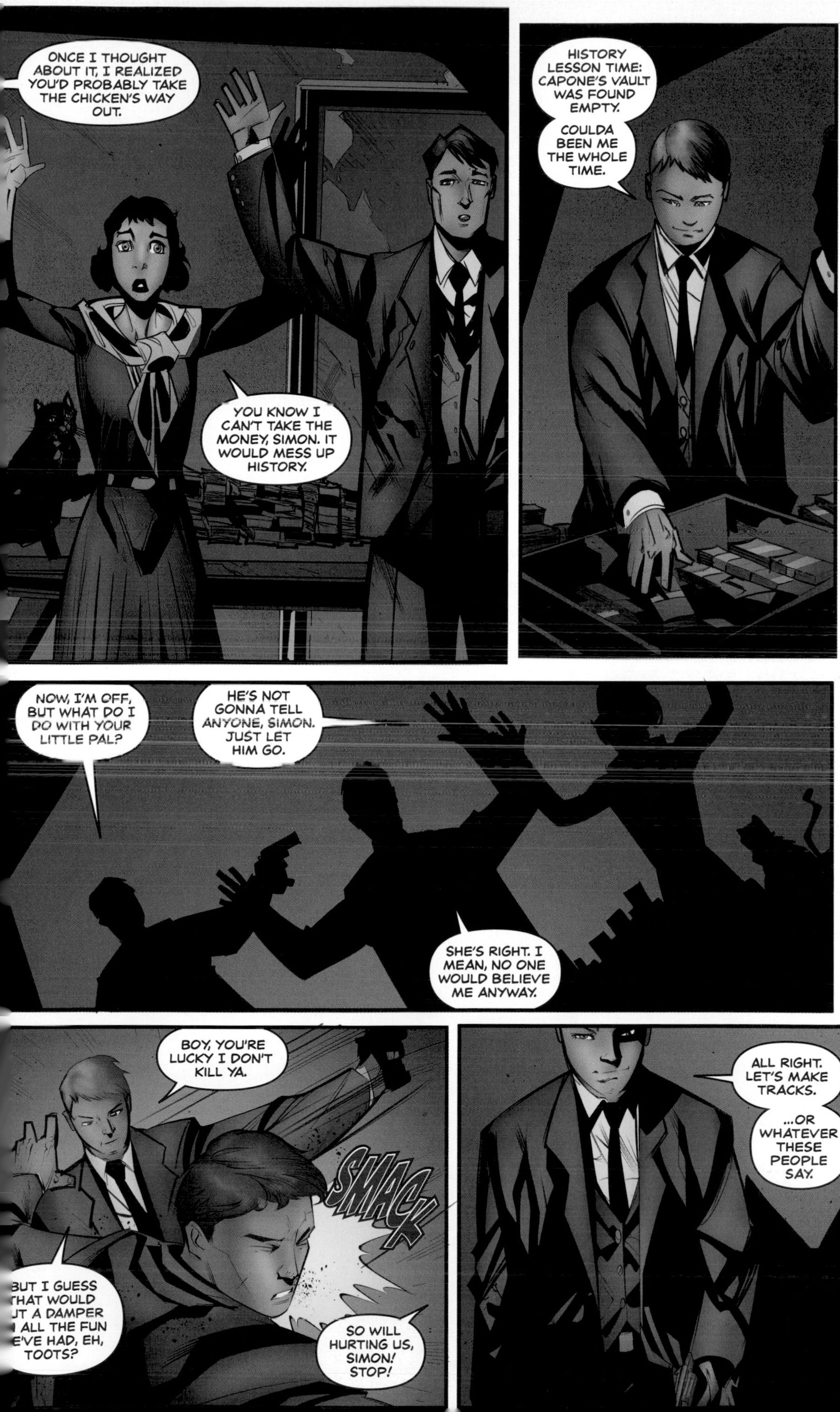
ONCE I THOUGHT ABOUT IT, I REALIZED YOU'D PROBABLY TAKE THE CHICKEN'S WAY OUT.
YOU KNOW I CAN'T TAKE THE MONEY, SIMON. IT WOULD MESS UP HISTORY.
HISTORY LESSON TIME: CAPONE'S VAULT WAS FOUND EMPTY.
COULDA BEEN ME THE WHOLE TIME.
NOW, I'M OFF, BUT WHAT DO I DO WITH YOUR LITTLE PAL?
HE'S NOT GONNA TELL ANYONE, SIMON. JUST LET HIM GO.
SHE'S RIGHT. I MEAN, NO ONE WOULD BELIEVE ME ANYWAY.
BOY, YOU'RE LUCKY I DON'T KILL YA.
SMACK!
BUT I GUESS THAT WOULD UT A DAMPER I ALL THE FUN E'VE HAD, EH, TOOTS?
SO WILL HURTING US, SIMON! STOP!
ALL RIGHT. LET'S MAKE TRACKS.
...OR WHATEVER THESE PEOPLE SAY.

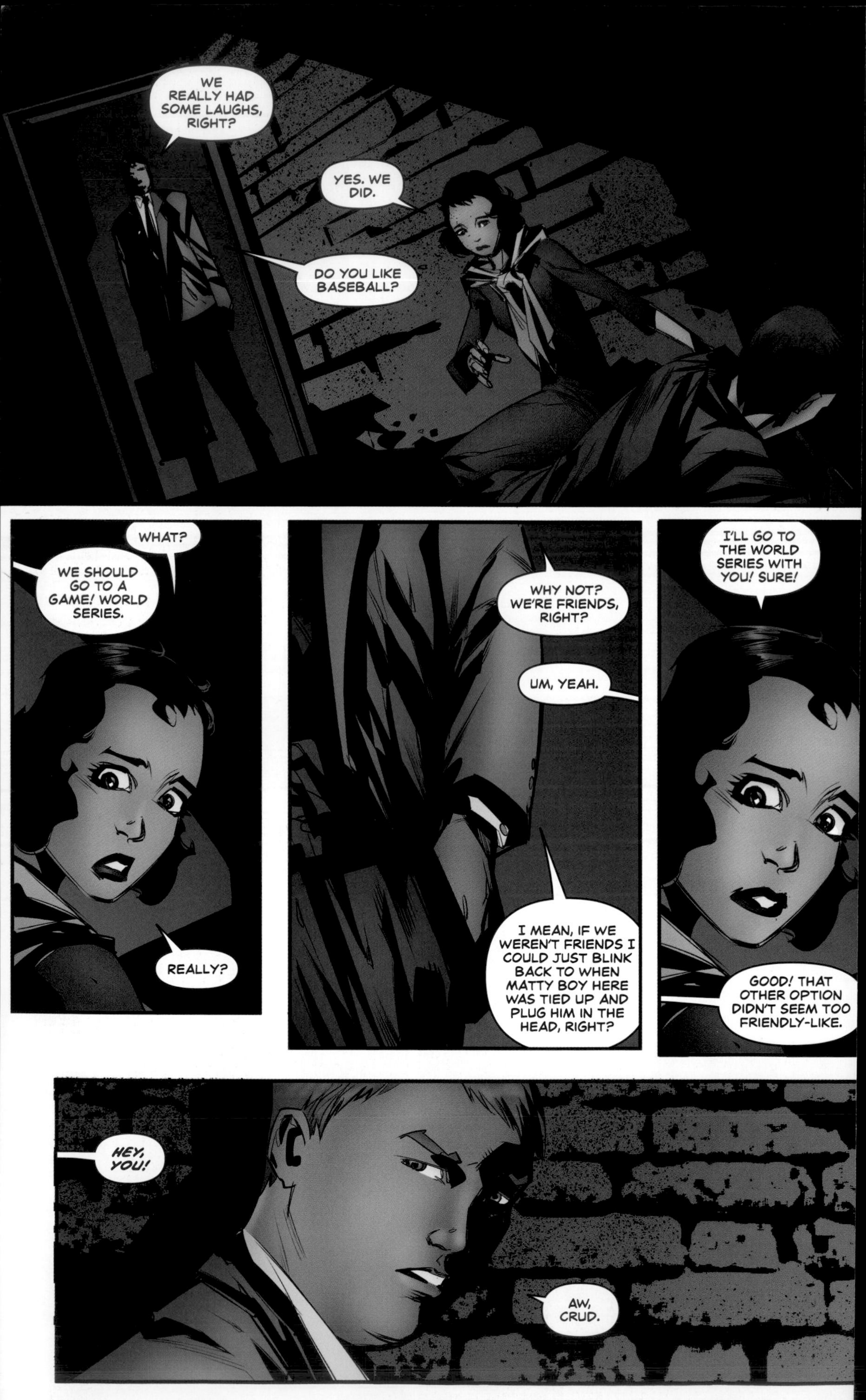
WE REALLY HAD SOME LAUGHS, RIGHT?
YES. WE DID.
DO YOU LIKE BASEBALL?
WHAT?
WE SHOULD GO TO A GAME! WORLD SERIES.
REALLY?
WHY NOT? WE'RE FRIENDS, RIGHT?
UM, YEAH.
I MEAN, IF WE WEREN'T FRIENDS I COULD JUST BLINK BACK TO WHEN MATTY BOY HERE WAS TIED UP AND PLUG HIM IN THE HEAD, RIGHT?
I'LL GO TO THE WORLD SERIES WITH YOU! SURE!
GOOD! THAT OTHER OPTION DIDN'T SEEM TOO FRIENDLY-LIKE.
HEY, YOU!
AW, CRUD.

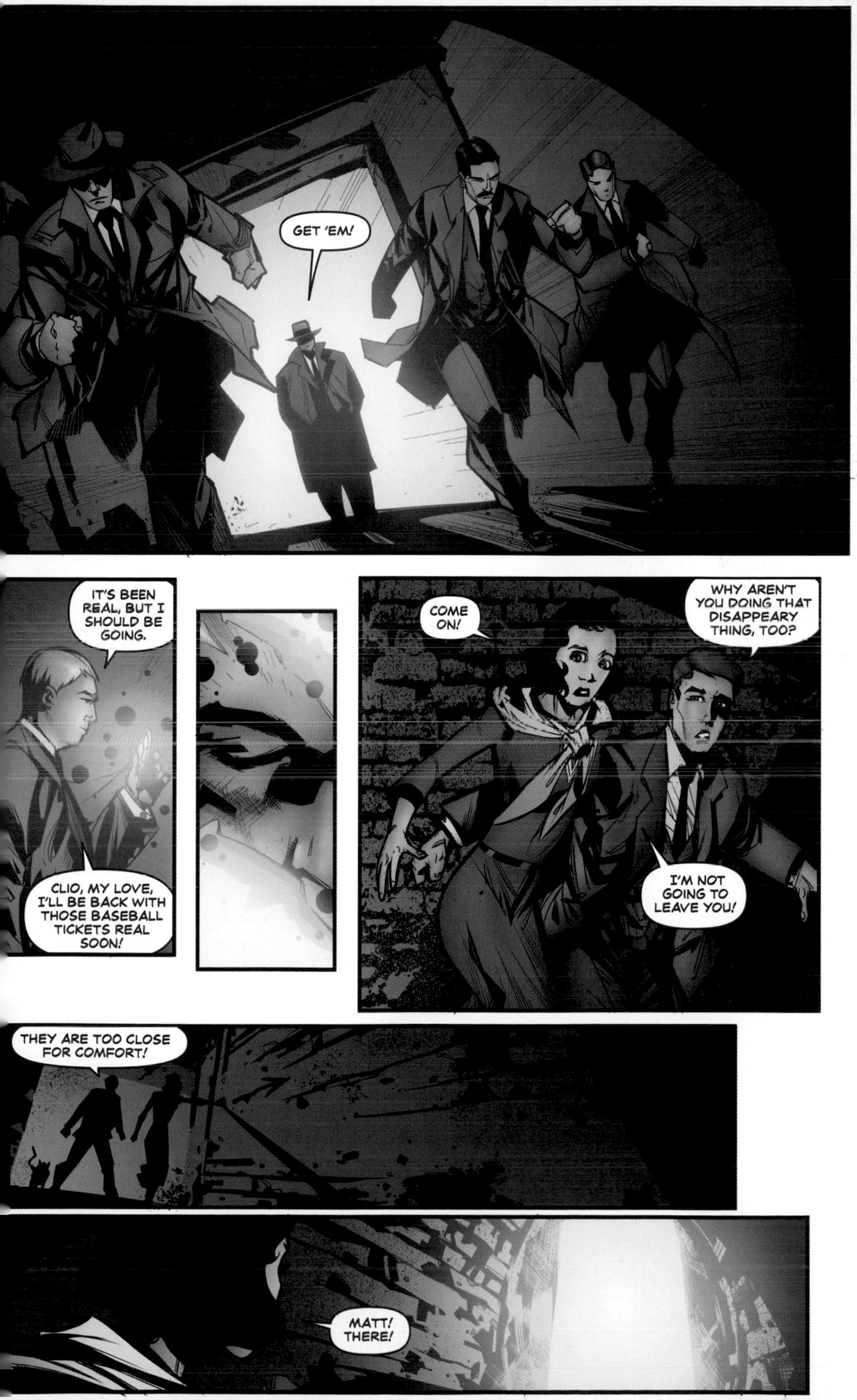
GET 'EM!
IT'S BEEN REAL, BUT I SHOULD BE GOING.
CLIO, MY LOVE, I'LL BE BACK WITH THOSE BASEBALL TICKETS REAL SOON!
COME ON!
WHY AREN'T YOU DOING THAT DISAPPEARY THING, TOO?
I'M NOT GOING TO LEAVE YOU!
THEY ARE TOO CLOSE FOR COMFORT!
MATT! THERE!

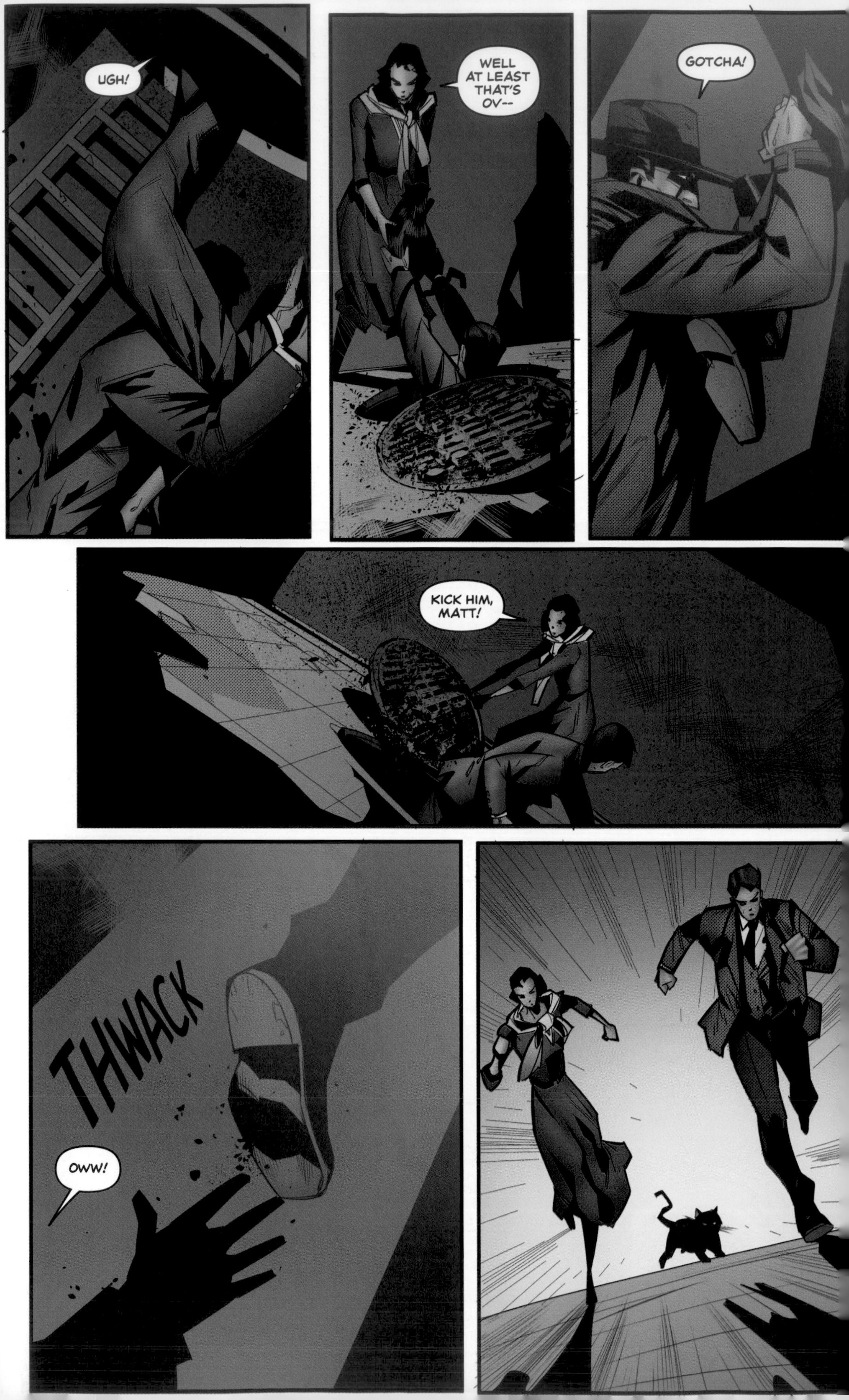
UGH!
WELL AT LEAST THAT'S OV--
GOTCHA!
KICK HIM, MATT!
THWACK
OWW!

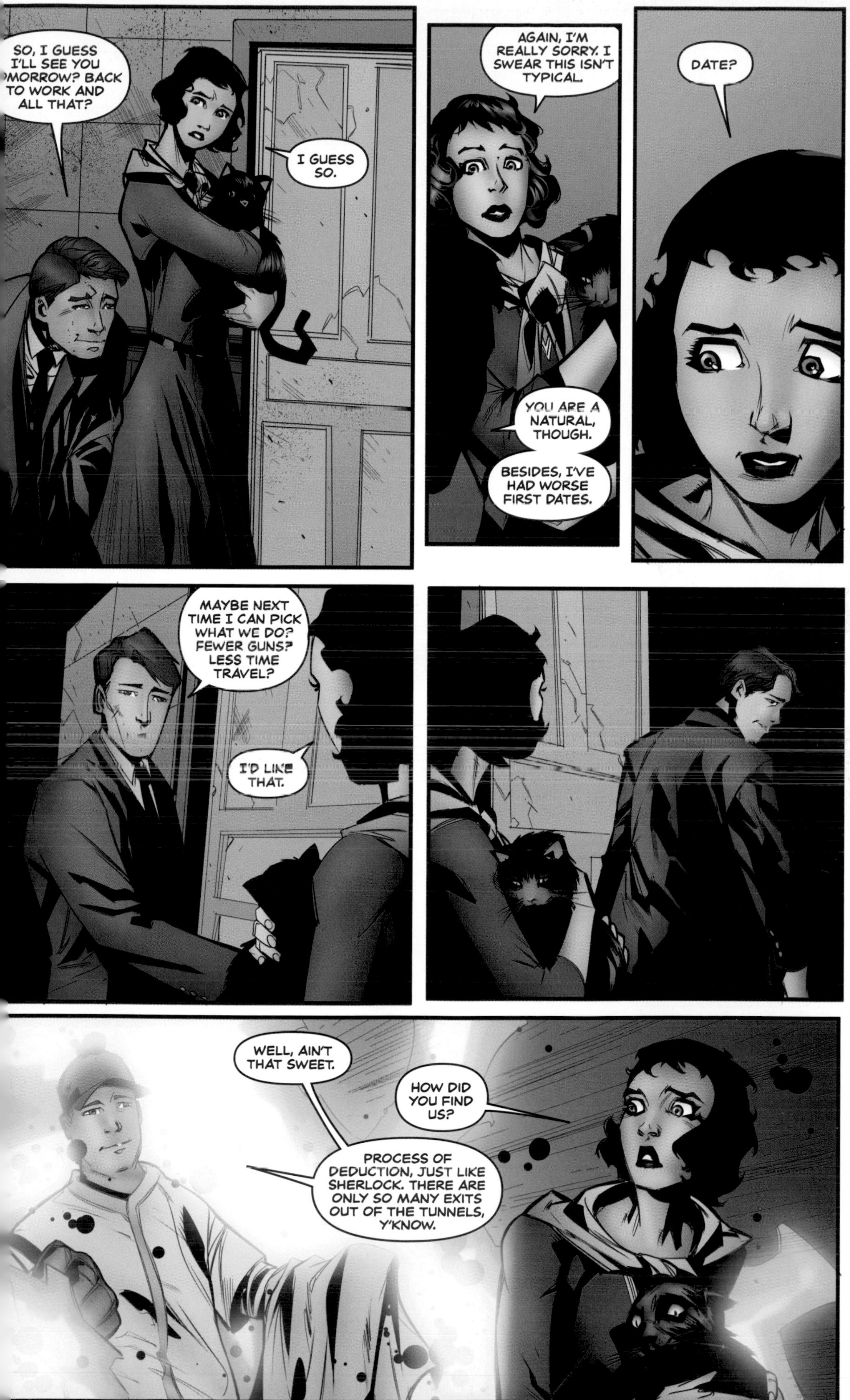
SO, I GUESS I'LL SEE YOU OMORROW? BACK TO WORK AND ALL THAT?
I GUESS SO.
AGAIN, I'M REALLY SORRY. I SWEAR THIS ISN'T TYPICAL.
YOU ARE A NATURAL, THOUGH.
BESIDES, I'VE HAD WORSE FIRST DATES.
DATE?
MAYBE NEXT TIME I CAN PICK WHAT WE DO? FEWER GUNS? LESS TIME TRAVEL?
I'D LIKE THAT.
WELL, AIN'T THAT SWEET.
HOW DID YOU FIND US?
PROCESS OF DEDUCTION, JUST LIKE SHERLOCK. THERE ARE ONLY SO MANY EXITS OUT OF THE TUNNELS, Y'KNOW.

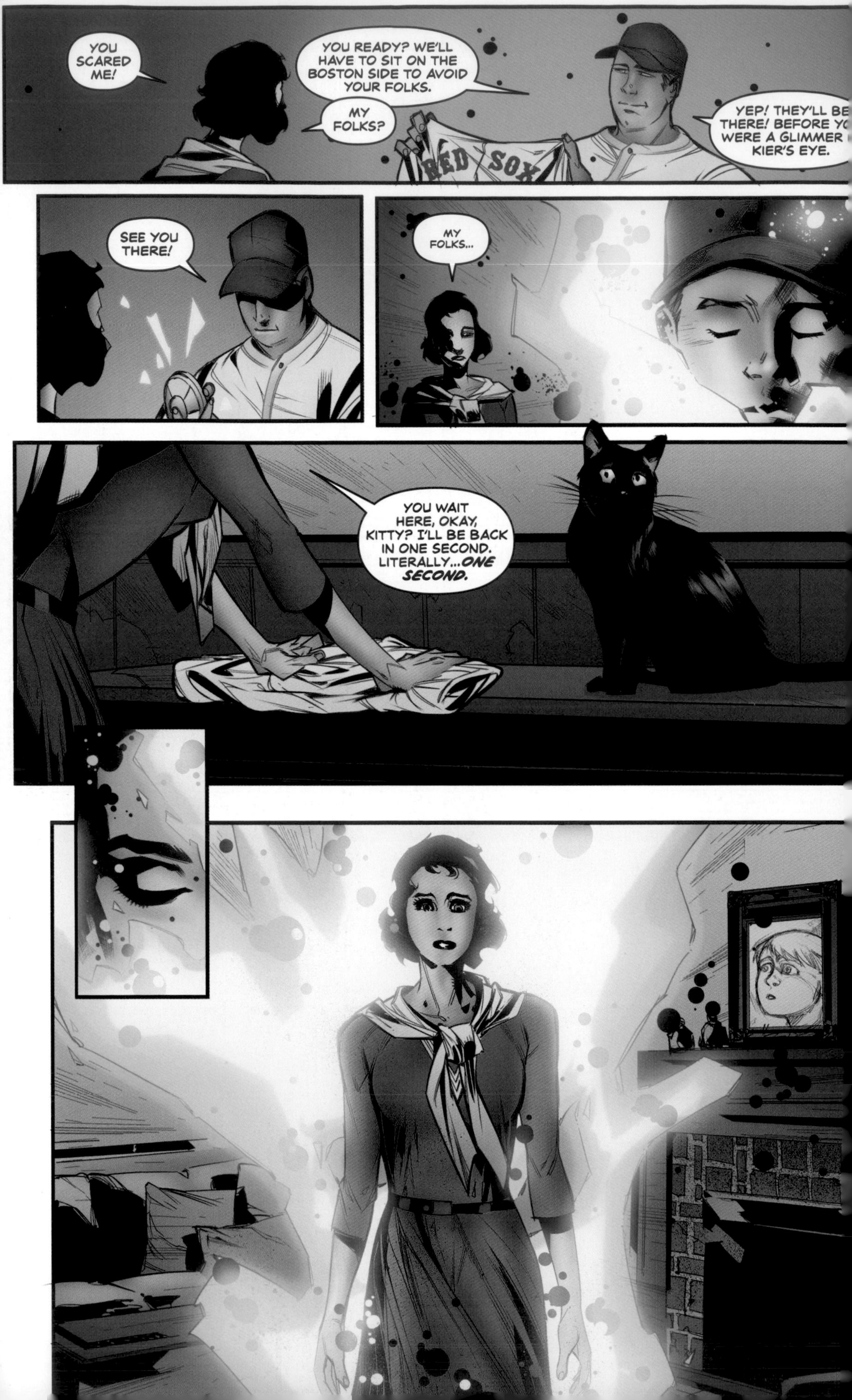
YOU SCARED ME!
YOU READY? WE'LL HAVE TO SIT ON THE BOSTON SIDE TO AVOID YOUR FOLKS.
MY FOLKS?
YEP! THEY'LL BE THERE! BEFORE YO
WERE A GLIMMER
KIER'S EYE.
RED SOX
SEE YOU THERE!
MY FOLKS...
YOU WAIT HERE, OKAY, KITTY? I'LL BE BACK IN ONE SECOND. LITERALLY...*ONE SECOND.*

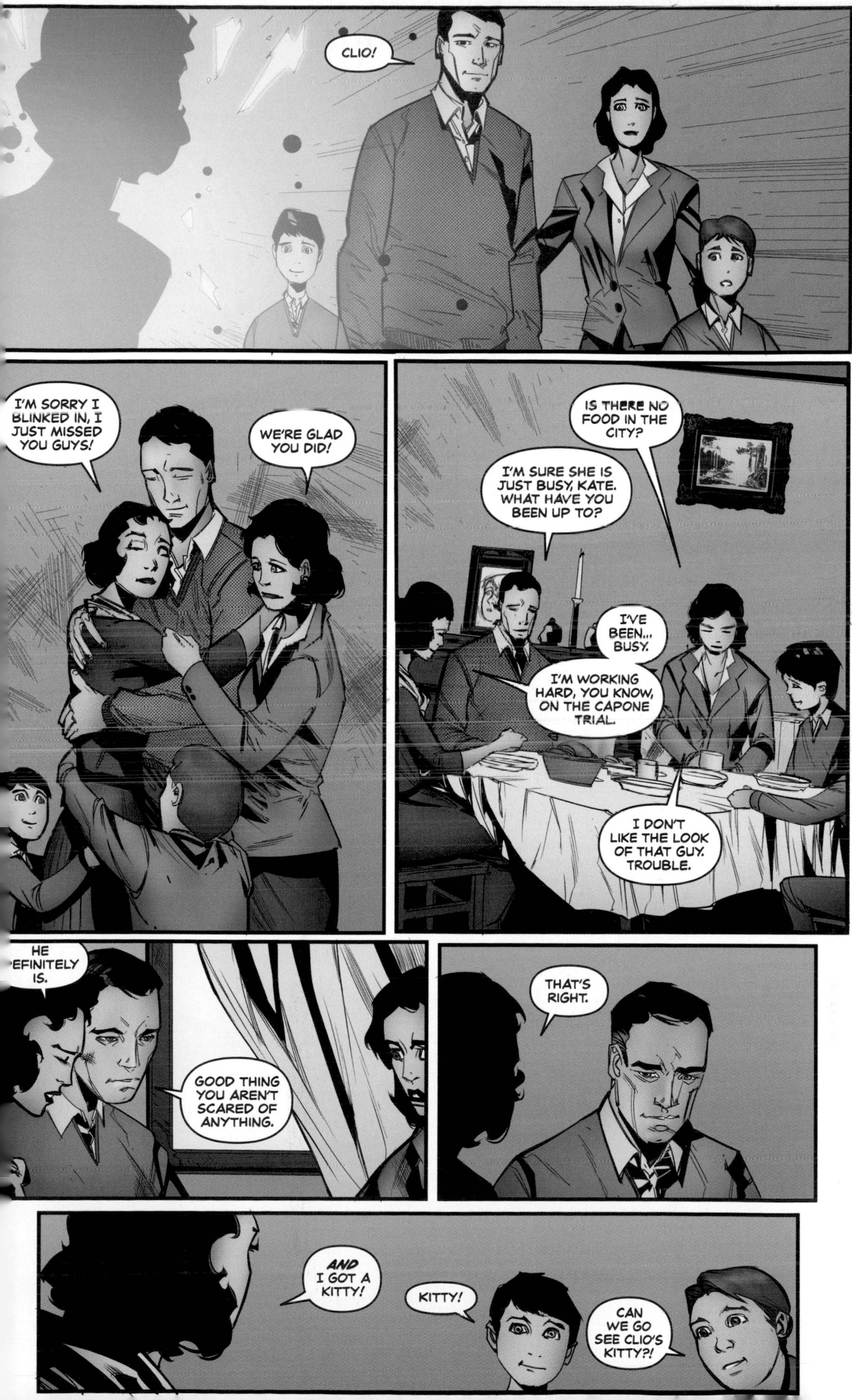
CLIO!
I'M SORRY I BLINKED IN, I JUST MISSED YOU GUYS!
WE'RE GLAD YOU DID!
IS THERE NO FOOD IN THE CITY?
I'M SURE SHE IS JUST BUSY, KATE. WHAT HAVE YOU BEEN UP TO?
I'VE BEEN... BUSY.
I'M WORKING HARD, YOU KNOW, ON THE CAPONE TRIAL.
I DON'T LIKE THE LOOK OF THAT GUY. TROUBLE.
HE EFINITELY IS.
GOOD THING YOU AREN'T SCARED OF ANYTHING.
THAT'S RIGHT.
AND I GOT A KITTY!
KITTY!
CAN WE GO SEE CLIO'S KITTY?!

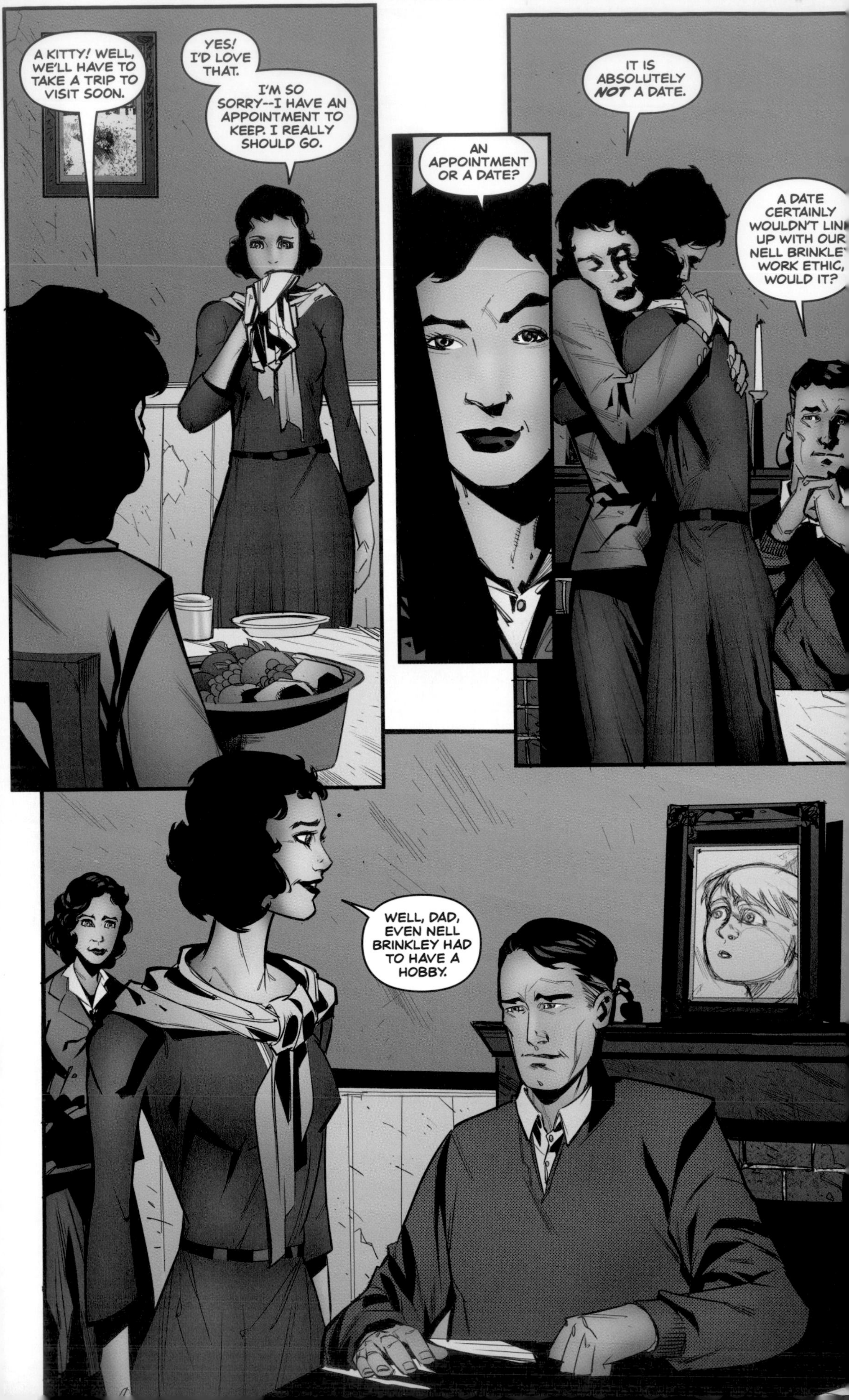
A KITTY! WELL, WE'LL HAVE TO TAKE A TRIP TO VISIT SOON.
YES! I'D LOVE THAT.
I'M SO SORRY--I HAVE AN APPOINTMENT TO KEEP. I REALLY SHOULD GO.
AN APPOINTMENT OR A DATE?
IT IS ABSOLUTELY *NOT* A DATE.
A DATE CERTAINLY WOULDN'T LIN UP WITH OUR NELL BRINKLE WORK ETHIC, WOULD IT?
WELL, DAD, EVEN NELL BRINKLEY HAD TO HAVE A HOBBY.

CLIO'S JOURNEY HAS COME TO A CLOSE,
BUT RYSA WALKER INVITES YOU TO READ THE
CHRONOS FILES
NOVEL TRILOGY FOR ADDITIONAL ADVENTURES
FEATURING CLIO'S FAMILY!

TIMEBOUND
RYSA WALKER

TIME'S EDGE
THE CHRONOS FILES
BOOK 2
RYSA WALKER

THE CHRONOS FILES BOOK 3
TIME'S DIVIDE
RYSA WALKER

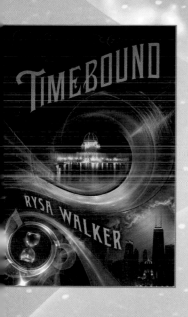

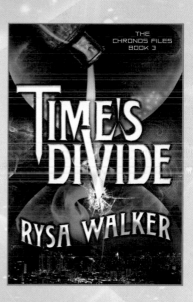

FROM THE VAULT:
AGUSTIN PADILLA'S SKETCHBOOK

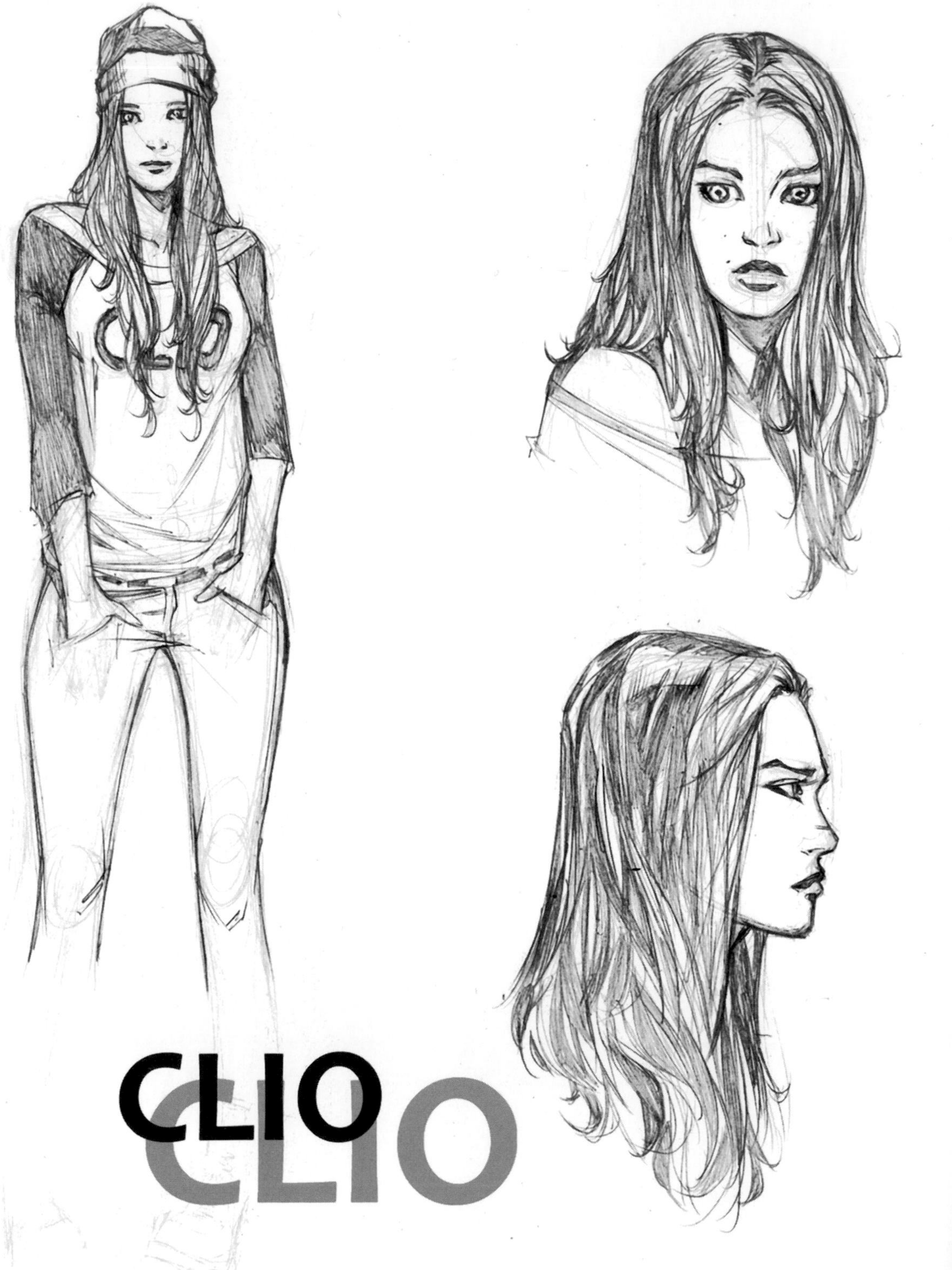
CLIO

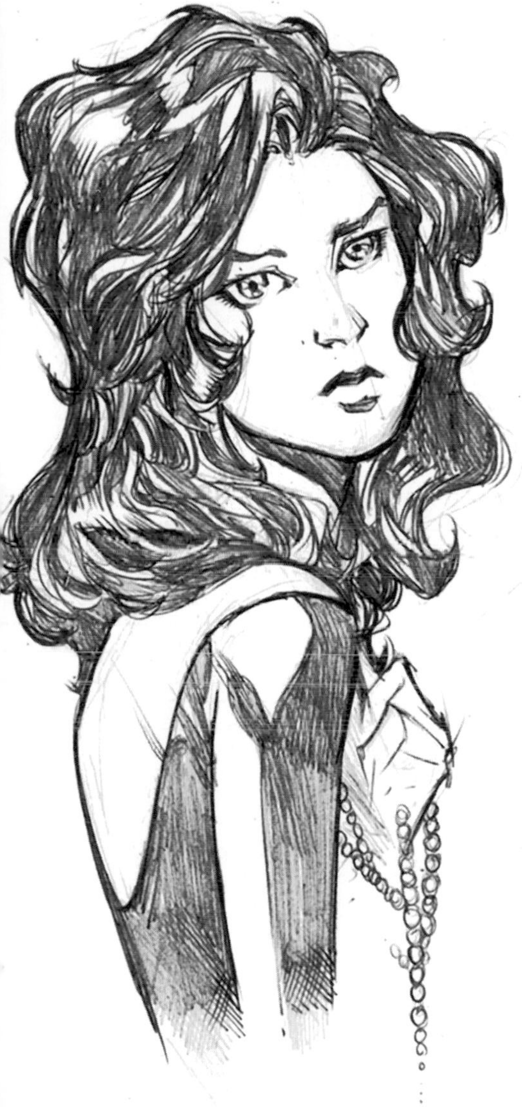

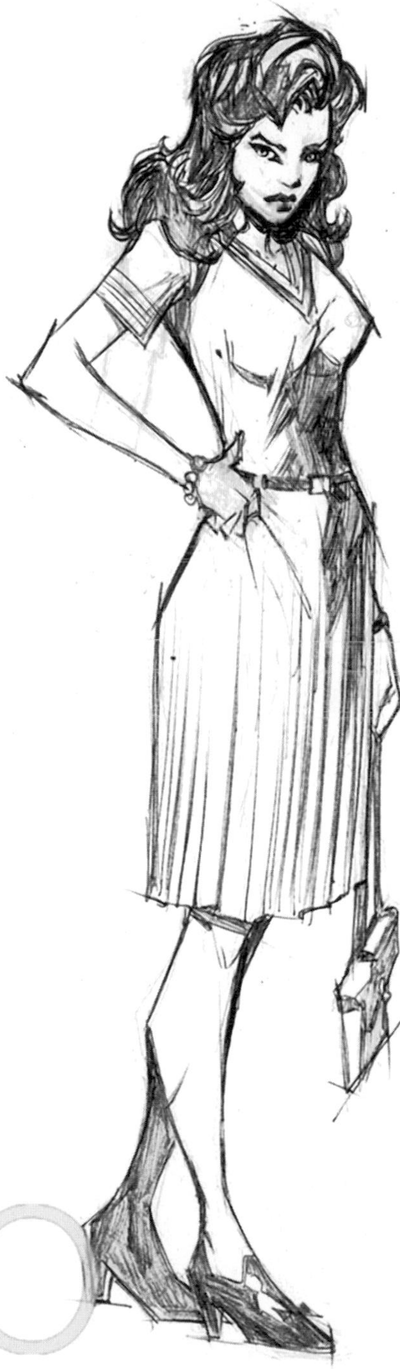

CLIO

CLIO

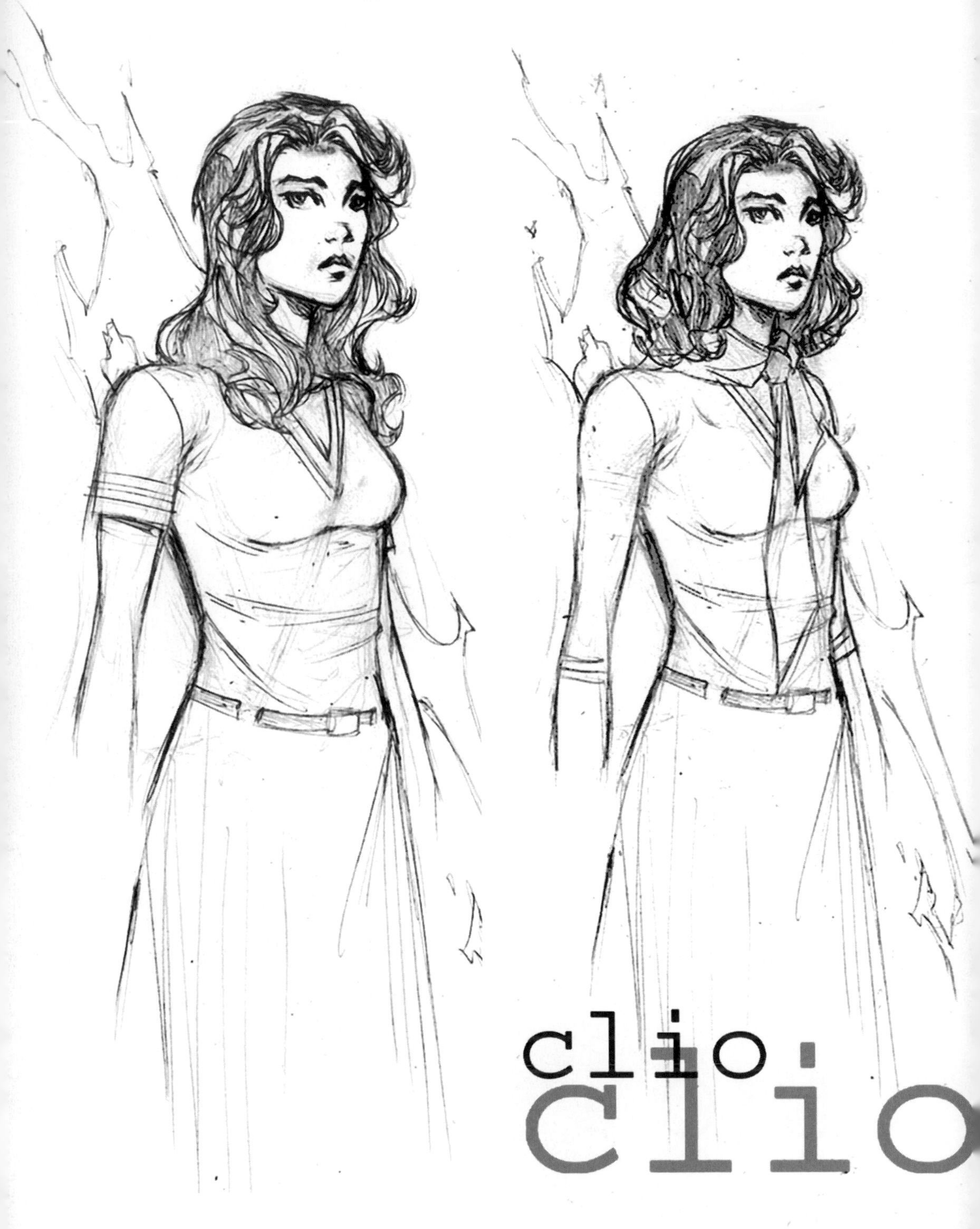
clio
clio

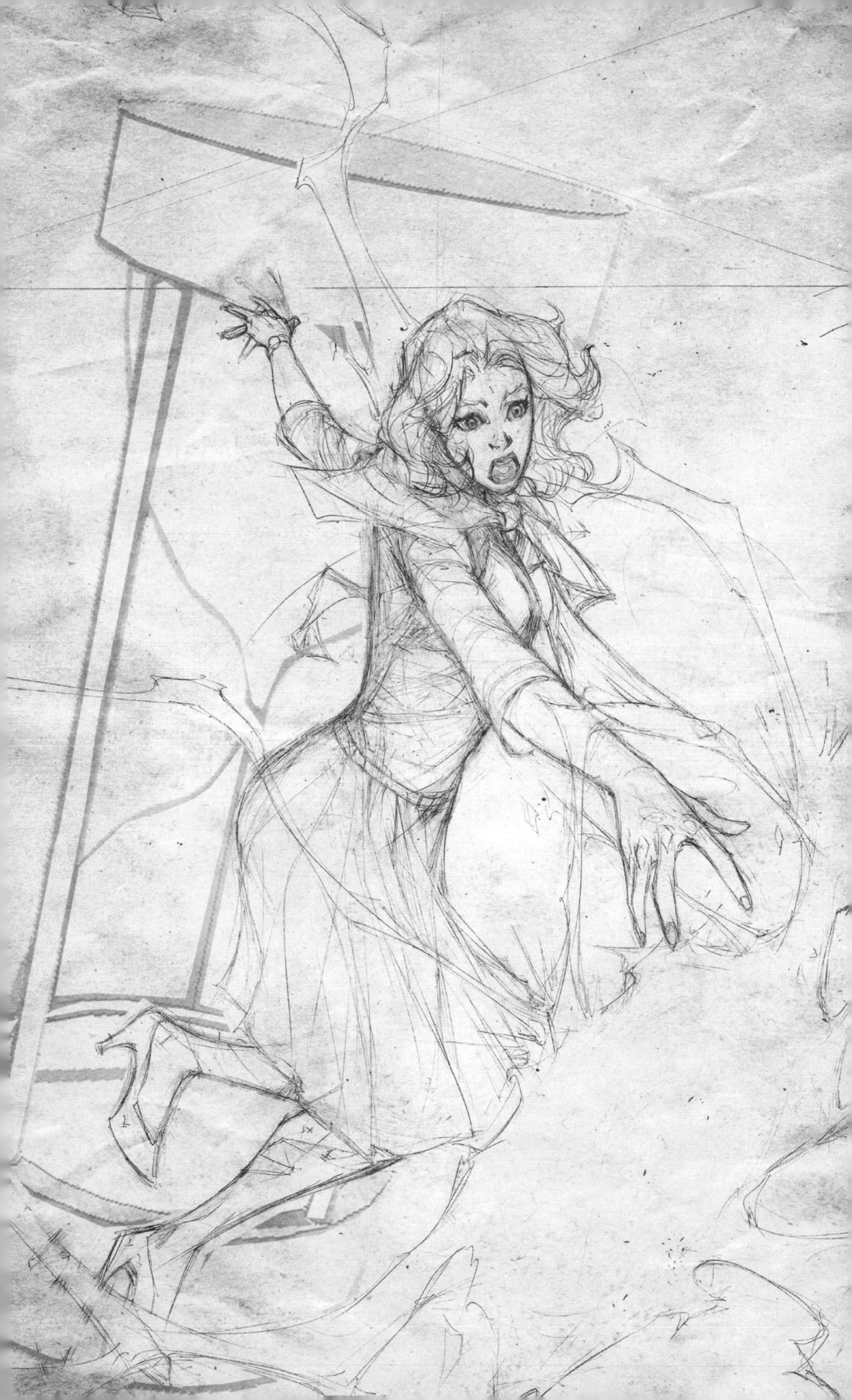

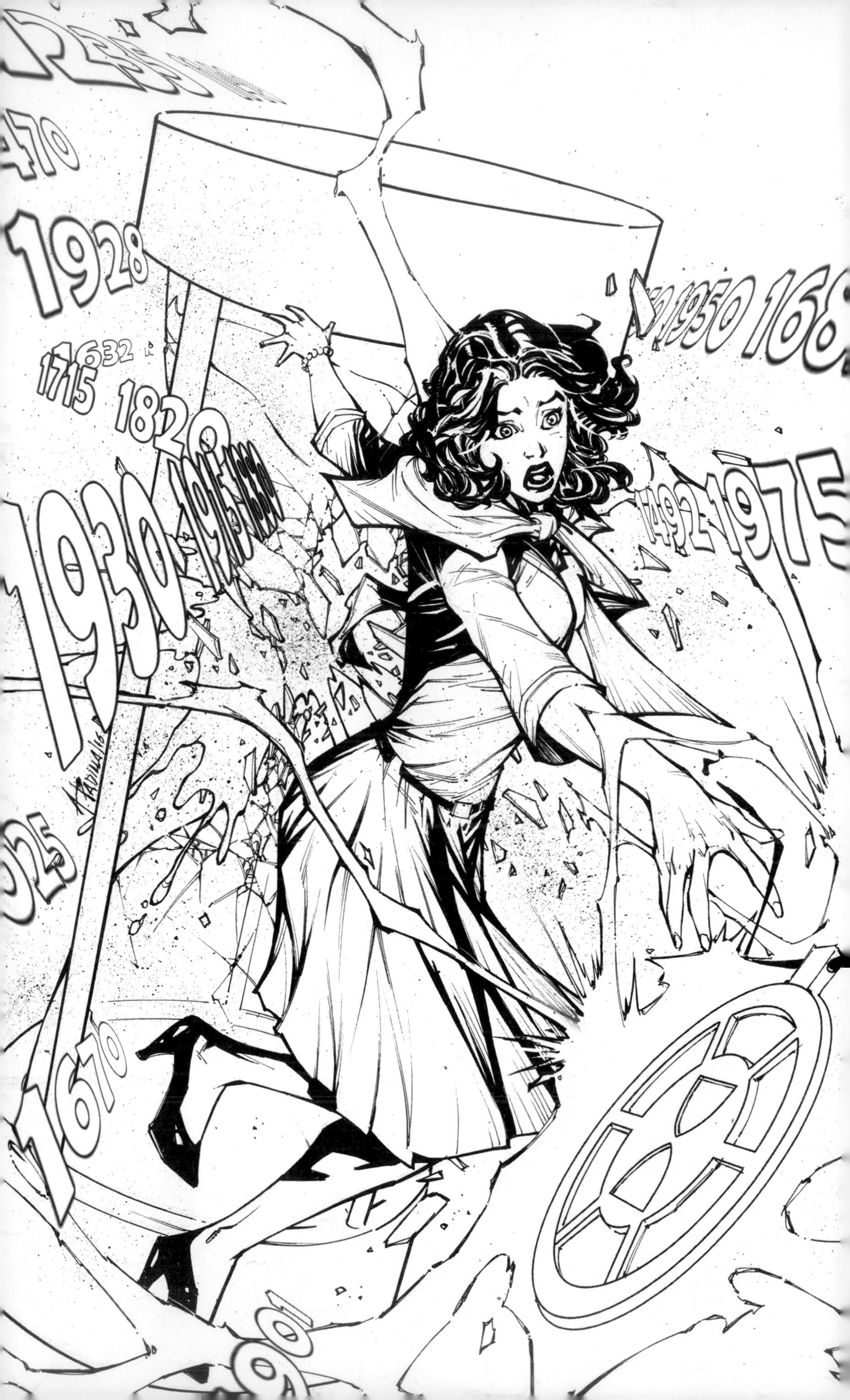
1928
1632
1715
1820
1930
1950
1492
1975
1670

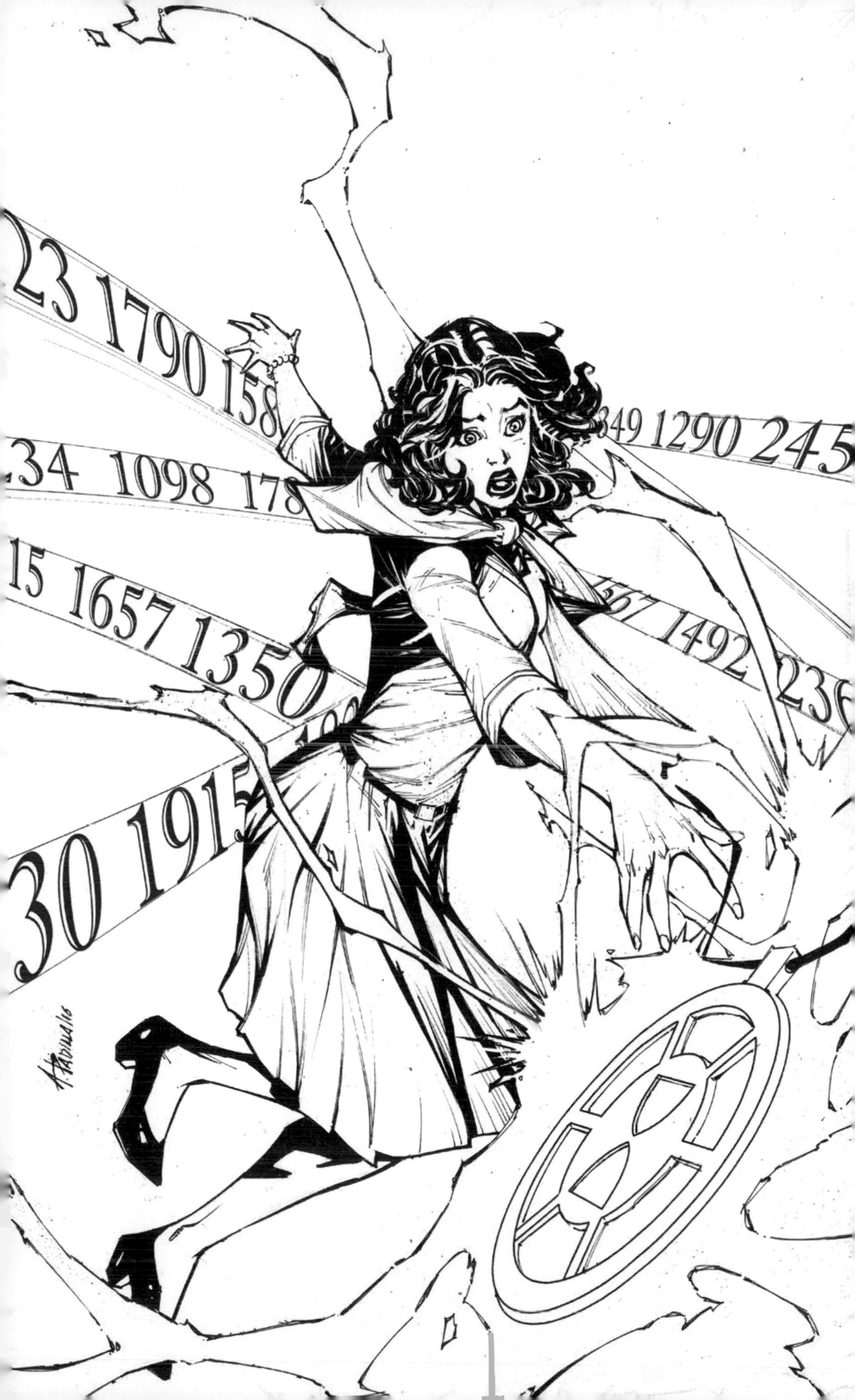
23 1790 158
34 1098 178
15 1657 1350
30 1915
349 1290 245
1492 236

JET CITY COMICS PRESENTS
AN EXCERPT FROM GWENDA BOND'S

CIRQUE AMERICAN
GIRL OVER PARIS

After a high-profile tumble, Cirque American's star wire walker, Jules Maroni, has a lot to prove—and her invitation to an exclusive exhibition in Paris looks to be just the opportunity to put her back on top...

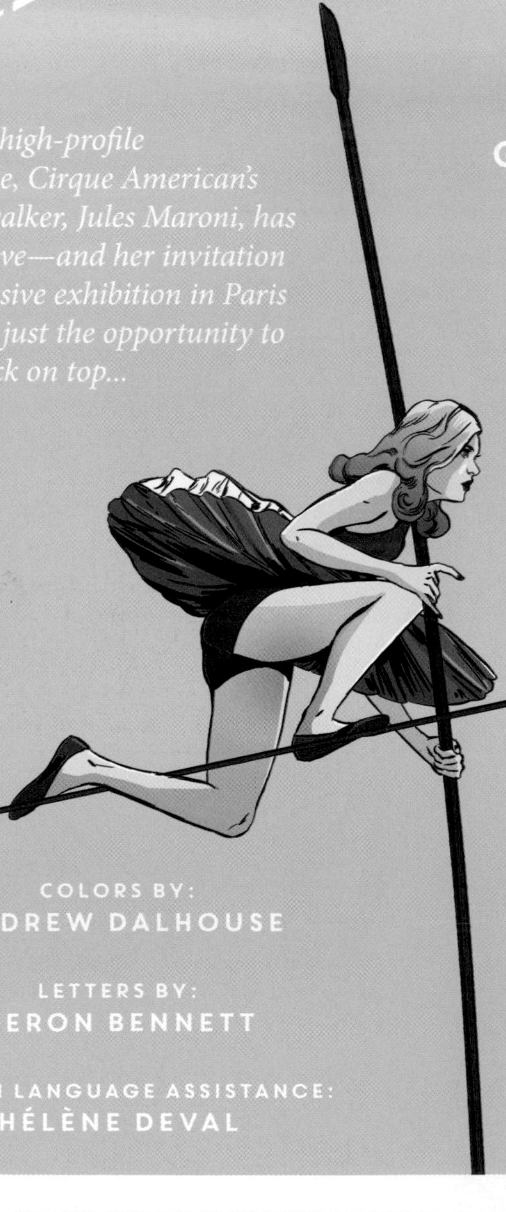

STORY BY:
GWENDA BOND

WRITTEN BY:
KATE LETH

ART BY:
MING DOYLE

COLORS BY:
ANDREW DALHOUSE

LETTERS BY:
DERON BENNETT

FRENCH LANGUAGE ASSISTANCE:
HÉLÈNE DEVAL

EDITOR:
PAUL MORRISSEY

SENIOR PRODUCTION MANAGER:
JILL TAPLIN

AVAILABLE NOW!

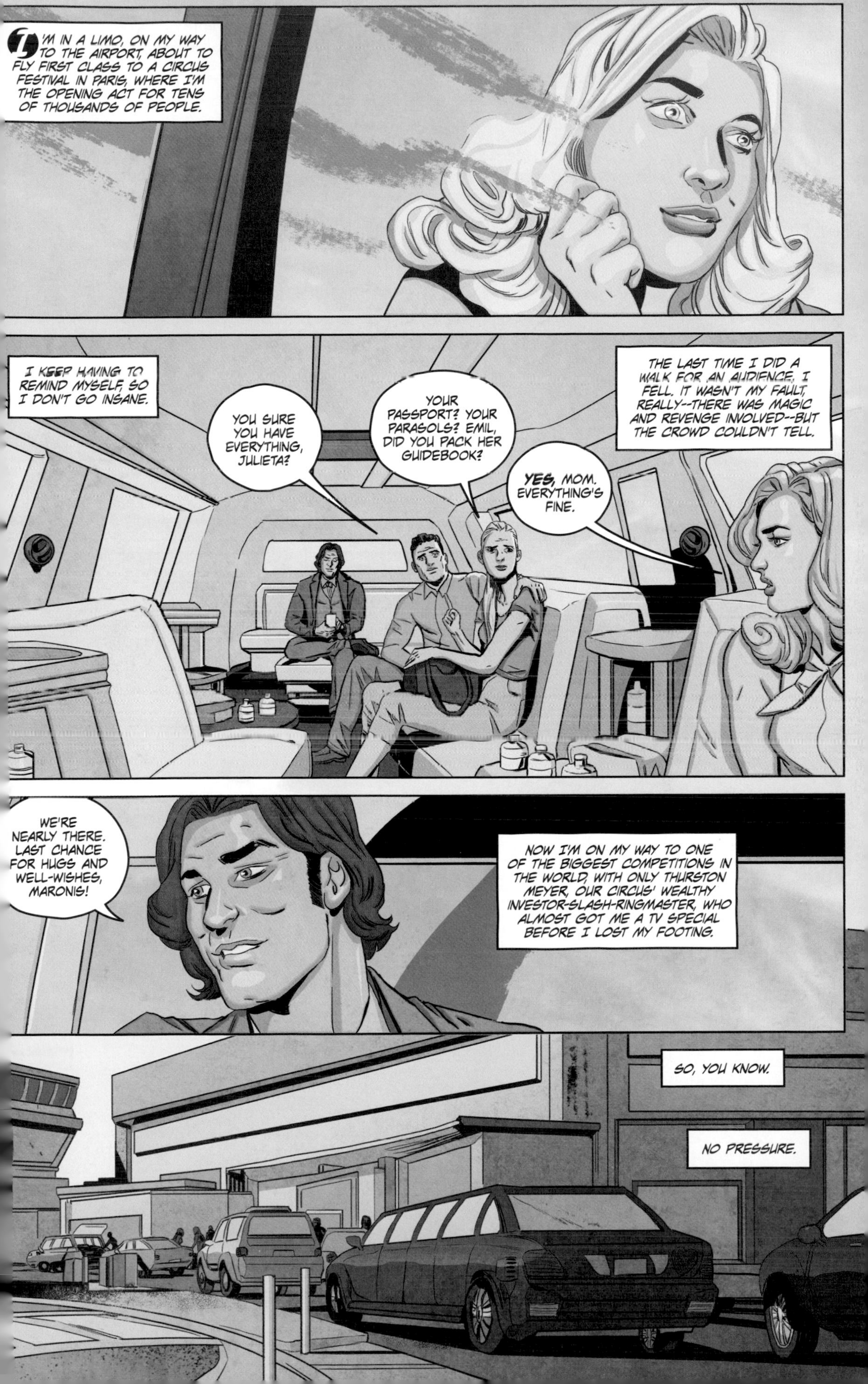
I'M IN A LIMO, ON MY WAY TO THE AIRPORT, ABOUT TO FLY FIRST CLASS TO A CIRCUS FESTIVAL IN PARIS, WHERE I'M THE OPENING ACT FOR TENS OF THOUSANDS OF PEOPLE.
I KEEP HAVING TO REMIND MYSELF, SO I DON'T GO INSANE.
YOU SURE YOU HAVE EVERYTHING, JULIETA?
YOUR PASSPORT? YOUR PARASOLS? EMIL, DID YOU PACK HER GUIDEBOOK?
YES, MOM. EVERYTHING'S FINE.
THE LAST TIME I DID A WALK FOR AN AUDIENCE, I FELL. IT WASN'T MY FAULT, REALLY--THERE WAS MAGIC AND REVENGE INVOLVED--BUT THE CROWD COULDN'T TELL.
WE'RE NEARLY THERE. LAST CHANCE FOR HUGS AND WELL-WISHES, MARONIS!
NOW I'M ON MY WAY TO ONE OF THE BIGGEST COMPETITIONS IN THE WORLD, WITH ONLY THURSTON MEYER, OUR CIRCUS' WEALTHY INVESTOR-SLASH-RINGMASTER, WHO ALMOST GOT ME A TV SPECIAL BEFORE I LOST MY FOOTING.
SO, YOU KNOW.
NO PRESSURE.

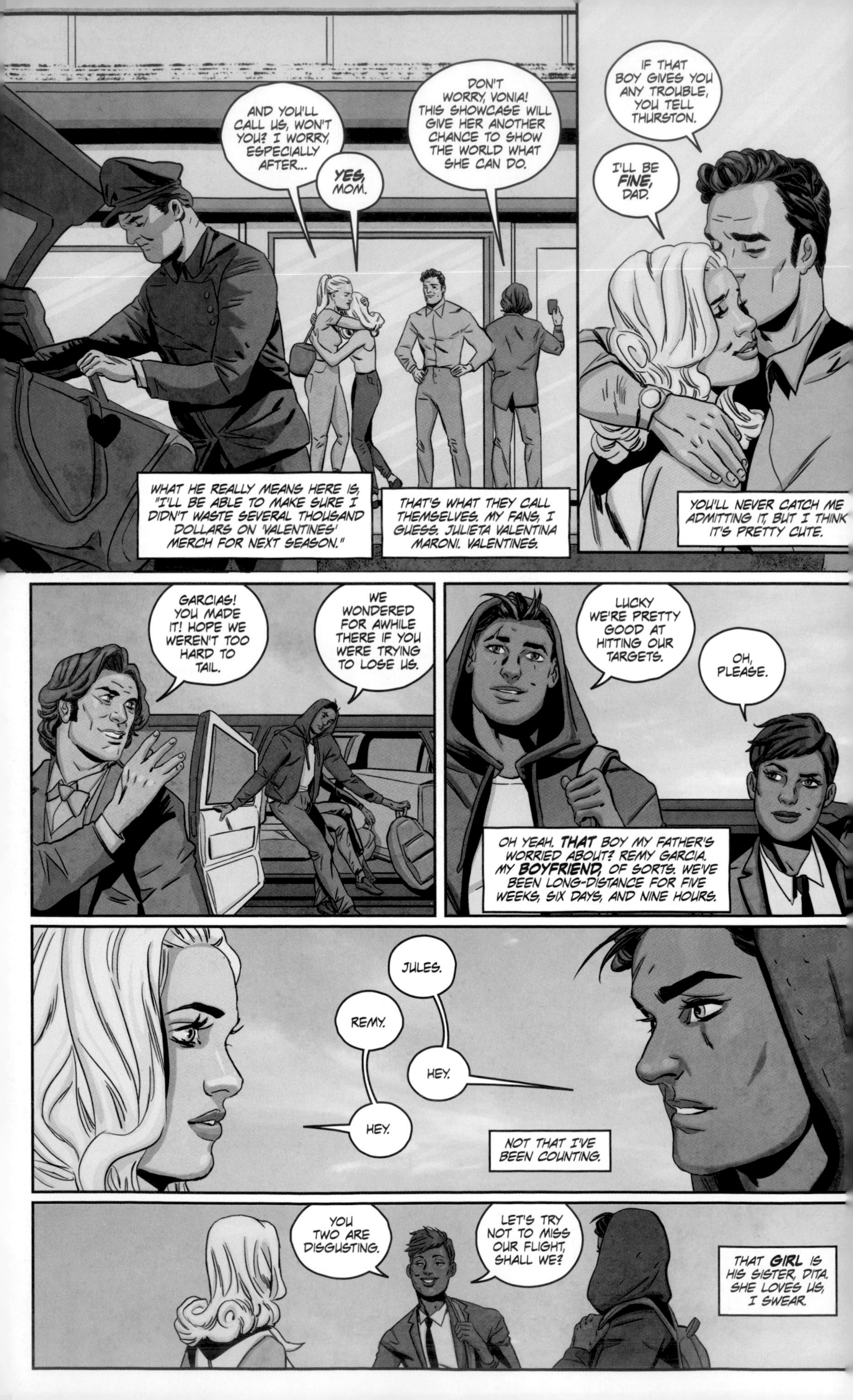

AND YOU'LL CALL US, WON'T YOU? I WORRY, ESPECIALLY AFTER...
YES, MOM.
DON'T WORRY, VONIA! THIS SHOWCASE WILL GIVE HER ANOTHER CHANCE TO SHOW THE WORLD WHAT SHE CAN DO.
WHAT HE REALLY MEANS HERE IS, "I'LL BE ABLE TO MAKE SURE I DIDN'T WASTE SEVERAL THOUSAND DOLLARS ON 'VALENTINES' MERCH FOR NEXT SEASON."
THAT'S WHAT THEY CALL THEMSELVES. MY FANS, I GUESS. JULIETA VALENTINA MARONI. VALENTINES.
IF THAT BOY GIVES YOU ANY TROUBLE, YOU TELL THURSTON.
I'LL BE FINE, DAD.
YOU'LL NEVER CATCH ME ADMITTING IT, BUT I THINK IT'S PRETTY CUTE.
GARCIAS! YOU MADE IT! HOPE WE WEREN'T TOO HARD TO TAIL.
WE WONDERED FOR AWHILE THERE IF YOU WERE TRYING TO LOSE US.
LUCKY WE'RE PRETTY GOOD AT HITTING OUR TARGETS.
OH, PLEASE.
OH YEAH. THAT BOY MY FATHER'S WORRIED ABOUT? REMY GARCIA. MY BOYFRIEND, OF SORTS. WE'VE BEEN LONG-DISTANCE FOR FIVE WEEKS, SIX DAYS, AND NINE HOURS.
JULES.
REMY.
HEY.
HEY.
NOT THAT I'VE BEEN COUNTING.
YOU TWO ARE DISGUSTING.
LET'S TRY NOT TO MISS OUR FLIGHT, SHALL WE?
THAT GIRL IS HIS SISTER, DITA. SHE LOVES US, I SWEAR.

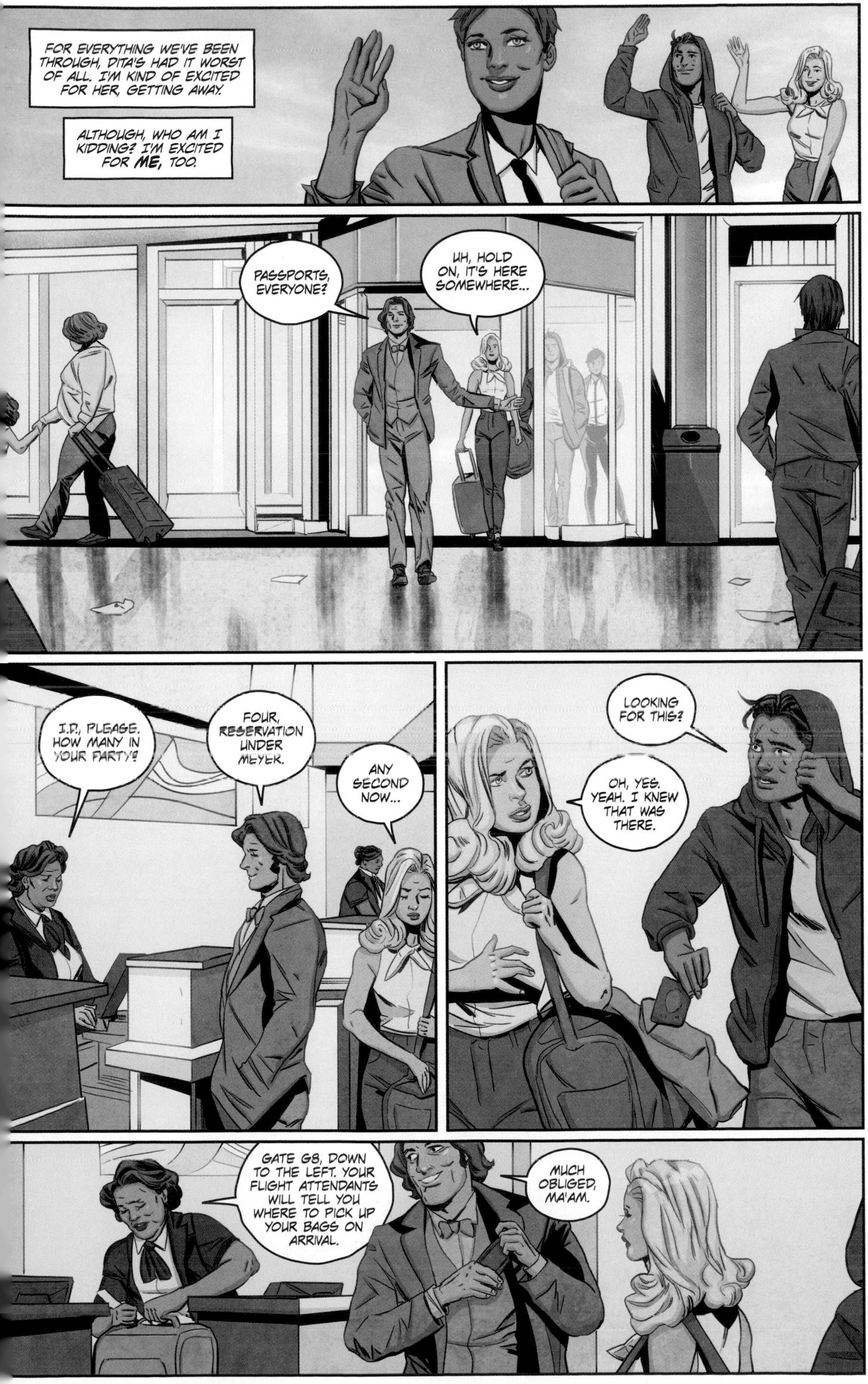
FOR EVERYTHING WE'VE BEEN THROUGH, DITA'S HAD IT WORST OF ALL. I'M KIND OF EXCITED FOR HER, GETTING AWAY.
ALTHOUGH, WHO AM I KIDDING? I'M EXCITED FOR **ME**, TOO.
PASSPORTS, EVERYONE?
UH, HOLD ON, IT'S HERE SOMEWHERE...
I.D., PLEASE. HOW MANY IN YOUR PARTY?
FOUR, RESERVATION UNDER MEYER.
ANY SECOND NOW...
LOOKING FOR THIS?
OH, YES. YEAH. I KNEW THAT WAS THERE.
GATE G8, DOWN TO THE LEFT. YOUR FLIGHT ATTENDANTS WILL TELL YOU WHERE TO PICK UP YOUR BAGS ON ARRIVAL.
MUCH OBLIGED, MA'AM.

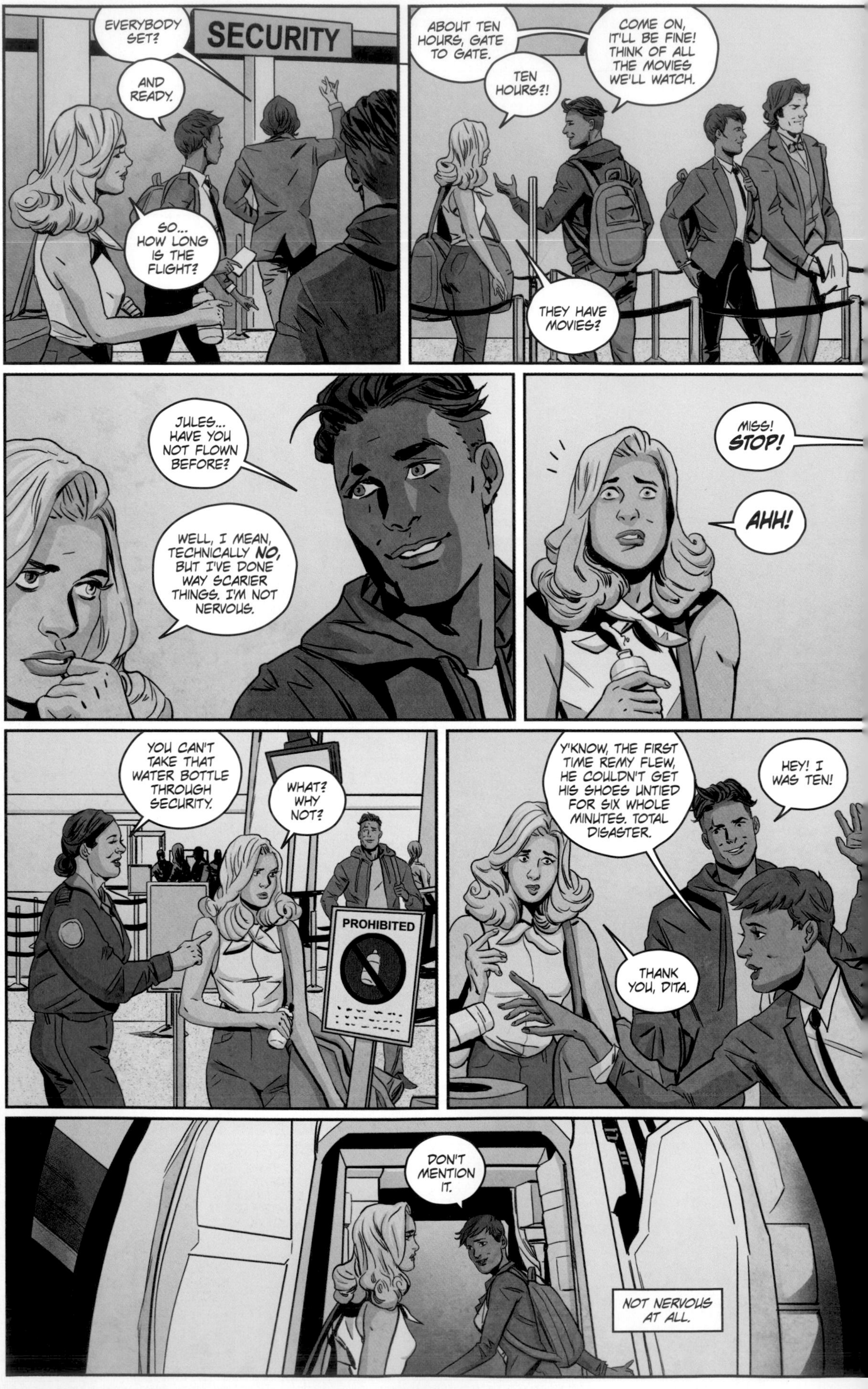
EVERYBODY SET?
SECURITY
AND READY.
SO... HOW LONG IS THE FLIGHT?
ABOUT TEN HOURS, GATE TO GATE.
TEN HOURS?!
COME ON, IT'LL BE FINE! THINK OF ALL THE MOVIES WE'LL WATCH.
THEY HAVE MOVIES?
JULES... HAVE YOU NOT FLOWN BEFORE?
WELL, I MEAN, TECHNICALLY NO, BUT I'VE DONE WAY SCARIER THINGS. I'M NOT NERVOUS.
MISS! STOP!
AHH!
YOU CAN'T TAKE THAT WATER BOTTLE THROUGH SECURITY.
WHAT? WHY NOT?
PROHIBITED
Y'KNOW, THE FIRST TIME REMY FLEW, HE COULDN'T GET HIS SHOES UNTIED FOR SIX WHOLE MINUTES. TOTAL DISASTER.
HEY! I WAS TEN!
THANK YOU, DITA.
DON'T MENTION IT.
NOT NERVOUS AT ALL.

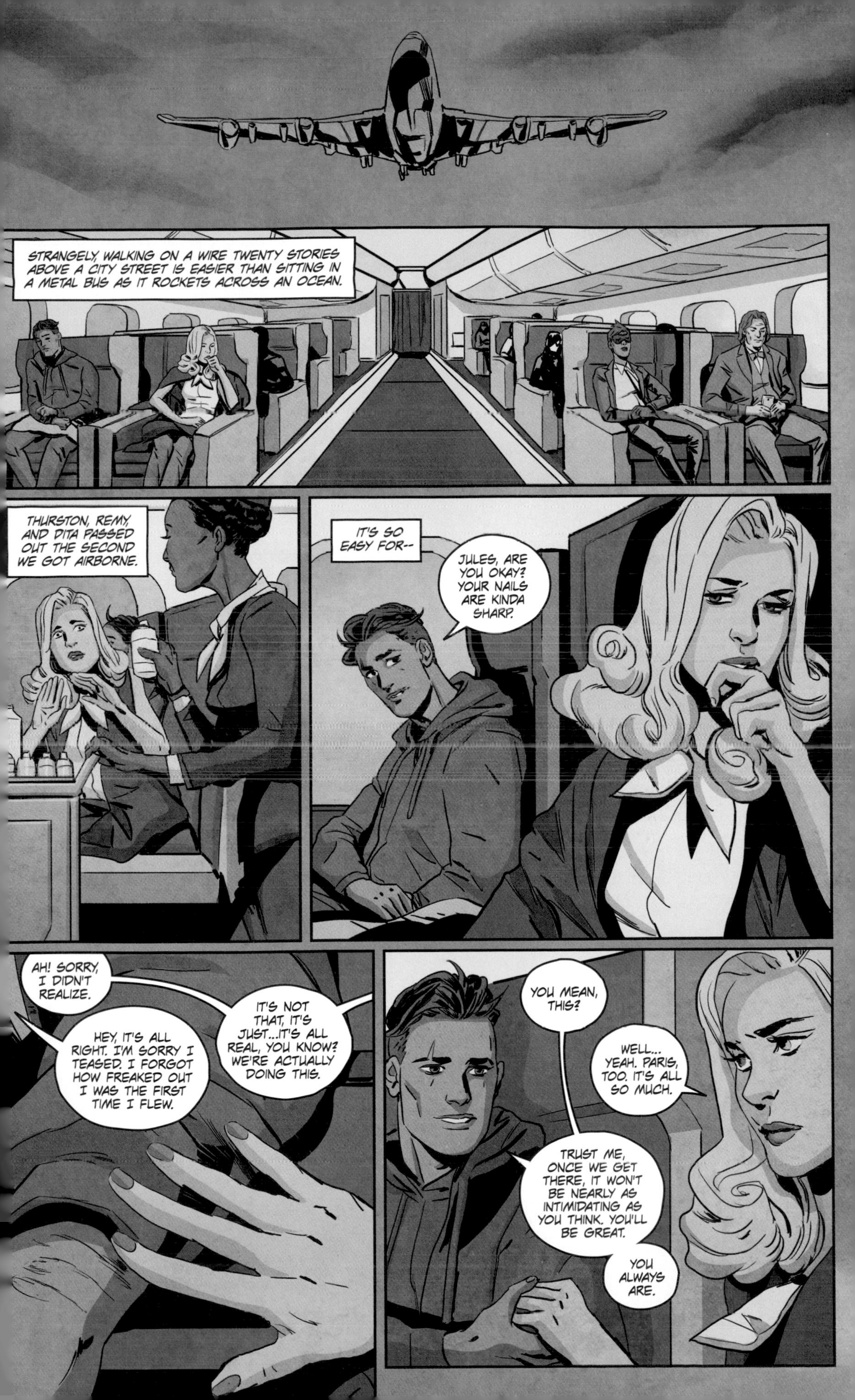
STRANGELY, WALKING ON A WIRE TWENTY STORIES ABOVE A CITY STREET IS EASIER THAN SITTING IN A METAL BUS AS IT ROCKETS ACROSS AN OCEAN.
THURSTON, REMY, AND DITA PASSED OUT THE SECOND WE GOT AIRBORNE.
IT'S SO EASY FOR--
JULES, ARE YOU OKAY? YOUR NAILS ARE KINDA SHARP.
AH! SORRY, I DIDN'T REALIZE.
HEY, IT'S ALL RIGHT. I'M SORRY I TEASED. I FORGOT HOW FREAKED OUT I WAS THE FIRST TIME I FLEW.
IT'S NOT THAT, IT'S JUST...IT'S ALL REAL, YOU KNOW? WE'RE ACTUALLY DOING THIS.
YOU MEAN, THIS?
WELL... YEAH. PARIS, TOO. IT'S ALL SO MUCH.
TRUST ME, ONCE WE GET THERE, IT WON'T BE NEARLY AS INTIMIDATING AS YOU THINK. YOU'LL BE GREAT.
YOU ALWAYS ARE.

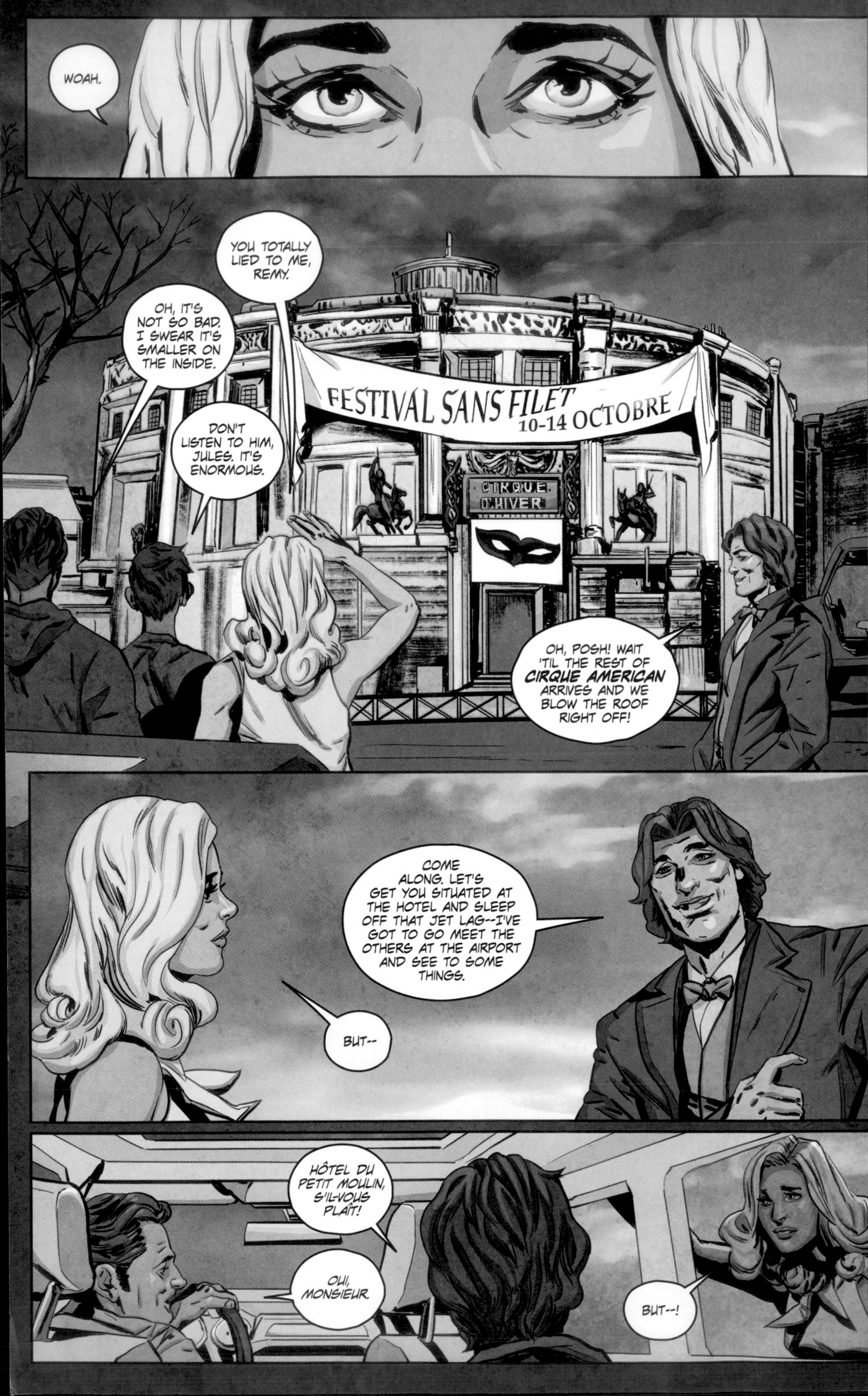

WOAH.
YOU TOTALLY LIED TO ME, REMY.
OH, IT'S NOT SO BAD. I SWEAR IT'S SMALLER ON THE INSIDE.
FESTIVAL SANS FILET 10-14 OCTOBRE
DON'T LISTEN TO HIM, JULES. IT'S ENORMOUS.
CIRQUE D'HIVER
OH, POSH! WAIT 'TIL THE REST OF CIRQUE AMERICAN ARRIVES AND WE BLOW THE ROOF RIGHT OFF!
COME ALONG. LET'S GET YOU SITUATED AT THE HOTEL AND SLEEP OFF THAT JET LAG--I'VE GOT TO GO MEET THE OTHERS AT THE AIRPORT AND SEE TO SOME THINGS.
BUT--
HÔTEL DU PETIT MOULIN, S'IL-VOUS PLAÎT!
OUI, MONSIEUR.
BUT--!

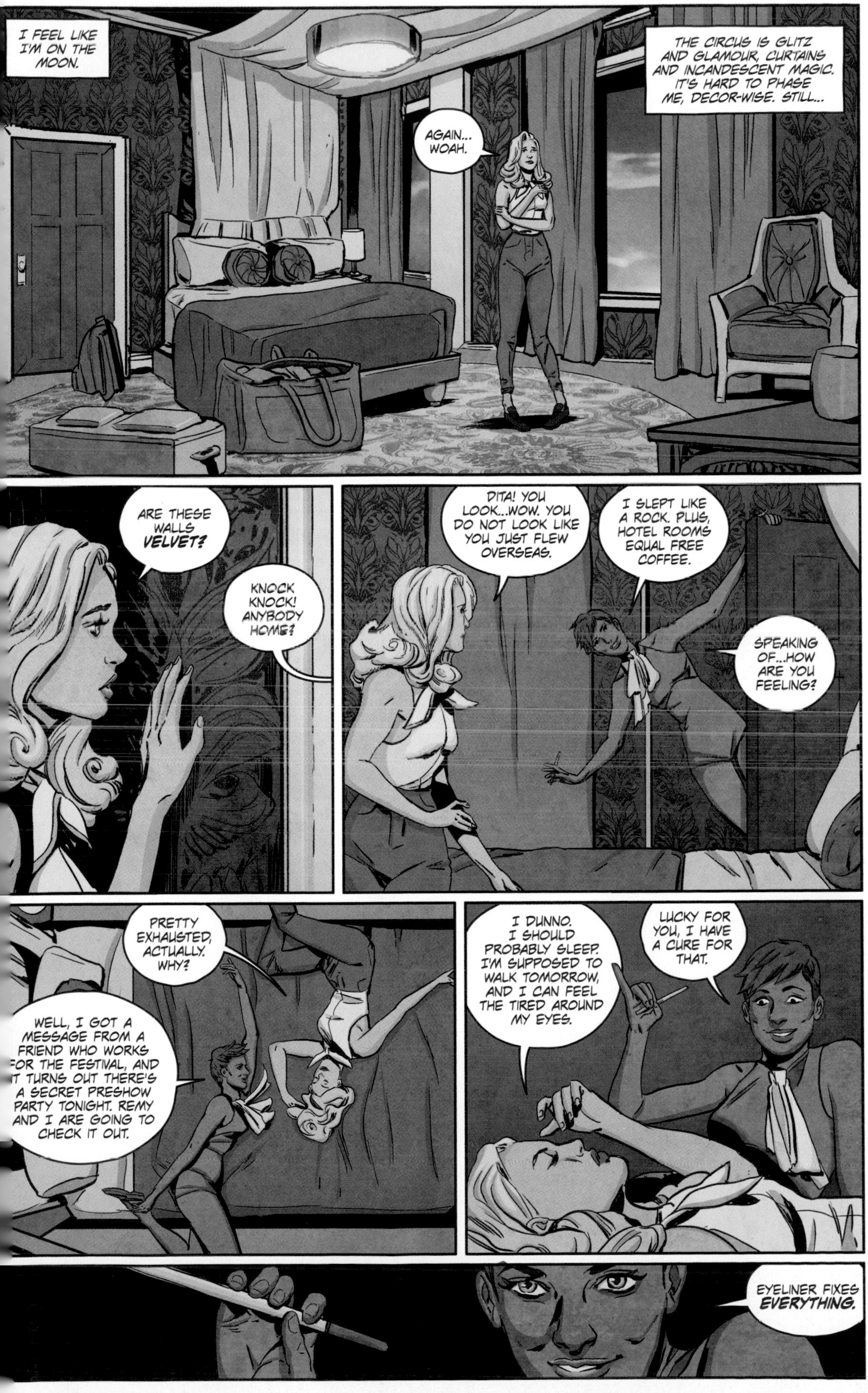
I FEEL LIKE I'M ON THE MOON.
THE CIRCUS IS GLITZ AND GLAMOUR, CURTAINS AND INCANDESCENT MAGIC. IT'S HARD TO PHASE ME, DECOR-WISE. STILL...
AGAIN... WOAH.
ARE THESE WALLS **VELVET?**
KNOCK KNOCK! ANYBODY HOME?
DITA! YOU LOOK...WOW. YOU DO NOT LOOK LIKE YOU JUST FLEW OVERSEAS.
I SLEPT LIKE A ROCK. PLUS, HOTEL ROOMS EQUAL FREE COFFEE.
SPEAKING OF...HOW ARE YOU FEELING?
PRETTY EXHAUSTED, ACTUALLY. WHY?
WELL, I GOT A MESSAGE FROM A FRIEND WHO WORKS FOR THE FESTIVAL, AND IT TURNS OUT THERE'S A SECRET PRESHOW PARTY TONIGHT. REMY AND I ARE GOING TO CHECK IT OUT.
I DUNNO. I SHOULD PROBABLY SLEEP. I'M SUPPOSED TO WALK TOMORROW, AND I CAN FEEL THE TIRED AROUND MY EYES.
LUCKY FOR YOU, I HAVE A CURE FOR THAT.
EYELINER FIXES **EVERYTHING.**

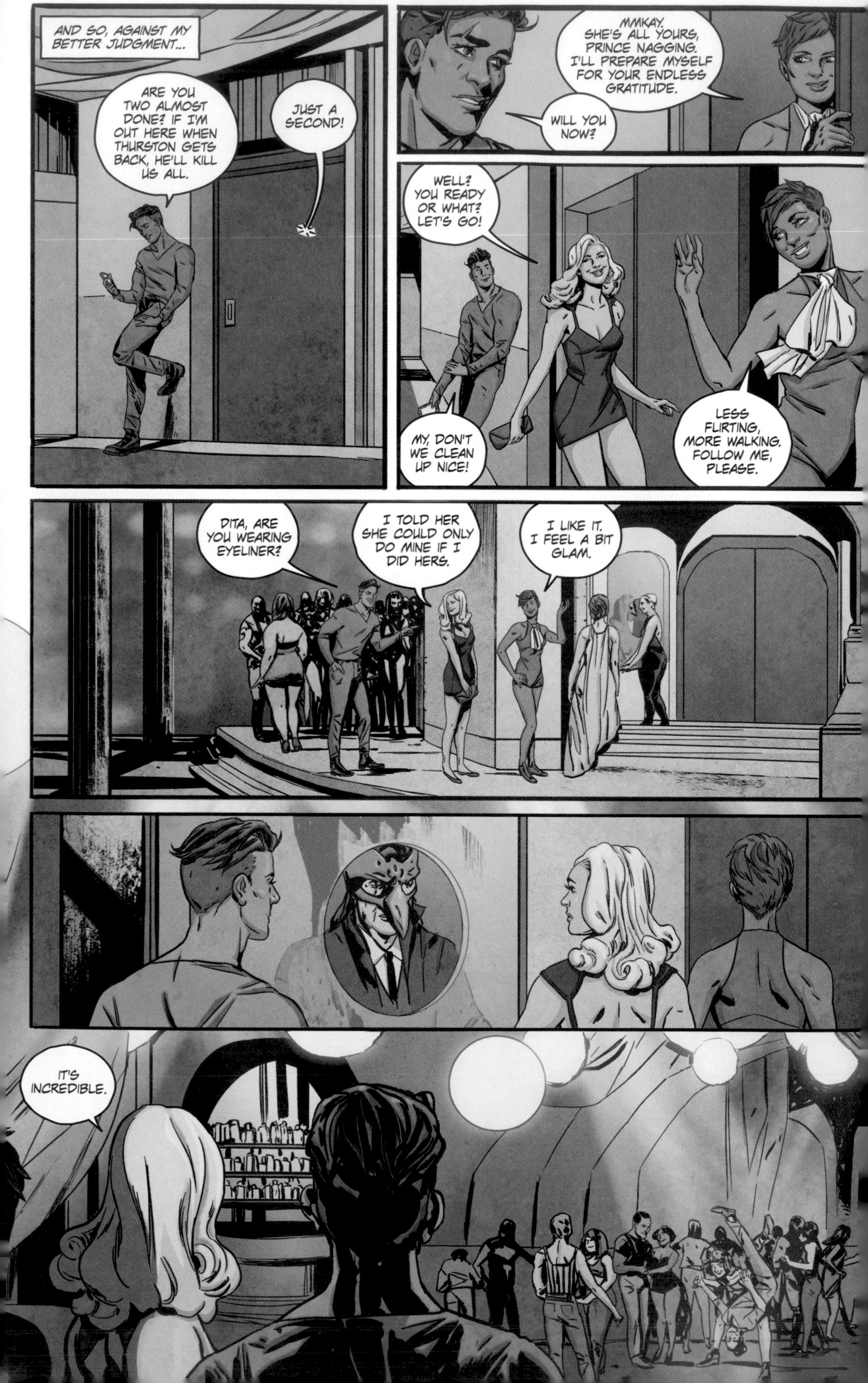
AND SO, AGAINST MY BETTER JUDGMENT...
ARE YOU TWO ALMOST DONE? IF I'M OUT HERE WHEN THURSTON GETS BACK, HE'LL KILL US ALL.
JUST A SECOND!
MMKAY. SHE'S ALL YOURS, PRINCE NAGGING. I'LL PREPARE MYSELF FOR YOUR ENDLESS GRATITUDE.
WILL YOU NOW?
WELL? YOU READY OR WHAT? LET'S GO!
MY, DON'T WE CLEAN UP NICE!
LESS FLIRTING, MORE WALKING. FOLLOW ME, PLEASE.
DITA, ARE YOU WEARING EYELINER?
I TOLD HER SHE COULD ONLY DO MINE IF I DID HERS.
I LIKE IT. I FEEL A BIT GLAM.
IT'S INCREDIBLE.

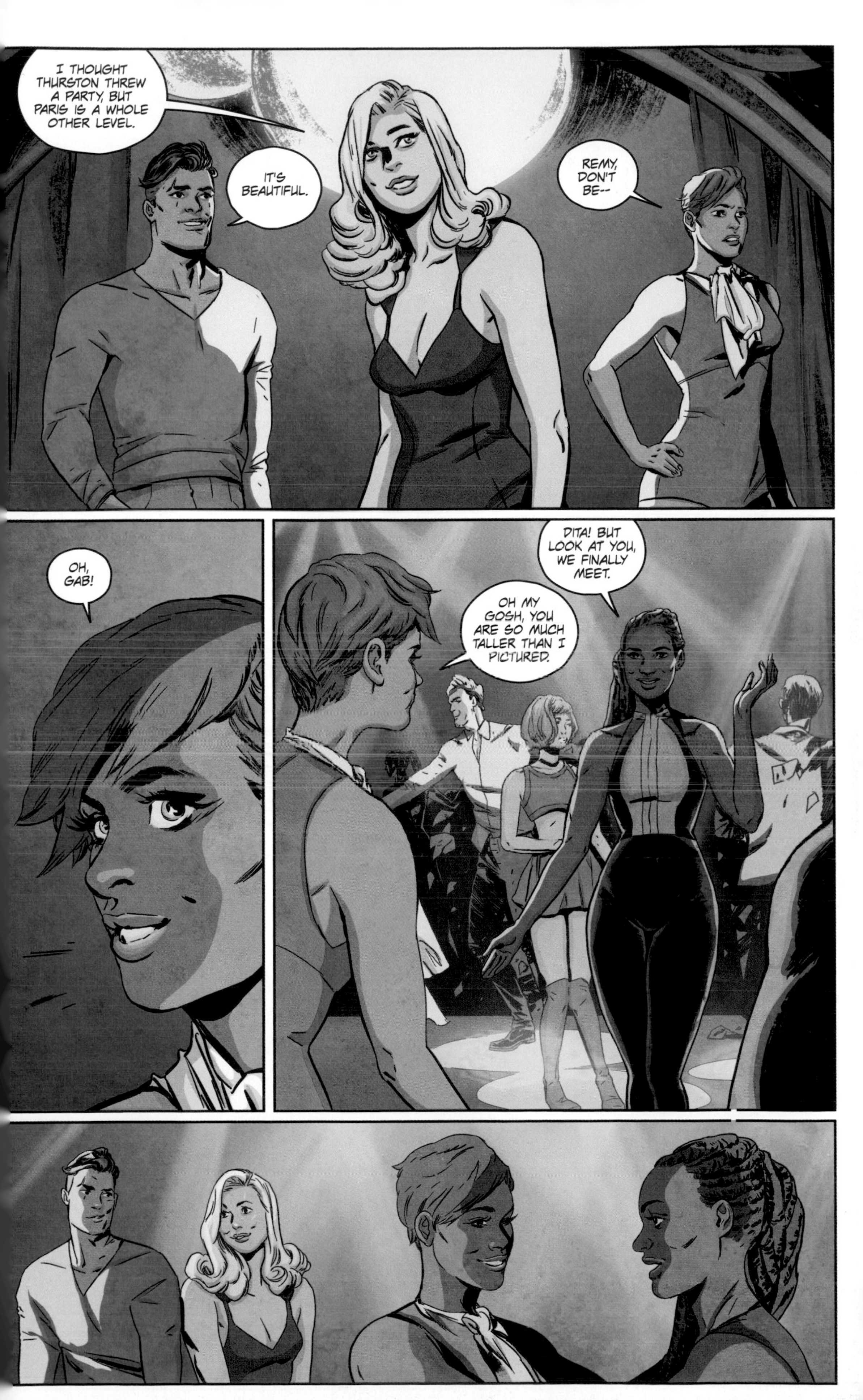
I THOUGHT THURSTON THREW A PARTY, BUT PARIS IS A WHOLE OTHER LEVEL.
IT'S BEAUTIFUL.
REMY, DON'T BE--
OH, GAB!
DITA! BUT LOOK AT YOU, WE FINALLY MEET.
OH MY GOSH, YOU ARE SO MUCH TALLER THAN I PICTURED.

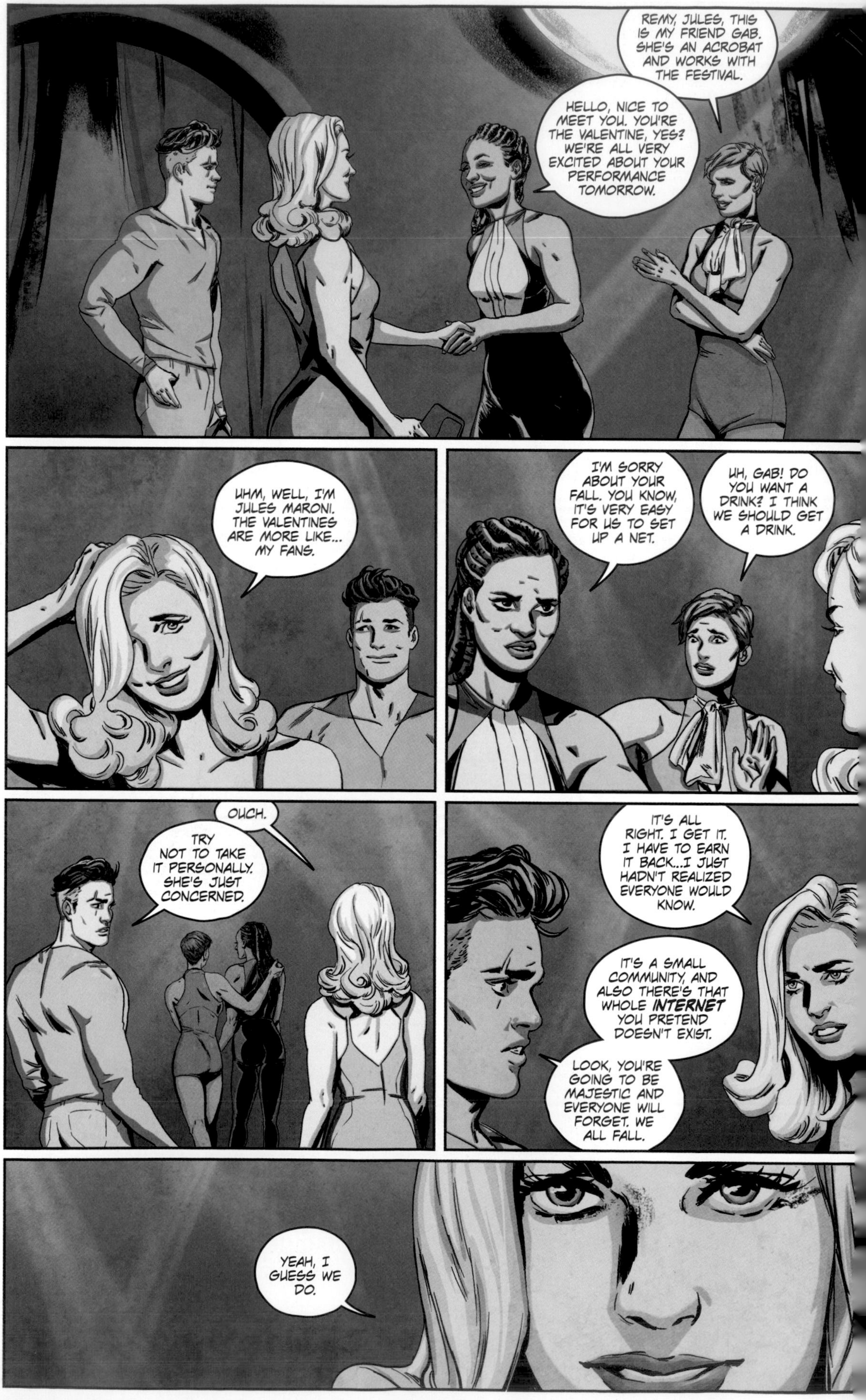
REMY, JULES, THIS IS MY FRIEND GAB. SHE'S AN ACROBAT AND WORKS WITH THE FESTIVAL.
HELLO, NICE TO MEET YOU. YOU'RE THE VALENTINE, YES? WE'RE ALL VERY EXCITED ABOUT YOUR PERFORMANCE TOMORROW.
UHM, WELL, I'M JULES MARONI. THE VALENTINES ARE MORE LIKE... MY FANS.
I'M SORRY ABOUT YOUR FALL. YOU KNOW, IT'S VERY EASY FOR US TO SET UP A NET.
UH, GAB! DO YOU WANT A DRINK? I THINK WE SHOULD GET A DRINK.
OUCH.
TRY NOT TO TAKE IT PERSONALLY. SHE'S JUST CONCERNED.
IT'S ALL RIGHT. I GET IT. I HAVE TO EARN IT BACK...I JUST HADN'T REALIZED EVERYONE WOULD KNOW.
IT'S A SMALL COMMUNITY, AND ALSO THERE'S THAT WHOLE **INTERNET** YOU PRETEND DOESN'T EXIST.
LOOK, YOU'RE GOING TO BE MAJESTIC AND EVERYONE WILL FORGET. WE ALL FALL.
YEAH, I GUESS WE DO.

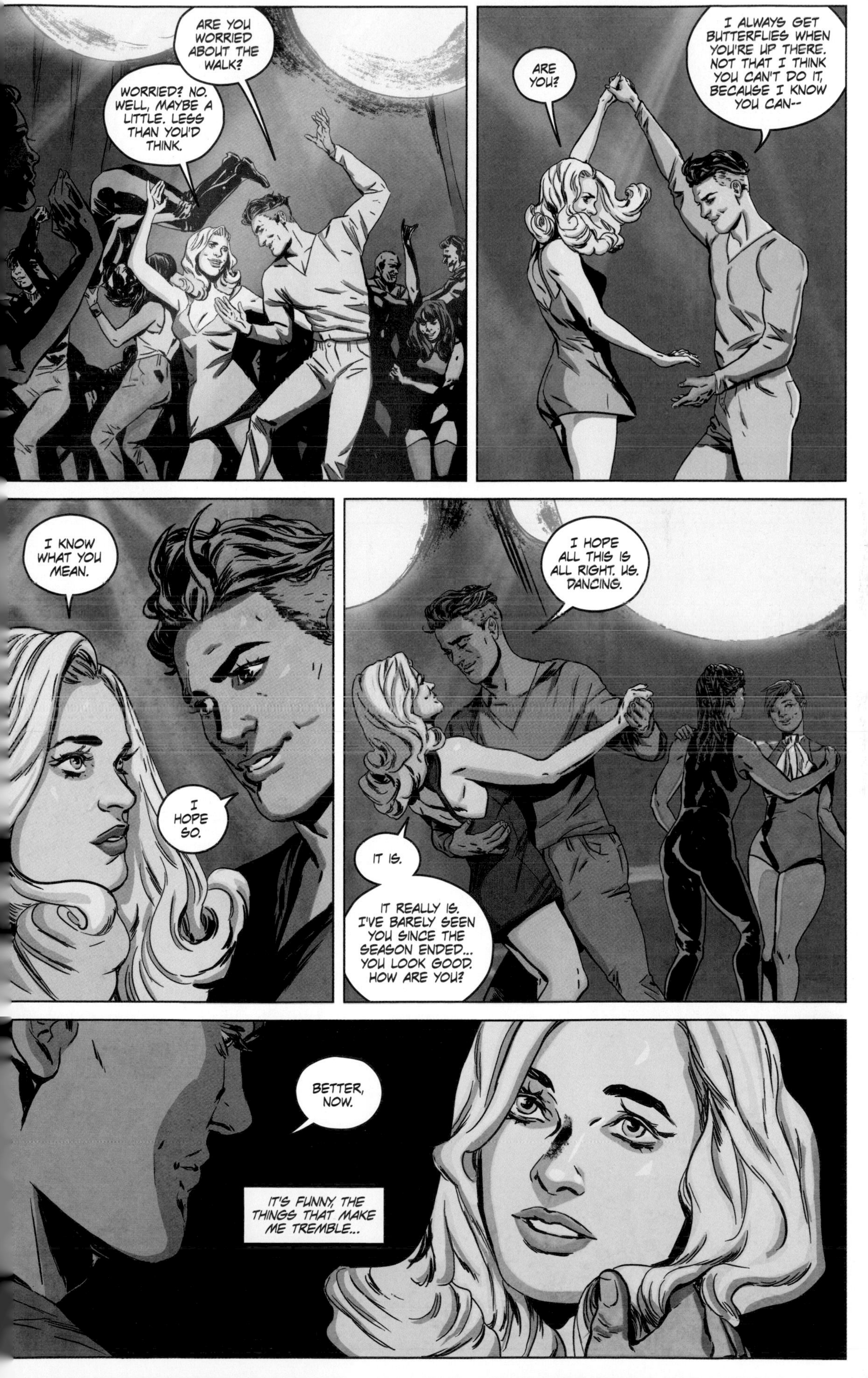

ARE YOU WORRIED ABOUT THE WALK?
WORRIED? NO. WELL, MAYBE A LITTLE. LESS THAN YOU'D THINK.
ARE YOU?
I ALWAYS GET BUTTERFLIES WHEN YOU'RE UP THERE. NOT THAT I THINK YOU CAN'T DO IT, BECAUSE I KNOW YOU CAN--
I KNOW WHAT YOU MEAN.
I HOPE SO.
I HOPE ALL THIS IS ALL RIGHT. US. DANCING.
IT IS.
IT REALLY IS. I'VE BARELY SEEN YOU SINCE THE SEASON ENDED... YOU LOOK GOOD. HOW ARE YOU?
BETTER, NOW.
IT'S FUNNY, THE THINGS THAT MAKE ME TREMBLE...

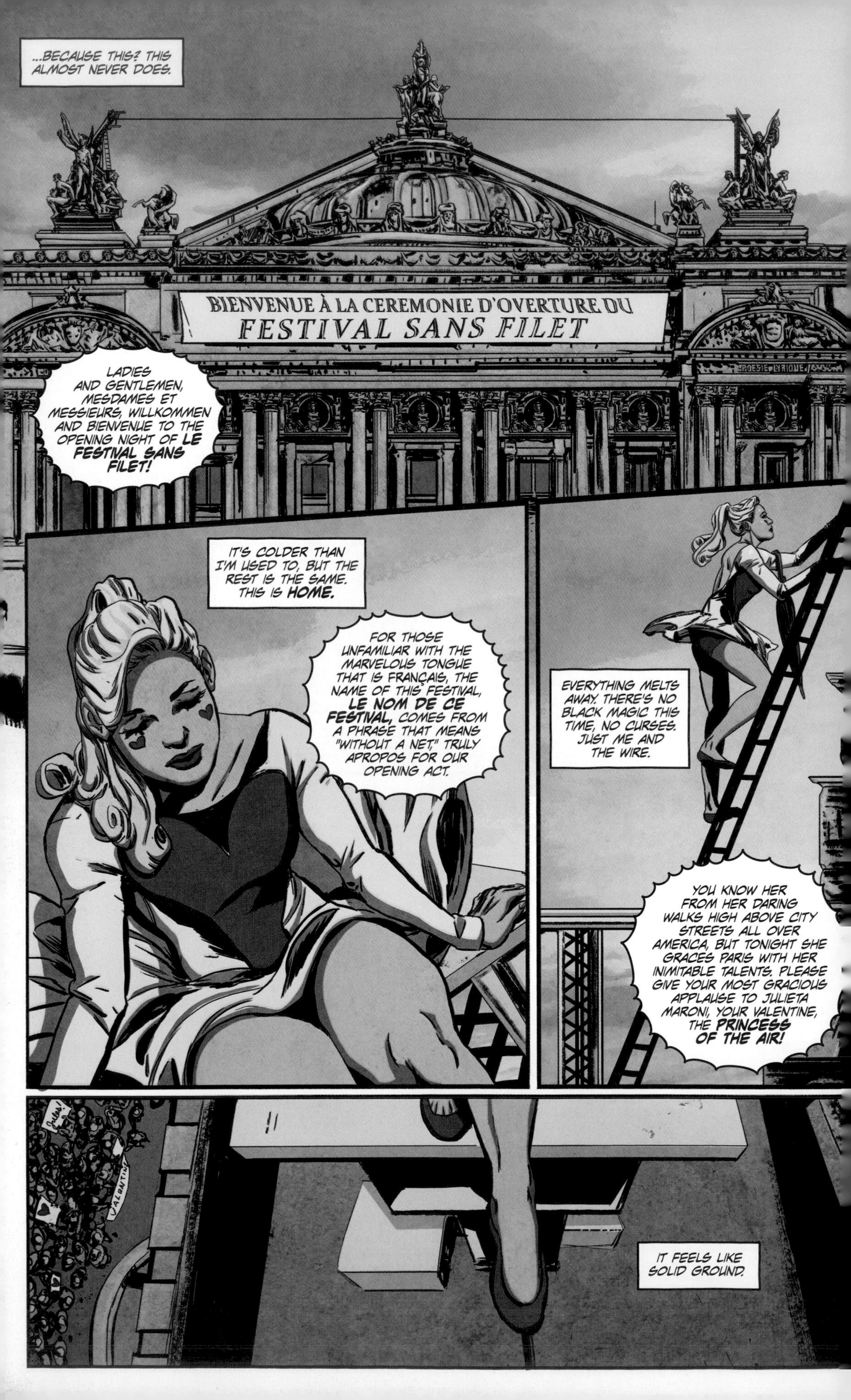
...BECAUSE THIS? THIS ALMOST NEVER DOES.
BIENVENUE À LA CEREMONIE D'OVERTURE DU FESTIVAL SANS FILET
LADIES AND GENTLEMEN, MESDAMES ET MESSIEURS, WILLKOMMEN AND BIENVENUE TO THE OPENING NIGHT OF LE FESTIVAL SANS FILET!
IT'S COLDER THAN I'M USED TO, BUT THE REST IS THE SAME. THIS IS HOME.
FOR THOSE UNFAMILIAR WITH THE MARVELOUS TONGUE THAT IS FRANÇAIS, THE NAME OF THIS FESTIVAL, LE NOM DE CE FESTIVAL, COMES FROM A PHRASE THAT MEANS "WITHOUT A NET," TRULY APROPOS FOR OUR OPENING ACT.
EVERYTHING MELTS AWAY. THERE'S NO BLACK MAGIC THIS TIME, NO CURSES. JUST ME AND THE WIRE.
YOU KNOW HER FROM HER DARING WALKS HIGH ABOVE CITY STREETS ALL OVER AMERICA, BUT TONIGHT SHE GRACES PARIS WITH HER INIMITABLE TALENTS. PLEASE GIVE YOUR MOST GRACIOUS APPLAUSE TO JULIETA MARONI, YOUR VALENTINE, THE PRINCESS OF THE AIR!
VALENTINE
IT FEELS LIKE SOLID GROUND.

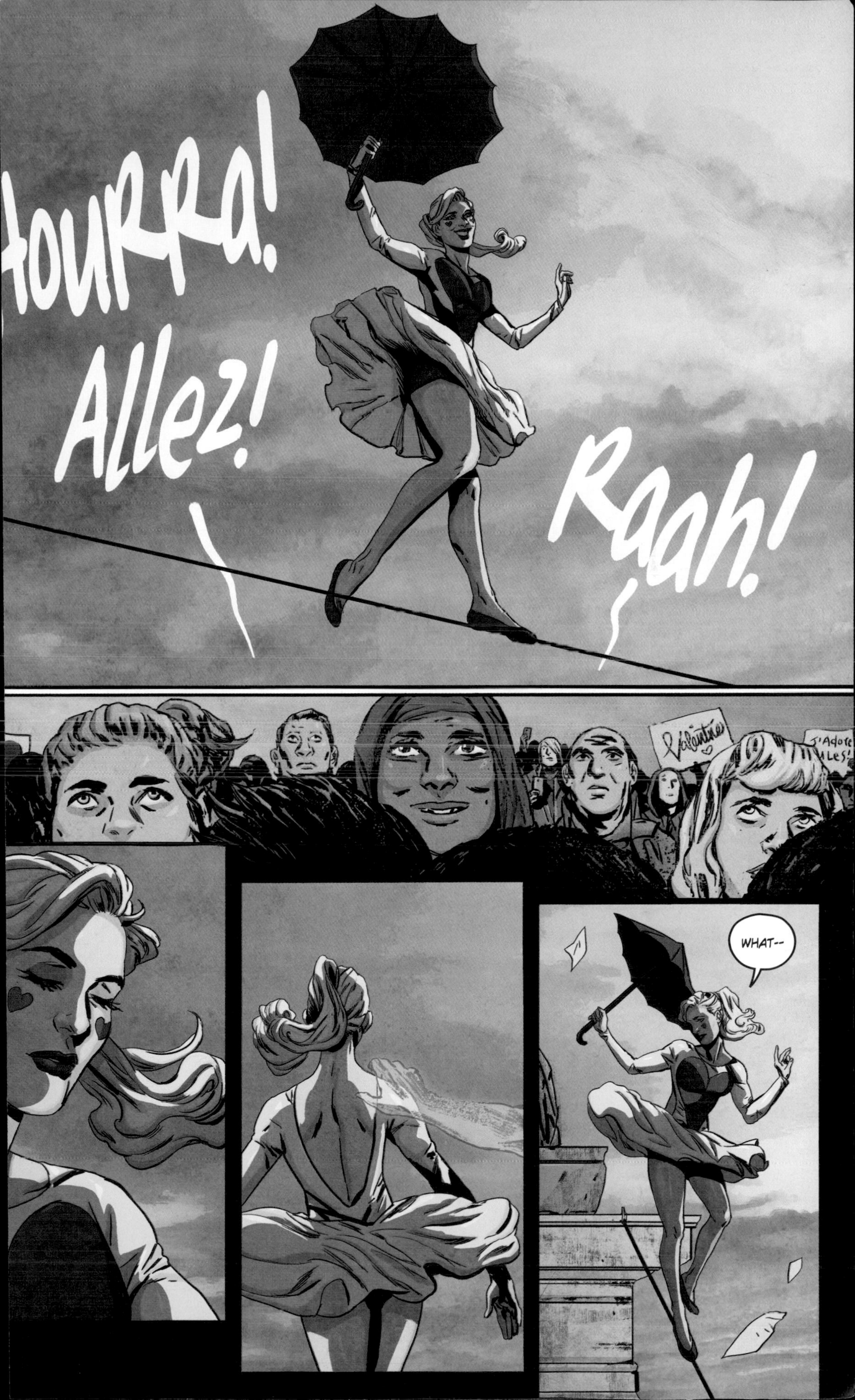
Hourra!
Allez!
Raah!
Valentine
J'Adore
WHAT--

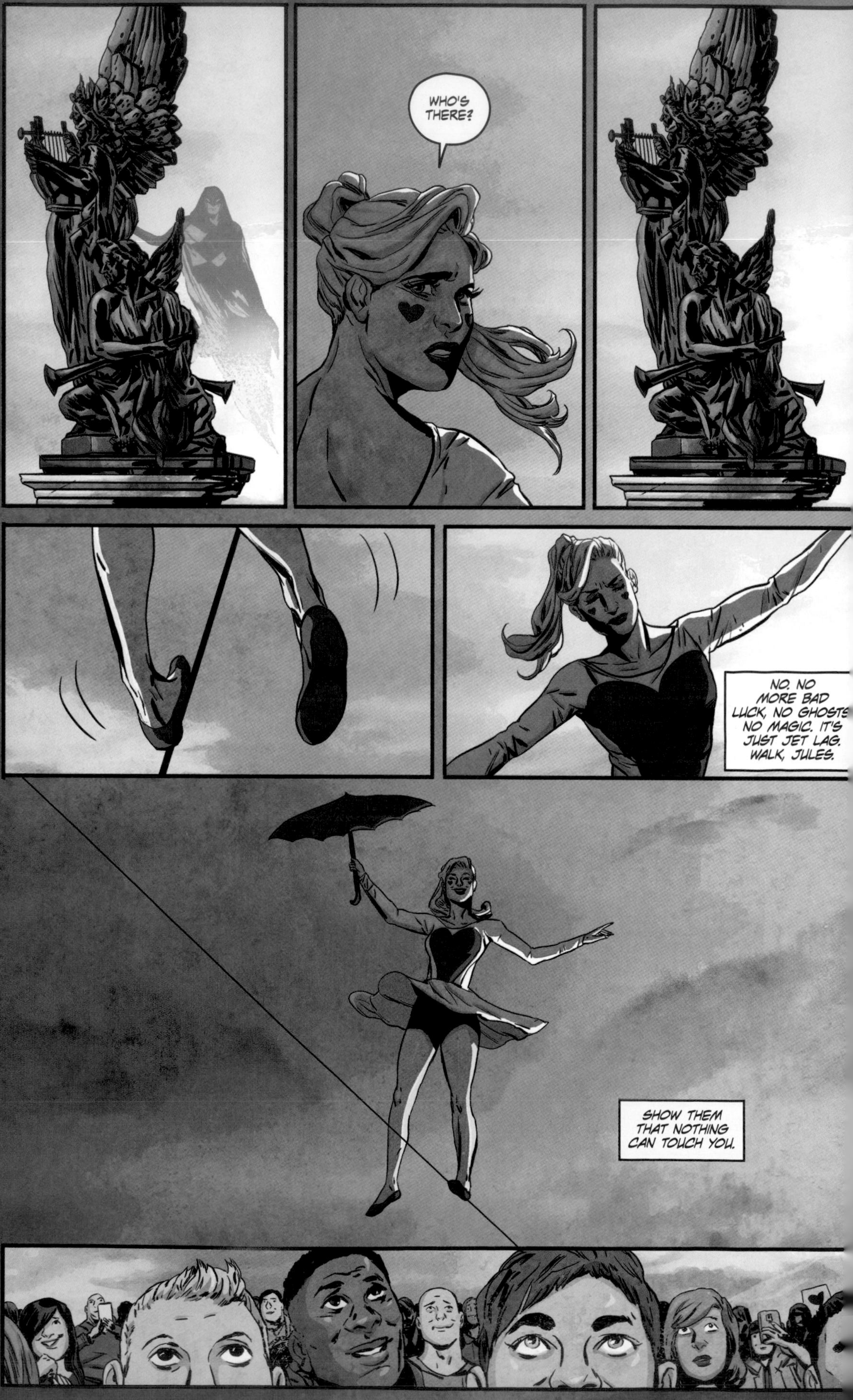
WHO'S THERE?
NO, NO MORE BAD LUCK, NO GHOSTS, NO MAGIC. IT'S JUST JET LAG. WALK, JULES.
SHOW THEM THAT NOTHING CAN TOUCH YOU.

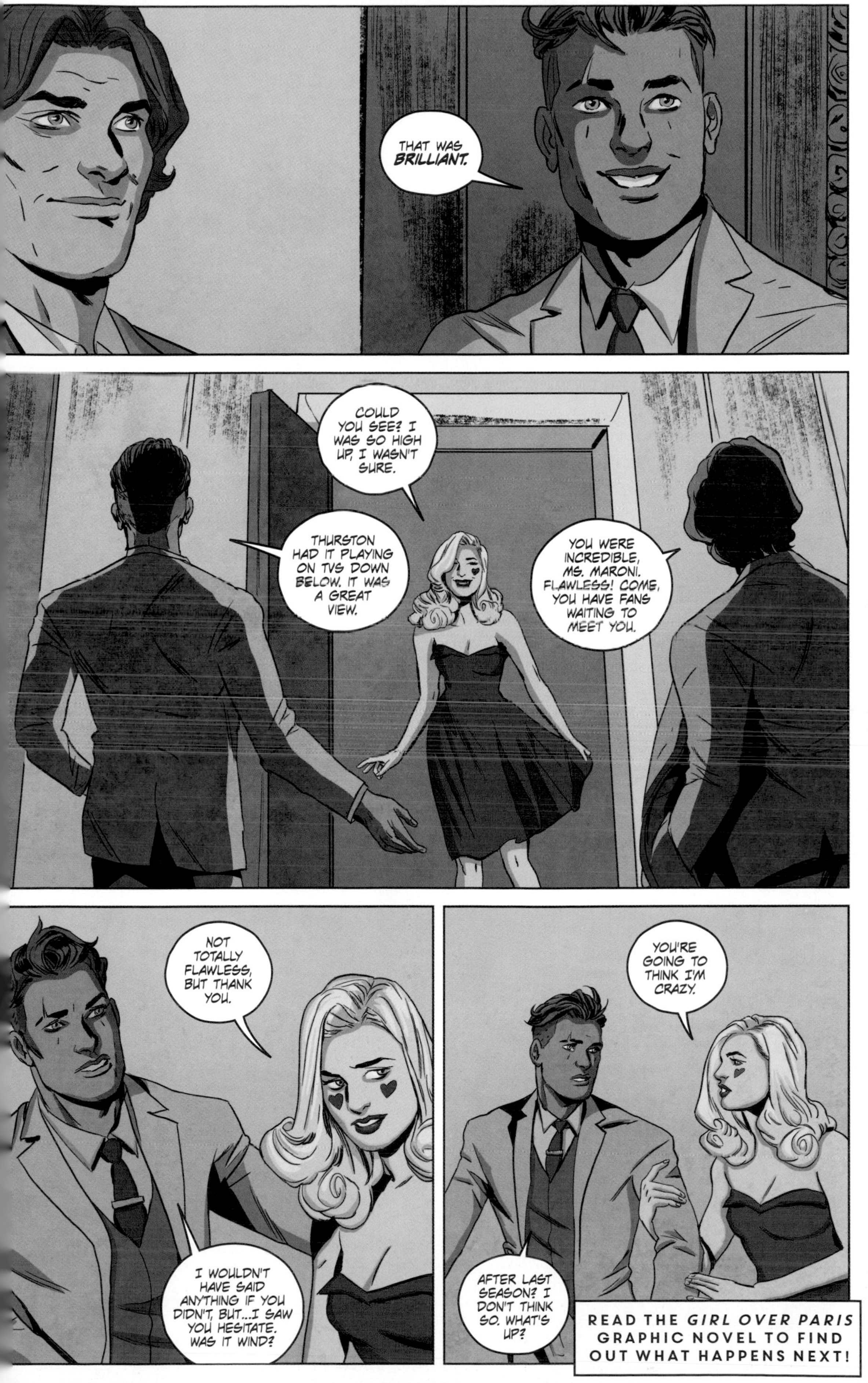
THAT WAS BRILLIANT.
COULD YOU SEE? I WAS SO HIGH UP, I WASN'T SURE.
THURSTON HAD IT PLAYING ON TVS DOWN BELOW. IT WAS A GREAT VIEW.
YOU WERE INCREDIBLE, MS. MARONI. FLAWLESS! COME, YOU HAVE FANS WAITING TO MEET YOU.
NOT TOTALLY FLAWLESS, BUT THANK YOU.
I WOULDN'T HAVE SAID ANYTHING IF YOU DIDN'T, BUT...I SAW YOU HESITATE. WAS IT WIND?
YOU'RE GOING TO THINK I'M CRAZY.
AFTER LAST SEASON? I DON'T THINK SO. WHAT'S UP?
READ THE GIRL OVER PARIS GRAPHIC NOVEL TO FIND OUT WHAT HAPPENS NEXT!

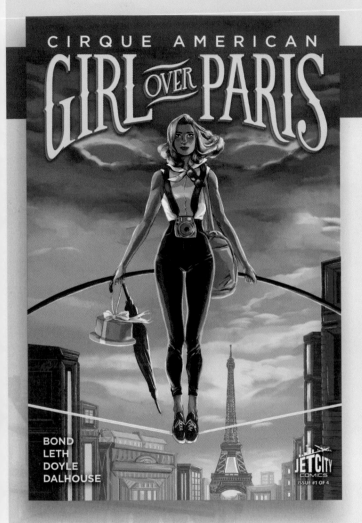

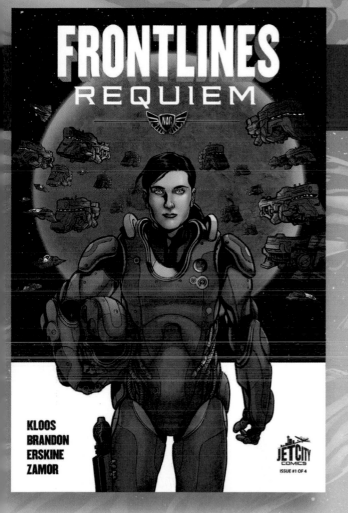

KLOOS
BRANDON
ERSKINE
ZAMOR

ISSUE #1 OF 4

FRONTLINES: REQUIEM

From acclaimed writer
IVAN BRANDON
(*Drifter, Viking*), this four-issue comic book series features a new stand-alone story set within the action-packed military sci-fi world of **MARKO KLOOS'** bestselling **Frontlines** novels.

Includes stunning artwork from
GARY ERSKINE
(*Star Wars, Dan Dare, Doctor Who, Judge Dredd*)

WHEN EARTH IS IN THE CROSSHAIRS, THERE'S ONLY ONE THING STANDING BETWEEN SURVIVAL AND DESTRUCTION: DUTY.

Colonel Soraya Yamin, commander of the battle-ravaged space control cruiser *Phalanx*, engages the Lankies, a merciless alien species, in an apocalyptic assault over Mars. The Lankies, who have outgunned, outmaneuvered, and outfought humanity at every turn, have been menacing Earth's colonies. But now they're suddenly in our solar system, decimating the NACS fleet and swarming toward Earth itself. Facing insurmountable odds, Soraya must make a fateful choice between her sworn duty and the loved ones she desperately wants to protect.

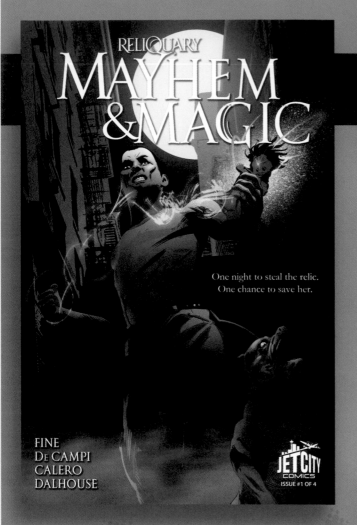

MAYHEM & MAGIC

Bestselling author **SARAH FINE** (*Marked, Sanctum*) gives hard-boiled noir a magical edge in this stand-alone four-issue comic book adventure—where crime collides with conjuring in the spellbinding world of her Reliquary series. Featuring an action-packed script by **ALEX DE CAMPI** (*No Mercy, Grindhouse*), and stunning art from **DENNIS CALERO** (*X-Men Noir*).

ONE NIGHT TO STEAL THE RELIC. ONE CHANCE TO SAVE HER.

Freelance thief-for-hire Asa Ward's latest job is heisting a powerful magic relic from a gangster's lair. But what should be an easy payday quickly becomes larceny the hard way—when he's dragged into a three-way crime war where mind-bending, body-racking magic is the most lethal weapon of all. And just when Asa thinks he's scored, the ruthless kingpin he's ripping off strikes back... threatening the only life Asa values more than his own.

FROM JETCITY COMICS

From the writer of THE BUNKER and the artist of GREEN LANTERN CORPS
KING
HO LYWOO
INTERSTATE
CALIFORNIA
405
JETCITY COMICS
FIALKOV
CHANG
MAIOLO

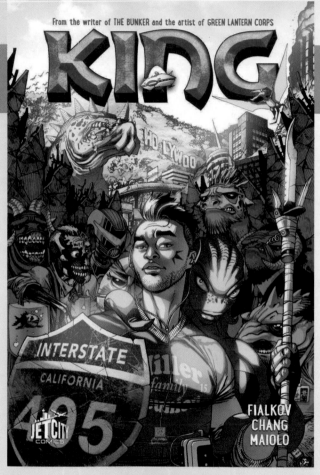

KING

From critically acclaimed writer
Joshua Hale Fialkov
(The Bunker, Echoes, and I, Vampire)
and superstar artists
Bernard Chang
and Marcelo Maiolo
(Green Lantern Corps, Batman Beyond)
comes an action comedy about surviving the global apocalypse

KING just wants what anybody wants: not to get fired, eaten, or forced to mate with a cheetah lady. As Earth's sole human survivor after the apocalypse, life among Los Angeles's strange new populace ain't easy. Working for the LA Department of Reclamation, King gets a lot of crappy jobs going on quests and searching for artifacts from the "old world," which can range from the mythical (Excalibur!) to the absurd (an iPod Shuffle—which, let's be honest, was a terrible, terrible invention). The work commute can be a real pain in the asphalt. The 405 freeway is filled with mutants, monsters, mayhem and tentacled Elder Gods. And that's all before you hit the horrors of the San Fernando Valley. As the world's freakish inhabitants battle for supremacy, King searches for the "seed of life," which may give Earth the second chance it probably doesn't even deserve.

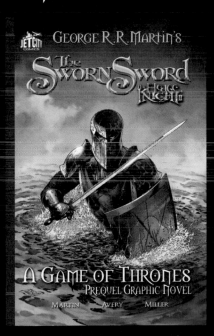
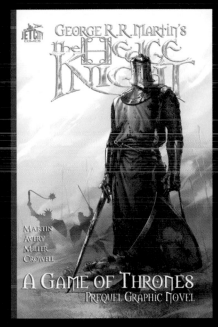

BIOS

RYSA WALKER is the author of the bestselling CHRONOS Files series. *Timebound*, the first book in the series, was the Young Adult and Grand Prize winner in the 2013 Amazon Breakthrough Novel Awards. Rysa grew up on a cattle ranch in the South, where she read every chance she got. On the rare occasion that she gained control of the television, she watched *Star Trek* and imagined living in the future, on distant planets, or at least in a town big enough to have a stoplight. She currently lives in North Carolina, where she is working on her next series, The Delphi Project. If you see her on social media, please tell her to get back into the writing cave. For news and updates, subscribe to the newsletter at www.rysa.com/contact.

HEATHER NUHFER writes children's books and graphic novels for all ages. She has penned numerous original stories for comic book titles such as *Scooby Doo*, *Wonder Woman*, *Teen Titans GO!*, *Fraggle Rock*, *Lisa Simpson*, and *Monster High*. Her *My Little Pony: Friendship Is Magic* graphic novels are international bestsellers. Recently, she wrote *WeirdEST*, her first prose novel. When she isn't writing, Heather loves to knit while watching bad 1990s action movies with her beloved furbaby, Einstein.

AGUSTIN PADILLA is a Spanish comic book artist who got his big break working on IDW's *G.I. Joe* comics. His other IDW work includes *Star Trek*, *Dungeons & Dragons*, and *Borderlands*. He has also worked for Marvel Comics on various titles, including *Captain America: Theater of War*, *X-Men*, *Spider-Man*, and *Hulk Smash Avengers*, and for DC Comics on the likes of *Batman*, *Green Arrow*, and the *Flashpoint* series.